SAYONARA BAR

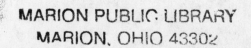

SAYONARA BAR

Susan Barker

St. Martin's Griffin
New York

www.stmartins.com

Library of Congress Cataloging-in-Publication Data

Barker, Susan, 1978–
    Sayonara bar / Susan Barker.
      p. cm.
    ISBN-13: 978-0-312-36210-2
    ISBN-10: 0-312-36210-2
     1. Women graduate students—Fiction. 2. British—Japan—Fiction.
3. Bars (Drinking establishments)—Fiction. 4. Yakuza—Fiction.
5. Japan—Fiction.

PR6102.A7635 S39 2007
823.92—dc22

2006037626

First published in Great Britain by Doubleday,
a division of Transworld Publishers

First St. Martin's Griffin Edition: March 2007

10 9 8 7 6 5 4 3 2 1

To my parents and sister

ACKNOWLEDGEMENTS

Many thanks to everyone at Transworld: Marianne Velmans for her support and guidance, Judy Collins, Deborah Adams and Gavin Morris. Thanks to the Manchester Novel Writing MA Class of 2003 and Martyn Bedford for his encouragement and advice. Thanks to John Saddler. I am grateful to Eleanor Bradstreet for her valuable input at every stage and to Zakia Uddin, all-round troublemaker and friend. Thanks to my dad for many years of conversations about space and time, and to Mum and Carol for all the love and enthusiasm.

Two books, *Beyond the Third Dimension* by Thomas Banchoff and *Hyperspace* by Michio Kaku, I am indebted to for sparking my imagination.

I

MARY

Shinsaibashi wakes for business, metal shutters clattering upwards, broom bristles scratching concrete. Dribs and drabs wander round, salarymen reading menus in restaurant windows, high-school drop-outs killing time till dusk. Edged by the aerials and billboards is a sunset the shade of blood oranges.

The building where I work is in the grimy end of the entertainment district. The chef from the grilled-eel restaurant on the floor below us slouches in the doorway, easing dirt from beneath his thumbnail with a toothpick. We nod hello as the sign for the Big Echo karaoke blinks on, and its fluorescent palm trees hum.

The Sayonara Bar is empty; only the spectral drone of Spandau Ballet drifts over the empty stage and dance floor. Every table sits in a pool of jaundiced light, the tasselled lampshades hanging low, making the place look ready for a séance or psychic convention.

In the changing room, shoes, magazines and crumpled balls of lipstick-stained tissue litter the floor. Blouses with deodorant-stained underarms hang from the sagging curtain rail. In the midst of it all stands Elena, peering into the slanting mirror, dotting concealer under her eyes. We bounce smiles and greetings off the glass. My back to her, I start to undress, flinging my T-shirt and jeans onto the mound of clothes in the corner. I zip myself into the gold-sequinned top that Katya lent me and a black knee-length skirt.

Elena budges sideways to give me room at the mirror. 'Nice sequins,' she says.

'I know. Couldn't get away with it anywhere but here. Did you have a good day?'

'Same as usual: up at seven to get Eiji and Tomo ready, then I had to clean up after the pair of them . . .'

Elena is petite, jaded and prone to world-weary sighs. She came to Japan with a TEFL qualification and a four-month English-teaching contract. Six years on, she has a Japanese husband, a five-year-old son and a vast catalogue of cross-cultural grievances. She makes me feel young, lightweight as flotsam. I watch her pull an eyelid taut and drag a sharpened kohl pencil along her lashes.

'Did you hear about the trouble I had last night?' she asks.

'Yeah. I hate that creep. He should be made to wear a muzzle or something.'

Last night this salaryman laddered Elena's tights, then stuffed a thousand-yen note down the front of her dress, telling her to buy herself a new pair. Elena told him her tights cost more than a thousand yen. So he ripped the other leg and tried to stuff another thousand yen into her dress.

'When I complained to Mama-san she told me to get a sense of humour.'

'That's disgusting.'

'I know. I am leaving at the end of the month.'

'You should.'

I really wish she would, but she has worked here for two years already and I bet she will be here long after I'm gone.

Her hand shakes, jolting her eyeliner upwards. '*Shit*. Can

you pass me a tissue? . . . First I quit this place, then I divorce Tomo.'

'Hmmm,' I murmur, not really in the mood to listen to her marriage problems.

We stare ahead at our reflections. I smudge on some MAC Purple Haze eye shadow. Elena traces her lip line in berry red.

'Did you get up to anything today?' she asks.

Today I woke at Yuji's place around two-ish. We tried to get up but were sunk in his bed like quicksand. So that was where we stayed, in a tangle of mouths and limbs. A whole afternoon with the curtains drawn, rutting from one end of the bed to the other, the television chattering in the background. I am sure there were things that mattered before I met him, but Yuji has this way of making me forget what they are.

'Nothing much,' I say.

In the mirror Elena clips on a gold earring and smiles.

The other hostesses arrive while I am setting up the bar. Yukiko negotiates a shift swap with me so she can see her boyfriend's band play at the Metro next Friday. Mandy shows off the henna tattoo she had done on her navel in Bangkok. Katya walks in late, clutching a take-away bag and pushing a french fry between her lips. Her hair is swept back into a silk headscarf, and a faux fur coat flaps at her too skinny calves. When she sees me she heads over. She smiles and grazes my temple with a greasy, menthol-cigarette-scented kiss. 'Wow,' she says, 'that top is hideous. Glad I gave it away.'

'Thanks, Katya. Appreciate your honesty.'

'Where are you tonight?'

'Bar duty. You?'

'Karaoke booth. Mr Shaky-hands has booked it for his ninety-seventh birthday. Do you want to swap?'

I reject the offer with a rueful smile. Mr Shaky-hands has Parkinson's – Katya can be quite cruel sometimes. She narrows her eyes and stalks away to the changing room, sinking her teeth into another french fry. We fight tooth and nail for bar duty here because you spend the whole evening airlifting drinks to the lounge and small talk is limited to short, near-painless bursts.

Waiting for things to get busy, I slice up a lemon and watch Supermodel TV. Mama-san put it on the wide screen because our Wednesday night keyboard player called in with stomach flu. Supermodel TV is this satellite channel that broadcasts nothing but fashion models charging up and down catwalks all day long. All these ethereal beings with jutting hips and swan-like necks. Not sure of Mama-san's strategy here. Perhaps she hopes we will absorb their glamour by osmosis – I do develop this 'sashay' in my walk whenever it's on. But there is something too innate about our imperfections; our bedraggled, lipstick-on-teeth, taut-seams-at-the-hips slovenliness. Something no amount of exposure to beauty will fix.

One of the first customers is Mr Mitsui, the head of some corporation in the Umeda Sky building. He and his companions take up a table by the cigarette machine and I watch him twist his neck about in search of me. Mr Mitsui bought me a Gucci handbag once; burgundy leather, it was, with a golden clasp that fastened with a sophisticated click. But Yuji hates it when I accept gifts from clients, so I gave it to Katya. The handbag was a reward for participating in his ongoing English-speaking scam. Mr Mitsui knows a smattering of English and he likes to use it to impress his business associates. He'll call me over, introduce me to his friends and then we begin to chat.

'Mary, in your country do you have sushi?'

'Yes. In Japanese restaurants and sometimes in supermarkets too.'

'Ah! And your country. Winter. Colder or warmer?'

'About the same, I think.'

And so on. The whole time his friends make admiring noises in their throats and exclaim things like: 'Isn't

Mitsui-san's English skilful?' He always has different associates in tow, so they have no idea that we run through the same dialogue every time. Tonight I carry over some Martinis and we do the routine for the benefit of two starry-eyed assistants. We have it down pat, word for word, except when Mr Mitsui throws me by substituting 'sushi' with 'escalators' in a rare spurt of improvisation. Afterwards he chomps on the olive from his Martini and looks proud of himself. He slips me a thousand-yen note and whispers I am not to share it with the other hostesses.

When I told a friend back in London what I was doing out here she was shocked. She thought hostess was a polite synonym for prostitute or something. I had to explain to her that it's nothing like that. Salarymen don't go to a hostess bar to purchase sex; it's sexual charisma they're after, a different thing entirely. Most of our clients are the older, mid-life-crisis types. Men loaded with prestige and greatness within the corporation, but invisible to young women they pass by on the street. Our job is to sit with them, act interested in them, laugh at their jokes. Create a make-believe world where they are attractive again. And the more exalted a customer's ego, the more generous the tip. Mama-san likes to recite this old proverb at the end of our more lucrative evenings: 'With flattery even a pig can be made to climb a tree.'

Flattery isn't easy, though – it takes stamina and fatigue-proof smile muscles. Sometimes the sound of my simpering turns my stomach. But whenever my thoughts turn to quitting, the money reels me back in. We earn three times what you'd get teaching English at some boot-camp conversation school and I am trying to save to travel round Asia. My savings are pretty meagre so far, but another three months or so should do it. Yuji hates the idea of me leaving. I hate the idea of leaving him too; every one of his embraces squeezes a little more of the wanderlust out of me. Still, I am determined to go. I have invited him along, but he needs to think it over. When the time comes I am sure we will work out a compromise. We are too crazy about each other not to.

I have never known anyone like Yuji before. He's so energetic, always in motion, too busy living to get dark and analytical. I love that about him. That and the fact he is so handsome it makes my eyes hurt. Yuji says he knew as soon as he was old enough to think that he wasn't going to be some salaryman. He works for this yakuza faction in Shinsaibashi, riding his motorcycle round Osaka delivering drugs and collecting loan repayments for his gangster boss. Risky as hell, but a damn sight more exciting than kowtowing before some company altar. I am intrigued by what he does, the criminal allure of it, but he rarely talks about his job. I hear more from other hostesses, the girls who've had flings with Yuji's friends. Tales of ex-gang members with shorn-off ears, of bamboo strips driven under fingernails. Yuji laughed and choked on his noodles when I told him this, called my friends gullible. Yakuza mythology or not, hearing about it still quickens the pulse.

Distance has shown me how weak my bonds to England are, the scarcity of people I care about there. My mum and her boyfriend decamped to Spain while I was doing my A levels (not that I minded – he was too quick to use his fists and she too quick to defend him), and my university friends are all busy pursuing careers in law and accountancy, shifting onto sensible, humdrum wavelengths. I have no grown-up ambitions, no desire to rush back and train to be a barrister or whatever. It's liberating to think that I am free to roam the world as I see fit.

'Hey, Watanabe. One of these days you're going to load the dishwasher yourself and give me a heart attack, aren't you?'

Watanabe is hunched over a chopping board, his knife a silvery blur as he slices an onion. Watanabe the anaemic kitchen ghost, the teenage catatonic. Did he hear me? Does he hear anyone? The kitchen taps are on full and a potential landslide of dirty plates sits on the draining board. While I am skidding about trying to put things straight Mama-san appears in the doorway, swaddled in a red silk kimono. She surveys the mess, one hand on hip, the other resting against the door frame so the sleeve of her kimono hangs down, cascading embroidered waterfalls and mountain scenery. She is made up geisha-style, her face chalky with powder, her lips nipped scarlet. I admire her flamboyancy, the flair and festivity of her outfits. I hear she was a beauty in her youth – she is still a very striking woman.

'Watanabe: two orders of Kimchee noodles for table thirteen, please.'

Whenever I give Watanabe a food order I always repeat it twice, popping back at regular intervals to make sure he hasn't been distracted. Mama-san's army drill-instructor bark gets it through first time. She sees me scraping pizza crusts into the pedal bin and gives me a frosty nod. I counter with a lukewarm semi-smile. You'd think we'd be on friendlier terms seeing as I am the girlfriend of her only son. I reckon she doesn't like Yuji going out with one of her hostesses, or a foreigner, or both.

'Mary, come here.' She beckons me over to the doorway and directs my gaze to a couple of salarymen fumigating the lounge with cigar smoke. 'I want you to join those two men over there, Murakami-san and the doctor. It is too quiet a night to have you on bar duty.'

'OK.'

'Take them hot flannels and a menu. Recommend the teriyaki chicken.'

'Right.'

Mama-san gives me a quick up-and-down, her gaze hardening as something catches her eye. She pulls at the bottom of my sequinned top, where she's spied a fag burn. Shit. 'Mary, do you know how much money our customers pay for an hour of your company?'

I nod. How can I forget? She only reminds us every five

minutes. 'Yeah . . . I'm sorry. It's so small I didn't think anyone would notice – not in this light anyway . . .'

'The men who come here pay a *lot* of money. The least you can do is appear well groomed. Please don't wear this again. Go.'

Go? I walk away, indignant. Who does she think she is?

'Oh, and, Mary . . .'

What now? I turn back, straining a complaisant smile.

'If Murakami-san starts to blow on your neck, just remind yourself how well he tips for the privilege.'

The smile vanishes. Three months. I will be out of here by then.

I walk over to Murakami and the doctor with a tray of sake and neatly rolled hand towels. The two men rise and bow with such exaggerated chivalry that I cannot help but laugh. Stephanie hurries over to join us, autumnal curls tumbling to her shoulders, which are bare in her strapless dress. They bow once more.

'Good evening,' we chime.

Stephanie seats herself next to Murakami-san, which saves me from having to deal with the neck-breathing thing. She has been really attentive to Murakami-san lately, ever since the night he promised to pay her tuition fees for this course in homeopathic medicine she wants to enrol on back in Florida. It's an empty promise, but she treats him like an emperor, just on the off-chance it might be true. Truly heartbreaking to watch.

I smile at the doctor and sit down, shivering and rubbing at my goose-pimply arms. The air conditioning is really fierce tonight.

'You look lovely, Mary,' he says. He beams and his eyes stray downwards from my face, making leisurely pauses en route to my knees.

It's like cockroaches scuttling over my flesh. Call me naïve, but doctors are meant to be pillars of society; decent, moral and devoid of lecherous impulses. The doctor is not generally like this: usually he's just chubby and jolly. When

I'm around him I always get this urge to reach out and tug at the flesh of his face, which gives the impression of being pliable, like dough. When he laughs he looks like a laughing Buddha, his cheeks bulging, his eyes diminishing into tiny gashes.

'Would you like some sake, Doctor?'

'Yes,' he says and pounds his chest. 'Sake makes me strong.'

A curious theory for a medic, but I smile and pour him a glass. 'So how has work been lately?' I ask.

'Very busy. It's hay-fever season,' he says. 'They come to the surgery in droves, wanting to be cured of their red, weepy eyes and dripping noses. "There is not much that can be done," I tell them, "short of leaving the country until June."'

'Or wearing a surgical mask,' I say. I saw two old ladies wearing them on the train yesterday.

'And how is the blossoming poet? Any new haiku?'

When I first got here I went through this phase of writing bad poetry, haiku that strained for the sublime but were hopelessly mired in the pathetic. Fortunately all my poetry-writing time these days is burnt up by Yuji.

I throw out something lame: '*Umeda at dusk, / Vending machines dispense porn, / Like bars of candy.*'

The doctor understands some English and cracks up at the word 'porn', clutching at his overhang of belly. 'Beautiful, Mary, just like Basho.'

I smile and nudge a ceramic dish of sweets closer to him. Though they are of the boiled variety he takes a handful and crunches them like popcorn. The doctor has a near-insatiable appetite, which he blames on the spirit of a starving Meiji-era peasant he encountered as a child. He says the spirit put a curse on him, so that at every meal he is compelled to eat with the might of ten men.

'Nao,' Murakami-san says, leaning his silvery head towards us, 'look at that television over there. Now, don't you agree that my Stephanie is far superior to any of those models?'

The TV shows a model striding down the runway, flaxen hair streaming. A caption scrolls along the bottom of the screen, deconstructing her into the following components: *Gretel. Swedish. 18. Aquarius. Volleyball.*

'Absolutely! Stephanie and Mary are far more beautiful!' Dr Nishikogi thunders. 'These models, pah! Anorexic, every last one of them. Not like Stephanie here – see how curvy she is? Yes, our girls are far more beautiful. And Mary is very clever too. Have you heard her haiku?'

Stephanie and I exchange furtive winces, to show that we don't buy any of this.

'Let's play a drinking game!' Stephanie suggests.

Drinking games are the secret money-spinners of this establishment. We play drinking games with cards, dice, ice cubes and beer mats, and sometimes more complicated games involving the phonetic alphabet and obscene hand gestures. The losing salaryman has to knock back his drink and buy the next round. Drinking games never fail to liven things up, getting the salarymen really sluiced and spending extortionate amounts on liquor. The down side is that I often end up getting drunk myself. Lately when I go to get more drinks I water my own whisky right down and charge them full price for it.

'Great idea!' I say. 'Let's play Queen of Hearts!'

There is a rumble of enthusiasm and Stephanie dashes to the bar to get a pack of cards. We shuffle our chairs closer round the table. Murakami-san's eyes brighten in anticipation of debauched mayhem. It never happens. The only sure-fire outcome is that he will be completely fleeced.

I top up our drinks and Stephanie deals the cards.

I dream about this place a lot. I dream of sloshing whisky into glasses, the hiss and click of a Zippo lighter. I have come to resent the invasion of my subconscious; it's like doing an unpaid shift in my sleep. I had a horrible dream recently, about one of our patrons, Fujimoto-san. In the dream I was sitting with him, listening to his golfing anecdotes, when his teeth began to fall out. Tapered pebbles of pearl grey hit the varnished wood of the table. I was alarmed but carried on as though nothing out of the ordinary was happening, listening as his words grew thick and incomprehensible. Then he turned to me with a knowing, toothless grin. I jerked bolt upright at that, my heart thrumming in the darkness. Sometimes I wake with dim memories of being kissed by clients, of letting hands roam where they shouldn't, of being aroused by them. But dreams are often without rhyme or reason; it's just the brain chewing over the events of the day. I'm no expert on dream analysis, but I'm sure it doesn't mean I latently crave any of this.

When I leave Osaka my dreams will teem with foreign landscapes. Vast skies of obscene blue, tortuous valleys and ramshackle villages. Rickety train journeys to bustling cities, dense with heat and people. Sometimes I don't know what agonizes me more, the itch to take off or leaving Yuji. It mystifies me, his lack of desire to travel. If I stay in one place for too long the world begins to narrow, like the sky viewed through a straw.

2

WATANABE

I can see you all from way up on high. You're like amoebae slithering over the surface of a slide, oblivious of the eyes that tunnel down upon you. From here I am privy to your secret yearnings as you strain for the sublime, ache in the search for meaning, gnash your teeth in boredom and frustration. I can see the sushi slurry mulching through that client's small intestine; his blood, rushing loin-bound through arteries and capillaries as he talks to Katya, aroused by the scent of her perfume and her husky Ukrainian accent. I can see the tiny alveoli of Katya's lungs deflate as she heaves a sigh of boredom. I can see the beer gurgling through the pipes, the laser skimming over the surface of that CD, the electrical impulses generating sound waves that oscillate at the frequency of Chris de Burgh's 'Lady in Red'.

I float in the realm of the Unified Field theory and Platonic forms. I could educate mankind, scatter beams of light where scientists and philosophers grope in darkness. Humanity has spawned thousands of religions and not one has hit the truth jackpot. I am no tambourine-shaking God-botherer though I have found Him. So allow me to enlighten you: God is the next phase of human evolution. And I have residency of his mind.

*

There was a time when I was as enslaved as the rest of humankind. Although it pains me to do so, I will describe my former life in the three-dimensional universe. My name is Ichiro Watanabe; most people call me Watanabe. My father told me at an early age I was destined for a life of high achieving. From the day I waddled into elementary school to the final day of my university-entrance exams, I sold my life-blood in the pursuit of academic excellence. After-school clubs were shunned in favour of hours studying at a private cram school. Home offered no reprieve – in fact, in the privacy of my bedroom my masochism was able to flourish. I toiled deep into the night under my self-devised study regime, joylessly committing to memory facts I was indifferent to: the laws of thermodynamics, photosynthesis, Japan's annual export of car parts. I would persevere with demoniac drive until a glance at my clock would reveal it to be 4 a.m. I would be exhilarated by the knowledge that my classmates were now entombed in the deeper stages of the sleep cycle. I felt triumphant, like I was pole-vaulting over those lazy sleeping bastards to scholastic brilliance.

I loathed myself, chastised myself and told myself that I needed to study harder. I sustained only one friendship during my high-school days: with Tetsuya, an ardent ping-pong player with a speech impediment. My eyesight became diminished by myopia and my spine ravaged by a curvature brought on by hours hunched over my books. I got the grades I needed to get into Kyoto University. But I flunked the interview. My father hacked into the interviewer's files, to find the panel had described me as 'severely introverted'. My father, a town hall official in our putrid suburb of Osaka, had whitened and convulsed. 'Ichiro Watanabe,' he had roared, fists clenched, drawing himself up to his full 160 centimetres, 'you freak! Your grandfather went to Kyoto University, I went to Kyoto University . . . Damn it, if I have to march in there and bribe every last member of the political-science faculty myself, you are going to Kyoto University!'

My father's nepotism proved successful. At Kyoto University I joined the crème de la crème of the Japanese education system. My fellow nerds and I rejoiced. Gone were the boisterous extroverts who mocked our feeble batting on the baseball pitch and slacked off during cleaning duty, leaving us to scrub lavatory bowls and clap blackboard dusters. Kyoto University marked the beginning of our trajectory to power and revenge. The waking hell of high school behind us, we rubbed our palms and cackled like Lex Luther, knowing world domination would soon be ours.

My self-image also underwent a paradigm shift. I realized that my scrawny torso and legs weren't a social disaster after all. A glance at some fashion magazines informed me that my malnourished androgyny was quite hip. I switched to contact lenses and got a jagged, asymmetrical haircut. Girls who before had paid the high-school Watanabe the same attention as they would carpet lint now began to smile at me. The first girl I took back to my student dorm was an Archaeology student called Aiko, who wore thick tortoiseshell glasses. Yukie came next, then Yukiko with the slender calves that hooked over my shoulders. Sometimes while they slept I would watch them in disbelief, gently prod them to make sure they were real.

It was during my second semester that I began to transcend the ordinary world. My terror was on the scale of awakening one day to find the Earth's tectonic plates have shifted to form a continent-long sneer into the crust of the planet. The most ludicrous things began to happen to me, things that I couldn't reveal to a soul. Not to the girls I invited back for clammy trysts beneath my dormitory sheets. Nor to Tetsuya, who, like myself, had undergone metamorphosis and had swapped the ping-pong paddle for a bass guitar, and was now fronting a band called The Eunuchs. I knew the futility of explanation.

From nowhere a strange fatigue came and seeped into my life. My appetite diminished to a memory. The only thing I could ingest without being wrenched by a brutal riptide of nausea were vitamin C tablets. I began to have murky, distorted dreams that lodged in my waking consciousness like a steak knife. It was as though something had come undone in my mind, as though aliens were probing me while I slept, snipping away at the cords that anchored me to reality. Then one morning I awoke and the doubt that had been so quietly incubating exploded into something I could no longer ignore.

I watch as Katya purrs up against an elderly client, lets the chiffon of her translucent blouse caress his skin, tormenting him. 'Playing golf must keep you *really* fit, Mr Suzuki. Your triceps must be in splendid condition.' I can see fierce tides of frustration swell within him. He is a sociopath and wants to snap her neck. Fortunately for society, he is too cowardly to obey these vicious impulses. Katya purrs on, oblivious. Mary is also watching Katya. Jealousy curdles within her stomach and she convinces herself she could never stoop to Katya's vulgar sycophancy. I watch as urea filters through her kidneys; she has to empty her bladder but is waiting for a lull in the conversation with her salaryman. Ah . . . there she goes.

Katya and Mary . . . I just need to be in the same room with them to know the thoughts that whirl through their minds and the secrets their bodies keep. Lately Mary has been agonizing over her boyfriend's sexual demands; he asks her to remain perfectly still during sex, as though she were a corpse and he a necrophiliac. And Katya hasn't had a period since she was eleven; she thinks the flow has been stemmed by the years spent training to be a gymnast back in the Ukraine, but the truth is she has an ovarian cyst. I can see it, clinging inoffensively to her ovary, like a pearl.

Nothing shocks me any more – not the thousands of diseases I see festering in the flesh, not the crazed, perverted thoughts I see lurking in the minds of ordinary people. By now I've seen it all.

'Watanabe, could you make up a couple of pepperoni pizzas for the Mitsubishi men? They're back again tonight. I hope they don't stay until four a.m. this time!'

It's Mariko. I nod and instantly see that Mariko is having an affair with the chairman of the Ministry of Fisheries, who came here last week. It is not with detached indifference that I observe the pitifully barren personal lives of the hostesses. During my time as the chef at The Sayonara Bar, a fondness has germinated for each hostess. I intend to concoct a subtle plan to get Katya to see a doctor (though sometimes even doctors can miss the ailments that I see).

This is the paradox of the position of enlightenment that I find myself in. I have the wisdom to alleviate every ill in society, and yet I am powerless. There are paths of elucidation, but they require the abandonment of every prejudice your senses have taught you; the suspension of every belief threading your existence into neat, comprehensible bundles. Even a deranged wino, discovering new worlds as he forages through the city bins, might think me insane.

Sirens resound across Japan, alerting the nation to a nuclear attack. A group of wealthy, apocalypse-fearing friends climb down a 100-metre shaft to their secret underground nuclear bunker. Just as the ten-inch lead door slams behind them the sirens stop and the Japanese public are informed that it has all been a false alarm. Paroxysms of relief flood the nation.

The bunker assemblage, however, have no idea that the all clear has been given. 'There will be nuclear fallout and then a nuclear winter,' *frets the chief apocalypse-phobic.* 'We should wait at least three years before we resurface!'

Unfortunately, during the three years their fear of the surface escalates and when the time comes to emerge they are too scared to leave. Before long the electricity generator breaks, so they have to live in darkness. Then the food supplies are exhausted, so they have to dig for earthworms and grubs.

Generations later, the descendants of the bunker pioneers are still living in the permanently dark underground lair. They dig tunnels to expand their underworld and become adept at farming grubs (an exceptional source of protein). They enhance their world in many ways, but an ancestral legacy of surface terror has been instilled within their community. There is a road directly above them and they often hear the rumbling of an overhead heavy-goods vehicle. They believe this rumbling to be the footsteps of one of the fire-breathing dragons that came to inherit the earth. The lair-dwellers are not dissatisfied with the dank squalor of their world of tunnels. They have an aphorism that slips from their lips in times of doubt: 'A man tired of Tunnel World is tired of life itself, for in Tunnel World there is all life has to afford.'

One day, while digging himself his own private lair a young man penetrates the original shaft that leads to the surface. 'How odd!' *he thinks.* 'A vertical tunnel! How can this be when in Tunnel World only horizontal tunnels are permitted?' *Curious, he climbs up the shaft and into a sewer. He pops open a manhole cover, to be confronted with a roaring Japanese metropolis.*

The escaped lair-dweller's mind detonates with astonishment. Eyes encountering light for the first time scald and blister. Machines of inconceivable colours zoom over the surface, his nasal cavities are flooded with petrol fumes and the succulent aroma of hotdogs wafting from a nearby stand. His eardrums shudder with the chaotic din of city life. He longs for the womb-like sanctuary of Tunnel World. 'Deliver me from hell!' *he cries, his sanity in shreds.* 'What are these strange creatures that charge to and fro?'

Horrified, he realizes that the strange creatures and the lair-dwellers are one and the same.

The escaped lair-dweller's mind gradually reorientates. The initial chemical peel of sunlight subsides to a more tolerable chlorinated sting. 'I have discovered the reality that exists beyond Tunnel World!' *he exclaims, his chest tightening with joy.* 'I must go back and tell the others.' *Unfortunately his attempts to explain to the lair-dwellers about the world above are met with incredulous laughter.* 'The fire-breathing dragons don't exist . . . People walk upright . . . The surface world has colours radically different from the seventeen shades of darkness! . . . Yeah . . . Right!' *Their minds unable to assimilate what they have never perceived before, the lair-dwellers remain unconvinced. Psychologically shackled, leaving Tunnel World to investigate for themselves is out of the question.* Screw it! This is a waste of time, *thinks the escaped lair-dweller.* I pity them and wish them freedom but I'm not going to hang around here for a moment longer. *After all, a butterfly sprung from its chrysalis is far too busy soaring the stratosphere to worry about the grubs it has left behind.*

I, Ichiro Watanabe, am the liberated lair-dweller, and the madness that snatched me from the sleazy prime of my undergraduate days was my ascent into a new reality. But I didn't have to climb up a 100-metre shaft to reach this new domain. This higher realm is superimposed upon the sphere of human experience. It is tantalizingly close and permeates our every move. Scientists, spiritualists, philosophers and madmen have all hypothesized upon it before. They have called it many things, but the name I deem most appropriate is this: the fourth dimension.

'Watanabe, how are those pizzas coming along? The Mitsubishi men are getting impatient. They've already eaten five bags of cashew nuts and are about to start on the drink mats!'

Mariko shatters my concentration like a juggernaut swerving into plate glass. I see the red blood cells being pumped around her arteries: her haemoglobin seems a touch pallid today. Later I will make her a spinach salad to boost her iron levels.

'Watanabe? The pizzas?'

I sniff the kitchen air and catch nothing more than the odour of drain sediment and washing-up detergent. Drat! The pizzas.

'Watanabeee!' Mariko wails. She mock-pummels my chest with her fists. 'How am I going to break the news to the Mitsubishi swine that their pizzas will take another twenty minutes? They'll flay me alive!'

Her tone is light, but the fourth-dimensional representation of her mind is a Van de Graaff generator of panic and dismay. Mariko suffers abysmal mental anguish from this job. Unlike the other hostesses, she is unable to dislocate her self-worth from the subservient nature of hostessing. I can see the tentacles of resentment knead her psyche.

With a pang of shame at my higher-realm preoccupation, I empty a package of dried squid onto a plate. 'Please accept my apologies,' I soberly announce to Mariko. 'And take them this squid. The pizza will be ready in fifteen minutes.'

I execute a 180-degree bow and she backs out of the kitchen bemused, my fanatical humility soothing her.

I have often pondered upon the spatial position I occupy. I guess you could call me an intermediary between the third and fourth dimension. When I speak of the fourth dimension, I do not speak of time but of the next dimension of space. Think of a two-dimensional universe sketched out upon a sheet of paper. A person looking down on that two-dimensional universe would be able to observe every event in that universe, like an omniscient god. It follows that if you transcend to the fourth dimension you are granted that same panoramic, divine view. And what does this entail? I can penetrate minds. I can perceive the visceral events of any corporeal entity. I can see the sap oozing up through the stem shaft of a three-hundred-year-old oak; cathode rays pinging against a computer monitor. I can see that one of Mariko's Mitsubishi clients wears a nappy beneath his suit because he loves the caress of its dry-weave fibres.

To propel oneself into the magnificence of fourth-dimensional reality, a sixth sense must be liberated. This portal or capacity for interdimensional travel exists within everyone. There lies a dormant 'muscle' inside your mind; if it is found and flexed your perception will explode. But the human race must locate this sixth sense before it can evolve . . . and therein lies our problem. *In a universe of absolute darkness a single street light glows. If you are searching for something, where is the only possible place you can search?* Answer: *Under the street light.* Problem: *That's not where it is.*

The day it happened I was supposed to be in my Introductory Statistics seminar. Instead I was at my local Lawson's trying to jolt my appetite out of a month-long cessation. A Tokyo Boyz ballad pervaded the convenience-store aisles like flatulent airborne bacteria. At the neat rows of refrigerated rice balls, my stomach winced and cowered. No change there, then. I sauntered up to the magazine rack and flicked through a TV guide. The girl beside me was scanning the advertisements for liposuction at the back of a fashion magazine. I glanced at her and smiled. She edged away with a haughty flip of her hair. I selected a packet of vitamin C tablets and waited by the cashier, tapping my foot. 'That will be 120 yen,' the Lawson's automaton bleated. Her bar-code scanner then crashed to the counter as I began to scream.

Thus marked my first ascent into hyperspace. Imagine, if you will, that, having spent a lifetime burrowed into the hairs of a lion, one day you're ejected from your cosy abode to be confronted with the lion in its roaring entirety. Imagine absentmindedly staring through an innocuous, gum-snapping Lawson's clerk and then, right before your eyes, she transmutates into a grotesque, thousand-headed demon. Imagine her head exploding into an infinity of aggregate layers, into layers of skin and flesh and cartilage and skull and brain. Imagine her head blown wide open so that every internal angle is externalized in macabre, bloody grandeur. Imagine suddenly being able to 'see' the fourth-dimensional representation of every thought and emotion pounding within her skull. (*Oh God! He's screaming like a wild animal. I hope he hasn't got a knife. I don't want to get hurt. Oh please, God, don't let him hurt me!*)

Imagine a hand descending from the sky and wrenching you, as you flail and cry, from the amniotic fluids that cocoon you through life; watching all physical boundaries fall away, as concepts such as 'inside' and 'outside' are rendered obsolete. Imagine calmly computing this million-fold splurge of sensory input and calmly acknowledging that you have just perforated the next level of the physical world, a level that your mind had conspired to shield you against. But despite this seamless mental transition, you can hear the screams of your infinitely inferior, third-dimensional self. Great lung-rupturing screams. Screams of raw human suffering; those of a woman in childbirth or a man in an aeroplane plummeting from the sky.

I crash to my knees, screams trampolining from my bleeding diaphragm, my fingertips gouging at my temples. 'Stop! Stop! Fucking stop!' I beg. And then, all of a sudden, it does.

The utter embarrassment! I wreaked enough pande-monium to convince everyone Armageddon was in the vicinity. I succeeded in scaring seven shades of shit out of the Lawson's clerk, the liposuction girl and some builders browsing the porn section. Once the universe had con-tracted to regular size I sat gibbering like a traumatized ape for a few minutes while the clerk called the emergency services. Then, with an amazing display of initiative, I picked up my chewy vitamin C tablets and scampered back to my student residence.

'Hi, Watanabe. It's really quiet now the Mitsubishi men have left. But I'm glad they've gone. Lecherous creeps. Always trying to tease a few inches off my hemline with their beady eyes.'

Katya has slunk into the kitchen while I'm chopping some spring onion to garnish a bowl of Udon noodles. My fight-or-flight reflex lurches. I have the same irrational fear of Katya that my mother has of microwaves – she will always scuttle to another room when one is nuking stuff.

'Watanabe . . . your company is so refreshing after all those salarymen gawping and pawing at us. You're so shy . . . always hiding under that baseball cap of yours . . .'

I am cutting far more spring onions than a bowl of Udon could possibly need. Why does Katya always succeed in making me blush? She enjoys terrifying the socially inadequate: it reinforces her ranking in the pecking order and offers cheap distraction from her vapid inner monologue. I decide to flex into the fourth dimension. Katya's dulcet tones are much less intimidating when juxtaposed with her lower bowel movements. As I transcend, Katya explodes into a million shattered mirror fragments, each one reflecting a different physical and mental aspect of her. Her thoughts trail along dimly, like a myxomatosis-ridden rabbit. (*I bet he's never had sex at all . . . I bet he wants to have sex with me . . .*)

'Hmmm, Udon.' She lowers her head to the bowl and slurps, 'hmmm-ing' as though the Udon broth is giving her much sexual gratification. I will have to wipe away the fuchsia lipstick with a dish rag before I put that through the serving hatch. 'Delicious! Bravo, Watanabe!'

Fire crackers combust in my cheeks. Here is something no one knows about Katya: she is anorexic, and judging by the acid bile eating through the walls of her contracted stomach she hasn't eaten for the last fourteen hours. I slide the Udon through the serving hatch.

'Y'know what, Watanabe . . .' Katya lisps peevishly '. . . you never look me in the eyes!' She crosses her arms and pouts. 'What colour are they, Watanabe? Get it right and I promise to scrape the crap from that pile of dishes for you.' She gestures towards the washing-up and closes her eyes.

The opportunity to shift Katya to the other side of the kitchen presents itself. So what colour are her eyes? Well . . . I could describe to you the texture of her vitreous humour (gloopy, like hair gel) or the interlocking pattern of rods and cones on her retina (honeycomb) or the angle of light refraction at her corneas (43.2°). I could relay to you the images that dance along her optic fibre to the surround-sound, wide screen of her mind. And the colour . . . The irises of her eyes hang like a frozen mineral substance, the palest, devil-may-care shade of . . . 'Blue.'

'Shame on you! They're brown!'

Excuse me? Brown?

'I knew I wouldn't have to get my hands dirty!' she meows and sashays out to the bar, her hips in a figure-of-eight victory swivel.

Brown? My fourth-dimensional radar sweeps over the kitchen. Everything is as it should be. Detergent spurts inside the dishwasher, the electric coils of the oven cool and contract. Every angle, internal and external, of the walk-in fridge is laid out. Every nook and cranny, every aubergine and onion and leek. Mould liquefies a bag of carrot detritus on the second shelf. From my fourth-dimensional vision, nothing is clandestine. So how did Katya manage to hide the colour of her eyes?

As I became accustomed to dimensional transcendence, I learnt to isolate distinct hyper-objects from the chaos. In hyperspace, internal organs inhabit the same plane as external features such as skin, hair and clothes. Each human body is shrouded by a four-dimensional,

31

machine-gun splatter of hyper-gore. Imagine all of the blood geysers from all of the slasher movies you've ever watched in your whole life compacted into one. Then project it into four dimensions. By my tenth visit to hyper-space I was able to recognize organs and biological functions, and now after several months of hyperspace I can read blood-sugar levels, recognize the malfunctioning of organs and diagnose diseases.

When you shift up a dimension the thoughts of other creatures are as easy to translate as the scratching of thirst in your own throat. The fourth-dimensional realm is electrified with the mental activity of all animal life. Thousands of internal monologues clamour relentlessly for your attention. I have squandered many hours riding on the Osaka underground, mesmerized by the cogitations of strangers, transfixed by the neuroses and perversions darting about the confines of our subterranean capsule.

It was Mary who unwittingly lured me to The Sayonara Bar. By then I had officially quit university and chosen to spend my days tramping about Osaka. I first encountered Mary in a bank vestibule in Shinsaibashi station. It was the lunch-time rush and I was waiting to withdraw my 1,000 yen daily allowance for a salmon rice ball and a pack of Lucky Strikes. Impatient electrical pulses twitched about my fellow queuers as they waited in ten-deep lines at each cash dispenser. A spectrograph of stress and tension grew as they shifted from foot to foot, cracked knuckles and made critical mental appraisals of one another.

C'mon, you senile old witch! Move it! *C'mon, you Alzheimer's infested moose!* What? *How many times does she have to insert her card?!*
                                        Momoko Yamada, 20, office lady

If that insipid Malibu Barbie clone doesn't stop screeching into her mobile . . . Hey! What was that look for? Jesus! If you don't like people looking at your legs, then wear a longer skirt.

Noburu Yoshikawa, 28, telesales executive

Is there enough time to decode the Andromeda Corporation microchip before I smuggle it out of the country in my prosthetic arm? Or should I wait until the team pick me up in Brazil?

Kaori Tanizaki, 36, housewife and flower arrangement teacher

Many pairs of eyes spun towards Mary as she stepped into our air-conditioned vault. En masse, the private cogitations of those around me skidded to a halt and with a chaotic jangle homed in on her Amazonian proportions. We Osakians are used to Westerners, but even by Western standards Mary is a giantess. She strutted through the dense nebula of curiosity to join a queue. She stood with her shoulders thrust back and her vertebrae set poker-stiff, as though her mutant stature was a lifestyle choice, not a blow dealt by the gods of genetic inheritance.

I bet if Spiderman and Godzilla and the Yakuza and that big American lady had an Ultimate Death match, the American lady would pulverize them all!

Yuu Kawagawa, 11, accompanying his mother on a trip to the Hankyu department store

I too was intrigued by Mary. She gazed stoically into the middle distance as she waited in line. Her mental activity was negligible, practically flat-lining. All her thoughts had been displaced by a melody – the most haunting melody that I have ever heard, a bittersweet refrain to the indignity and pathos of life.

I trailed Mary from the ATM annexe so I could cling onto that melody for a few moments longer. I pursued her past Laundromats and Pachinko parlours. I followed the swish of her leather jacket and her lion's mane of golden hair, my heart somersaulting every time her profile dipped into view. The melody continued as though in abhorrence of a silent vacuum. We pushed through the noonday crowds of Shinsaibashi and cut through a urine-breathing alley. We clambered up six flights of stairs (me stealthily wheezing a flight behind). When I emerged on the sixth floor the last strains of melody disappeared behind heavy double doors. Ahead, the Amazonian girl was now shedding her jacket and talking in excellent Japanese to a burly matron presiding over the bar. Etched upon the glass and shaded with gilt were the words *THE SAYONARA BAR*.

The door swung open. The matron loomed upon me. 'Oi!' she growled through her tar-pit larynx. 'Are you here about the job?'

Behind her, Mary appeared and smiled at me for the first time. Pheromones glided through the air in a Viennese waltz. Desire galloped across the pastures of hyperspace. My heart flared as I suddenly realized what that melody was. I nodded wordlessly and she ushered me inside.

3

MR SATO

I

How quiet it is at night. Nothing more than the rumble of distant factories and the shiver of trees in the breeze. And the moon, a pale orb in possession of the sky, scattered with tarnished constellations.

I find this wakefulness, this hyperactivity of mind, very frustrating. It must be the green tea I drank earlier: green tea always leaves me overstimulated. The silhouette of the hedge obscures my view, unruly prongs of foliage reaching into the dark. Must remember to give it a trim on Sunday.

The geraniums, by the way, are flourishing. We have Mrs Tanaka to thank for that. They'd have withered right away if it wasn't for her efforts with the watering can. She's always been an old fusspot, hasn't she? Every morning she'll wait until I am leaving for work before scuttling out of her house, hair in pink curlers, her quilted dressing gown flapping about her ankles. This morning she gave me two salmon rice balls wrapped in a gingham handkerchief. She told me that I need to get more sunshine, that death from overwork is epidemic these days. 'I've never been fond of sunshine,' I told her. She didn't believe me. 'Mr Sato! How can you not be fond of sunshine? It's the source of all life.' Then she continued to make enquiries about my well-being, brushing aside my insistence that I am in good health. She usually makes me late for work. I've begun to leave the house several minutes earlier to allow for these daily inquisitions.

I don't agree with Mrs Tanaka's opinion that I work too hard. Her generation had a much more resilient work ethic than ours does. Her generation made Japan into the economic powerhouse it once was. This generation is simply treading water . . . and I fear things are in decline. Every year the new intake of graduates at Daiwa Trading seem a little more dismissive of company etiquette, a little too eager to escape their desks at the 5 p.m. chime. It's been hectic at the office lately and I find myself putting in a lot of overtime to take up the slack, racing to catch the last train, which leaves Umeda at 11.30. I can just see those frown lines puckering your brow! I know how you disapprove. I promise to slow down in May, once the quarterly shareholders' report is out of the way. Then I might take a holiday, maybe in China – you always wanted to go to China, didn't you?

Anyway, I finished work at seven tonight. We all got sent home early, as the whole computer network has been infected with a virus from South Korea, which brought things to a standstill. It was strange to leave the office while it was still daylight outside. Some of my colleagues went out drinking. As always they invited me and as always I apologized and made my excuses. I am sure my co-workers think me very odd and antisocial, but, as you know, I do not care for bars and discothèques and suchlike. I found myself home by eight with nothing more for my evening's entertainment than some take-out sushi and the television remote. How that wretched, glowing box gives me a headache! All those flashing lights and cheering studio audiences. After dinner I turned it off and looked about the house for some chore to do, but as I take care of everything on Sundays there was nothing left to fix or clean. So I've been sitting at the kitchen table instead, drinking green tea and listening to classical music on the radio. They played

Elgar earlier. It reminded me that I still haven't done anything about your cello. It sits in the spare room, gathering dust. Maybe I should donate it to the local high school – I am sure that there are plenty of budding cellists who would appreciate it. It's been selfish of me to cling onto it for so long.

II

Mrs Tanaka is at it again. She ambushed me as I left for work yesterday morning. 'Mr Sato! Coo-eee! Mr Sato!' She hobbled across the dew-drizzled lawn, nearly slipping in her excitement. I was concerned because she had forgotten her housecoat, but despite the frigid morning air she was very sprightly.

'Mr Sato! Guess who is coming to Osaka!'

Apart from the residents of our neighbourhood Mrs Tanaka and I have no other common acquaintances that I know of. 'I have no idea, Mrs Tanaka,' I replied.

'Oh yes, you do!' she insisted, her eyes sparkling mischievously. 'It's my niece Naoko!' She clapped her hands with a delight I could not partake in. 'Her company has transferred her to their Osaka branch!'

'That's wonderful news,' I said, smiling politely.

'Isn't it just?' she replied with a crafty grin.

A frozen smile masked my torment. I sensed an invitation to dinner in the offing. Naoko and I would soon be seated opposite each other, stiff with mutual disinclination, awkwardly eating Mrs Tanaka's simmered dumplings. Then Mrs Tanaka would slyly slip away to attend to some urgent chore she'd claim to have forgotten . . . Oh, the wretched embarrassment! Naoko may be a lovely girl, but an atmosphere of discomfort lingers between us. It is not that I dislike her. What is there not to like? It is just that I will never like her enough. Not nearly enough to consummate Mrs Tanaka's silly romantic plans.

*

My encounter with Mrs Tanaka was just the beginning of a very peculiar day. At about mid-morning I was summoned to the Deputy Senior Managerial Supervisor's office. Murakami-san's office was very pleasant and spartan, save for a display cabinet resplendent with golfing trophies. He took great pains to make me comfortable, dispatching his secretary to make a pot of barley tea and inviting me to sit in his plushly upholstered wing-back chair. He even offered me a cigarette, which I of course declined. The young secretary returned and bustled about in a fricative murmur of nylon tights, pouring us tea. Murakami-san sat in the chair behind his desk. Behind his broad shoulders stretched Osaka's dirty skyline, gauzy clouds misting the tops of skyscrapers. As his secretary left he grinned widely, revealing teeth like broken china, colliding at hazardous angles. The skin around his permanently bloodshot eyes crinkled.

'Sato-san,' he began, 'I want to voice my appreciation of all the hard work you have been putting in lately. We are delighted to have you join our department. You have exceeded your reputation as a dedicated, first-rate employee by far.'

'Thank you,' I said and bowed my head in humble pride. Upper-level management at Daiwa Trading rarely dole out praise, even to the most diligent of employees. To be praised by Murakami-san is to be picked out by a celestial spotlight.

'But I am concerned that you have been working too hard.'

My head snapped up in surprise. I have never heard a superior express such sentiments before. 'I . . . I apologize . . .' I stammered. 'But last week we lost some computer files so I had to organize—'

He dismissed my defence with a backhand flap. 'Those files weren't that important; besides, we got a repair man to recover them from the hard drive last night. You did all that work for nothing.' He patted his immaculately coiffed silver hair. Perhaps he expected the revelation that my labours had been meaningless to aggrieve me. It didn't in the slightest.

'Oh,' I said.

'Sato-san,' he said, smiling gently, 'your promotion means that you are now able to delegate responsibility. Yet you insist upon wearing yourself out, overseeing everything, right down to the most menial of office chores.'

My jaw descended. It had never once occurred to me that my commitment to Daiwa Trading could elicit such criticism.

Murakami-san leant forward and adopted a low, confidential tone. 'Allow me to make a suggestion. I think you would work more efficiently if you took some time out to relax . . . Do you know our department has an entertainments account for guests and senior management?'

I nodded. I had heard rumours of this debauched account.

'How long have you been with us in the Finance Department, Sato-san? Three months? We still haven't had the opportunity to socialize together, have we? How about I take you out for a night on the town, courtesy of this generous account?'

I squirmed in my chair. 'Tonight?'

'Yes, tonight. I have tonight free in my schedule.'

'Forgive me, Murakami-san, but tonight may be difficult. It is my intention to have the Kawazaki files ready by Wednesday . . .'

'Now now, Sato-san. You can't wriggle your way out of this one. Today is the day you learn to delegate.' Murakami-san beamed triumphantly.

I pushed my spectacles up the bridge of my nose. I was flattered that my boss had taken such an interest in me, but the mere thought of an evening of drinking and carousing made my stomach shrivel in trepidation. 'I . . . er . . .'

'I'll come for you at six,' he announced.

Twisting my fingers in my lap, I smiled back awkwardly, flushed with defeat.

All afternoon I hoped that Murakami-san would forget. At five to six I sneaked away to the water fountain. I wasn't thirsty, but I thought if I loitered there Murakami-san would grow impatient and leave without me. Many of my colleagues were queuing at the vending machine, purchasing coffee to fuel the hours of overtime that stretched ahead. How I envied them! I hadn't been hiding there long when Murakami-san came striding down the corridor towards me, his heavy over-coat billowing behind him.

'Ah! Sato-san. Thought I'd find you here!' he thundered. 'I brought your briefcase and jacket.' He thrust them into my arms. 'Now, what do you fancy for dinner? I know a restaurant in Shinsaibashi that serves battered squid so sublime it'll make your toes curl!'

A giant plastic crab sat on the roof of the restaurant, waving its mechanical claws at passers-by. Inside, it was overcrowded and noisy. Murakami-san ordered plate after plate of skewered seafood for us to cook on the grill in the centre of our table. The grill glowed with heat, baking Murakami-san's complexion to terracotta. He also requested a large jug of sake. My stomach gave a nauseous tremor at its paint-stripper fumes, but I took a couple of polite sips anyway. Through mouthfuls of squid and tiger prawns Murakami-san told me of his recent golf tournament. He invited me to participate in the next one, turning a deaf ear to my protestations that I am an awful sportsman. The laughter and chants of the college students at the next table rang in my ears. They were terribly rowdy, and even the girls swigged beer and sat with their knees pulled up to their chests. I remember the folk clubs we used to go to in Tokyo, how we used to sit and talk quietly with our friends, appreciating the music. There was none of this incessant gossiping into mobile phones or using chopsticks to pop the tops off beer bottles.

Murakami-san was growing disgracefully tipsy. His eye-lids were bee-stung and his cheeks had taken on an unsettling burgundy hue. This reassured me. Surely now, considering his inebriated state, he would want to go home to bed. When we received the bill I suggested that perhaps we should call it a night, especially as we both had work the following day. Murakami-san blinked at me, in-credulous. 'Nonsense!' he boomed. 'It's only nine thirty! . . . Now, tell me, Sato-san, how's your English?'

In the smoky lounge, many businessmen sat in groups encircling the low, wooden tables. Lampshades with tasselled fringes dangled above them, and the chairs were scattered with soft, velvet cushions. Not that the décor was the first thing to command your attention. Dotted about the lounge, evenly dispersed between the groups of salary-men, were four or five foreign hostesses. The lounge had a very gay and frolicsome atmosphere, laced with peals of feminine laughter. 'Mariko! Oi! Mariko!' Murakami-san bellowed. A dainty Japanese hostess whisked up to our table and took our drinks order. Despite my protests, Murakami-san ordered me a double whisky.

He leant forward, invigorated by our exotic surround-ings. 'Sato-san. Tell me . . . what do you think of these foreign women?'

At that moment a blond girl in a red dress stood up to accompany a group of departing businessmen to the door. She was very reluctant to see them go, teasing and cajoling them to stay a bit longer. The blond girl was uncommonly tall, at least a head taller than a couple of the men she was saying goodbye to.

'They are very tall,' I ventured.

Another foreign girl emerged from the kitchen, seemingly shrink-wrapped in her black lycra dress. She wore im-practical shoes with dangerously high heels that must have put crippling pressure on her toes. When she spotted

Murakami-san she waved and hurried towards us. Her hair was orange and piled on top of her head.

Murakami-san and I both stood and bowed in greeting.

'Murakami-san! What a surprise! How are you?' she cried in halting Japanese. This impressed me enormously. Japanese-speaking foreigners are very rare.

'In excellent health as always, my princess! Excellent health! Now, allow me to introduce my company subordinate, Sato-san. Sato-san, this is Stephanie. She is from Florida.'

'You work for Murakami-san! How nice!' she said and smiled warmly. She looked very radiant and healthy, full of Florida sunshine and vitamins.

We all sat down. The little Japanese hostess served us our whiskies and slipped back to the bar again. I noted with interest that Stephanie from Florida had orange eyebrows. She also had orange freckles, sprinkled across every square inch of skin, from her forehead to her wrists. She seemed unabashed by these freckles and had made no attempt to camouflage them. Stephanie was terribly fond of Murakami-san, positively enthralled by his every word. When he brought a cigar to his mouth she quickly held aloft a silver lighter, to spare him the inconvenience of lighting the cigar himself. On the stage some men had begun to shunt about heavy speakers and tighten guitar strings.

'So how are things at work?' Stephanie asked, generously addressing both of us, even though I am of lesser company ranking.

'Work bores me!' Murakami-san complained. 'Day in, day out: the same tedious drivel.'

I bristled with disapproval. A Deputy Senior Managerial Supervisor should know better than to make flippant remarks injurious to the reputation of Daiwa Trading.

'Let's not talk about work. It's all stuffy board meetings and broken photocopiers. Let us drink whisky and talk about golf instead! I have a tournament coming up next week, you know.'

'How exciting!' Stephanie exclaimed, leaning across the table in her eagerness to hear about the golf tournament. As she did so her ample cleavage tumbled forwards, disclosing far too many secrets of the female flesh for comfort. I examined some potted ferns by the door.

'I had a tournament last week too. The Daiwa Trading team were ranked ninth in the Osaka prefecture. We would have finished higher if it wasn't for my dratted shoulder injury.'

Stephanie's face fell in dismay. 'Never mind. You'll do better next time.'

'Yes, we will. Sato-san has offered to join us next week, haven't you, Sato-san? I'm going to take him to practise his swing.'

Fortunately another hostess materialized at our table and the conversation shifted from the perilous subject of golf. It was the statuesque, blond girl in red I had spied earlier. Murakami-san and I stood and bowed once more.

'Murakami-san! Long time no see. How are you this evening?' Her Japanese appeared to be fluent, but her accent was very coarse and unladylike.

'I'm in marvellous health, thank you. Allow me to intro-duce my company subordinate, Sato-san. Sato-san, this is Mary.'

We exchanged How-do-you-dos? and with a perfunctory smile Mary sat herself in the chair beside me. This seemed to please Murakami-san, who gave the distinct impression of wanting to talk privately with Stephanie.

Suddenly stranded, I was very nervous of this tall, blond girl – so nervous, I took a grimacing sip of whisky. She tucked her chair in, her face drifting into the light. With a start I realized that this girl was terribly young, far too young to be working in a hostess bar. I wondered if her parents knew what she did for a living, so many thousands of miles away from America. Blond hair cascaded down to her shoulders in feathery layers, a few strands oddly static and levitating about her head. Her fine, young skin was suffocated beneath thick foundation and her mauve eye shadow had migrated to the creases in her eyelids. She tapped a cigarette from a packet she had with her, lit it and inhaled with relish.

'I would like to congratulate you on your Japanese,' I began, somewhat timidly. 'It is exemplary.'

'Thanks,' she replied, blowing smoke into my eyes.

'If I may presume, you are an American?'

Mary flinched slightly, her smile tightening. 'No. I'm English.'

Well, I was delighted to hear she was from England. 'I am a great fan of Sherlock Holmes!' I exclaimed. 'I have read every book in the series. More than twice!'

'Really?' Mary said, her eyes flickering with interest. 'Wasn't he an opium addict?'

I stared at her blankly. I know nothing of this opium addiction. 'I also greatly admired your Princess Diana,' I added sombrely. 'I am very sorry she died.'

'That's OK. I think we've just about got over it,' Mary said.

I may be mistaken, but her lips seemed to twitch in amusement. Her callousness stunned me and I had to look away.

On stage the band had finished their preparations. The band members didn't look Japanese at all, more like immigrants from the Philippines or Indonesia. I thought them very smart with their lilac tuxedos and neatly Brylcreemed hair. Without introduction they launched into a splendid rendition of 'Hotel California' by the Eagles. It was very pleasant and melodious and I soon began tapping my foot in time to the music. Across the table Murakami-san and Stephanie, ensconced in their tight cocoon of intimacy, exchanged urgent whispers. Mary wore a glazed expression as she picked scarlet varnish from her fingernails. Sensing my gaze, she jerked from her reveries. She glanced at the band and gave me a 'thumbs up' of smiling approval. Then, remembering her duties as a hostess, she asked if she could get me another drink.

I glanced at my glass. It was three-quarters full. 'That is not necessary. Thank you,' I said.

Then Mary did something very peculiar. She began to laugh and throw her head about as though I had made a joke. I smiled uncertainly. 'So . . . Tell me about your job!' she blurted with sudden enthusiasm.

I blinked. 'I am sure you will find it very dull.'

'Oh no!' she protested. 'I like hearing about other people's jobs.'

She then looked anxiously towards the bar. I turned, curious as to the source of her distress. At the bar stood a plump and burlesque Mama-san, who was beckoning sternly to Mary. A halo of black curls framed the Mama-san's head. Her dress sense was highly eccentric for a woman of her advanced years: a velvet dress with a plunging neckline and an extravagant, floor-sweeping skirt. Just like a heroine from those historical romance novels you liked to read in the bath. Clutched tightly to her bosom was a tiny dog with bouffant hair. The dog stared at me, unnerving me with its fierce little eyes.

'Is that the proprietress?' I asked Mary.

'Erm . . . yeah,' she said. 'I'd better go.'

Trailing her spiked heels as she went, Mary crossed the lush maroon carpet to speak to the Mama-san. After a terse exchange of words, punctuated by the fraught yaps of the tiny dog, Mary was sent into the kitchen. I did not see her again after that.

In spite of the fact I had no one to talk to I was quite content. I ordered a lemonade from the little Japanese hostess and she brought me one with a jaunty parasol and a curly drinking straw. We shared a chuckle over this frivolity. The immigrant band were superb and played a variety of popular tunes. I think you would have enjoyed them very much.

Several couples twirled about the dance floor, including

Murakami-san and Stephanie from Florida. A glittery disco ball revolved from the ceiling, shifting pretty shafts of light over the faces of couples. I have to report that Murakami-san was not very skilled on the dance floor. He shuffled drunkenly in Stephanie's arms in a manner hardly suggestive of dancing. Fortunately for Murakami-san, Stephanie's sturdy Western frame supported him like scaffolding. Despite Murakami-san's drunken condition Stephanie smiled serenely as he drooled and slurred gibberish in her ear. The smile persevered even as she gently removed a wayward hand from her behind.

After an hour or so the lounge began to empty. One by one businessmen, giddy with philandering and liquor, bid their farewells and swung out of the double doors. The immigrant band played their final song of the evening – a gloriously heartfelt rendition of 'Unchained Melody' – and began to pack up their equipment. After returning to the table Murakami-san slumped in his seat, occasionally patting Stephanie's thigh or gazing at her affectionately. She sat quietly, the tranquil smile never slipping from her lips. The hour was shockingly late – about one o' clock. I was about to ask Murakami-san if I should call a taxi to take us home, when the petite Japanese hostess appeared at our table.

'I am sorry to interrupt,' she said, though we had been sitting in deathly silence, 'but we are closing in thirty minutes. So it's last orders for the drinks.'

Murakami-san's unfocused pupils roved in a lazy gyroscopic spin as he cultivated a spit bubble between his lips. Stephanie was smoking a cigarette and looking at her watch.

'I don't think we need any more drinks, thank you,' I said.

The Japanese hostess looked at Murakami-san and tittered. 'No, I don't suppose you do!' she giggled, modestly raising her fingertips to her mouth. 'Shall I just bill your company account, then?'

'Yes. Thank you. It's Daiwa Trading . . .'

'Yes. I know.'

She didn't leave immediately. She stood there for a moment, her eyes resting upon me. She looked even younger than Mary, her hair in a sleek bob, her eyes wide and gazelle-like. 'Well, then . . .' she said, and, with a wry smile, moved on to the next table.

Outside, the entertainment strip was awash with revellers still in pursuit of sleazy distraction. The sight of so many salarymen amazed me. However do they concentrate at work the next day? Neon signs flashed with the promise of topless cabaret and exotic dance acts incorporating pythons. It was all so bright and mind-fuddling that I wanted to locate a dimmer switch. Murakami-san flailed about on his fifth attempt to thread his arm through the sleeve of his overcoat. Then he stumbled into an alleyway to urinate against some wheelie-bins. As I stood listening to the drumming of urine against plastic I burnt with an in-explicable shame. Going to that hostess bar had been a terrible mistake. And it had cost the company 50,000 yen. If that's how much Murakami-san likes American women he could have bought himself an aeroplane ticket to the United States instead! When Murakami-san reappeared from the alleyway, cheerfully zipping up his fly, I could barely look him in the eye. My glum mood bounced off him completely.

'So, Sato-san!' he cried, slapping me on the back, 'how d'you like The Sayonara Bar?'

I resisted a stubborn urge to ignore him, reminding myself that he was the Deputy Senior Managerial Supervisor. 'I very much enjoyed the band,' I said.

'I mean the girls, Sato-san. The foreign bitches!'

'They were very tall.'

Murakami-san cackled with laughter and paused beneath the awning of a noodle restaurant. Tattered red lanterns swayed above his head. 'How about some noodles?' he asked, squinting at the grease-tinged menu.

'Actually, Murakami-san, thank you very much for your kind hospitality but I think I will take a taxi home now. I want to be fresh for work tomorrow,' I said apologetically.

'Don't be ridiculous! It's still early! I promise you . . . the whores at this next place will blow your mind.' His eyes glinted and he lowered his voice to a stage whisper. 'How d'you like massages?'

'Murakami-san, I am most grateful for the hospitality you have shown me this evening, but I really should return home.'

'Sato-san,' he said, his face hardening slightly, 'as your boss, I officially grant you the day off tomorrow. There. Now you can stop panicking about the dratted office and enjoy yourself.'

'No,' I said.

'What?'

'I am going home.'

Murakami-san sighed, his voice softening. 'Sato-san, I am only trying to help you.'

Well, I was entirely flabbergasted. It was *he* who needed help! Indulging himself in these lubricious pursuits night after night. I suddenly thought of his wife, a sweet, homely woman who always provides picnic hampers for the annual cherry-blossom viewing. How hurt she would be if she knew!

'I am in no need of help,' I asserted, stony-faced.

Murakami-san leant against the window of the noodle shop and hiccuped. He pointed at my hand, at the wedding band on my finger. 'C'mon, Sato-san,' he wheedled. 'How long's it been already? Maybe things would be easier if you just took that off.' He smiled encouragingly, his stance wobbly, his head lolling slightly.

I glimpsed my reflection in the noodle-shop window and recognized the belligerence smouldering behind my spectacles. I remembered walking along a beach in Okinawa and impaling my foot upon a nail; the searing pain and shock of seeing the rusty apex of that nail poking through my shoe. As I smiled back at Murakami-san a tourniquet tightened across my chest.

'Ah! That's more like it, Sato-san!' Murakami-san said, beaming with staunch approval. 'How about we give the food a miss and move straight on! What do you say?'

And what did I say, my sweet? I said nothing. Smiling grimly instead, I turned my back and walked away.

4

MARY

Tonight Yuji turns up just after one, hair hanging in his eyes, jeans sliding down his hips. The only salaryman left in the lounge sips neat gin; he's sunken into the sofa cushions, heartbroken and dazed. Despondently he lifts his feet so Stephanie can vacuum beneath them.

Yuji strolls behind the bar. 'Jesus, he looks like he's lost everything, twice over,' he murmurs.

I am kneeling on the floor, restocking the fridge with Asahi and Budweiser, but I know who he means. 'That guy is going through a really nasty divorce at the moment.' I raise my voice over the *clink clink* of beer bottles.

Yuji shakes his head, like the salaryman has disgraced his team or something. 'He needs to pull himself together. Be a man about it.'

I close the fridge and haul myself upright. Yuji kicks aside the empty beer crate that sits between us. He grins, his teeth white against bronzed skin, more handsome than I care to admit. How does he stay so preternaturally healthy? So resilient to the regime of Marlboros, amphetamines and junk food?

'Save the advice for yourself,' I say. 'Don't think it won't happen to you one day.'

'Divorce is nothing that a trip to a strip joint can't cure,' Yuji jokes.

'Such maturity,' I marvel. 'Such wisdom.'

Yuji's grin broadens. His sense of compassion may leave much to be desired, but that smile of his is beyond reproach. I slide my hands inside his jacket, over the cotton of his T-shirt, down to his waist, skimming beneath the waistband of his jeans. I move closer, breathing in cigarettes and citrus shower gel, and that other indefinable something he always carries about with him.

'Mary . . . You know my mother's probably watching us on her TV.'

The tiny camera above the bar has its red blinking eye on us. I smile at the thought of it.

'It's gone one – she'll be too tanked-up on vodka to care.'

Something flickers across Yuji's face. Irritation? A wry smile chases it out. 'Listen, Mary, how long are you gonna be exactly?'

Outside, the rain is barely perceptible, filling the pavements of Shinsaibashi like a blotchy rash. The bar fronts are awash with neon and customers bellowing into mobile phones, Korean hiphop and reggae filtering out from behind them. At the taxi rank a long queue wobbles; Uniqlo-clone college students, droopy-headed salarymen sleep-queuing, two curfew-violating schoolgirls collapsing against each other, helpless with braying laughter. Yuji strides ahead, pulling me by the hand. Katya's heels click their come-hither click alongside me, the sleeve of her faux-fur coat silky friction against my arm.

'Your pulse is twenty beats per minute, sir. You're practically a dead man! Come inside. We'll get one of our nurses to revive you.' A girl in an undersized nurse's uniform stands, hand on hip, in a red-lit doorway, a syringe tucked into her suspender belt, a toy stethoscope hooked round her neck. She wags her finger at the salarymen she has just flagged down, their faces cleaved by grins of carnal delight.

'Someone should tell Florence Nightingale she has to plug that thing in her ears,' Katya nit-picks in English.

'Oh, I'm sure the men don't mind.' I answer in Japanese, so Yuji doesn't feel excluded.

'The men don't mind what?' Yuji asks.

My Japanese vocabulary doesn't stretch to stethoscope, probably never will. 'That nurse,' I say.

'Oh, her . . . I know her. They didn't mind her pistol-whipping them back when she was a cowgirl at Hiday's either . . . OK, left here . . . This is the place.'

The Under Lounge is a lush, velvet-lined womb. Helmut Lang-swathed space cadets smoke clove cigarettes and waft expensive perfume about the bar. The DJ resides in the basement below, techno thudding through the floorboards like a subterranean heartbeat. I'm keen to go down and check it out, but Yuji leads us to a wrought-iron, double helix of a spiral staircase. The bouncer stationed at the top nods at Yuji and unhooks a gold rope to allow us through to the VIP area, a mezzanine overlooking the main bar space. The so-called VIPs are gathered around low, curvy tables, lit by trembling candles. Yuji homes in on the sofa where Kenji, Shingo and this much older guy sit. The older guy stands and engages Yuji in an affectionate bout of backslapping and handshaking. 'Yuji, you rascal, we thought you'd stood us up!'

Kenji and Shingo stand too, all labels and designer stubble. The older guy is impeccably attired, his shirt crisp and the crease in his trousers knife-edge.

'Yamagawa-san, this is Mary. Mary, Yamagawa-san.'

'Wow, Yuji! Fine piece of eye candy you've got there.'

'Erm, she can understand Japanese. She studied it at university.'

Kenji and Shingo laugh. Yamagawa's grin stretches to breaking point. Isn't Yuji going to introduce Katya? Unperturbed, Katya unclasps her handbag and looks for her cigarettes.

'Beauty and intellect, eh? Why are you knocking about with an old shit-for-brains like Yuji?'

I smile and shrug. 'I ask myself the same thing.'

Yamagawa-san laughs uproariously. 'That makes us even. I often ask myself what the scoundrel's still doing in my employment.'

We sit on the sofa opposite them. A waiter glides over and takes our drinks orders in automated solemnity, before gliding off again. Yamagawa-san begins lecturing the boys, his earthy Kansai dialect gargled through a throatful of catarrh. I listen, catching only fragments of his spiel – high-flown stuff about samurai loyalty and ethics. What relevance this has to three motorcycle couriers is beyond me.

'Oh, how he adores the sound of his own voice,' Katya whispers.

'His accent is so strong,' I say, 'I only understand every other word.'

'It's boring as hell. But look at the boys. So well behaved!'

We share an indulgent smile. Katya tells me about a junk shop she discovered in Kyoto that sells dirt-cheap old kimonos. She knows I like to cut up kimono fabric and make my own stuff: skirts, shift dresses, handbags. I'm a shitty seamstress, though, my creations wonky-hemmed and full of rents. Yuji says the clattering of the sewing machine makes his head hurt, makes him think of sweat-shops packed with illegal immigrants. 'You look like a gypsy,' he jokes, whenever he sees me dressed in my own couture.

Sometimes I think Katya would make a more fitting girl-friend for Yuji. Katya with her shampoo-ad sensuality and steely veneer of glamour; her never-chipped nail polish and designer shoes. But I've never detected any sexual fris-son between them. On the rare occasions the three of us end up in a bar together, they direct their comments to me, never to each other. I'll return from the toilet to find them smoking in silence, conversation suspended in my absence. I don't know whether to be flattered or unnerved, whether their silence is one of mutual indifference or complicity. I remember lying on the sofa with Yuji one afternoon, drowsing in front of a Hanshin Tigers game, my dress hitched up round my waist. 'Katya's really pretty, isn't she?' I said, trying for a light and breezy, unjealous tone. Yuji yawned and replied: 'What? Katya? Yeah, I suppose . . . if you like your women made of ice.' Then he drew his hand up between my thighs and said: 'I'm getting tired of all this baseball, aren't you?'

Yamagawa-san sounds like the background drone of a radio tuned into a tedious evangelical broadcast. Yuji, Kenji and Shingo listen raptly, *hhmming* in the right places. Shame they can't understand English. They'd find what Katya is saying far more fascinating. She is telling me about a client at The Sayonara Bar who paid her 30,000 yen to walk on a glass coffee-table in a skirt as he lay underneath.

'Tsuru-san?'

'Yes, Tsuru-san.'

'*The* Tsuru-san? The company chairman who always does Johnny B. Goode on karaoke?'

'The one and only.'

'You're joking! And you let him look up your skirt? Katya, *please* tell me you were wearing something underneath!'

'Five minutes was all he wanted. The easiest 30,000 yen I have ever made. He offered me 40,000 extra if I peed on him.'

'You peed on him?'

'I drank two litres of Evian from the minibar, then we sat on the hotel bed and watched the news on cable until I was ready.'

I bristle with incredulity and furtive awe. 'Katya, you are full of shit.'

'I am not.' Then, smiling, she says, 'Well . . . maybe a little.'

It hardly matters. Katya lies so beautifully that I still half believe her. She takes a Marlboro and strikes a match on a slim box with THE SAYONARA BAR printed on the side. A fleeting shadow of concentration crosses her face as she holds the flame up to the cigarette. Yuji's hand descends on my knee. A swift, proprietorial squeeze and then it is gone, as though it had never strayed. But Katya notices as she exhales, a Cupid's-bow smile framing her crooked teeth.

It's 3 a.m. and the dance floor is strobe-lit chaos, stewing in its own infernal heat. We watch tonight's consolidated clique of humanity; saucer-eyed in a sea of limbs, jerking as if conducted by manic puppeteers. Soon the seismic *thud thud thud* proves too hard to resist and we weave our way onto the dance floor. I dance self-consciously at first, but after a while I get into it, decorum swept away with my inhibitions. Katya is more constrained; she dances practically on the spot. Shimmying, I call it. I think it might be the way they dance in Ukrainian discos, but always forget to ask. Though Yuji is only sitting upstairs I miss him. I miss his broad-shouldered self-assurance, his hand on my knee. I can't think of a single person I would admit this to.

Dancing sober quickly becomes as boring as waiting for a bus. Katya and I go and sit with our vodka-tonics on two of the primary-coloured beanbags strewn about the chill-out room. The music here aims to sedate and only a few girls dance, slow and introspectively. The smell of weed, enticingly pungent, drifts from a group of boys with fluorescent dreadlocks.

I tuck my legs beneath me, and say to Katya: 'If you could go anywhere in the world, where would you go?'

It's a question asked for conversation's sake but Katya *hmmms* and pretends to give it some serious reflection. 'The seventh floor of the Hankyu department store.'

'I'm offering you anywhere in the world. Back to the Ukraine . . . China . . . Sri Lanka . . . anywhere.'

'I once found a Christian Dior dress marked down eighty per cent in the Hankyu, I'll have you know.'

'The Hankyu department store is three train stops away. Where's your sense of adventure?'

'I came to Japan, didn't I?' Katya protests.

'You've been here almost three years. Aren't you bored of it by now?'

'Bored? Never!'

'Well, you can't stay here for ever. You must have something planned.'

'Maybe I'll make a pilgrimage to a Tibetan mountain top. Fly to Florida to swim with the dolphins. Find a filthy-rich salaryman to marry. Fuck knows.'

I laugh. Best not to pursue this line of conversation if it makes Katya so tetchy.

Her hand brushes the nape of my neck as she lifts a handful of my hair and says: 'You should have your hair like that girl over there. It would really suit you.'

Before long Yuji appears, escorting Yamagawa-san on a tour of the club. They pause for a moment in the doorway, Yuji the taller by an inch or two.

'Yamagawa-san is way too old to be here,' I whisper to Katya.

Ageist, I know, but upstairs in the world of plush sofas and candle-lit sophistication, Yamagawa-san belonged. Down here among the nubile, fashion-obsessed youths, he's a blaring impostor. As they make their way over I haul myself up off the beanbag, then lend a hand to Katya.

'We thought you were dancing. We were searching for you in the other room,' Yuji says, touching my shoulder.

He smiles and the rest of the room vaporizes out of existence. I tell myself to get a grip.

'We got tired,' Katya says.

She twirls the ice cubes in her vodka-tonic with her straw. I realize that this is the first time she's spoken to Yuji tonight.

'Yeah, I am about ready to go home,' I say, hoping Yuji will be sensitive to the fact I worked an eight-hour shift before coming out.

Instead he says: 'Mary, Yamagawa-san was telling me earlier that he wants to dance. I said you'd dance with him. You don't mind, do you?'

What! Does Yuji think that I work for him as well as his mother? I shoot him a sharp look that should leave him in no doubt as to whether I mind or not. His eyes flash back impatience.

'Of course I don't mind!'

Smiling warmly, I hand Yuji my vodka-tonic and take his boss by the hand.

The music has downsized to drums, bass and genderless vocals spun from helium. Two girls sway like sunflowers with over-long stems. One of the dreadlocks brigade whacks at an imaginary drum-kit in hopeful approximation of dancing. Everyone else lolls about, brains frazzled martyrs to hedonism. With a crinkly smile Yamagawa-san puts his arms round me. I remind myself that everyone in the room is far too wasted to pay us any attention, that Yuji will be grateful I indulged his boss's eccentric whim.

'Do you come here often?' I ask as we shuffle back and forth.

'Rarely, and when I do I stay upstairs. But Yuji wanted to know where his pretty English girlfriend had got to, so I thought I'd stretch my legs.'

My wrists rest lightly on Yamagawa-san's shoulders; his broad hands span my waist. Up close his face is fissured and grainy-textured, his eyebrows threaded with grey. His aftershave smells like Old Spice, reminding me of pipe-smoking uncles and bygone family gatherings.

'Your Japanese is excellent for a foreigner, Mary.'

'Thank you.'

'Do you take lessons over here?'

'I pick up a lot from working as a hostess.'

Yamagawa-san beams. 'Splendid. And how do you like Japan?'

Truth is, I don't know how I like Japan. I have a scattered appreciation. I like the bowing shop assistants and being serenaded in the night by cicada song. On the other hand, I don't like the elementary-school kids trailing me around Izumiya, commenting on what I put into my shopping basket: 'Look! Americans eat Japanese sushi too' and 'Foreigners use tampons!' That, I can live without.

'I like the contrast between old Japan and new – y'know, sumo and *kyogen*, and, er . . . bullet trains and *anime*.'

The answer lacks my usual aplomb. I sound like I am feeding random words into a Japanese-sentence generator.

'*Kyogen*, eh? What a cultured young lady you are! Y'know, my daughter loves *kyogen*.'

'Really?'

'Yes. The two of you should meet up. I can get tickets so you can go and see a *kyogen* play together.'

'I would love that.' I really would. I don't have many female Japanese friends.

'I must warn you, though, she will probably bother you for English-conversation practice.'

'Oh, I don't mind one bit. I can give you my phone number . . . I'm free most afternoons.'

'Perfect. My daughter is a student so she is also free most afternoons . . . and mornings and evenings.' He chuckles.

I smile and our gazes lock. His eyes are packed with tiny red fuses, and have an oddly narcotic glaze. His jaw judders, reinforcing my suspicions. It throws me, the contradiction of thoughtful father and yakuza coke-head. At my waist his fingers move, brushing the inch of bare skin between my skirt and top. Alarmed, I look over his shoulder, to signal my unease to Yuji. But I only see Katya curled up on a large orange beanbag, her dark hair veiling her sleeping face. Yuji must have wandered off somewhere. Typical.

*

It was mid-October, the tail end of the rainy season, when Yuji walked into The Sayonara Bar. He was wearing jeans and a hooded sweater, DKNY or something, and his face was set in a fiercely handsome scowl. I had been working there for only seven days and thought he was a client. Ignoring everyone, he strode straight into Mama-san's office. Then, five minutes later, he was out again. Gone without a backwards glance. 'Who was that?' I asked the nearest person. The nearest person was an American hostess who obviously bore a grudge against Yuji because she said: 'That arrogant fucker is Mama-san's little boy.'

After work that night, sheets of rain crashed down on my cheap umbrella as I made my way to the taxi rank. Enough rain to drown yourself in, I thought. Teeth chattering, I found my mind stuck on the slant of his shoulders, the way his features fell in the proportions equivalent to perfection.

I did some background research and found out about his gangster connections, that his arms and shoulders swarmed with tattoos. Among the Sayonara Bar hostesses the jury was out. Opinions ranged from 'he's a good kid – good to his mother' to 'Yuji treats women like disposable chopsticks: use them once, then throw them away'.

It was a fortnight before I saw him again. I was in a bar in Namba, pressing buttons on the jukebox to make the CD sleeves flip round, when a voice behind me said: 'Hey, new girl. Put "Tokyo Boyz" on and I swear I will have my mother fire you and pack you off back to England before the jukebox finishes playing your song.'

He was wearing a leather jacket this time. Up close, the impact of his face was a thousand-fold.

'Really? I wasn't going to put "Tokyo Boyz" on, but you've just reminded me how much I love them.'

He grinned at this. So you don't scowl all the time, I thought.

I turned back to the jukebox. 'What is it now?' I jagged my finger across the glass. 'F-17 . . . F-17 . . .' I made to type in the code.

Yuji lunged at the keypad from behind me, punching numbers at random to mis-select another J-Pop song instead.

I turned back, mock-aghast. 'That's 100 yen you just wasted,' I said.

'A hundred yen?'

'Yep, 100 yen. Gone.'

'Then, let me buy you a drink.'

I woke the next morning and saw he'd left his digital watch on my nightstand. Opaque plastic with the Nike logo swooshing across its face. And there was other evidence too: an empty bottle of Stolichyna, Marlboro stubs in the ashtray, carpet-burn on my back. Had I given him my phone number? Even if I hadn't he knew where to find me. But then a whole week of nothing passed. Another week and I told myself not to take it personally. Mariko agreed: 'He did the same thing to Tanya. Forget about him. And keep his stupid watch.' Then one night three weeks later, I left the changing room after work and saw him sprawled in the lounge. I'd had a tough shift. Mascara was panda-smudged round my eyes, and my throat was hoarse from smoking. *Why should I care if he thinks I look like shit?* I thought.

I eyed him with all the composure I could afford. 'Come to see your mother?'

'Yeah. And you. Been a while, hasn't it? I'm sorry I haven't been in contact – my boss packed me off to Okinawa, and I didn't have your phone number . . . You ever been to Okinawa?'

I shook my head.

'You should go, really. Sandy beaches, laid-back pace of life . . .'

What did I care about Okinawa?

'I have your watch if you want it back,' I said.

What happened later that evening was predictable. What happened the evening after that wasn't. He came back. I walked towards him after my shift, wary of the eyebrows arching behind my back. 'What are you doing here?' I asked, genuinely confused. His failure to disappear for another three weeks or so felt like a breach of etiquette. But then he came back the night after that, and the night after that. And before long it stopped occurring to me to wonder why.

It's chilly, but the duvet stays scrunched up at the foot of the futon. Yuji is wrapped tightly around me, his arms covering mine, his leg drawn over my thigh. I'd had him down as a back-turner, so it surprised me after the first time, when he'd clung to me like this. The darkness is thinning out. Soon the mailboxes in the lobby will begin to clatter, one after the other, as the papers are delivered. I feel the rise and fall of Yuji's chest against my back, a rhythm soothing and familiar.
   'Yuji.'
   There's no reply, but I think he's listening.
   'Yamagawa-san wants me to meet his daughter.'
   'Hmmm . . .'
   'I really hated dancing with him, Yuji.'
   No reply. He's probably too tired to speak.
   I hear the back gate creak and close my eyes.

Mama-san forces us to do *kyaku-hiki* once a week; more, if business has been slow. She scans her computer database for the phone numbers of patrons who've been lax on the attendance front and prints them out. Then we call them, using our feminine wiles to tempt and cajole them back into customer loyalty. Mama-san knows which clients have 'special relationships' with which hostesses, and she allocates the names and phone numbers accordingly. Commission is made for every client lured away from our rival hostess bars. After I had been at The Sayonara Bar for a couple of weeks Mama-san summoned me into work early. 'Come in at five today,' she'd said. 'You can sit with Katya and listen to her until you understand what you have to do.'

I didn't know much about Katya back then. While most of the other hostesses seemed keen to forge an intimacy with new hostesses early on, Katya treated me with polite detachment. When I arrived that afternoon, she was already sitting beneath the bar spotlights, winding the phone cord round her fingers as she squealed into the receiver.

'Mr Kobayashi! It's been weeks since I've seen you. Aren't you going to drop by and say hello?' Katya paused to let the receiver transmit his garbled strains. 'Don't be silly!' she chided. 'I am wearing the charm bracelet right now. I wear it all the time.' Her voice grew husky. 'I never take it off, not even in the shower . . .'

I clocked her bare wrists and wondered how she'd explain them if her client showed up. I sat down on the bar stool next to her as she said goodbye and hung up. She crossed the *kanji* for Mr Kobayashi's name off her list.

'He'll come,' she said. 'You can get away with all kinds of crap over the phone. It's easier to lie when you're not face to face.'

She spoke stilted English with an East European inflection, like a Bond villainness. I asked her where she was from and she said, 'The Ukraine.' When I told Katya her English was really good she shrugged and began to explain how to keep client phone calls down to under three minutes. It was weeks before Katya told me about herself.

Katya's mother is English. She moved to the Odessa with Katya's father when she was eighteen. I love the sound of that place: Odessa. It has the coarse glamour of frozen vodka and fur hats. Katya says her mother was unhappy in the Ukraine, driven near mad from loneliness. She had no one to speak English to, only Katya and a husband prone to long stretches of absenteeism. She eventually fled back to the UK when Katya was twelve.

'Your mother just left you behind?' I asked. 'Did you ever see her again?'

Katya didn't lift her eyes from the wineglass she was polishing. 'Never.'

'Do you want to see her again?'

'Not really.'

I could relate to that. Our backgrounds, both of us being shunned by our mothers, have a lot to do with why Katya and I get on. My mum has barely been in contact since she left for Spain. I haven't even bothered to tell her I am in Japan. What difference would it make? Katya had it much worse than I did, though.

She had to leave school at seventeen to work as a super-market checkout girl but was far too ambitious to accept this dreary fate. After two years of bar-code-scanning monotony Katya found an ad in a local newspaper recruiting girls to work in Japan. It didn't matter if you couldn't speak Japanese, the ad said, and you could earn the equivalent of a year's wages in a month. A fortnight later Katya and two other Ukrainian girls arrived at Kansai International Airport. She says it was rough at first, she didn't know a word of Japanese and worked for a shady yakuza-run hostess bar. I am not sure how exactly, but she broke free after a few months. She doesn't talk about it, but if I ever complain about blistered heels or arrogant clients, Katya will say: 'Quit whinging. You don't know how good we have it here!'

Katya wanted to know what I did before I came to Japan. I told her I'd studied Japanese Literature. That I'd come to Japan after splitting up with my boyfriend. He'd cheated on me with my friend. 'Histrionics are not my style,' I told Katya, wishing this were true. 'I went and got my passport renewed instead.'

When I got to Osaka I spent three days tramping through the alleys and arcades of the entertainment districts, gnawed at by loneliness, the straps of my backpack gouging my shoulders. Though my Japanese was pretty good, most places didn't want to risk employing someone with only a tourist visa and turned me away. By day I would haul myself from bar to bar, and at night I returned to the youth hostel where I was staying. I'd play a few lack-lustre rounds of Gin Rummy with the Australians in my dorm, before succumbing to abject despair in the non-privacy of my bunk.

Then I found The Sayonara Bar, on the sixth floor of a building crammed with a labyrinth of bars and private members' clubs. Mama-san eyed me carefully and said, 'I could probably organize some alien registration for you, get them to put down you're an English teacher or suchlike.' I said: 'Where from? The Department of Immigration?' Mama-san just looked at me and laughed. I started as a hostess that same evening.

5

WATANABE

As far as I know, I am the sole citizen of hyperspace. It may take several millennia for the mammalian brain to evolve the transcendental capacity that I have. I suspect there are extraterrestrial civilizations with minds as advanced as my own, but here in the primitive annals of Earth I am the sole figure of enlightenment. You might think me an outlandish liar. A freak of nature. But allow me to remind you: nothing happens in contradiction to nature. Only in contradiction to what we know of it.

Viewed through ordinary three-dimensional eyes, nothing remarkable can be said of this hostess bar. A weaselly pack of bankers sits in the lounge, the smoke from their cigars drifting in lazy Brownian motion towards the air vents. Hostesses slink panther-like between tables, bearing trays loaded with drinks and seaweed-flavoured delicacies. There is the usual animated chatter; the usual lies and banalities. As I stand upon this stepladder, wiping the dusty slats of the air vent, no one pays me much attention. Why should they? My baseball cap and ketchup-smeared apron hardly signify the deity of hyperspace that I am. Drained by my tedious surroundings, I begin to covet the sensory symphony, both beautiful and profound, that is the fourth dimension.

I lower my damp cloth into the bucket of water and, with a dextrous mental twitch, reach into the deepest catacombs of the human mind. In ontological warp speed the universe deconstructs before my eyes.

All at once I am flooded with omniscient comprehension. The hostess bar clientele become my own private anatomy lesson as they explode before me, resplendent with viscera and brains. The air is illuminated with mental activity. Thoughts flicker like fireflies, spark and flare like pyrotechnics in a jam jar. Electrical impulses accelerate along nerve fibres, synapses relaying bodily commands. Nothing escapes unseen in the realm of hyperspace. I could tell you the quantum fluctuation of every molecule in this bucket of water, the spin velocity of every electron. But why waste our time? Your underdeveloped minds cannot possibly process this information. Let me tell you some other things instead.

A row of salarymen lines the bar. The one in the navy suit is called Mr Yamashita. Mr Yamashita is an exports manager at Yasuka electronics. He has a gluten allergy and subsists on a macrobiotic diet. Digestive enzymes bombard the remnants of the green-bean salad he ate for lunch. His interests include amateur ornithology and ordering size 11 heels from an internet company catering for female impersonators. Mr Yamashita is currently sitting in the clutches of resident preying mantis Katya Kischel. Her blue eyes widen in a mimicry of sincerity. 'I'm working seven shifts a week now, I'm so desperate to raise money so my brother can have his life-saving kidney transplant.' Back in the Ukraine, Katya has five pig-farming brothers, the only physical defects among them being syphilis and mild schizophrenia. Mr Yamashita, the sentimental fool, is moved by this fabricated plight and intends to make Katya a generous donation. In the dark, cancerous recesses of her soul, Katya purrs. She nibbles a pistachio nut, a fragment of which gets caught between a premolar and incisor. She eases it out with her tongue and swallows. It free falls down her oesophagus to land in a corrosive pool of stomach bile.

There is a ripple in the fabric of space-time. Mary dashes into the bar. Beautiful Mary, with her pale, sapphire eyes and hair spun from gold. Her heart trills with anxiety as she scans the room for Mama-san, her tongue spring-loaded with apologies for her lateness. Mary's psyche is besieged by problems at the moment as she frets over an overdue rent cheque and the demands of her vile, necrophiliac boyfriend. Yet she finds the time to pause by my stepladder and smile up at me. The soft flesh of her lips pulled taut, her beauty soars to its zenith. For a moment there is nothing else. Nothing but an infinity of smiling Marys, swirling through hyperspace.

'Hello, Watanabe,' she says.

Smile back at her! I urge myself. Say hello!

But I am sadly bereft of vocal chords. With a lustrous shimmer of golden hair Mary walks away. She disappears into the changing room, a path of molecular insurrection blazing behind her.

Yesterday was my nineteenth birthday. My parents of the lower dimensional realm sent me a card adorned with a picture of a fluffy kitten. They also enclosed a photograph of themselves, standing to attention in the shade of a persimmon tree, boring into me with their unsmiling eyes. The photograph was unnecessary as I still remember what they look like. My father also wrote that he expected me to be fully engrossed in my studies by now and in the top one per cent of my class. If he knew how his son marked the new evolutionary phase of mankind, my grades would quickly wither into insignificance. It saddens me that he judges me by criteria my higher dimensional excursions have long rendered irrelevant.

I placed my birthday card on the mantelpiece. The kitten made me uneasy. It seemed to stalk me with its pathetically foetal eyes. I could bear only a few minutes of this before I was compelled to tear the card into many pieces and flush it down the toilet. I yanked hard on the lever several times so it would be flushed deep into the bowels of the Osaka sewage system. I then sank to my knees, trembling, ashamed of my ingratitude.

During my formative years, my father laboured to toughen me up. He knew how cruel the world could be and prepared me for it as best he could. My first brush with brutality came when I was in the fourth grade. I was taking a short cut home from school through the wooded area behind the playing fields when Michio and Kazuo Kaku, twin brothers notorious for their pre-pubescent savagery, dashed out from behind a thicket and began to belt me with their satchels. I was more shocked than hurt. Owing to the absence of books, the satchels lacked real clout. Once they had had their fun with the satchels, Michio, the smaller of the two, began to remove his jacket.

'C'mon, freak boy,' he taunted. 'Show us what you've got! I'll even let you get the first punch in.'

Sunlight filtered through the leafy canopy and dappled his lawless face. He handed his jacket to his brother Kazuo, who hastily stepped aside, eyes glinting with blood-lust. I stood there stunned. My spindly pipe-cleaner arms hung limply by my side.

'C'mon! Are you ready or not?'

Needless to say, I was not. Two minutes later I was face down on the track, curled like a wood-louse in defence mode. I had become one with pain: gut-flaying, lip-swelling, bloody-nosed pain.

Michio booted my unprotected backside a couple more times before announcing to his brother: 'Right . . . I think that should do it.'

He squatted beside me. I was playing dead at this point, a tactic I had seen endorsed on wildlife documentaries. '*Faggot*,' he whispered in my ear. 'We'll be back for you next month.'

They had begun to retreat down the path, when there came an almighty rustle from the bushes. The foliage parted and out stepped my father. Dusty tears of joy snaked down my face. *My father had come!* He nodded grimly at the twins and they halted before him. He then withdrew his wallet from the inside pocket of his suit and handed Michio a thousand-yen note. The Kaku twins bowed respectfully to my father before fleeing down the path, feral laughter cackling in their wake.

'Father?' I asked, fearful this was some cruel impostor.

His sombre shadow drifted across my face. 'Get up, Ichiro,' he ordered. 'That was abysmal. You have one month to learn how to put up a decent fight. I don't want to have to watch a rerun of that appalling performance.'

Some fathers pay for piano lessons. Others take their kids fishing. My father was committed to toughening me against the world. Every month until my senior year of high school, through cherry-blossom fall, snowstorm and blazing sunshine, I would be violently skirmished by the Kaku twins, each punch and kick that rained down upon me a fiery testament to paternal love.

Birthdays are nothing but a meaningless vanity. What significance are nineteen years to the great celestial time-piece in the sky? The whole of human civilization, in fact, is nothing more than a fleeting moment of the universe. Why should we exalt birthdays with presents and celebration? Why? Yesterday afternoon I climbed out of my bedsit window and onto the roof of my apartment building, where I sat, sucking on an effervescent vitamin C tablet and gazing upon the brownish haze of sulphur dioxide that swathed the Osaka skyline. I contemplated the millions of people living and working in Osaka. All 12,900,467 of them. I could see the office workers bustling about in those grey, pollution-smeared monstrosities they call skyscrapers. In Osaka City Hall I saw Mayor Takahashi accepting a bribe from a Sumitomo bank official. I saw a yakuza boss in Tennoji discipline a dissident gang member by severing his middle finger with a hacksaw. In the NHK television studios I saw popular talk-show host Yoko Mori snorting cocaine from her vanity mirror seconds before air time. I remained on that roof for several hours. I would have stayed up there longer if Mr Fuji, the landlord of my building, hadn't brought me out of my trance by dousing my feet with the fire hose.

'Watanabe. A moment of your time.'

There is a lush metallic clatter as Mama-san deposits a bucket of cutlery on the kitchen counter. My nasal receptors recoil from the stench of lavender talcum powder and canine incontinence. I put down the knife I am using to slice shiitake mushrooms and wipe my hands on my apron. Mama-san fixes me with her harsh, unyielding eyes. Fault lines and fissures score her face where her wrinkle-proofing foundation has cracked. Copious cleavage spills from her low-cut bodice, threatening to break ranks at any moment. As always Mr Bojangles, her tiny chihuahua, is nestled in her arms, moulting white fur over her velvet dress. Sheltered by Mama-san's formidable bulk, Mr Bojangles peers down his nose at me, haughty as visiting nobility.

'We have had complaints,' Mama-san announces brusquely.

Again? What fastidious bastards these salarymen are.

Mama-san extracts a fork from the cutlery bucket and holds it before me. 'Look at this fork, Watanabe. Now, what is wrong with it?'

The light glints from its slender metal prongs. It looks like a normal, healthy fork to me. I activate the depths of my advanced hyper-mind. In a billionth of a second the barriers of space and logic blast away as my surroundings detonate into a greater reality. The fork breaks down into its component matter and energy. The iron ions vibrate in their loosely knit lattice, like a lazy swarm of gnats. Even at a sub-atomic level everything is in order.

'There is nothing wrong with the fork,' I inform Mama-san.

'Watanabe!' she shrills, jabbing the fork in hazardous proximity to my eyes. 'It still has cheese on it.'

I take the fork from her and squint at it. There does appear to be some congealed substance clinging to the stem.

'I apologize. The dishwasher must be low on detergent.'

I bow my head for the appropriate length of time to demonstrate remorse. I must be having a rare off-day. Such is the dazzling complexity of hyperspace that it can occasionally induce mental fatigue.

'Watanabe, I want you to do that whole bucket again. This establishment has standards of hygiene to maintain. Once you have finished the cutlery the oil in the deep fryer needs changing: we cannot continue serving brown french fries to our customers . . .'

Mama-san nags with uninhibited abandon. Though her sour reprimands are unpleasant to the ears, I bear it. I recognize the true source of Mama-san's anger and frustration. A swift hormone analysis of her blood tells me her oestrogen levels are at an all-time low. The onset of the menopause. Her subliminal thought waves are restless with anxiety, turbulent with fears of hot flushes and osteoporosis. She waves a spatula in my face and persists in her raging discharge. Mr Bojangles yaps excitedly, delusions of supremacy bouncing within the confines of his tiny canine skull. Contained within the stomach of Mr Bojangles are the following: half a pound of rabbit-liver paté, the nozzle from a hairspray canister and a small colony of threadworms. I shift my weight from my left foot to my right, waiting for Mama-san's sabre-rattling to wind down. I remind myself that her scolding is nothing more than an attempt to reassert control when confronted with the deterioration of her body. I experience a twinge of sympathy. I may be a mere kitchen hand but at least I have my youth and the glorious omniscience of hyperspace.

'. . . And don't forget to clean the grease from the extractor fan!'

I nod. Mama-san turns on her heel and starts towards the bar. The clip-clop of her heels and the protruding bustle of her dress remind me of a centaur. And then . . . silence. My eardrums rejoice in the absence of pain. I return to slicing the shitake mushrooms, watching as the knife dissects each spongy fungal pore. In the far corner of the kitchen lives a family of cockroaches. They scuttle about behind the grime-coated skirting board, black armour gleaming, serrated mandibles twitching. I pause for a moment to observe them.

Beyond the belt of Orion, beyond the spiralling arms of Alpha Centauri, at the very periphery of space, there is a zone where anarchy reigns. Where the forces that govern the universe revolt and run amok, bringing chaos to all physical laws.

It is in these dark regions of the universe that there came to be a planet as flat as a disc. This planet is inhabited by a species called the Omegamorphs, a species with an entirely two-dimensional mode of existence. This means that they are completely flat, and when I say flat I don't mean flat like paper. I mean they have absolutely no 3-D projection.

Despite this handicap the Omegamorphs have evolved into highly intelligent life forms, blessed with a peaceful, educated civilization. They move about their planet by sliding across its flat surface. When they arrive at the planet's edge they simply flip themselves over to the other side.

One day Omegamorph 245HQK is sliding on his way to college, minding his own business, when a thunderclap resounds above him, a great cosmic echo reverberating through the skies. Omegamorph 245HQK is puzzled but he cannot look up to see what it is. In his world there is no such thing as vertical perception, only horizontal. But he can hear a voice, booming down from the heavens.

'Greetings, Omegamorph 245HQK. I am the intergalactic astronaut god of the third dimension. And I have come to liberate you from your tedious, flat little world.'

Omegamorph 245HQK is intrigued. He thought the third dimension existed only in comic-book mythology.

'As intergalactic astronaut god I am invested with the power to elevate you to the next level of reality, though I must warn you: the process is very risky and may be accompanied by dizziness, nausea and headaches. Sometimes nosebleeds too. Worst-case scenario is you go insane.

'And even if your mind is robust enough to cope you will suffer exquisitely. Unique in your genius, you will become isolated from the rest of the Omegamorphs, cast adrift as the sole figure of enlightenment.'

Omegamorph 245HQK finds the idea of this rather appealing.

'So happy, ignorant fool or prodigious son of the third-dimensional gods? Which is it to be? I will give you a moment to mull it over.'

Omegamorph 245HQK, who is not particularly keen to attend his afternoon lecture on Keynesian economics, does not hesitate in his decision. 'I would like to be a prodigious son of the third-dimension gods – if you don't mind.'

No sooner have the words been uttered than the fabric of space-time wrenches apart, and Omegamorph 245HQK is yanked into the third dimension.

In the span of a heartbeat he possesses perfect knowledge. Though he still rests upon the flat surface of his planet, his senses float in a perpendicular realm, bestowing on him a bird's-eye view of his planet, enabling him to witness all his fellow Omegamorphs sliding about their business. To his horror he realizes that he can now see inside them, the visceral events of their flat bodies exposed in excruciating detail. His new perception withholds nothing. He spots his mother pruning her bonsai, his little brother, Omegamorph 783HTY, snivelling because his

Digimon cards have been stolen. His mind begins to crumble beneath the enormity of it all.

'Either this is madness or this is Hell!' he bellows to the intergalactic astronaut god. With his new panoramic vision Omegamorph 245HQK casts his eyes skyward for the first time. He spots the astronaut god's spacecraft, hovering like a giant silver kidney-bean above.

'I've changed my mind,' he cries. 'Being able to see everything like this is really freaking me out!'

'Too late,' replies the astronaut god. 'We have to get going. Enjoy your new powers of cognition.'

And with an eardrum-perforating sonic boom the spacecraft vanishes, leaving Omegamorph 245HQK alone to deal with the terrifying consequences of his new gift.

The history of science involves the acceptance of concepts beyond your imagination. But discovering hyperspace is akin to waking one day to find the earth careering from its solar orbit into deepest space. Reality as I knew it was for ever changed. I had stumbled upon a realm two millennia of bungling scientific investigation had completely failed to detect.

I soon learnt that all the scientific theories mankind has assembled are mere *shadows* of the truth. That the truth in its entirety lies in hyperspace. Here in the fourth dimension quarks and neutrinos perform with the brazen abandon of circus seals. The Unified Field theory – the much coveted Holy Grail of physics – flaunts itself like a debutante at a charity ball. So why, I hear you ask, am I withholding this infinite wisdom? Why don't I go ahead and alter the landscape of modern physics for ever? My silence is not of my choosing. My transformation into a higher life form has placed a conceptual chasm between myself and the rest of civilization. Human language simply lacks the range and power to communicate the reality of what I see. I could speak for all eternity and not convey a thousandth of it.

*

We are alone, Mary and I.

I mop the floor and watch as Mary moves about the dank gloom of the lounge, radiating her soft nebulosity. She is busy ferreting behind the sofa cushions; a private ritual for her ever since she found a ten-thousand-yen note tucked away there last month. All kinds of stuff falls from the pockets of the clientele into the sofa's dark crevices: gold cufflinks, business cards, vials of Viagra. I should tell Mary that she is wasting her time, that the only thing the sofa will yield tonight is a defective plastic lighter. But I like to watch her as she flings the cushions aside, fluff and grit collecting in her French-manicured nails.

A schmaltzy, instrumental version of 'Norwegian Wood' plays in the bar, sound waves billowing the sentimental melody into our ears. In the fourth dimension, music is an enigma solved. Why does a rising crescendo exult the spirit? Why does a minor chord evoke sadness? Because music stirs the ether in which our emotions float – a metaphysical feat witnessed only in hyperspace. I watch the melody tiptoe across the threshold of Mary's subconscious. She looks up from her scavenging, wondering what has come over her. I heave the slimy tendrils of my mop back and forth, feigning ignorance.

My hankerings for Mary may smack of juvenile infatuation, but that is not the case. Sure, I used to get crushes on girls when I was a naïve high-school student, but those crushes were incited by superficial features, such as hair and eyes and personality. The perspective of hyperspace allows me to appreciate Mary's inner beauty; the fine vaulted architecture of her mind; the way the right hemisphere of her brain lights up as she scrawls left-handed upon the food-order pad. While most people marvel at her svelte figure and blond hair, I am busy admiring the tightly coiled python of her intestines; the vivid, fiery arteries spurting blood to the extremities of her flesh . . .

'Something the matter, Watanabe?'

I start at Mary's voice, its serrated edge cutting through the gentle waves of Muzak. 'No.'

'It's just that you were staring at me.'

'Oh. Sorry.'

Mary has begun to emit powerful pulsars of suspicion in my direction. I duck beneath the rim of my baseball cap and grip the mop handle, my knuckles whitening, sweat clamouring to evacuate the palms of my hand.

'By the way, could you put some more detergent in the dishwasher? The glasses keep coming out stained.'

I penetrate the stainless-steel exterior of the dishwasher and see that detergent levels are sufficient, but I nod, put my mop into the bucket and wander into the kitchen.

I lug the heavy six-litre container of detergent back into the bar. The scene before me wrenches me apart. Mary's boyfriend has arrived in my absence and the pair are now canoodling. I stall in the doorway, debating whether to slip back into the kitchen, then Yuji spots me.

'Hey, Watanabe-san,' he says, releasing Mary. 'How's it going?'

I grunt ambiguously.

'I'll just get my jacket,' Mary tells Yuji. She walks away, throwing him a backwards smile – the happiest smile she has smiled all evening. A dull, toothache throb of suffering consumes me.

Yuji wanders over to the bar, his brawny musculature rippling. I cheer myself by surveying his puny walnut brain and the flaccid tar receptacles embedded in his chest (left lung: 540 ml tar deposits; right lung: 612 ml).

'Hey, Watanabe, can you pass me that bottle of sake? No, the larger one. Thanks.'

Yuji smiles, but I refuse to indulge his cheap camaraderie. I only have to pierce the fog of testosterone shrouding his brain to see how he disrespects Mary, how he tells his friends she is his English whore. Hidden away in his memory depository I see the broken wrist he once dealt his ex-girlfriend and seethe. Yuji grins, mistaking it for an expression of sociability.

'Y'know what, Watanabe, you should come out drinking with us some time. D'you remember Aiko? Hot little number, isn't she? She was asking after you last week . . .'

I baulk at the mention of Aiko. Aiko worked here last autumn. She had a mania for Hello Kitty friendship bracelets.

'Hey, Mary. What do you think about taking Watanabe out with us tonight . . . introducing him to the ladies?' He winks at me.

Mary walks towards us, tightening the belt of her jacket. She smiles, raising a quizzical eyebrow. 'Yeah, why not? It'll be fun. We're going to the Atrium. Do you want to come?'

'I have work to do.'

'Don't worry about it. I'll have a word with the old lady. You can finish it tomorrow,' Yuji insists, anticipating the hilarity quotient of mission Get Watanabe Laid.

I refuse. Yuji continues to harass me until Mary, embarrassed on my behalf, begs him to stop. Then they leave, the double doors swinging shut on Yuji's laughter. Harsh, metallic, empty laughter.

More than anything I wish I could liberate Mary from the evolutionary ghetto of mankind. To usher her into the magnificent kingdom of hyperspace, introduce her to the nether realm beyond the tangible senses. We would communicate at the speed of light through the mutual interception of psychic emissions. We would race through the intoxicating wilderness, make the whole of hyperspace our playground.

We would know happiness in its purest form.

In hyperspace many secrets of the cosmos are divulged; how many angels can dance upon the head of a pin? What proportion of the clientele at The Sayonara Bar wear toupees? In the fourth dimension all this is revealed – and more.

Life as omniscient prophet of hyperspace has many rewards, but unfortunately ability to read the future is not one of them. I remain as ensnared in the present as the rest of mankind, the future just as mysterious to me as it is to you. This said, I do possess one avenue into the future: my meta-readings of other people's intentions.

I saw something last week. A glimmer of evil to come, incubating in the mind of Yuji Oyagi. Since I saw it, some 174 hours 36 minutes ago, I have been trailing Mary. Before work, after work – it has become a full-time occupation. I am her scrawny shadow as she lugs her laundry to the coin-op, as she throws breadcrumbs for the ducks in Osakako park. This may seem excessive, but I cannot rest so long as the potential danger is there. I need to keep her under constant surveillance. I need to be there if anything should happen.

At The Atrium I sip at a bottle of Asahi beer and lean over the balcony railing, peering down at the intoxicated masses below. Hundreds of bodies, writhing in their youthful prime. The flailing motor co-ordination, the alcohol-heightened promiscuity – it's all too familiar. The mass of shiny, smiling faces does not disguise the reek of despair and nihilism that pervades these places. Mary dances alone on the outskirts of the dance floor, her hands scything the air with breathtaking fluidity. When she dances, her mind slips free of whatever is troubling it, floating in a sea of endorphins. Yuji and two of his friends occupy a sofa at the other side of the club. They sit like feudal lords, legs fanned out, working their hoodlum image, letting everyone in the vicinity know who the resident alpha males are.

Look at those geeks over there, jealous of how hard we are. This Tommy Hilfiger shirt makes me look like the Japanese Tom Cruise.

Yuji Oyagi, 23, gangster's lackey

When Yuji's hand brushed my thigh just now it felt like . . .
electricity. Christ, this is driving me insane. I have to tell
him how I feel. Oh please, God, don't let him be repulsed!
Kenji Yamashita, 26, gangster's lackey

No, mother! I won't do it! I won't put bleach in her drink.
She's a nice girl. She hasn't done anything to us . . . No!
That's not true. I could never love anyone more than you!
Hiroya Murasaki, 32, bartender

After assessing the bland mental emissions of Yuji and his cohorts I decide that they pose no real threat tonight. I'd better stick around, though. If I left and something were to happen to Mary I would never forgive myself.

6

MR SATO

I

And here I am again. At the kitchen table, deprived of sleep for a second night in a row. Watching the darkness listlessly succumb to an ashen grey dawn. I keep replaying the incident over in my mind, trying to distinguish between waking and dreams, attempting to rationalize that which shuns explanation.

Yesterday morning I woke in a terrible state. I had spent the night dozing, waking every few minutes to find my limbs in all manner of contortions, and my muscles were knotted, as if tied up by a mischievous troop of boy scouts. But despite this I was up at six thirty as usual, in time for the daily radio callisthenics broadcast. Mid hamstring stretch it dawned on me that I had neglected to iron my workshirt the night before. I erected the ironing board and grouchily ran an iron over a crumpled shirt, scalding my hand with steam in the process. That will teach me! The little omissions prove very troublesome later.

My lack of foresight cost me precious minutes. I left the house in a rush, anxious to catch the 7.45. If I missed the 7.45 there wouldn't be another express until 8.13. Barely had I reached the front gate when my progress was thwarted.

'Mr Sato! Mr Sato!'

I lamented my bad luck. Mrs Tanaka couldn't have picked a worse time to accost me. She came limpingly towards me, her artificial hip no doubt aggravated by the cold weather. Her slippers left a trail of footprints across the frost-laden lawn.

'I'm sorry, Mrs Tanaka, but I cannot stop and talk. I am very late.'

'Tssk!' said Mrs Tanaka. 'This will take only a minute. Besides, when else can I talk to you? You didn't get home until 10.45 last night!'

To Mrs Tanaka my being late for work is a trifling and inconsequential thing. I resigned myself to a lengthy delay.

She looked me up and down, taking no pains to conceal her displeasure. 'You look very peaky and anaemic, Mr Sato,' she commented.

'Really?'

'Yes. Most unhealthy.'

With each word a puff of mist was dispatched into the icy morning air. I brought my fingers to my face, as though the truth of her statements could be deduced through touch. Mrs Tanaka pulled her patchwork shawl tightly around her shoulders.

'You obviously haven't been eating enough red meat. Why don't you come to my house for dinner on Sunday? I will cook you a beef steak. And I'll ask my niece Naoko if she'd like to join us also.'

Mrs Tanaka spoke earnestly, but as she pronounced her niece's name her sobriety was plundered by an impish grin. As you know, never is Mrs Tanaka more in her element than when she is being meddlesome.

'I think I might be busy . . .'

'Nonsense. You never go anywhere at the weekends.'

'Well, I might have to . . .' I floundered, stricken by a drought of suitable excuses.

'Splendid! Let's make it seven thirty, Sunday evening, then.' She beamed, with a candid, childlike joy.

'Seven thirty, Sunday evening,' I echoed miserably.

'And Naoko's favourite flowers are pink roses,' she added with a jubilant wink.

I watched as Mrs Tanaka trotted back to her house as buoyantly as her artificial hip would allow, leaving two parallel slipper trails melting in her wake.

I was in a gloomy frame of mind all day today. Whenever I began to feel normal again I would remember the ordeal that lay ahead of me on Sunday and the gloominess would return. To make matters worse Taro, the graduate trainee, had forgotten to fax the dividend yield analysis to Head Office as I had instructed last Tuesday. How irresponsible that boy is! Deputy Senior Managerial Supervisor Murakami came down in person to ask why Head Office had been kept waiting. Though Taro hung his head as I chastened him I could tell he took none of my words to heart. He waited impatiently for the lecture to end, eager to slouch back into his leisurely routine of taking lengthy cigarette breaks and teasing Miss Hatta, the office assistant. The other day I caught him listening to pop music on a Walkman he had secreted in his desk drawer. I shudder to think that the future of Daiwa Trading rests in the hands of Taro and his ilk.

Murakami-san said not to worry about the delayed fax and that he would apologize to Head Office on our behalf. Murakami-san has been surprisingly pleasant to me since our sojourn to the hostess bar. He was obviously too inebriated to remember my bad temper at the end of the evening. To my relief he hasn't asked me out since, though sometimes I notice him smiling at me in an inscrutable manner. Perhaps I underestimate the strength of his memory. As you always used to say: 'A clever hawk hides its claws.'

I arrived home from work at 11 p.m. tonight and, determined not to repeat this morning's disorganized muddle, immediately set about ironing the remainder of my shirts.

Then, after a light supper of rice and miso soup, I took myself to bed. Owing to my restless exertions of the night before I fell into a deep, merciful slumber the moment my head sank into the pillow.

Hours later, I jolted upright on my futon. I awoke with a gasp for air, heart clamouring, like a man surfacing from a long time underwater. My digital alarm clock shone 3.19. I sat, trembling in the darkness, trying to resurrect the substance of my dreams.

For many minutes I waited, my pulse still quick in my ears. I remembered that you had been there – in your white cotton sundress, straw hat and gardening gloves, pale in the shade – that summer we grew tomatoes in the garden. But what had unsettled me so? Surely not that. I sank down beneath my duvet. Perhaps it was better not to know.

Then it came. A single note. The low, sepulchral product of a bow being drawn across a string of your cello. I leapt out of bed, snatched the hefty marble paperweight from the nightstand and flew, as though catapulted by adrenalin, towards the spare room. The paperweight held high above my head, I pushed aside the sliding door.

The curtains were wide open. A soft lunar glow bathed the tatami mats and illuminated the objects in the room. Moonlight winked from the burnished curves of the cello. It reclined against the bookcase, mute and regal, and seemingly undisturbed. The bow was nowhere to be seen – no doubt packed away in the box with your sheet music. I assured myself that the music I had heard could not have been produced without the aid of a bow. But despite this robust logic I remained staring at the cello for a long time, shivering as the cold made a mockery of my thick winter pyjamas.

The moon had shifted position in the sky by the time I tired of gazing at the cello. When I went downstairs to make some tea, my hands shook and fumbled with the kettle and tea leaves. The ravenous cold had made quite a feast of me, gnawing the sensitivity from my fingers and toes.

It is sunrise now. The tea has calmed me somewhat, but the fear has given way to maddening confusion. I am too old to fall for spooks and such nonsense. It couldn't be you, could it? You would never toy with my sanity in such a way, would you?

II

I marched myself into the office this morning, caffeinated to within an inch of my life. I proceeded to plough through the accounts ledgers at my desk, a jittery whirl of enterprise. Unfortunately, at about eleven o'clock my caffeine reserves plummeted, rendering the simplest of tasks onerous. The gossip and keyboard clatter of my co-workers began to crash in my ears, like the rush of waves inside a seashell.

Miss Hatta, the office assistant, observed my behaviour with consternation and tactfully suggested that I return home to rest. I thanked her for her concern, then explained to her that this was out of the question. Summoning every last reserve of strength I managed to remain at my desk until 6 p.m., by which time my energy gauge had slumped to zero.

As I walked to the underground station I felt great relief that the following day would be a Saturday. I will rest diligently over the weekend and return to the Public Accounts office of Daiwa Trading on Monday an efficient, indefatigable worker. All thoughts of dinner at Mrs Tanaka's on Sunday I conveniently repressed.

I took a short cut through Umeda's brightly lit underground shopping mall. As I always commute early or late in the day I rarely pass through the mall when the stores are open. The mall swarmed with women – throngs of office ladies, and giggling high-school girls stampeding from shop to shop. They twirled before mirrors, sprayed perfume samples on their wrists, and sought out each other's opinions on the latest fashions. Observing these frivolous hordes of women evoked a pang of nostalgia. Nostalgia for all those occasions you would return home exhilarated from a shopping spree. The way you delighted in showing off your purchases: a silk scarf or a cashmere sweater for yourself, a handsome tank-top or a pair of socks for me. The way you would nervously conceal the price tags with your thumb.

I can't tell you how much I have come to regret my miserly reproaches.

As I neared the exit to the shopping mall I was assailed by a mobile-phone salesman, a stocky, cocksure youth with an earring and spiky, mousse-stiffened hair. Drained and enervated, I was unable to fight off his impassioned sales pitch, nor the advice on payment plans and demonstration of ring tones that followed. The youth waved the tiny piece of gadgetry about, entirely heedless of its harmful gamma radiation. When I finally freed myself from him I hurried away. It was then I heard a small voice call out, almost lost in the rowdy hubbub of the shopping mall: 'Mr Sato! It's Mr Sato, isn't it?'

I looked over my shoulder. A young girl stepped tentatively towards me and smiled. Her face was framed by a glossy curtain of chestnut hair and a department-store carrier bag swung gently at her side.

'Hello. Do you remember me? I work at The Sayonara Bar. You paid us a visit a couple of weeks ago.'

Indeed I remembered her. She was the only Japanese hostess working that night. It amused me to realize that she is actually a girl of ordinary height. Her petiteness of that evening must have been an illusion caused by proximity to such tall American hostesses.

'Yes, of course. You took excellent care of us that evening.'

I suddenly became conscious of my haggard appearance, of the greyish bruises that encircled my eyes. In contrast, the young girl looked as fresh as a daisy. She wore a smart jacket of brown corduroy and a modest plaid skirt. On her feet were shiny red buckle shoes.

'I must apologize for my appalling memory,' I said, 'but I am afraid that I have forgotten your name.'

'It's Mariko,' she said. 'And there's no need to apologize. We weren't introduced.'

A flurry of office ladies swept past us, homing in on a conveyor-belt sushi restaurant. Reluctant to compete with their gossipy clamour, I waited until they had passed.

'Are you working tonight, Mariko-san?' I asked.

'Yes,' she replied. 'I work every night except for Sunday night.'

'You work very hard indeed!' I praised.

Mariko shook her head in self-conscious effacement of her labours. 'Not nearly as hard as I ought to . . . Have you just finished work, Mr Sato?'

'Yes. I am on my way home now.'

'Do you intend to visit The Sayonara Bar again?'

I shook my head. 'No. I don't think I will.'

Mariko tilted her head, her expression a blend of disappointment and curiosity. 'Oh. Why?'

I was at a loss over how to reply. I did not want to insult her chosen place of work. 'I am not a very sociable person. Neither do I take well to drink.'

Mariko nodded, seemingly accepting of this. 'Well, if you should ever change your mind you are always welcome at The Sayonara Bar. You don't have to sit with a hostess if you don't want to. If you prefer to be left in peace to enjoy the music, we will be considerate of this. And I can prepare some excellent non-alcoholic cocktails.'

Well, persuasive skills as impressive as that should be put to use in a business corporation, not squandered on a hostess bar.

'That's very kind of you. Perhaps I will visit you again one day,' I said. I shifted my spectacles further up the bridge of my nose, guilty in the knowledge of this unlikelihood.

Mariko brightened. 'Well, I'm looking forward to it.' She glanced at the clock suspended above the Uniqlo outlet. It was 6.27. 'You'll have to excuse me,' she apologized. 'I am late for work.'

We bid each other farewell and she squeezed from me a last-minute assurance that I would return to The Sayonara Bar. Then Mariko hurried away, her step brisk and smart, her shiny red buckle shoes disappearing into the anonymous fray.

That is about the sum of my day. Though it is barely eight o'clock, my jaw aches from yawning. I think it best that I turn in now.

But first I might go into the spare room and wrap a scarf around the neck of the cello. That should muffle the strings nicely . . . To hear me talk! Is this really what I have become? A foolish man, taking silly superstitious precautions?

Perhaps it would be better to muffle my imagination – the only logical source of this folly. Perhaps it would be better to go straight to bed.

III

I awoke on Saturday morning, grateful and rejuvenated after twelve hours of uninterrupted sleep. I sat at the kitchen table for a while, rousing my stomach ulcer with a cup of coffee as chill sunlight seeped into the kitchen. After breakfast I donned a warm cardigan and a pair of casual slacks and departed for the hardware store, a pleasant fifteen-minute stroll away. As I paused at the front gate to check the contents of our mailbox, Mrs Tanaka took the opportunity to stick her head out of her upstairs bathroom window.

'Good morning, Mr Sato,' she called.

'Good morning, Mrs Tanaka.'

'I can't come down, Mr Sato. My hair is still in curlers.'

'That's quite all right, Mrs Tanaka.'

'I bought some beef at the butcher's yesterday. Prime-cut steak. For tomorrow evening.'

'You really shouldn't have gone to any trouble.'

'Nonsense! What's a little trouble for my favourite niece and favourite next-door neighbour?'

My smile at that moment was a masterpiece of pretence.

'And what are you up to today, Mr Sato?'

'I am going to the hardware store to buy paint. I plan to paint the living-room ceiling.'

Mrs Tanaka's lips shrank into a thin line of disapproval. 'Don't you tire yourself out, now!' she cautioned.

'Of course not.'

'It's seven thirty sharp. Don't forget.'

'Of course I won't, Mrs Tanaka.'

Mrs Tanaka began to slide the upstairs window down, but then, having remembered something, she popped her roller-festooned head out once more. 'And remember . . . pink roses!'

My day passed exactly according to plan. I went to the hardware store and purchased a tin of magnolia paint. Then I ordered some fleur-de-lis patterned tiles for the bathroom. That will keep me occupied next Saturday. It is imperative to keep oneself busy. *You* never lazed about watching soap operas like other housewives, you were always crocheting or baking or learning your Spanish verbs. A fine example. When I returned home I covered the furniture and tatami mats with sheets and set to work at noon.

Dusk fell as imperceptibly as dust. One moment it was daylight, and the next thing I knew I was painting in darkness. I turned on the light and had the job finished by seven o'clock. Then I stood for a while, admiring my handiwork. The ceiling didn't look discernibly different, but it had a fresh cleanliness I found cheering.

*

After dinner the house became very quiet. A stillness only accentuated by the hum of the fridge and sporadic drips from the tap. I traipsed upstairs to run a bath, eager to soak my aching joints. I secured the plug and let both hot and cold taps run, dipping my hand in every so often to check the temperature.

Halfway through unbuttoning my cardigan I froze. I turned off both taps and listened carefully. From outside came the distant clanging of the level crossing, the slam of a back door, the mellow knocking of bamboo wind chimes. But nothing more. I leant over the tub, intending to resume preparations for my bath. But I froze once more. This time I had heard it distinctly. It came from a floorboard in the spare room. A loud, excruciatingly drawn-out creaking sound.

Unsteady legs took me into the hallway, where I stood, meditating beneath the sallow light. This is an old house, I told myself. Timber floorboards age. They weaken until they expand and contract at the slightest provocation, at the slightest fluctuation in temperature.

One more creak, and then another quick at its heels. I felt my pulse gallop beneath my skin. I edged towards the spare room, barefoot and clammy with dread.

From behind the screen door came a low, scraping sound, the sound of a heavy object being dragged across the reed mats. A sound that transgressed the very boundaries of my belief. Suddenly incensed, I thrust aside the sliding door, in a surge of reckless confrontation.

The empty room seemed to jeer at my outrage. The cello reclined against the bookcase as guilelessly as it had done the night before. All that was altered about the room were the shadows, which were stouter, and set at more obtuse angles. My anger quickly gave way to relief. Then to fear. I will take myself to see a doctor, I promised myself. I will even take Monday morning off work. I will tell my superiors that it is an emergency. Anything to put an end to this torment.

Abandoning my bath, I walked downstairs, put on my loafers and overcoat, and left the house.

I hovered indecisively at the entrance to the hostess bar. The butterflies in my stomach had proliferated at such a rate I was fearful that they all might come fluttering out of my mouth. What had possessed me to come here? Unaccompanied, no less! I was on the verge of fleeing when the doors opened.

'Good evening. Can I help you?'

It was Stephanie from Florida, with her orange hair piled helter-skelter on top of her head. It pleased me to see that she had swapped her clingy black dress of the other evening for a modest silk gown the colour of crushed pearls. It was reassuringly high-necked and skimmed down to her ankles.

'Hang on. You're Murakami-san's friend, aren't you! Are you coming in?'

'Yes. Thank you,' I said, finding my tongue.

Stephanie took me by the elbow and gently tugged me inside. The heavy glass door thudded shut behind us. As she glided ahead of me, with a backwards smile encouraging me to follow, I reddened to the tips of my ears. Stephanie's silk gown, so chaste and becoming when viewed from the front, was entirely backless. Her shoulder-blades and bumpy protuberance of spine were laid bare for all to see. Orange freckles danced from the nape of her neck right down to her lower back.

'Would you like to be seated at the bar?' she asked.

'The bar will do nicely, thank you.'

The hostess bar was quieter than on the evening of my first visit. Salarymen must reserve the weekends for their families, I presume. Upon the stage an American man with hair teased into an Elvis quiff played an electronic keyboard. His outfit was an unhappy marriage of snakeskin suit and white T-shirt. He warbled into the microphone: 'Bob bob bob bob bob aran, oh bob araaan, oh bob araaan . . .'

In front of the stage a Japanese hostess moved sedately in the arms of a salaryman, his cigar clasped between teeth bared in a rictus grin. They danced beneath the colourful circles of light that swept about the dance floor.

'Is there any particular hostess you would like to talk to?' Stephanie asked as I hoisted myself upon a bar stool.

My thoughts turned to Mariko. The smart red buckle shoes she wore in the underground shopping mall.

'No, no, thank you. I am quite happy to sit and listen to this American gentleman sing his songs. You girls must be very busy.'

Stephanie smiled sweetly. I noticed how pretty her eyes were: green and diaphanous, the hue of mentholated cough sweets.

'No problem. But any time you want to talk, you let me know. Don't be shy, now!'

She squeezed my shoulder – rather overaffectionate for a girl I scarcely know – and slipped away, many pairs of eyes monitoring the progress of her freckled back through the lounge.

On stage the voice of the Elvis-quiffed singer crept up to a falsetto. His thigh shook indecorously as the heel of his pointy shoe slapped the stage in time to the music. All around me salarymen chattered, the laughter of the hostesses tinkling along like crystal bells. Although not the environment I usually like, the lively surroundings soothed me. I began to feel foolish about my hasty departure from the house. Like a silly old man, afraid of his own shadow. Whatever would people think if they knew of my cowardice?

'Mr Sato!'

I turned to see Mariko smiling at me from the other side of the bar. She laughed in disbelief.

'Mr Sato. You decided to come.'

'Yes. You will have to excuse my unkempt appearance: it was a last-minute decision and I neglected to change.'

'You look fine,' Mariko reassured me. 'What can I get you to drink, Mr Sato?'

I selected from the menu a non-alcoholic cocktail called a Blue Lagoon. Mariko deftly prepared this for me, her movements lithe and graceful. She wore a beige, sleeveless dress, and her hair was held back from her face with a broad Alice band. I chuckled when she presented me with the turquoise concoction, complete with tropical parasols and glacé cherries. I took a single, tentative sip and my taste buds were instantly concussed by its staggering sweetness.

'You have been painting today,' Mariko remarked.

'Yes, I have,' I said, surprised. 'How could you tell?'

'You have paint flecks on your glasses.'

I removed my spectacles at once and was startled to see that Mariko was right. How could something literally right in front of my eyes have escaped my attention thus? I rubbed ineffectually at the lenses, only to add a liberal smudging of fingerprints. With a sigh of resignation I put them back on.

Mariko giggled, amused by my plight. 'Do you know you have paint on your ear lobes too?'

Again I sighed. 'Well, that will teach me to rush out of the house without consulting the mirror first.'

We laughed at this and I took another sip of my syrupy cocktail.

'You are not with Mr Murakami tonight?'

'No, not tonight,' I said, hoping she would not probe any further.

She was astute enough not to. Instead she said, 'You know, Mr Sato, you don't have a very strong Kansai accent. Where are you from originally – if you don't mind my asking? Tokyo?'

'Yes, that's correct: Tokyo. I moved to Osaka in 1984.'

'I thought so!' Mariko exclaimed, taking girlish delight in her guesswork. 'And what brought you to Osaka?'

'My wife's mother was dying. We moved here so my wife could nurse her.'

'Oh, I'm sorry.' Mariko lowered her eyes, genuinely sad to have unearthed this piece of family history.

'But we ended up staying. My wife grew up here. She says that Osaka is the friendliest city in Japan, that Tokyoites are too uppity.'

Mariko tittered demurely, fingertips pressed to her lips. 'That can't be true, Mr Sato – you're not uppity in the slightest!'

I glowed, pleased by this, although certain that you and my work colleagues would beg to differ.

'And you don't have a Kansai accent either, Mariko-san. Where is your home town?' I asked.

'Fukuoka prefecture. But right out in the sticks. Where I come from, well, you couldn't even call it a village. My father is a rice farmer.'

Funny how a mere handful of words can impart far more information than the teller would ever wish to disclose. Country folk are very conservative and rightly suspicious of the city. No farmer would let his daughter move to Osaka to embark upon a career in hostessing. She must either have left without her parents' consent, or be concealing the truth of her occupation from them.

'Fukuoka. That's a long way to travel home for the holidays.'

'Yes. I tend to stay in Osaka.'

'Did you come to Osaka by yourself?'

'More or less.'

What a wishy-washy answer. I wanted to know more about the circumstances of Mariko's leaving Fukuoka, but she was called upon to make a Long Island iced tea for a whiskery gentleman at the far end of the bar. Just as well, I told myself: it is rude to pry. By poking at a bamboo thicket one can draw out a snake.

Two more couples were dancing now, but in a jaunty, upbeat fashion. One of the girls was Mary from England, her blond ponytail bouncing about as she jitterbugged along to the rock-and-roll music. The quiffed singer had also grown very animated, the heel of his pointy shoe hammering the stage floor at the speed of a pneumatic drill, his body jerking behind the electronic piano. Perspiration glistened upon his curled upper lip: 'Oooo whooo, ooo whee, ooo whee, ooo woooo . . .'

I turned to Mariko to ask what the strange American was singing, but she had disappeared. Seconds later she emerged from the kitchen, carrying a plate of chicken impaled upon wooden skewers along with grilled green peppers and tomatoes.

'Watanabe made an extra order of these kebabs by mistake. Please help yourself,' she said.

'I couldn't possibly,' I protested. 'I am sure they are delicious, but I cooked dinner earlier. There is nothing worse than eating when you have no appetite.'

At this Mariko broke into a beatific smile, like kindling bursting into flame. 'You cooked for yourself? I'm impressed. The only time my father and brother turn on the stove is when they need to light a cigarette.'

'That's a shame. Cooking is such a wonderful pastime.'

'Absolutely. All men should know how to cook. Especially when they live alone like you do.'

Something felt amiss. I thought back over our conversation of that evening. 'Mariko-san,' I asked, 'how do you know that I live alone?'

Mariko blinked, her smile faltering. She toyed with a loose strand of hair. 'Didn't you mention it earlier?' she asked.

'No. I don't believe that I did.'

'Didn't you say something about your wife? I mean, I can't think why I thought that . . .'

I fell quiet for a moment. Mariko ran a limp rag over the surface of the bar counter, blushing pinkly. Murakami-san must have told her, I thought. He must have told her everything he knows about you and me.

Mariko gave a tense, impromptu laugh. 'Forgive me. I should learn to mind my own business . . .'

'I make no secret of the fact I live alone,' I said, smiling to ease her discomfort. So she had heard some gossip about me. She is not to blame for having ears.

'Can I get you another drink?' Mariko asked.

'No, thank you. I should be returning home now.'

Mariko seemed dismayed by this. 'Already? But it's so early . . .'

At that moment Stephanie appeared beside me, fluttering a thin sheet of paper. 'Hey, Mariko. Can you run into the kitchen and get Watanabe to do these orders?'

Mariko hurriedly snatched the paper, oblivious to the puzzled eyebrow Stephanie raised.

'Can you wait a moment?' Mariko asked, pleading with her eyes. 'I won't be a minute. There is something I want to ask you.'

I nodded. But the second she was gone, I gathered my overcoat and left.

7

MARY

I wake to tepid sunlight and radio static, my sheet twisted round me like a vine. I lie in limbo for a moment, before the cluttered reality of my room swoops in. Empty cigarette cartons and semi-read paperbacks breed on the tatami, a puddle of red beside my futon, where I unfastened my dress last night and let it drop to the floor. I dreamt of work again last night. These days I dream of little else.

My alarm clock tells me most of the day has already gone. I pull on a crumpled T-shirt and pad barefoot into the kitchen. Mariko stands in front of the cooker, thrashing about the contents of a sizzling wok, housewife-like in her plaid headscarf and prim skirt.

'Hello.'

Mariko leaps about four feet out of her skin. She turns round, one hand clutching a spatula, the other her heart. 'Mary! You scared me.'

'Sorry.'

I raise myself on tiptoe and try to discern the contents of her wok.

'It's spinach and aubergine. You can have some if you like . . .'

Mariko turns back to the cooker and the last of what she

says is sucked into the extractor fan with the steam. First thing, even the simplest Japanese can confuse me. I sink down at the kitchen table and extract a Lucky Strike from a scrunched-up pack on the table. Mariko scoops some rice into a bowl and puts it in front of me. 'I bet you're hungry,' she says. 'It's not good to smoke on an empty stomach.'

She crowds our table with miso soup, lacquered chopsticks and a plate of vegetables. I get the feeling Mariko doesn't like eating alone and she times her cooking to coincide with my waking.

'Did Mama-san find out what set the fire alarm off at the hostess bar last night?' I ask.

'Someone broke the hallway alarm. Maybe one of her enemies.'

'Who are her enemies?' I ask, intrigued.

'Oh, you know, ex-hostesses . . .'

I was in the karaoke booth, at about midnight last night, when this salaryman's rendition of 'Close to You' was cut short by the squall of the fire alarm. A second later the ceiling sprinklers sprang into action. Everyone panicked. This geriatric millionaire in the booth with us began hyperventilating. He kept saying, 'Earthquake? Earthquake?' again and again as Katya steered him outside by the arm, soothing him with the baby talk he is so notoriously fond of. Paler than I've ever seen her before, Mama-san shepherded everyone from the bar. Deafening and drenching the clientele is not good for business.

The shrill of the alarm emulsified the air. Most people evacuated with their hands clamped over their ears, but I didn't mind it so much. The water from the sprinklers was refreshing as a cloudburst on a muggy afternoon. When no one was looking I closed by eyes and raised my face to the ceiling.

'Last night I never thought that there was a real fire,' I say. 'I thought the alarm was not real, a . . .' I search for the right word, but my vocabulary is sleep shrunken.

'A fire drill,' Mariko says.

I repeat this to myself, to lodge it in my memory. Mariko puts her hands together, as though in prayer, and says thanks for the food. I echo her words then attack my bowl with my chopsticks. I spear some aubergine, the flesh indigo where its skin bled in the wok.

'It was real to me,' Mariko says. 'I could practically smell the smoke. I remember thinking: *There have to be better places to die than in a hostess bar.*'

'There have to be better places to work than in a hostess bar,' I say.

Mariko smiles, the dimples in her cheeks like punctuation marks. 'Three months,' she says, 'is all I need to pay off my father's debts, then I can go back to Fukuoka.'

'I'll be out of here in three months too,' I say. 'Maybe we should throw a joint leaving party.'

I eat at twice the speed of Mariko and finish before her. I poke my chopsticks into the remainder of my rice so they stand upright like wooden stilts. Then I push the bowl aside and reach for the cigarette I took out earlier. Mariko lifts her eyes over the rim of the bowl she sips from, spilling soup on the table as she snatches my chopsticks from the rice.

'You must never do that,' Mariko says severely, as though I'd just jammed a screwdriver into a plug socket. 'It is very bad luck . . . That is how we offer rice to the dead.'

'I'm not superstitious,' I say.

'Do you think it makes any difference to them,' Mariko says, 'whether you are or not?'

She returns to her soup and the room falls quiet, the only sound the kitchen clock, each tick the disparaging cluck of a tongue.

Hostessing is not Mariko's first choice of career. Mariko is an elementary-school teacher *manqué*. A year into her teaching degree, her father's farm ran into financial difficulties. He had to take out a huge loan and Mariko came to work as a hostess in the city in order to help him make the monthly repayments. She has never really specified whether this was her decision or her father's.

Mariko is a popular hostess, though she never flirts or puts on a sexy act for the clients. Uncontrived sweetness is her strength; she assumes the role of drinks-server and confidante as though it were second nature. Some men come here for sexual provocation; others, for feminine nurturance: to be consoled for the brutal, corporate lives they lead. While I tend to discourage melancholy behaviour with drinking games, Mariko always listens patiently to their whining, and then, with a few skilfully chosen words, persuades them their problems aren't so bad after all.

I forget that Mariko is still a teenager. Her lack of interest in music, or fashion, or people her own age, fascinates me. During the day she will go for a walk or watch television, and wants for little else in the way of distraction. She cooks her meals, cleans the flat, and is generally pleasant and unobtrusive. The only time we have clashed over something was when Yuji smoked a joint in the kitchen. She stormed out of her room at 4 a.m. in her Snoopy nightdress to tell us that she would not abide drugs in the flat. Yuji was so taken aback by her outburst he stubbed it out at once, apologizing like a madman. Mariko doesn't mind me smoking cigarettes, though. She says she is used to the smell because practically everyone in her family smokes. Sometimes I come home from work to see my ashtrays washed and placed upside down on the draining board to dry.

After I've showered and changed, Mariko and I leave for work. We get there just before it starts to rain, and stand in the foyer of our building watching the pedestrians whisk by beneath an undulating sea of umbrellas. We stall for as long as we dare, then go up in the musty lift. Up on the sixth floor there are no windows, so you don't know when it's raining. It could be as sunny as Dubai and we'd be none the wiser.

My shift begins in the bar, where I make drinks and small talk with the loners who congregate there. Tonight's entertainment is a Japanese guy in a stetson playing an acoustic guitar. I polish a stack of ashtrays and watch him sing beneath the sickly yellow spotlight. His bittersweet version of 'Country Roads' brings on a seldom-felt pang of homesickness for England.

The first hour or two passes slowly. I mix whiskey sours for a heavyset construction-firm boss and ply him with overpriced bar snacks. He asks me if I can use chopsticks, so I find a pair and gamely demonstrate my skill, transferring peanuts from one bowl to another. Then he asks me if I have ever screwed a Japanese man, and I laugh politely and tell him that is 'private'. The air conditioning is on full but his face is slippery with sweat.

At about nine o'clock Mama-san does her tour of the lounge, pausing at each table to chat to the clientele and jokingly ask if the hostess present is 'behaving herself'. Decades of hostessing have bestowed on Mama-san great intuitive powers when it comes to determining a customer's conversational needs. She knows when to ask after a client's family, when to get misty-eyed over 'old times', when to cackle bawdily, and when to bitch about the Nikkei Index and government policy. Watching her I can see echoes of the talented, exuberant hostess of her youth.

Mama-san makes a stop at the bar, Mr Bojangles nestled against her creamy silk blouse. She greets the construction-firm boss, screeching like a parakeet: 'Miyata-san! Long time no see! How is little Takuma-chan? In junior high school? Already! They grow so fast . . . Tell me, has Mary-chan been behaving herself?'

She pinches my waist and tells him I am too skinny. I laugh as though this is perfectly OK. In retaliation I roughly tousle the tiny head of Mr Bojangles. 'Such a cute little doggy!' I coo. Then it is Mama-san's turn to laugh as if no lines have been crossed. Mr Bojangles, not fooled for a second, stares back at me with black, vengeful eyes.

'How's your boy these days?' the construction boss asks. 'He must be in college by now.'

'College? God, no.' Mama-san lets out a thorny burst of laughter. 'Yuji's got himself a job as a motorcycle courier.'

The construction boss nods approvingly. 'Smart boy,' he says. 'Why waste four years at college when there is experience and opportunity to be had straight away? Good-looking fellow too. I bet the girls are throwing themselves at him.'

Mama-san laughs. 'Barbed wire couldn't keep them away. He has more girlfriends than I can keep up with. Still, the rascal can get away with it – he's still young, after all.'

The smile slides from my face. Mama-san wishes the construction boss a pleasant evening and moves away to Katya's table. I watch her greet the clients there, all big-hearted smiles, flesh jiggling beneath the silk of her blouse. What do I care what she says or thinks anyway? It's not like she has the power to will me out of Yuji's life.

The construction boss begins telling me some likely story about how he runs six kilometres every night with a backpack full of bags of rice. He must have one *hell* of a sluggish metabolism to do all that exercise and still be that pot-bellied. 'I wear ankle weights as well,' he adds. 'Two kilograms each.'

Over his shoulder I can see Mama-san walking to the office, Katya trailing behind like some disgraced handmaiden. Mama-san only calls a hostess into her office during a shift if she has committed an offence (like the time Sandrine told this high-school principal that he was a pervert unfit to work with teenage girls). But Katya is too self-possessed to do anything like that. The door to Mama-san's office closes, then opens a minute later as Katya strides out, her chin held at an angle suggestive of wounded pride. She heads for the double doors. I excuse myself and follow.

Katya is standing in front of the lift, punching the call button repeatedly, her face clenched in agitation. The lift cables groan as they crank between the floors.

'Katya! Where are you going?' I ask.

'Down. If the lift ever gets here. I'll probably be as old and mean as Mama-san before it does.'

The lift doors open with a metallic ping. The polished interior reflects us both; me with my silver hoop earrings and high ponytail, and Katya with her shiny dark hair, her shoulders, wiry and bare in her strapless top.

'What's wrong?' I ask. 'Have you been sacked?'

Katya turns and faces me. Her make-up, so rich and smoky in the lounge, is garish in the stark light of the corridor. Purple eye-shadow, streaks of pink blusher. I want to take out some tissue and wipe it all away.

'No, nothing so dramatic. Mama-san scheduled too many hostesses to work tonight, so she called me into the office and pointed to where she'd erased my name from the rota five minutes ago. Then she told me I had made a mistake by coming in.'

'Are you sure you were meant to work?'

'Positive. My night off this week is Sunday. Not tonight.'

The lift doors threaten to slide shut. Katya curses in Ukrainian and hits the call button again.

'Did you tell her you knew what she'd done? That you were definitely scheduled?' I shake my head. 'She treats us so badly. No wonder everyone here hates her.'

Katya sighs and taps her foot. 'I don't have a visa to work in this country. I am in no position to argue my rights. Besides, I have worked for far worse than Mama-san. She was just being sly tonight, trying to save herself some money.' Katya looks at me, shakes her head and laughs. 'Don't look so upset, Mary. I'm the one being sent home, not you. At least I can watch TV now. And I get paid for the hours I've been here. You should get back before you get into trouble . . .'

She squeezes my arm and steps into the lift.

My mood takes a nosedive after Katya leaves. There has been a reshuffle in my absence and Mariko has taken my place at the bar. She tells me that I have to join the youngish businessmen Katya had been attending to. I really can't be bothered and start out being as rude to them as I can get away with. I yawn hugely, pour myself a whisky and scratch at a mosquito bite on my leg – all code-violating stuff. My clients titter uneasily. It turns out they are elementary-school teachers who have come to Osaka to attend a seminar on teaching children with learning disabilities. They regale me with eccentric English ('I play karaoke every night because I have bachelor freedom') and I warm to them despite myself. I end up teaching them English nursery rhymes to sing to their kids.

Before long the country-and-western singer is packing away his guitar and the elementary-school teachers get up to leave, in tipsy high spirits. They hand over the 35,000 yen they owe without so much as a flinch and thank me for 'very much good time'. I escort them to the lift and wave goodbye until the doors shut on their smiley faces. Alone in the corridor, I feel the fatigue set in.

Leaden legs take me to the kitchen. Watanabe is grating cheese onto the counter – an artist's palette of ketchup and mayonnaise and God knows what else. Poorly aimed projectiles circle the bin; empty milk cartons, eggshells, vegetable peelings. I'm no hygiene freak, but *really* . . .

'Hi, Watanabe,' I say. Was that a glimmer of acknowledgement there, or did I imagine it? 'Can you make me something to eat? A sandwich would be fine.'

Watanabe nods, nervous tics leaping beneath his skin like tiny, high-voltage fleas. He slaps butter onto bread and adds some cheese. He eyes the floor tiles as he presents me with my sandwich, cut into four dainty triangles. I take it from him, alarmed to feel the hummingbird vibrato of his pulse trembling through the plate.

I bite, chew, swallow and say: 'Mmmm . . . delicious.'

Watanabe contemplates his trainers. I wonder, not for the first time, if he is mildly autistic.

'Well . . . thank you,' I say.

I head off to the bar, but steal a backwards glance from the doorway. Watanabe throws a tomato at the bin. It splats against the wall, spilling seed and watery pulp as it slides to the floor. He can't have been much of an athlete in high school.

I sit behind the bar, on the foot stool used to reach the Navy Rum and Amaretto, eating my sandwich. Elena comes over and tells me I have clients waiting for me in the karaoke room. Through a mouthful of bread and brie I explain to Elena that I am saving my voice for *Talent Search Japan* and ask if she would take them instead.

'They made a specific request,' Elena says, deadpan. 'For you and Katya.'

'Katya's gone home,' I say. 'Would you like to come with me?'

Elena is unenticed. She points at the clock and tells me her shift finishes in five minutes. She tells me she steers well clear of yakuza – she has her son to think of. 'But you're quite attracted to gangsters, aren't you? One of them has bandages on his face. Gunshot wound, I bet. Very sexy.'

I sigh and get up from the foot stool.

Another hour of small talk won't kill me. I walk past the last drunken dregs in the lounge, ribbons of smoke unfurling from their cigarettes. Low in the background Patsy Cline sings 'Crazy', making me nostalgic for another time and place.

The first thing I see through the window of the karaoke booth is the man with the bandages, rigid on the leather sofa, hands in his lap. The left half of his face is masked by plump cotton dressing secured with surgical tape. The hair above the bandages is tufty and fine, like black dandelion fuzz.

The man next to him waves at me. With a queasy jolt I recognize Yuji's boss, Yamagawa-san. I push open the karaoke-booth door, wondering why he is here.

They rise to greet me, formidable in dark designer suits. Yamagawa's companion is young, in his early twenties. The clinical whiteness of his bandages is stark against the tanned, exposed side of his face.

I bow deeply. 'Yamagawa-san! Good evening,' I say. 'This must be the first time I have seen you here.'

'Good evening, Mary. Sorry to call on you so late,' Yamagawa-san says, with melodious warmth. 'We thought we'd stop by for a drink. See, what did I tell you, Hiro? Speaks perfect Japanese and beautiful to boot. Yuji is a lucky man.'

'Please!' I protest, all flattered scepticism. 'It's not late at all. I am delighted that you came.'

Yamagawa-san glances at the door. 'Will Katya be joining us?' he asks.

'I am afraid that Katya is not here,' I say. 'I could fetch another hostess if you like . . .'

Yamagawa-san's smile burrows right down to his gold-capped molars. He rests a hand on the bandaged guy's shoulder. 'Ah, well,' he says. 'We'll just have to do without the Ukrainian tonight. Let's all sit down, then. Mary, allow me to introduce Hiro, the prodigal son.'

For a second I think Yamagawa-san means 'son' in the biological sense, then I remember that he refers to all his employees as sons.

'Nice to meet you,' I say.

Hiro extends his hand and we share a wordless handshake. He betrays nothing in the way of emotion, and a blank stare deflects my smile. From what I can see of his face he is not that bad-looking. The bandages cover his injuries thoroughly and give no hint as to their nature. Burns? Cuts? Is that left eye swollen? Morbid curiosity demands I know.

'Well,' I say, sitting opposite them, 'how are you both for drinks?'

The leather of the sofa is cool and sticks to the back of my knees.

'A hostess with fiery hair brought us whisky,' Yamagawa-san says, pointing to a crystal decanter and four empty glasses. 'Where do girls with orange hair come from? No! Don't spoil it for me. I want to imagine a land of flame-haired beauties.'

I laugh and pour two triple measures of whisky for Yamagawa-san and Hiro. Yamagawa-san pours one for me.

'A toast,' Yamagawa-san says. 'To the return of my prodigal son.'

We clink glasses and '*kampai*'. There is a lull as we sip our whiskies.

'I suppose you are itching to know what happened to Hiro's face, Mary,' Yamagawa-san says.

'No, I . . .' I am caught off guard. For one irrational moment I fear that he read my mind. '. . . It's none of my business.'

He chuckles at how flustered I am. 'Hiro, perhaps you should explain to Mary what happened to you.'

Hiro looks at me. 'I was in a car crash. My face caught fire.' He speaks with the bored detachment of a student reciting from a textbook.

'Boy racers, eh!' Yamagawa-san says.

I swallow a dry pocketful of air. It must have been horrific. 'I am sorry . . .' I say. 'I hope you make a fast recovery.'

'He will be scarred for life,' Yamagawa-san assures me.

'I'm sorry,' I say again.

Hiro looks entirely unmoved by any of this. He takes a packet of American Spirit cigarettes from his jacket pocket, lights one, drags on it and exhales towards the ceiling. Yamagawa-san unwraps a cigar. He holds it in front of his mouth until I realize that he is waiting for me to light it. Apologizing, I scramble to rectify my inattentiveness.

Yamagawa-san picks up the laminated song directory from the table.

'Do you want to pick a song to sing?' I ask.

'No,' Yamagawa-san says, turning the pages. 'We each

come into this world with a small amount of dignity and I
am not going to squander mine singing into a machine.'

'Hiro?' I ask him purely out of duty – he really doesn't
come across as the karaoke type.

Hiro looks at me like I've asked him to paint his tongue
blue and do a Maori war dance. Why choose the karaoke
booth if they both find it so objectionable? Yamagawa-san
taps a number into the remote. It appears digit by digit on
the box above the karaoke screen. The artist and title flash
up: Madonna, 'Material Girl'. He hands me the microphone. 'We would be really honoured, Mary, if you could
sing for us.'

On stage I grip the microphone self-consciously. The
intro starts up, as do the disco lights on the edge of
the stage, splashing me with colour. The lyrics glide
across the bottom of the screen and I strain to sing in key.
In the low-budget video a Japanese girl in a wedding dress
skates about on rollerblades, tossing Monopoly money into
the air.

Yamagawa-san claps his hands out of time, his cigar
clasped between his teeth. Hiro breathes smoke about like
a dry-ice machine, his good eye heavy-lidded with boredom. My singing is joyless and I do not dance. I may have
been railroaded into this, but I still have some degree of free
will.

'Good,' Yamagawa-san says as the song fades out.

I step down from the stage.

'Wait,' he says. 'We are not finished yet.'

He points the remote at the control box and taps in a
number: 6132. Madonna, 'Material Girl'.

I shoot Yamagawa-san a look of confusion. Has he
tapped in the same number by accident?

He leans back in his seat, watching me in a leisurely way.
'Once more,' he says.

It all starts up again: the disco lights; the synthesizer
beats; the actress in the wedding dress.

I sing 'Material Girl' three times in a row. I am

thoroughly sick of the tuneless whine of my voice. Can't they see how much I am hating this? Yuji will be *furious* when I tell him.

'Good,' Yamagawa-san says after my third performance. 'Why don't you sit down and have a rest.'

I sit on the leather couch, short of breath, trying to remember the prerequisite face muscles for smiling. I reach for my whisky. I can't gulp it down fast enough.

'Well sung, Mary,' Yamagawa-san praises. 'She's a good singer, isn't she, Hiro?'

'Forgive me, Yamagawa-san,' Hiro replies, 'but I am a poor judge of these things.'

'It's OK. I know my voice is awful,' I understate, wildly.

Hiro elects to remain silent. I swallow more whisky.

'Do you find Hiro attractive?' Yamagawa-san asks, apropos of nothing, except maybe cruelty. 'Even with half his face gone?'

This turns my stomach. Why humiliate him like that?

'I really shouldn't be checking other men when I have a boyfriend.' My laughter is light and unconvincing.

Yamagawa-san also laughs. 'And how about me?' he asks. 'Am I attractive?'

'Really, you're embarrassing me!'

Yamagawa-san drains the last of his whisky. He takes up the remote control again and runs his fingers over the buttons as if picking out a message in Braille. Is he going to make me sing again? I will have to tell him no this time. I will have to tell him my throat hurts.

Pointing the remote at the screen, he looks at me and smiles.

8

WATANABE

The sun smirks down, hot and heavy, irradiating the epidermal cells on the back of my neck. I am three storeys high, flat on my belly like a sniper, gripping the over-jut of apartment-block roof. In the parking lot below the tarmac sizzles. The cars gleam; red Honda, magenta Nissan, blue Toyota with a squirming nest of baby rats in its boot. I never learnt to drive. Traversing this grimy pockmark of a city in a flattened metal box has never appealed to me. Freedom? You might as well be a hamster on a treadmill for all the freedom owning a car affords . . .

Here she comes.

This morning Mary wears her hair in a high ponytail. A majestic fountain of golden jets, resonating in the sunlight like fibre optics. She yawns, a wide and powerful lioness yawn. She wears a pale sundress, tatty plimsolls and no socks. A small leather bag is slung over her shoulder. In the bag is a mobile phone and a dog-eared copy of *Zen and the Art of Motorcycle Maintenance. Today*, she thinks, *I'd like to be by the sea.* Mary emits a sigh of discontent. Though it has only been two days since she last saw her Neanderthal boyfriend, she yearns for him – a romantic longing as misplaced as an ectopic pregnancy.

Little does she know how his absence keeps her safe.

She resolves to seek him out later this afternoon, to make him a surprise visit.

A pall descends upon my heart.

She sets off across the parking lot and I proceed to the fire escape.

I stick close to the walls, the soles of my trainers slapping against the paving slabs, sending shoe-shaped quasars into the echelons of hyperspace. I deftly time my footfalls to coincide with Mary's. A petty yet pleasurable pleasure. If Mary knew of the valiant exertions I am making on her behalf I am sure that she would be thankful, that she would begin to view me in a new, vastly improved light. Perhaps then I could help her make that first paraspatial leap . . .

We continue along the cherry-tree-lined avenue, footfalls in perfect synchrony.

Among the tree-tops, sparrows perch in twittering clusters. Leaves flutter, green and juicy and rampant with chlorophyll. Fractal patterns explode, micro-organisms feast, tiny veins sprawl across leaf surfaces like electrified dendrites. Nature never premeditates. Its erratic rhythm simply pounds on. Since the throat of hyperspace opened before me, my sense of awe has never wavered. So eternally rich is the world I have come to know.

Reality is a pack of cards, infinite in number. Our three-dimensional universe is but a *single* card dealt by the hand of God. Compare this with the fourth dimension – an infinity of cards laid bare, suit upon endless suit, like an everlasting game of Patience. The disparity defies articulation. Dimensional impediments eliminated, my once stunted, embryonic knowledge of the universe has soared into the divine realm. It would be audacious of me to claim that I know as much as God, but I know at least as much as He did when He was my age.

*

I lurk by the tobacconist's as Mary purchases her ticket. Commuters glance up from their workaday scuttle to behold this Venus in plimsolls, moving in her aurora borealis of beauty. They stumble on their way, dazed by the encounter.

As Mary walks down to the platform I loiter by the ticket barrier, scoping the crowds. An old man in a green pullover dodders up to the barrier. I rush up behind him as he fumbles his ticket into the slot, and together we pass through, the most unlikely of conjoined twins. On the other side the man wheels round in bewilderment. I guiltlessly stare him down, zipping through his DNA to see his recessive genes for Tourette's and ingrown toenails. The man shakes his head and walks away. The medication he takes for his Tourette's cripples all confrontational impulses.

'Oi! Where d'you think you're going without a ticket?'

Shit. Just what I need. I keep going, head cowed, hands rammed deep in my pockets. Behind me a station attendant marches to the ticket barrier, boots polished to a military sheen, standard-issue Japan Railways cap perched importantly upon his head.

'Boy in baseball cap! Get back here now.'

All around me, dozens of law-abiding commuters swivel their heads, their gazes crossing like searchlight beams as they look for this boy-in-baseball-cap. Cursing, I turn round and trudge back to the ticket barrier. Better they get me up here than down on the platform where Mary can see. As I walk towards him the station attendant folds his pudgy arms over his shirt button-wrenching paunch. His expression is stern, but inside he is giddy with executioner's delight. Down on the platform Mary drags on a Mild Seven and squints down the track for the next train. It is approximately 1.69 km away and due in 29 seconds. Damn this bastard.

'C'mon, sonny. Either you haven't got a ticket or you're training for the Olympic turnstile-barging event. Now, which is it?'

'I . . . er . . .'

A quick psychogenic scan tells me Station Attendant Morimoto is a bureaucratic zealot with a lowest-common-denominator morality. A dangerous combination. He will exploit my misdemeanour for all it is worth.

'What are you? Mute? Deaf and dumb? Either you conjure up a ticket for me or you can crawl back under that barrier and come and fill out some forms for me in my office.'

From the platform below comes the rattling traction of train wheels against track, the headlong squalling of brakes. I rummage through my pockets for my imaginary ticket. Below us, train doors hiss apart. I take a step towards the barrier, ducking down as though I have every intention of traipsing obediently into the arms of criminal retribution. Then I spin round and begin to sprint the fifty metres down the tunnel to the platform.

Behind me Station Attendant Morimoto shouts: 'Oi! You cheeky scrag! Hey! Stop!'

I whizz past a scandalized old lady with a poodle on a leash. I swerve round a gang of truanting high-schoolers, who cheer encouragement as I careen towards the soon-to-close-on-me train doors. Not far now, I tell myself, my cardiovascular system lambasting every last lung-shattering step. I dive into the carriage, a millisecond before the door mechanism activates and swishes them shut behind me. Relief roars in my ears as the train heaves out of the station.

The inland sea is bruise-coloured and froths around the pier struts. I squint at the sun shining innocuously above; round and yellow as a child's Crayola rendering. A solar flare leaps out from its swirling photosphere, then vanishes, witnessed by no one other than me.

The sea-front entrance to the Osaka Aquarium is stark and exposed. The only hiding place is an Asahi beer vending machine, which I slot myself behind, squeezing past the wiring, the refrigerator motor chugging gently against my thigh. My hypervision circumnavigates the hulking machinery to see Mary purchase a green-tea ice cream from the refreshments stall. Ice cream in hand, she gazes out to sea, the grey undertow and hypnotic undulation of waves pulling her under.

For a moment Mary forgets herself, mesmerized by 14,792,090 litres of cold, drab water. If this bland feature of the ordinary world moves her so, how awestruck would she be gambolling across the quantum pastures of hyperspace? If she encountered Planck's constant, or felt an electron whizz past her nose at a quillionth of a coulomb?

She teeters at the entrance to the rabbit's hole. I must be the one to tug her through.

The aquarium is dank and shaded. Sunlight diffuses through the fish tanks, casting rippling, subterranean shadows across the walkway. From the next floor comes the distant pandemonium that is class 4a of Ashihara elementary school running amok in the tropical-fish section. Thirty-five yelpy, whelpy, scab-eating, blowfish-impersonating eight-year-old runts. I feel a stab of pity for their teacher Mrs Kobayashi. It really isn't her problem that little Tesuka-kun has forgotten his asthma inhaler, or that Aki-chan has a purple M&M jammed up her right nostril. Mrs Kobayashi's nine o'clock Valium hasn't yet worn off, but she prudently decides today's excursion calls for another half.

I monitor the Cartesian co-ordinates of Mary's movements until they remain stationary outside the emperor-penguin enclosure. When I arrive Mary is watching the penguins waddle about. She laps absentmindedly at her ice cream and licks up the drips sliding down her knuckles. I squat some ten metres away, behind a small tank of echinoderms and sea urchins. Mary thinks she is the only person in the penguin enclosure. Here are some other things she thinks: *Is it true that penguins fall over backwards when they look up at aeroplanes? I wish an*

*aeroplane would fly overhead so I can see. I probably
shouldn't mention to Yuji that I came here today. He will
think I am strange for coming here by myself . . .*

Little does she know lack of intimacy is the least of her
problems with Yuji. Knowledge of her innermost thoughts
can be agonizing at times – akin to watching a girl stumble
spellbound along the edge of a snarling wolf pit as their
fangs snap at the air by her feet.

Mary presses her nose to the glass of the penguin
enclosure. One of the emperor penguins peers myopically
back at her. He sees her blurry pink face and the fountain
hairdo, spurting from her head like effluent from the blow-
hole of a killer whale. A shiver creeps through Innuk. He
sidles closer to his sister Iglopuk, who is sleeping with her
bill tucked behind a feathery flipper.

I slink amid the shadows, diligently dogging Mary's
movements from the pamphlet vending machine to the
coin-operated submarine. In the tropical-fish section I stow
into a pitch-black cleaning supplies cupboard. Through the
balsa-wood door I watch, light-headed from bleach fumes,
as Mary dawdles past the Indo-Pacific angelfish. She taps
her fingers against a tank, trying to attract the attention of
some tiny, stripy anemone zigzagging stupidly about. We
proceed to the walrus enclosure, where Mary develops a
curious affinity with a 1,206 kg oestrus female of cinnamon
brown, whom the aquarium-keepers have named Marilyn.
Marilyn reclines, supine on the damp concrete, stretching
her fore-flippers and wrinkling her whiskery snout in the
sun. The myoglobin percentage in her muscle tissue is
hazardously low, afflicting her with the walrus equivalent
of Chronic Fatigue Syndrome. She spends 94.8 per cent of
her day on this same patch of concrete.

At the entrance to the main tank I hunker down beneath
a cylinder wall attachment containing an aluminized Mylar
fire blanket.

'Look, Granddad, it's Jaws!' The little girl's Pocahontas
plaits bounce excitedly as she skips alongside her

grandfather towards Osaka Aquarium's star attraction: Oscar the albino killer whale.

Granddad halts in front of me. 'Hello, there. Have you lost something? Can we help you look for it?' he asks in a very loud voice.

Interfering old . . .! I '*Shuush!*' vehemently at him. Fortunately Mary is transfixed by Oscar the albino killer whale, and fails to notice. Frowning, the old man draws his granddaughter closer to his side and moves quickly away.

In his 24 by 18-metre salt-water tank Oscar glides in elliptical circles, sleek and agile, averaging 34.2 kph, a specimen of perfect albino health. In the perspex tunnel that cuts through the tank, Mary gawps upwards as Oscar's deathly white ventral surface passes overhead. Mary imagines Oscar smashing through the tunnel wall, his jaws clamping down on her flesh. She shudders in delight. In truth, nothing could be further from Oscar's mind. He is too busy being lonely and confused. The tank screws up his echo-location system; all the sonars he sends out rebound meaninglessly back and forth between the tank walls. For the past fifteen months Oscar has been endlessly trying to navigate a maze of mirrors, turning this way and that, searching for the passage back to the Norwegian Sea. Frustrated, Oscar shoots to the top of the tank and lob-tails the surface with his tail fluke. He trills and whistles before submerging again.

Mary watches enviously. *He's having so much fun. It must be great to be a killer whale, to be able to fly up through the water like that.*

Mary does not realize exactly how kindred she and Oscar truly are. Oscar tail-spins and arcs through hoops in return for fish. Mary trusses herself up in slinky dresses night after night, to sweet-talk money from salarymen. Both the hostess bar and the aquarium are zoos, catering for different sections of the public.

*

In the provinces of hyperspace, the darkest penetralia of the universe are uncloaked, heralding the end of quantum privacy.

Mary tucks a stray strand of hair behind her ear as she watches hermit crabs scuttle across their sandy compound. From the first moment I cast my hypergaze upon her, I have possessed perfect knowledge of Mary. Imagine knowing someone so intimately that you know the rate at which her fingernails grow (0.000001 mm/s), that without even having kissed her you know the flavour of her saliva (nicotine and honeysuckle), that you've seen her deepest, darkest phobias clamouring at the walls of her psyche (frogs and stepladders).

It is a popular myth that one's lover should possess an aura of mystery, that to demystify is to throw stagnant pond water upon one's infatuation. But passion kept alive by mystery cannot be pure . . . Passion that can endure the sight of colon muscles propelling your lover's last meal towards its timely exit . . . now, *that* is purity of passion.

Our afternoon at the Osaka Aquarium comes to an end when Mary has to go to work. On the Midosuji line into Shinsaibashi I realize that I have left my chef's uniform at home. I alight at the station before Mary's and travel back to my bedsit. I arrive at mission base camp T–30 minutes before my shift. Afflicted by the neurological effects of sleep deprivation, I decide to stretch out on my futon for ten minutes of neurone regenesis. Precisely 103 minutes later I am woken by the angry *brring-brring*-ing of the telephone. I must have misprogrammed my metaspatial sleep monitor. 7.38 km due east, Mama-san cradles her office phone. She wears a purple kaftan and varicose-vein-support tights. Mr Bojangles is also present, reclining on his rosetta day-bed, chewing at his crocheted booties.

I lift the receiver and hold it cautiously to my ear.

'Good evening. Have I reached the residence of Watanabe Ichiro?' Mama-san coolly enquires.

I gulp in an affirmative manner.

'Oh, good! I am just phoning to check whether Mr Watanabe intends to come into work this evening. Because if Mr Watanabe does not intend to come in for his shift, the management need to know so they can commence searching for the lazy good-for-nothing's replacement.'

'I overslept,' I say.

Mama-san takes a deep breath. Then she warps into high-gear control-freakery. 'You have fifteen minutes to get here.'

'I—'

'We have given the clients seaweed crackers and told them their food is delayed because our kitchen boy is a useless oaf. If you are not here in fifteen minutes, we will tell them their food is delayed because our *ex*-kitchen boy is a useless oaf.'

Mama-san slams down the receiver, leaving me nursing third-degree frost-bite in my ear. Heady from her power-trip, she leans over to smooch Mr Bojangles, a conga procession of germs dancing from his fur onto her Chanel-rouged lips.

I pop an effervescent vitamin C tablet and pull on my trainers. Luckily for Mama-san my job at The Sayonara Bar is a vital façade for my protection of Mary. If it wasn't for Mary I wouldn't have picked up the phone.

I slip through the mirrored double doors, an impressive 23 minutes, 34.2 seconds later. The murky, twilight lounge is strangely free of pestilence tonight. The vermin scourge is limited to three City Hall officials, two postal clerks and a superintendent from the local sewage-treatment plant. It doesn't take long to get to the bottom of this peculiarity. A mutant strain of Influenza A(H5N2) has been circulating through the air ducts of several major office buildings in the district. It was planted there by biotechnology lab technician Yoshi Kawakata, 27, in a masterful strike against the corporate drones.

'Hey, sleepyhead! There's a pizza and a teriyaki chicken platter waiting to be made in the kitchen.'

Mariko, the Fukuoka farmer's daughter, is perched on a bar stool next to Sewage Superintendent Ishida. Ishida puffs on his cigar and fantasizes about plying Mariko with oysters and champagne before crudely defiling her atop the main control-panel at the sewage-treatment works. Mariko bats her eyelashes and asks him if he would care for another drink. A whimper catches in his throat.

I go to the kitchen and put my apron on. An hour slogs by. I am watching over Mary, incarcerated in the karaoke booth, joylessly caterwauling 'La Isla Bonita' at the de-moralizing behest of the two postal workers, when Katya struts into the kitchen. Finding it preferable to scrub filth from the dishes of the dissolute than to converse with Katya, I remain hunched over the sink. My failure to be suitably awed by her presence torments her.

'Hey, loverboy,' she drawls. 'What happened to you earlier? Girlfriend wouldn't let you out of bed?'

Katya chews aniseed-flavoured gum. A salivary solution of sorbitol, glycerine and E320 compounds swills about her mouth. She reminds me of a camel with earrings. I rinse a plate and put it on the draining board.

'How am I going to break the news to Mary, Watanabe? She'll be devastated to hear you've met somebody else . . .'

Katya tightens the thumbscrews with a smirk. Panicky quarks fly from my solar plexus. Fortunately, Katya's alpha emissions possess no knowledge of my inner pledge to safeguard Mary. She suspects I am attracted to Mary, but regards my attraction as rudimentary and third-dimensional. I pity Katya. This squalid type of love is all she will ever know. I rinse some cutlery and place it on the draining board.

'You know, she's wanted you since your first ever shift . . .'

With a stroke of luck the millionaire electronics magnate Ohara-san steps into the bar. Rich, decrepit, and possessed of a soft spot for the milky curves of Western ladies, Ohara is Katya's current undertaking. Her nostrils twitch as she detects his presence (her nasal receptors are highly attuned to the scent of wealth – a formidable olfactory skill). And she trails her nose into the lounge, determined as a blood-hound closing in on its prey.

Time drips on like a festering stalactite. I prepare a Greek salad with a side order of octopus tentacles drizzled in soya. I prepare an order of fried potatoes and chilli sauce. I skim crumbs from the oil in the deep-fryer with a metal spatula. I yelp with pain as a spiteful speck of oil bespatters my wrist.

I decide it is time to take flight from this God-forsaken kitchen.

In a single metaspatial bound I shoot up into hyperspace. I pirouette upon the shroud of light pollution cloaking the city, up where the stars are strung across the sky like in-candescent paper garlands. Eternal truth floods my cranium as I hurtle through the brilliant, lunatic realm where epistemological warfare has human logic in shreds. I see the tumult of humanity down below, a million destinies unfolding, like poorly enacted classroom dioramas.

Way down below, buildings are crammed cheek by jowl, town planning reduced to a game of Tetrus. Families sit hypnotized, captivated by the subliminal urgings of their television sets; pubescent vampires prowl the grounds of Osaka castle; lesbian arsonists race from a blazing building as the smoke-stifled cries of a woebegone husband fade out of earshot.

Way down below, Mary sits in the Sayonara Bar karaoke booth. Cigar smoke prickles across her corneas like static electricity. Her smile muscles atrophied hours ago, surrendering themselves to a fatigued grimace. The salaryman next to her, his cheeks flushed with more units of alcohol than his body can metabolize, tells her she reminds him of a famous actress.

Ohara-san is up on the stage, singing 'New York, New York'. He punctuates the rising crescendo of New York, New York, with kicks, his joints protesting with rusty creaks. Katya sways reverentially, smiling as though enraptured by his singing, when really she is enraptured by his wealth. Palms clash in fervent accolade as he returns to his seat.

'That was wonderful!' Katya breathes as though his performance had been a spiritual journey and Ohara-san her Svengali.

His liver-spotted hand gives her thigh a firm, appreciative squeeze. Ohara-san thinks: *Yes, I will take the blond one tonight . . . but will she be willing? My Katya will persuade her, trick her if necessary. My Ukrainian princess has never let me down before.*

An icy splinter penetrates my heart. What kind of a man is this Ohara-san? I enter his memory depository and witness the grisly history of his yakuza-assisted electronics empire, his violent intimidation of rival firms into bankruptcy. While his wife, a blubbery, medicated wreck, stumbles about their hill-top mansion, Ohara-san and his cronies comb the red-light district for nubile bitches to use and abuse. Sometimes he'll take a few Polaroids, which he'll leave about the house the next morning to taunt Mrs Ohara.

I need to get Mary out of there. Now.

Across the ceiling runs a network of copper piping – the Pyrosafe Ltd sprinkler system Mama-san installed after a spectacularly bleak fire-risk assessment. Any one of the three fire alarms in the hostess bar will activate the sprinkler system, but only the corridor alarm is beyond the range of Mama-san's CCTV cameras. I hang up my apron and sneak towards the exit, monitoring the people in the lounge. Absorbed as they are in their meaningless social and monetary transactions, I don't even register as a peripheral blip.

The fire alarm outside is a manual, break-glass affair.

Buildings like this one are notorious death traps. The reprobates will be ditching their laptops in the scramble to get out. I would be rubbing my palms in anticipatory glee were I not so preoccupied by Mary's welfare.

I count backwards from three and ram my fist into the glass of the fire alarm.

The glass remains intact. Owing to a lethal manufacturing blunder its tensile breaking point is excessively high. What if there was a real fire? What then? Frustrated, I pull off a trainer and hammer the glass with my heel until it shatters. There is an interim of a 1/30th of a second as electrons speed round the electrical circuit. Then the deafening, air-raid squawk of the fire alarm. In an additional 2.4 seconds hydraulic pressure builds up in the sprinkler pipes and activates the irrigation system. The spray is discharged with a satisfactory range of 3.2 metres, dousing all and sundry.

I allow myself a moment to bask in the gentle radiance of a job well done, before hot-tailing it to the stairwell. My ingenuity results in a complete minesweep of the lounge. Clients and hostesses hasten exit-wards, hearts drumming a panicky cadence. Psychosomatic responses include amplified pulse-rate, hyperventilation and weakened sphincter muscles. Mama-san gathers abandoned coats, her face a frozen masque. Stephanie begs a drunken postal worker to get off his stool, but he continues to sip whisky and remark: 'It's raining indoors! A miracle! Fetch me my umbrella.' Other salarymen hurtle pell-mell down the six flights of stairs. Ohara-san clutches the arm of Katya on the way down, scowling because his suit is wet.

Hidden from view in the foyer of the Big Echo karaoke, I watch the Sayonara Bar evacuees file outside to dripdry on the pavement. The collective mind lattice buzzes as mental corpuscles jolt and jangle. Scintilla illuminates the air with psychedelic sparks. Cerebral kinematics, animated by the unexpected calamity, have leapt up a notch.

Emigrés from other bars in the building also mill around. Heads crane upwards, eagerly seeking flames, a wisp of smoke, anything to justify their ordeal. Mama-san walks round, distributing sodden coats among her shivering customers. Ohara-san's assistant calls the chauffeur on his mobile phone, instructing him to take the boss for a rub-down at another hostess establishment. 'It looks like a false alarm,' people remark to one another. Those amorous for disaster lament their lot.

In the entire building, only one person remains.

I hyperzoom up to the lounge. Mary stands beneath a sprinkler, dark-blond hair plastered to her scalp, her face marmoreal beneath streaming rivulets. Though the wailing fire alarm is only 7.5 decibels below the pain threshold, Mary welcomes it. It bulldozes all memory of the night's customers from her consciousness.

Mary has never felt so calm. She closes her eyes and lifts her face to the sprinklers. The white light of her soul disperses into a wild, iridescent spectrum of colour, streaming from her sternum. I pass through her, slithering amid her psychic entrails, and see something that astounds me. Mary *knows* there is no fire. She knows because a latent, un-developed faculty has told her so. It is a faculty she will remain unaware of until it explodes. As unexpectedly as it did for me.

A shiver creeps down my spine. The time for Mary to join me is growing near.

9

MR SATO

I

As you know, Sunday has never been a day of rest in the Sato household. It has always been a day of sizeable undertakings, such as the painting of the garden fence, or the clearing of leaves from the gutters. I remember how keen you were to don your headscarf and go from room to room, polishing every stick of furniture to an immaculate sheen. Resolute in the division of labour, you insisted that I attend only to the outdoor chores. If I offered to mop the floor or wipe the slats of the venetian blinds you would brandish your feather duster and cry: 'No husband of mine!' Of course, since you are no longer here, the responsibility to maintain our household's exceptional standards of cleanliness has fallen upon me. I think you will find I am doing a fine job.

After breakfast I changed into my tracksuit and set to work. The grey, morning drizzle scuppered my plans to trim the hedge bordering the Tanaka property, so I mopped the stairs and polished the banister. Then I took up the broom and ventured into the spare room. In daylight it was hard to understand what had caused my fear and my subsequent flight to the hostess bar the night before. And as I swept I had to concede that the floorboards were remarkably squeaky. It wouldn't surprise me, I thought, if they were capable of squeaking of their own accord. Reassured thus, I moved on to the master bedroom.

As always, I left the upkeep of the Sato family shrine until I was satisfied that order had been restored within the rest of the house. Kneeling before the shrine, I dusted the ancestral memorial tablets and swept the fallen pellets of incense ash from the platform. You observed me from within the confines of your gold lacquered frame, expressionless in your high-collared dress. I would much rather have used the photograph I took of you on the ferry to Kyushu – the one of you leaning against the ferry railings and smiling fit to burst, your hair in flight in the wind. However, common sense dictated I select a sober photograph that wouldn't rouse the disapproval of our respective mothers, sternly flanking you in their own gilded frames. I squirted everyone with Windex and polished the glass until it gleamed.

The sky had all drizzled out by noon. I set off for a stroll about our sun-brightened neighbourhood, the earth springy with moisture beneath my feet.

As I passed the paddy-field backing the Hideyoshi property my thoughts turned, with some mortification, to the night before. I hoped Mariko had not been upset by my silent departure. After all, it is Murakami-san I am cross with, not her. It is troubling that a girl barely out of high school is working until the early hours in a smoky hostess bar. And deplorable to think that she may be corrupted by the alcohol and men typical of these establishments. I must have been in a very aberrant mood to go there. I will never go back. Not now I know that we have been the subject of idle gossip.

My wanderings about the neighbourhood had inspired a considerable thirst. When I reached the Circle K on Tomo-Oka lane, I stopped to purchase a bottle of grapefruit juice. As I stood outside the convenience store drinking my beverage (loath to adopt the ill-mannered trend of drinking while walking), two boys sharing a bicycle came wobbling across the parking lot towards me. One boy clutched the handlebars and pedalled, while the other stood on the back-wheel pivot, gripping the shoulders of his friend. They wore T-shirts and trousers in desperate want of belts (for each boy exhibited the waistband of his boxer shorts). They stopped a metre short of me, and the boy who had hitched a ride on the back wheel jumped down. He extracted some coins from a baggy pocket.

'Hey, mister. Can you get us a pack of Kools? We'll let you keep the change.'

The boy couldn't have been more than twelve, his companion younger still. He held the coins out in his palm, confident I would perform his illegal request.

'Smoking is very bad for you,' I said. 'It is best never to start. It may seem like fun when you are young, but it is highly addictive and causes all manner of diseases . . .'

The boy pulled an ugly face, not unlike that of a gargoyle.

'Put a lid on it, granddad,' he said with a sneer. 'C'mon . . . We don't need a lecture from this old man, we'll get them from the vending machine down the road.'

'Yeah. Go screw yourself,' added his recalcitrant young friend.

The boy remounted the bicycle.

For a moment their outburst of expletives robbed me of my tongue. But then, in a surge of indignation, I cried out: 'I know who your mothers are and I shall tell them of this!'

Of course, I haven't a clue who their mothers are, but my threat bared an Achilles heel. Gone was their bravado. Fearfully, they glanced back, before pedalling quickly away.

On my way home I stopped at the flower stall next door to the Nakayama funeral parlour to purchase the pink roses

Mrs Tanaka had requested. However, upon arriving home I realized that the bouquet was not freshly cut and the petals were wilted and browning at the edges. I fretted over this as I selected a tie and cuff-links for the dinner party.

I was standing on Mrs Tanaka's doorstep, my finger poised to ring the bell, when the door flew wide open as if assailed by an almighty gust of wind.

'Mr Sato!' Mrs Tanaka exclaimed. 'What a pleasant surprise! Don't you look dapper in your suit.'

Mrs Tanaka had forfeited her housecoat for a stylish purple dress. On the front pocket of the dress an em-broidered cat chased a ball of yarn – no doubt Mrs Tanaka's own nifty handiwork. Her soft grey hair had been stiffly waved and set with hairspray.

'Good evening, Mrs Tanaka. I hope I am not late,' I said.

'By a minute and a half,' she replied. 'But never mind, you're here, that is the main thing. Well, what are you wait-ing for? Come in, then.'

I removed my shoes in the reception area and slipped on a pair of peach guest slippers. A pair of spike-heeled leather boots caught my attention. As Mrs Tanaka's age and rheumatism ruled out such aggressive footwear, I could only infer they belonged to Naoko.

In a tizzy of excitement Mrs Tanaka pushed me towards the living room. 'Naoko, Naoko!' she cried. 'Mr Sato from next door is here!'

Naoko, sitting cross-legged on a floor cushion, was watching the seven o'clock news bulletin. She rose to her feet as I entered. Mr Tanaka snoozed in his wicker rocking chair, his mouth agape.

'Good evening, Mr Sato,' Naoko said, with a bow.

'Good evening, Miss Tanaka,' I replied, returning the bow.

'It's been a while, hasn't it?' Naoko said. 'You look very well.'

'So do you, Miss Tanaka.'

'Please, call me Naoko.'

Naoko's voice was as rich and commanding as I remembered. Her appearance was also faithful to memory: her face pale and angular, her auburn-dyed hair hanging loosely about her shoulders. Streamlined in a black shirt and trousers, Naoko looked every inch the modern career woman – most out of place in Mrs Tanaka's cosy den of crocheted seat covers and winsome cherub figurines.

I presented her with the roses, abashed by their tattered petals.

'Oh! You remembered I like roses! How sweet of you, Mr Sato.'

Mrs Tanaka winked, as discreet as a herd of pink elephants. 'Mr Sato has a masterful memory. Don't you, Mr Sato? He couldn't have worked his way up through the ranks of Daiwa Trading without it.'

'Is that so?' Naoko said with a quirk of the eyebrow.

Really! Such fibs Mrs Tanaka can tell.

'No, not at all. My memory is average at best.'

'Such modesty!' Mrs Tanaka marvelled. 'Well now, shall we adjourn to the table?'

Bending over her husband, Mrs Tanaka administered a sharp prod to his shoulder, launching his chair into a jerky rocking motion.

'*Mr Tanaka. Dinner!*' she shouted in his ear.

We sat upon the floor cushions positioned around the dining-room table. Steaming bowls of rice and *miso* soup were placed before us, along with dishes of grilled vegetables and tofu drenched in soya. The centrepiece of the table was a ceramic plate in the shape of a four-leaved clover, each leaf flaunting a glistening slab of steak.

The meal was beyond reproach. The steak was succulent and the vegetables mouth-watering. Naoko and I chorused an endless round of compliments, which Mrs Tanaka swatted away like pesky midges. Mr Tanaka, indifferent to his wife's culinary gifts, muttered under his breath as she used a knife and fork to cut his steak into manageable pieces.

'Mr Tanaka,' she scolded, 'your arthritis wouldn't be this bad if you did your physiotherapy every morning, like the doctor instructed . . . No! You cannot have any beer, you are only allowed orange squash.'

For one so lean and wraithlike Naoko had a vigorous appetite. She helped herself to a second bowl of rice, and piled her plate with asparagus as if she had just heard the vegetable was soon to be extinct.

'Naoko-chan,' I said, 'how are you settling into your new job?'

'Wonderfully, thank you. I have so much more freedom to experiment here than at the Tokyo office. I have picked up three new clients already, and I have barely been in Osaka a month.'

Naoko's dark eyes shone with enthusiasm. She obviously likes her job as an interior designer very much indeed.

'I am happy to hear it. It does one good to take pride in one's job.'

'How wise of you, Mr Sato,' Mrs Tanaka praised. 'Of course Naoko's artistic streak wasn't always the source of such pride. When she was a girl she'd scribble all over my walls with her crayons! Oh, she was so naughty!'

We all laughed at this, except for Mr Tanaka, who chewed his steak and grimaced.

'And you, Mr Sato? How is Daiwa Trading?' Naoko enquired.

'Each day has its challenges,' I said. 'Each day has its rewards.'

Naoko smiled at this. 'I guess when your job stops being a challenge then it's time for a new job.'

Well. This struck me as a rather slipshod attitude. If everybody abandoned their jobs simply because they are unexciting, then who would occupy the small yet essential niches society so depends upon?

'But to remain in a career that one finds unchallenging is a challenge in itself,' I retorted.

Naoko smiled again. 'Well, I suppose that's one way of looking at it . . .'

'More rice, Mr Sato?' Mrs Tanaka interjected, depositing a ladleful into my bowl. 'Did I mention that Naoko and her friend Tomomi recently completed a walking tour of Hokkaido?'

'Tomoko,' Naoko corrected.

'What, dear?'

'How many times do I have to tell you, Auntie? Her name is Tomoko.'

'Yes, of course it is. Anyway, I am always advising Mr Sato to take a holiday. He hasn't had one in years. A walking tour would do him the world of good.'

'Tomoko works in a travel agents',' Naoko said. 'It's really handy for finding cheap flights. I can give you her card if you like.'

I crunched on some *daikon* pickle. What could be more extraneous to my needs than a travel agent? I swallowed my pickle, and in the spirit of polite conversation said: 'I want to visit China one day. My wife always wanted to visit China.' But no sooner had the words left my mouth than I experienced the queer, inward revelation that, just as I will never sprout wings and fly to the moon, I will never visit China.

There was a silence as Mrs Tanaka twisted her napkin awkwardly. Then, 'Well, Naoko,' she said, 'you've always wanted to visit China, haven't you? And Golden week is coming up soon, isn't it? Why don't you two go together!'

This all came out of Mrs Tanaka in a breathless flurry. Perhaps she thought that if she got her suggestion out fast enough, we would agree before realizing how ludicrous it was.

Naoko laid down her chopsticks. Though she had been in good humour all evening, she now looked sharply at her aunt. 'Auntie,' she said crossly, 'Tomoko and I have already made plans for Golden week. You know this already.' Then she turned to speak to me, her voice softening. 'But, Mr

Sato, if you should require assistance finding inexpensive flights to China, then I will do my utmost to help.'

I thanked Naoko and Mrs Tanaka began to clatter together the dinner plates, clucking over Mr Tanaka's left-over steak. She shooed us away when we offered to help with the washing-up and went to the kitchen, noticeably smarting from Naoko's reproach.

Mr Tanaka rose from the table and limped back to his rocking chair. Soon the rumble of satiated snores drifted from the living room. Naoko and I remained at the table for a while, chatting though we have scant in common. I had never heard of any of the strange, arty films she had seen, and thought her plans to go jungle-trekking in Burma foolish. Naoko's eyes glazed over as I told her of my plans to re-tile the bathroom next weekend – a topic of conversation I was certain would appeal to an interior designer. We sat together until nine o'clock, by which time I decided we had bored each other quite enough.

Upon returning home I brushed my teeth and changed into my pyjamas. Then I sat at the kitchen table and listened to a radio programme on Renaissance art while trimming my nails with the nail scissors. It is odd how time spent in the company of others can magnify one's solitude rather than alleviate it. It probably wouldn't have occurred to me to feel lonely if the evening had been spent in my own company. Above the radio I heard Mrs Tanaka call good-bye to her niece, then the slam of a car door and the growl of an ignition. I swept my nail cuttings into my hand and scattered them in the kitchen bin. Perhaps now Mrs Tanaka has been discouraged from further romantic intervention. One can only hope.

II

I had planned to take some time off work to consult a doctor about the strange anxiety attack I suffered on

Saturday night, but arriving at work on Monday morning I saw that this was just not feasible. Mr Takahara, Assistant Section Chief, had left on a business trip to Hawaii, and Mrs Kawanoue had just begun her maternity leave (about time too; though her deft secretarial skills will be sorely missed, I was beginning to find the sight of her ever-swelling belly quite disagreeable in the office environment). If I were to step out of the office for an hour or two, Taro, the graduate trainee, would be left at the helm. Anxious to avert this catastrophe, I took great care to remain at my desk. Even trips to the bathroom and water fountain were conducted with haste.

Anyway, perhaps now a visit to the doctor's is unnecessary. I am pleased to report that my nights thus far have been undisturbed. All week I have been returning home from work at midnight, and tumbling exhausted into bed. The next thing I am aware of is the piercing shrill of my 6 a.m. alarm, rousing me in time for the morning callisthenics broadcast.

I left for work in good time this morning. The sky was pastel blue and delicately frothed with clouds. Two doors down, Mrs Ue's cherry blossoms were in joyous flower. The air hummed with regeneration, as spring dug its heels into our quiet suburb. I was quite relieved when I saw Mrs Tanaka standing sentinel at our mailbox, her quilted housecoat buttoned up to the collar. She had remained indoors Monday and Tuesday morning, causing me to worry that she had taken to heart her dashed romantic hopes for her niece and me. She waved a Tupperware container at my approach.

'Mochi cakes, Mr Sato,' she announced. 'I made them myself yesterday. Lovely weather, isn't it? I might take Mr Tanaka for a stroll around the carp pond later.'

'Thank you, Mrs Tanaka,' I said, accepting the cakes. 'I shall have these on my tea break.'

'Good. It is important to eat regularly, especially with the long hours you have been keeping of late. Five past midnight you got home last night!'

'My office has been very short-staffed lately.'

Mrs Tanaka tutted and shook her head. 'Then, you should tell them to employ more people.'

I nodded compliantly. Mrs Tanaka knows nothing of administrative organization and it is best not to quarrel with her about it.

'By the way, thank you again for dinner on Sunday,' I said. 'It was the most wonderful meal I have had in a long time.'

'I only hope my niece's bad manners did not spoil it for you,' Mrs Tanaka said. She was as bitter as a coffee bean.

'Bad manners?' I said. 'Naoko-chan is a thoroughly charming, uh . . . modern young woman.'

Mrs Tanaka lifted her eyes to the heavens and sighed. 'Modern, yes. But charming and young? She will be thirty-five next birthday. Thirty-five and not a squeak of a boyfriend. I only hope her biological clock will outlast her stubbornness. Oh, her poor mother—'

'Yes, well . . .' I interrupted, not wanting to be drawn into this intimate topic of conversation, 'I must be off, Mrs Tanaka: the seven forty-five won't wait. Thank you for the cakes.' I unlatched the front gate.

'Wait,' Mrs Tanaka said. Her fingers, marbled by poor circulation, clutched at the gate. 'How have you been sleeping these days?'

'Very well, thank you,' I said. 'Why?'

'I heard you pacing about your house at about four this morning.'

Impossible, I thought. She must have heard the Korean family on the other side of the Tanaka residence, and in her drowsy state confused the origin of the noise.

'Are you quite sure, Mrs Tanaka?' I asked. 'Are you sure it wasn't the Koreans? I was in bed.'

'Well . . .' Mrs Tanaka said, bristling in offence, 'I suppose one cannot be a hundred per cent certain that the Jeungs didn't break into your house to tramp on your floor-boards and play your old cello . . .'

'Cello?' A curious nausea swept over me. I tasted my morning coffee as my gorge rose. 'But I was in bed until six this morning,' I insisted.

'I was sitting up knitting when I heard it,' Mrs Tanaka said. 'I thought: *Why is Mr Sato playing the cello at this hour?*'

'I don't recall any of this,' I said.

'Then you were sleepwalking,' Mrs Tanaka decided.

Is this possible? Have you ever known me to sleepwalk? You would have mentioned it, surely. Could I have been playing your cello in my sleep?

Mrs Tanaka's gaze veered towards our empty house, towards the darkened upstairs windows. 'You make sure that you don't work too hard, Mr Sato,' she said, her usual abruptness dimmed by concern. 'We don't want your health to suffer now, do we?'

The idea of my having been sleepwalking, unbeknownst to myself, frightened me. As the 7.45 pulled out of Osakako station I decided that I was long overdue for a medical check-up after all.

However, as I walked into the office this morning I was confronted by the sight of Taro, the graduate trainee, with his head lodged beneath the cover of the photocopier. Fluorescent light flashed as the machine spat out sheet after sheet of the deviant boy's flattened profile.

'Taro!' I cried. 'What are you doing?'

Taro extracted his head, blinking woozily, bedazzled from prolonged exposure to the flash. 'Morning, Mr Sato. Heavy night at Karaoke last night. Thought this would wake me up.'

Well, as you can imagine, I kept Taro under close supervision all day. I will just have to wait until Mr Takahara returns from Hawaii before booking myself a doctor's appointment. To leave the office in the hands of young Taro would spell disaster for Daiwa Trading.

I returned home at 11.15 p.m. Having eaten nothing since lunch, my stomach has clenched into an angry fist, which I am now attempting to pacify with some clam soup. Preoccupied all day with the affairs of Daiwa Trading, I'd had little time to reflect on Mrs Tanaka's report of cello music. However, on the train home tonight I hit upon a technique to determine the truth of the matter. Tonight, before retiring I will sprinkle talcum powder on the floorboards beside my bed. This will expose me at once if I am the culprit.

I had best turn in now. But first I have a gift to lay by the family altar; some sugared almonds purchased from a subway kiosk on my way home from work. Though your mother, blighted throughout her life by diabetes, may object, I think you will enjoy them. You were always notorious for your sweet tooth, weren't you?

III

The bamboo forest at night thrums with manifold noises. Does the forest come alive after dark, or are our ears just boorishly imperceptive during the day? Though I took a stroll here just this Sunday, it is now an altered place – the dominion of beating insect wings, and snakes winding stealthily among the trees. Earlier I walked into the sticky, gossamer kiss of a spider's web suspended across the path. I swiped at my shoulders and head, fearful a vengeful spider had landed there.

A few kilometres along this path is the site where we camped. Do you remember? We hadn't been married long and it was your first camping trip. How excited you were! You waded in the stream as I fished, the legs of your dungarees rolled up, plucking from the riverbed any pebble that took your fancy. Later you cooked over the campfire the fish I caught, steaming rice in accompaniment. You declared it the most delicious fish you had ever eaten, remember?

A breeze stirs the calm night air. The cotton of my

pyjamas is cool against my skin. It is strange how at ease I am as the forest floor crunches underfoot. Walking out here clears my head. It offers reprieve from the torment encountered within our four walls.

When I woke this morning the first thing I did was inspect the talcum powder I had sprinkled round my bed. There were no footprints, not even a toe smudge. I must have lain in bed all night. As I swept the camellia-scented powder into the dustpan, the dream I had dreamt came back to me in bittersweet shards. I had been at the hostess bar, sitting on a bar stool. Mariko placed a cocktail before me, her glossy hair held back by two silver butterfly clips. The liquid swirled in the glass, a maelstrom of bewitching colours. I debated for a moment or two whether to drink it – such a kaleidoscopic beverage would surely be poisonous – then I lifted the glass and sipped. I do not recall the sensation of taste. But I do recall looking up to ask Mariko what I had just drunk. You were in her place.

As expected, today was another hectic day at work. To my dismay Mr Takahara sent us a fax informing us that negotiations in Hawaii were trickier than he had anticipated, and that he would be delayed for another week. Deeply concerned, I telephoned his Honolulu hotel room and left urgent messages on his answer machine.

After lunch, Deputy Senior Managerial Supervisor Murakami-san paid the finance office a visit. He had come to brief me on a new micro-management strategy for the transport department, but ended up staying for a couple of hours to look over some accounts. Needless to say I was still upset by his gossiping about us, and nettled by his presence. Fortunately my professionalism kept me civil.

Murakami-san's behaviour was not what one would expect from senior management. He whistled jazzy tunes as he flipped through the account ledgers and teased poor

Miss Hatta, the office assistant, until she blushed to the roots of her hair. He also encouraged Taro's malingering ways by inviting him for frequent cigarette breaks. Before he left the office, Murakami-san asked if he could take the Kawamoto files for closer inspection. When I insisted that the files were in perfect order, Murakami-san chuckled and said: 'I'm sure they are, Sato-san. A meticulous book-keeper such as yourself would never let these files fall into disrepair . . . Hey, how about joining Taro and myself for a few drinks tonight?'

I mumbled my excuses, and Murakami-san nodded understandingly before walking to the door, praising my tight management skills and clutching the Kawamoto files to his chest.

I was immersed in the micro-management spread sheets when Miss Hatta alerted me to a telephone call at about 4 p.m. I picked up the receiver, expecting Kojima-san from the loans department at the Fujitsu bank.

'Yes? Mr Sato speaking,' I said.

'Mr Sato, this is Mariko from The Sayonara Bar.'

The fever of shame crept up my cheeks. What could be more improper than a hostess contacting me at my work-place? I glanced about the office. Matsuyama-san, Assistant Accounts Adviser, was talking to a client on the other phone. Taro was staring into his Donald Duck screen saver. Only Miss Hatta was nearby, reloading the stapler on top of the filing cabinet. What if she had intuited the nature of this call?

'I . . . I am so sorry to bother you while you are at work . . . but it was the only way I could think to contact you.' There was a timorous tremor in Mariko's voice. She seemed only too aware of her transgression.

'How did you get my phone number?' I asked, at pains to keep my voice low. 'Did Murakami-san give it to you?'

'Oh no!' she said. 'I got the number for Daiwa Trading

from directory enquiries . . . I went through your company operator.'

'I see . . . I am afraid that I cannot talk now. I am very busy. In fact, I think it is best that you never call me here again.' I was sorry to speak to Mariko in so cold and impolite a manner, but I thought it very bad form to contact me at the office.

'OK,' Mariko said. 'But we must arrange a time to talk. Can you come by the hostess bar? I have something I want to tell you.'

What could Mariko, so remote from my day-to-day life, possibly have to tell me? I was impatient to terminate the phone call as Miss Hatta was still within earshot, now tending to the spider plants on the windowsill.

'What does this matter concern?' I asked.

There was a silence at Mariko's end of the line. Then a calm voice said: 'It concerns your wife.'

I left work at 8 p.m. with an ineptly feigned migraine. My briefcase knocked against my legs as I was borne along by the after-work revellers thronging their way through Shinsaibashi. What enticed them so was beyond me. Everything was drowning in brightness, each bar more crassly eye-catching than the next. Pachinko balls ricocheted and games arcades blared machine-gun fire. In the foyer of the Sea Breeze restaurant a girl clad in a shell bikini and scaly mermaid's tail swam about a giant fish tank. She stared vacantly at passers-by, her inky hair swishing about her head.

I approached The Sayonara Bar, my pulse unsteady. Mariko's telephone call had unsettled me as a fox does a henhouse. What could a child like Mariko possibly have to say? I replaced the handset when she mentioned you. Then I told Miss Hatta I would accept calls only from the Fujitsu bank. But it was too late. Mariko had robbed me of the ability to concentrate. I knew I wouldn't be at peace until I had spoken to her.

I lingered outside the noodle shop next door to the hostess bar. People jostled past, treading on my toes without apology. Inside the steamy window a chef prepared meat dumplings with thick, callused hands. I wondered what Mariko could possibly know about you. Nothing more than what Murakami-san has told her. And he only knows what he heard from the cruel Chinese Whispers that circulated after your death. No one knows you as well as I. No one knows you well enough to be certain you would never take your own life.

I decided that there was no need to speak to Mariko after all. I turned from the noodle-shop window and set off for home.

When I got back I took a hot bath and listened to the radio. Then I went to bed, eager to succumb to the soporific effects of my bath.

But at 2 a.m. the telephone began to ring, wrenching me from my contented slumbers. I got up and stumbled through the dark towards the hallway phone.

'Hello? Mr Sato's residence,' I said, my voice furred with sleep.

There was a click, then an empty dial tone.

This made me very cross. The gall of some people! They could at least have had the decency to apologize for their mistake. I began my ascent of the creaking stairs, grumpy as a bear disturbed during hibernation. It seemed unlikely I would sleep after this – my mind had been irritated into wakefulness. This will cost me dearly tomorrow, I thought bitterly.

The house was very still and quiet. On the upstairs landing I noticed that the door to the spare room was open a snatch. *How odd*, I thought: *I always shut that door tight.* I decided to take a quick peek inside.

The door slid smoothly open. The moon spread its muted glow through the parted curtains. I looked to the centre of the room and my heart gave a sickening lurch. Your cello had been moved.

It lay on its side, an air of decadence about the posture, as though it had been basking in the moonlight. My head swam with incomprehension. Had someone broken in and moved it? Who would do such a thing? My breath came in jagged rasps as I fumbled blindly for the light switch. Stark light leapt to every corner, and the cello was back in its usual place, against the bookcase.

So it had been a hallucination. I was astonished. Never have I been subject to such a vivid, convincing hallucination before. My feet were rooted to the tatami. I was scared to turn my back, or walk out of the room, lest the cello engage in further mischief. But one cannot stand about all night. To take a walk struck me as the most rational thing to do.

Once again daybreak finds me talking to you. I have wandered much farther than I intended – it will be a good hour's hike home. And just look at how high up I am! I scarcely noticed my uphill progress until first light showed me the bamboo forest, lush and green, blanketing the world beneath me. I had better start back now, or I shall be late for work. What a bizarre sight I will make for passing drivers as I hurry along the roadside in my pyjamas and mud-caked moccasins. I will have to sneak quietly back into the house to avoid Mrs Tanaka. I will be in too much of a rush to speak to her. I have a shirt to iron and a train to catch; a doctor's appointment to make and a cello to sell.

If I hurry I can still make the 7.45.

10

MARY

We talked all night and passed out at daybreak on sheets damp with sake and sweat. Neither of us could sleep past noon, so we came here for breakfast. Men in boiler suits line the counter, smoking, bantering, excreting tarmac and toil. A whiskery woman mans the noodle vats, garnishing lunch-time specials with cremains of the cigarette stuck to her bottom lip. We are unshowered, dazed by a dearth of sleep. Tiny red cobwebs thread Yuji's eyes, and his hair is pillow-pummelled. He takes a pair of disposable chopsticks and snaps them apart at the join. I watch him hoist his breakfast mouthwards; beautiful, even when his face swarms with noodles.

Last night he sent a message to my phone asking me to meet him at a bar in Namba. I took a cab there after work, out of sorts because the last place I wanted to be headed was a British theme pub where the carpets give off the stodgy fug of battered cod and real ale. Yuji and his friend Shingo were in a back room, playing pool. I sat on a tall stool, drinking beer and watching them whittle down the number of balls on the table. While Shingo was leaning over the table, lining up a shot, Yuji came over and said, casually: 'They trashed my flat today.'

I asked him what he meant. *Who* trashed his flat? He said he didn't know. They had broken his stereo and slashed his mattress with a knife, but taken nothing. He was bemused by my reaction, smiling at Shingo as if to say, 'Women, eh? Always stressing.' Shingo laughed at me. He told me that Yamagawa-san would soon get to the bottom of it.

Later, walking back to my apartment, Yuji was subdued. His arm was slung over my shoulder, and I leant against him, breathing in tobacco and the leather of his jacket. I was chattering drunkenly in not-so-quiet, broken Japanese, when we heard a heavy thud behind us. We jumped and looked round. Beneath the halogen glow of the street light was nothing more than cracked paving and recycling bins.

I laughed. 'Must have been a cat.'

'That scared the shit out of me . . .' Yuji said.

He surprised me. Yuji always acts like fear isn't part of his emotional spectrum. And walking the streets at night in Japan is safe, even on your own. The crime rates are low, and I've never seen any violence here, not once. Then I remembered why Yuji had reason to be jumpy.

'You thought it was the people who broke into your flat, didn't you?'

A motorbike revved on the other side of the railway tracks. Steeped in shadow Yuji's face was hard to read.

'What did Yamagawa-san say when you told him? Does he know who it was?'

'He didn't say much. Things haven't been good between us lately.'

'What do you mean? You were getting on fine that night at the club.'

My heels struck a drain cover, steel echoes denting the night. Yuji let his arm slide down from my shoulders.

'Something is wrong. I've pissed him off in some way. The other guys – Shingo, Toru – they sense it too. Everyone has been acting weird lately. And the jobs he's been giving me have been getting worse.'

'Worse how?'

Yuji shunned my gaze. I told him once about the yakuza films I saw before coming to Japan – the gunfights, punch-ups and amputated digits. Yuji had laughed and told me it wasn't like that, but seeing him so shaken up I had to wonder.

'This is not good, Yuji,' I said. 'You should leave. I mean, you don't have to work for Yamagawa-san for ever, do you?'

'It's not that easy,' Yuji said. 'He's invested time and money in me. It would make him angry.'

'So let him be angry. If you don't want to work for him any more, then you shouldn't. What can he do? Force you?'

'He will see my leaving as betrayal.'

'Betrayal of what?'

'You don't understand,' Yuji said. 'He will lose his temper and make things difficult.'

We fell into a silence. He was right: I didn't understand. Why would Yamagawa-san kick up a fuss? Any high-school drop-out this side of Amerika-mura can be trained to make deliveries and collect loan repayments. But since that night in the karaoke booth I could see how Yamagawa-san can make things difficult for a person.

'Sometimes I just want to take off and lie low for a while. It's been done before.'

'Where would you go?' I asked.

We were approaching the foyer of my apartment building. Cheap flyers for discount pizza delivery and call-girls spilt from the mailboxes onto the salmon floor tiles. Yuji shrugged, too tired to answer.

'You could leave Japan with me,' I said, 'when I go travelling.'

The silence said it all. To hide the hurt in my eyes I walked ahead of him, over the leaflet litter to the entryway. I jabbed my swipe card into the slot by the door. The door jerked open and the recorded voice urged us to enter. I went inside, but Yuji did not move. He stood, hands in pockets, staring in the direction of the car park.

I smiled tentatively. 'Aren't you coming in?'

And he looked at me and said: 'If I got the money together we could leave next week.'

Yuji pushes away his empty bowl and reaches across the table for my hand. I smile at him, full of doubt and in-security. Last night was the first time I'd ever heard Yuji complain about his job. I'd always thought it was im-portant to him. What if he only said what he did because he was demoralized by the break-in?

'Won't you miss your friends when we go?' I ask. 'And your mother? Everyone you know is in Japan.'

This is his get-out clause. A reminder of all that he is leaving behind. I brace myself for a change of heart. Plots hatched in the middle of the night are often fuelled by insanity.

'My friends are the property of Yamagawa-san,' Yuji says. 'And my mother is tough. We don't have to worry about her.'

'Will you tell her that we are leaving?'

Yuji shakes his head. 'We can't tell anyone. Not even her. She will be mad I kept it from her, but it's not worth the risk. And I want you to keep working at her hostess bar until it's time to go – everything has to stay normal.'

'I feel awful about not being able to say goodbye to any-one,' I say.

'Tell Katya and Mariko, then. Tell them that you are going back to England. But don't say anything until we are ready to go. It might take me a week or two to get the money together. Just be ready when I do.'

'I will.'

So he waived the get-out clause. I break into a smile, which Yuji cuts short by leaning across the table and kiss-ing me. He tastes of salt, the cracked asphalt of his lips tender and coarse. He pulls back too soon for my liking. Two of the boiler suits pitch Yuji a lewd grin. The noodle-shop owner pulls a wire basket from the vat and cackles.

You don't often see a Japanese guy with a Western woman; the reverse is more common. We sometimes find ourselves magnetic north of the public gaze. Yuji usually gets a kick out of it, but for once he is oblivious. I see my reflection in his eyes, dark and slick as pools of oil.

'We are not going to regret this one bit,' he tells me.

Yuji has to report to Yamagawa-san, so I go home and hum tunelessly beneath a scalding shower. I am not usually of the humming disposition, but I feel like I've just had an intravenous fix of happiness. After my shower I put on a second-hand kimono and wrap my hair in a towel. I badly want to talk to someone – though the only subject I want to talk about is off limits. I pad down the hall to Mariko's room, a grande dame in my towel headdress.

I tap on her door. 'Mariko, are you in?'

The door is ajar. I kick it so it swings open. The room is empty, everything stowed away, all the surfaces pristine. It is as though I have opened a door into a room in a meticulously ordered guest-house. A breeze seeps through the mosquito screens. I step back over the threshold, closing the door behind me.

Without Mariko to distract me I light a cigarette and pace the kitchen, buzzing with nervous energy. I hope Yuji can lay his hands on the money soon. I know I am selfish to be so excited when things are so unpleasant for him, but I can't help it. Besides, we'll be out of here before anything bad happens.

I am not without misgivings, though. Months of roach-infested hostels and the fatigue and confusion of travelling can take their toll on a couple. We could end up like those sun-burnt, travel-worn couples you see bickering their way through Japan. But travelling exposes you to new cultures, opens you up. Yuji will be freer away from the underworld machismo of his job. He doesn't say it a lot, but I know he loves me. I think Japanese men hide their emotions, the way Japanese women hide their giggles behind their hands. I don't need him to be demonstrative. His willingness to spend months on end travelling through Asia with me is confirmation enough.

I sprint into work late and charge into the changing room. After getting ready in record time I dash out to the lounge, hoping Mama-san is still in her office. Fortunately there aren't many clients yet – just two at the bar with Stephanie and Annoushka, and two with Katya. Shadows flock beneath a broken light in the lounge. On the jukebox Sting dirges on about being an Englishman in New York. If he feels alienated in America he should try it over here for a while.

Katya rises to greet me as I go over. She's wearing the long, red Chinese dress she bought on our jaunt last week to Kobe, her hair twisted into a topknot, oriental flicks of kohl tapering the corners of her eyes. She takes my hands and pecks me on both cheeks.

'This is Mary,' Katya announces. 'Mary is from England.'

'Good evening,' I say to the salarymen.

They stand and bow. One is venerable and grey, the other an office junior with the last vestiges of pubescent acne inflaming his forehead. I recognize the venerable grey one. Stephanie calls him 'the Octopus'. Apparently, to those who can tolerate his shallow breathing and frisky, wandering hands, he'll dispense 10,000-yen notes like a cash machine gone haywire.

'And these two handsome gentlemen,' Katya says, 'are Murakami-san and Taro.'

More bows all round. Katya sits next to the Octopus, so full of adoring smiles and honeyed devotion she almost has *me* convinced. I sit down next to the office junior.

'England, huh? Cool,' Taro says. He is whippet-skinny, bony wrists shooting past his shirtsleeves, like a schoolboy ambushed by an overnight growth spurt.

'Rains a lot,' I reply. 'Where are you from?' I put my elbows on the table, leaning forward like I can't wait to hear.

'Hiroshima,' Taro says. 'I came to Osaka to work for Daiwa Trading. You may recognize my esteemed superior, Deputy Senior Managerial Supervisor Murakami.' Taro gestures towards the Octopus. 'He is a regular client at this hostess bar.'

Katya is shelling pistachios and popping them in the mouth of the esteemed superior, smiling through his repellent attempts to suck her fingertips. He murmurs something, and Katya throws her head back in laughter, neck tendons flaring.

'I like pistachios too,' Taro says, hopefully.

I smile in a too-dense-to-take-a-hint kind of way.

'So what's it like working for Murakami-san?'

'He's the best. He's expanded the Graduate Trainee Programme to include private tutorials in Woman and Alcohol. I am learning from a master.'

'Lucky you.'

'He is way cooler than the other people at the company. Murakami-san really knows how to unwind after a hard day at the office. My office head is, like, this boring robot: "Please do the corrections I have made in red ink. No more cigarette breaks until I say so . . ."'

'Cigarette, Taro?' Murakami-san asks, proffering a pack of Winston Extra Strength to his charge.

Taro takes one and sticks it in his mouth. I light it for him and watch as he sucks smoke into his mouth and holds it there a second, before blowing it out. He tells me about his new hobby, golf, which he is learning under the supervision of Murakami-san. Then Taro asks me to teach him some English swear words. I oblige, helping him with his pronunciation.

Half an evening passes in this way. Taro puts away about three glasses of lychee *Chu-hi*; hardly enough to intoxicate a hamster, yet his cheeks fire like a kiln, and he succumbs to the inexplicable urge to whip off his tie and wrap it round his forehead, Rambo-style. I laugh politely.

Murakami-san claps eyes on the spectacle and booms: 'Bravo, Taro! The office clown strikes again!'

Katya and I titter girlishly. Our eyes briefly meet and unite in contempt. Murakami-san drags his pouchy eyes away from the thigh-high slit in Katya's dress long enough to tell her that he is ready for another Singapore Sling. Katya asks me to accompany her to the bar.

I measure out the Cointreau, cherry brandy and gin and tip it into the cocktail mixer. Katya adds pineapple juice from the carton. It's a lively night, with seven hostesses dispersed among the suits. All the girls have glittery hair and cleavage (I saw a can of that spray-on stuff in the changing room earlier) and Annoushka and Sandrine have white orchids tucked behind their ears. They look so pretty. As a client talks to her, Annoushka smiles, shredding a cardboard drinks mat under the table with her nails.

'You're quiet tonight,' Katya says. 'Has the ankle-biter been getting on your nerves?'

'I feel like a bloody babysitter,' I say. 'I wish I could just pack him off to bed or something. How's the Octopus?'

'I've had nicer things stuck to the sole of my shoe, but the little extras make up for it . . .'

Above the bar is Supermodel TV. A model struts down the runway in a top hat, trailing a magnificent fantail of ostrich feathers.

Katya smiles to herself. 'He asked me to ask you something.'

'What?'

Katya screws the lid on the cocktail mixer and gives it a couple of brisk, conger-eel shakes. 'He asked me to ask you if you'd sleep with that boy he brought. He says he's still a virgin, and Murakami-san got the impression you were hitting it off.'

'*What!*' I choke.

Katya is serious. 'He's offering three hundred thousand yen and will pay for the love hotel. The only thing is the boy mustn't know it's a set-up. He has got to think it's because you like him.'

Three hundred thousand yen. That is a month's salary for most people. I look over and see Taro and Murakami-san in a conspiratorial huddle. Murakami-san is talking. Taro is grinning from ear to ear.

'Katya! Are you serious? I'm not a prostitute . . .'

Katya drops the act. She creases up with laughter. 'Don't take it personally. Murakami-san propositions everyone.'

'Right.'

'Three hundred thousand yen, though – that would cover a lot of your travelling expenses!'

'Yeah.'

'And I lose out on the commission I'd make off you.'

I've had enough of Katya's joking around. I thump a silver tray onto the bar top, with slightly more force than I intended.

'Come on, Mary. Where's your sense of humour tonight?' she teases.

'I am sick,' I say, 'of men who assume the hostess bar is a front for a brothel.' This venom arises from nowhere, surprising me, surprising Katya. I look away from her.

'I heard Yamagawa-san was here the other night,' Katya says lightly, changing the subject.

'Yeah. He made me sing 'Material Girl' in the karaoke booth. Four times.'

Katya laughs, just like Yuji did when I told him. I suppose it is quite funny in retrospect. 'You should have said no . . . Or made him pick a better song.'

Katya pours Murakami-san's cocktail into a glass.

'He had this boy with him who'd been in a car accident. His face was covered in bandages.'

'Jesus. Poor guy,' Katya says. 'One thing about people who work for Yamagawa-san, they are definitely more accident-prone than most.'

She pours some more pistachios into a dish. I pick up a clean ashtray and add three thousand yen to the Daiwa Trading tab. Katya's grim remark has depressed me. She lifts the silver tray and balances it on the palm of her hand. As she walks out of the bar she turns and says with a rueful smile: 'About the Octopus . . . I didn't mean to offend you. I thought you'd think it was funny.'

'I know,' I say. 'I'm a bit tired tonight. Forget it.'

'Let's go for a drink after work,' she says, 'and we'll talk properly.'

I smile at her and think, *I'm really going to miss you when I'm gone.*

Murakami-san must have given Taro a pep talk in my absence, because I get back to find the boy remodelled on Don Juan. Murakami-san must also have warned him just how severe an impediment the Rambo look is to wooing the opposite sex, because he has removed the headband and opened a couple of shirt buttons, to air his skinny chest.

'Can you drive?' Taro asks.

I shake my head. 'Nah, I'm too lazy to learn. I'll probably be stuck with public transport for the rest of my life.'

'I'm taking lessons,' Taro says casually. 'My instructor says I'm the fastest learner he's come across in a long time. I should have my licence in a couple of weeks. I'll take you for a spin if you like. Nara is especially beautiful this time of year.'

'Thanks, Taro. That should be fun,' I say.

I reach for a cigarette. I wonder what season it is in China right now. Will Yuji need to bring his leather jacket?

'Allow me.' Taro lights my cigarette, suave as hell. I grimace my thanks, trying to inhale and smile at the same time. He takes a swallow of his lychee alcopop, emitting a silent belch before asking: 'Mary, do you have a boyfriend?'

'Yes,' I reply, lightning fast.

Taro weathers the news with a strained, skull-like grin.

The malicious pleasure I feel is quickly succeeded by

guilt. 'But it's nothing serious . . . you know, just a bit of fun.'

Taro's smile assumes a natural laxity. 'Oh! Right. I like having fun too . . . Maybe *we* could have fun together some time?'

'OK,' I say. 'Why not?'

No way in Hell! . . . but where's the harm in lying? It's not like I'm going to be around for much longer.

Taro is going on about Universal Studios Japan when the dizziness begins. I grip the table and wait for it to pass, but my skull tightens, as if clamped by an invisible vice. A blizzard of monochrome dots blights my vision. Taro's boyish squeak is suddenly as barbaric as nails driven down a blackboard. I want to tell him to shut up, but wait for a pause in his boring, second-by-second account of the Terminator II ride before excusing myself.

I lurch through the lounge, my vision like a detuned television; full of flickering human shapes, light and shade. I stumble my way from memory, ramming shoulders with a client by the bar, who apologizes in a deep baritone. I don't stop to see who he is. I need to get to where I am going before I pass out.

Beneath my feet the floor surface changes from carpet to tile. The air smells of charred pizza crusts and Korean pickles. I inch by the deep-fryer, oily convection currents settling on my skin. I pass the silent, human-shaped snow-storm of Watanabe, edging forwards until my hand, held out before me, meets the cool metal surface of my desti-nation. I grope for the handle, wrench open the door and enter the frigid air of the walk-in fridge. The door swings shut behind me. Upsetting a stack of pizza bases, I sink to my knees in relief.

I kneel with my forehead pressed against the cool, gritty fridge floor. Marooned in the darkness, I knead my temples and the vice loosens its grip.

Sound-proof, light-proof, salaryman-proof; I could stay

in here all night. I try to diagnose my dizzy spell. It can't be alcohol. After months in this boozy occupation, it takes seven whiskies even to put colour in my cheeks. The cold clears my head. Goosebumps have reared up all over, and my back teeth have begun a demure, staccato rat-a-tat-tat. Blood refrigerates in my veins, chilling me to the marrow.

A wrenching sound and a chink of bright kitchen light cuts across my floor-level field of vision. Despite the angry 'leave me alone' vibes I send out, the chink widens into a sizeable gap and a shadow enters. The silence indicates the shadow belongs to Watanabe. He closes the door and crouches beside me. He touches my shoulder and my head snaps up in surprise; Watanabe isn't the type to make physical contact. I sit up, shins against the cold fridge floor.

'Here, drink,' he whispers.

A glass is pressed into my hand. I take a sip of water, then another. I'm not remotely thirsty but the act of drinking eases me back into human functioning.

'Thank you,' I mouth into the darkness. 'My head hurts.'

'You will get used to it,' Watanabe intones gravely.

I laugh weakly. 'I want it to go away.'

There is a silence as Watanabe turns my words over. Then: 'That's what I thought,' he says, 'when it first happened to me.'

I laugh again and wonder, not for the first time, if Watanabe is altogether there.

We sit in quietude for a moment before the seal of the walk-in fridge breaks again. The door swings wide open. We blink at the silhouette of Mama-san, her little chihuahua tucked into her arm.

'Back to work, Watanabe,' she says.

Watanabe gets up and ducks past Mama-san, lowering the visor of his baseball cap like a protective shield.

'What is wrong with you, Mary?' Mama-san asks impatiently. 'Why are you sitting in the fridge? Are you drunk?'

I rise on wobbly legs. 'No. I just had a dizzy spell. I thought I would feel better if I sat in here for a while. Sorry.'

Mama-san does not verbalize her displeasure. She drinks in my frowzy satin dress and messy hair with a face most people reserve for sucking lemons. 'Where is Mariko tonight? Is she sick?'

'I don't know. I haven't seen her,' I say.

Mama-san shoots the vegetable rack a withering look. 'If you are sick, Mary, go home. If you can work, then work. I do not pay you to sit in my fridge all night.'

Watanabe listens, stooped at the sink.

Stephanie bounds into the kitchen, her auburn ringlets jouncing. 'Watanabe-san! Prawn tempura and a plate of nachos,' she says in her American-accented Japanese. 'Salsa dip.'

She clips up the order slip and sneaks an inquisitive look our way. It must look as though Mama-san is about to shut me away. Mr Bojangles slithers an inch down the front of Mama-san's red dress. She hoists him back up with the crook of her arm.

'I am better now,' I say. 'I can go back to work.'

'Good. Then, get back to table nine.'

Mama-san turns back to the lounge, her face still cast in a vinegary grimace. I wonder how she will feel when she discovers her only son has skipped the country without telling her. That he has chosen to elope with me is bound to add salt to the wound. I feel sorry for her, I really do. But if she was a nicer person he wouldn't keep it from her.

I sigh, daunted by the prospect of two more hours babysitting Taro. Watanabe stands motionless at the sink. 'I can't wait to get out of here,' I say.

The tap alone gushes its reply, but I am certain Watanabe wishes the same thing.

II
WATANABE

The glass department store stretches eight storeys high. Escalators zigzag through the centre of the building, up to the roof-top garden. Golden lifts voyage up and down like tiny beads of air in a crystalline plant stem. Outside this glorified greenhouse two foreign girls embrace, one blond, the other brunette. Tiny fibres from the brunette's mohair tank-top float up and tickle the blonde's nostrils. Static crackles across the breadth of air between them.

Mary and Katya cocoon themselves in the mellifluous tones of feminine interaction, pealing every so often with xylophonic laughter. Mary impregnates the air with oxytocin, a hormone conducive to trust and uterine contraction. The 2 parts per 17 million diffusion of this chemosensory signal causes Katya, whose biology serves purely Machiavellian ends, to wrinkle her nose.

I stand opposite the department store, beneath a giant azure-blue screen, upon which a famous actress chirrups the virtues of Maybelline Ultralash mascara. The signal at the pedestrian crossing beeps and a battalion moves towards me: necktie-asphyxiated salarymen; women clutching the hands of their pre-school offspring; drop-out youths roving from games arcade to pool hall. It is human cartography in motion; muscles manoeuvring ivory skeletons, bloody Medusan tentacles shooting into hyperspace. Each individual moves within a ghostly vortex of memory and emotion; psychic treasure-troves I dip in and out of at whim. In a flash of neutrinos they touch down on my side of the street, and continue towards their destinations, bodily microprocessors whirring, like tiny, electric cicada.

Greeting ritual consummated, Mary and Katya enter the building. I cross the road to join them. Some 2,758 whorling fingerprints besmirch the handle of the door they went through. I recognize Mary's thumbprint atop the smudgy miscellany. Touching my hand to this blazing vestige, I push open the door.

Shop automatons in red uniform and pill-box hats are posted throughout the ground floor. Each has a pearly smile and a compulsive bow. Blitzed by vibrant stimuli, Mary and Katya experience the kind of endorphin rush usually induced by extreme sports and recreational drugs. They descend upon a stall of silk scarves. To the horror of a nearby automaton, Katya wraps one round her head.

'I could wear this to work and earn extra money reading tea leaves,' she says.

Mary laughs and a nearby office lady glances over. Unlike me, the office lady cannot translate foreign sound waves into the universal metalanguage underlying all speech. They head towards a hatstand 7.2 metres away. I slip behind a pyramid of diamanté tiaras. It is easy to evade detection in a department store. Caught in the dazzle and glare of such a place, visuospatial senses are stunted and inattentive to peripheral activity.

I seldom set foot inside these hothouses of consumer vanity. I hate the smell for a start, that sickly candyfloss spun from manmade fibres and air fresheners. Nor can I tolerate the consumer will-to-power, the self-delusion of the hunter-gatherers stalking the DKNY summer collection. Take that girl over there for example – the one admiring the cashmere twinset. She thinks this 9,000 yen outfit will transform her into the airbrushed beauty of the advertising campaign. And see the girl in the white cotton gloves, with the calamine chalky face. She thinks the blue sash belt she fondles will draw the eyes of her unrequited love away from her psoriasis. That man with the lazy eye and razor-burnt cheeks. He thinks the green diagonal stripes on the tie he has selected will help him get a promotion.

But their concerns are trivial. At times like these I liken myself to an omniscient scarecrow, watching over a field of cabbages as they each primp and preen to be the best-looking cabbage. Blind to the fact they are still only cabbages.

Mary and Katya move up to ladies' fashions, where the mannequins wear day-glo tank-tops and combat fatigues. Katya secretes herself in a harem-esque corner, drawn to the fur-lined handcuffs. Katya thinks her dominatrix tastes are sired of her own will. But I can trace her bloodline back to the sixteenth century, back to a Ukrainian countess who bathed in the blood of her servants.

Watching Mary browse through a rack of T-shirts, my heart swells with tenderness and fear. One night last week I trailed Mary and her boyfriend home through her quiet neighbourhood.

I kept close behind, listening. And what I heard made my ears retch.

Every night since then Yuji has been fertilizing Mary's love for him with the fetid manure of his lies. Lies that distort Mary's emotional attachment, so it no longer corresponds to the brutish, numbskulled reality of him. It is agony to watch Yuji string her along for his own wicked ends.

And yet Mary's emancipation draws near. The other night *it* happened, flooding me with deep, immortal joy.

She sought me out as her reality blistered and we sat together in the darkness of the refrigerator. Mary thought she was ill, unaware she had seen the first ripples in the looking-glass. Only I can help her. I know the torment of those early days of transcendence only too well.

I must be there when the final exorcism sets her ablaze, freeing her of the unhappy mildew of mankind.

Mary and Katya move across the beige carpeting. Fingers thirsty for exotic textures, they stroke everything within stroking distance. Aroused by a new range of shrink-fit jeans, Katya strides ahead on anorexia-enervated legs. Personal gripes aside, my heart gags on a spasm of pity.

'What do you think of these?' Katya asks. 'Those with hips need not apply.'

Mary is not paying attention. 'Y'know, I haven't seen Mariko for two days now.'

'Hmmm . . .' Katya is assessing the quality of denim weave. Katya exists in a state of solipsism so extreme she disregards the existence of anything not in her presence. Therefore Mariko, who is not present at this moment in time, does not exist. And non-existent entities do not warrant Katya's concern.

'I don't know where she is. She might have gone back to Fukuoka, but then all her clothes are still in the wardrobe. And she wouldn't have gone anywhere without saying anything.'

'Maybe she's having an affair,' Katya says. 'Remember how Sandrine kept missing shifts when she took up with that high-school teacher?'

'Mariko is not Sandrine,' Mary says. 'I'm worried. I turned her room upside down last night looking for an address book. I couldn't even find her family's phone number. If she was seeing someone, she'd at least come home to pick up some clean clothes.'

'Look,' Katya says. 'You have nothing to worry about. Mariko will turn up . . .'

But Mary is full of dread. A vision of Mariko lying face down in a ditch explodes like a sordid, tabloid flashbulb in her head. I decide to get to the bottom of this mystery.

I cannonball through tetraspace on my quest to find Mariko. I catapult above the urban fortress of steel and bricks, hollering heavenwards, rupturing infinity. My hyper lens swings left and right, upsilon and phi. Every gluon and positron united in the construction of this cityscape screams itself hoarse for my attention. But ever judicious, I tunnel down upon the subject of my endeavours.

Mariko is nowhere near a ditch; she is not even lying down. She is standing in a shopping mall in the Osaka suburb of Juso. For the past 2 hours 14 minutes, she has been watching a salesman demonstrate how to carve roses from radishes using a special paring knife (retailing at 1,999 yen). Mariko has suffered a mild nervous collapse – the consequence of pimping her integrity night after night. She will be mesmerized by the salesman and the deft, silvery flash of his knife for a few hours yet.

Mary, Katya and I leave the department store and journey across the Chuo line to the suburb where Mary lives. They have three hours to kill before work, and intend to spend it sitting at the carp pond beside the town shrine, drinking sake.

'They will think we are dissolute women for drinking in the afternoon,' Katya teases.

'They can think what they like,' Mary replies.

Mary has always been careful to present a clean-cut image of herself to the residents of her town, but, heady with her imminent departure, she has grown careless. On Monday, at 11.41 a.m., Mary hung laundry out on her balcony wearing only her underwear. It sent the old man at the bamboo-shoot stall across the street completely agog, and he spent the rest of the day telling his customers of the foreign floozy on the second floor.

Mary and Katya sit down, roll up their jeans and dangle their bare feet in the sun-spangled water. Solar radiation unmitigated by ozone falls upon Mary's shoulders, inciting melanocytes to blossom darkly. The carp pond is encircled by azalea bushes, and a few pensioners in flopsy sunhats, taking gentle, constitution-improving strolls. They drink oolong tea from plastic flasks and admire carp shadows passing through the plankton murk. If only these pensioners could see the spectacular carnival of fins and scales that is the true carp reality, they would fall to their arthritic knees. Once Mary is a seasoned hyper-excursionist like myself, we will return to this pond, and watch the carp shimmer by like majestic airborne zeppelins. In the meantime she bats the pond water with her toes, and deep in the azalea bushes I swat at the mosquitoes dive-bombing my jugular.

Mary bites into a rice cracker, igniting the epithelium of her tongue with chilli flavourings. Katya takes a hardened swig of sake.

'You seem different lately,' Katya says to Mary. She senses Mary's transformation.

Mary bites her lip, unsure whether to confide the glitch in reality she has experienced. 'Different how?' she asks.

'Restless.'

'It must be because it's springtime.'

'How have things been with Yuji lately?'

'He's been busy this past week. I haven't really seen him.'

Good! He must be cheating on her, thinks Katya. A tintinnabulation of glee rings out in her cadaver's heart. 'Yamagawa-san works those boys hard,' she says.

Mary slaps a mosquito on her forearm. The mosquito's internal organs seep through its caved-in fuselage. Reduced to a brownish smear on Mary's arm, its tracheae continue to squeeze, like tiny bellows, driven by the cosmic imperative of life.

'I hate getting bitten,' Mary complains.

Katya hasn't much to say on the topic. As a child her

staple diet consisted of potatoes grown in plutonium-contaminated soil. The mosquitoes leave her well alone. Mary takes a sip of sake, and the anterior lobe of her liver groans, having scarcely metabolized the alcohol from last night.

As the silence yawns between them, Mary asks: 'Do you ever get the feeling that there's more to it than this?'

'More to what? The carp pond?'

'To everything.'

'Everything? Do you mean spiritually? Like religion?'

Katya's vapidity is as boundless as the sea. Sensitive to her disdain, Mary says: 'Oh, I don't know. Just ignore me.'

Mary self-consciously closes her eyes and lifts her face to the sun. Katya stares into the water, recommencing the ongoing love affair with her reflection. Oh, to hurtle from these bushes and tell Mary that I understand *exactly* what she means . . .

A gentle breeze billows sun-baked dust over the pond.

But I must practise restraint. I must be patient until the time is ripe.

There is little to recommend the barren wasteland of Argonon. The planetary atmosphere is so thick with clouds of zinc and nickel that the sun can scarcely penetrate it. Even on a mild day visibility never exceeds a metre or two. The metallic dust of Argonon has achieved galaxy-wide notoriety. Propelled by the power of starlight, it wafts across the frozen darkness of interstellar space, settling on any planetoid it meets. Did you know five per cent of all dust on Earth originates from Argonon? It frosts our shelves and furs our skirting boards and radiators. It dances in shafts of light among the rafters of empty suburban attics.

Mortality rates on Argonon are high, and what little of life there is is generally understood to be nasty, brutish and short. Despite this Argononians have a reputation for kind-ness that puts the creatures of more inhabitable planets to shame. Though a tourist destination for the clinically insane, anyone who has been there will tell you the same thing: if you're in a fix, an Argononian will cut off his fourth arm to help you.

Owing to the poor quality of life, long periods of birth prohibition are imposed upon the Argononians. It was during one of these times of prohibition that a girl and a boy had the misfortune of being born. The parents of the twin siblings tried to cover up the birth, but rumours escalated until a Depopulation Enforcement Officer was sent to investigate.

'This is a serious violation,' he said as he paced about the living room.

A titanium squall whipped against the windowpane. The two mothers and three fathers hung their heads.

'It was an accident,' Father no. 3 piped up. 'How can we be guilty of a crime we did not know we were committing?'

'You cannot profess ignorance in this day and age,' the Depopulation Enforcement Officer barked back. 'The eight stages of the reproductive process cannot be completed without a certain degree of premeditation.' He looked at the babies sleeping in the crib, respiratory filters clamped against their faces. 'I am afraid I am going to have to take them both.'

The three fathers went limp with despair. Mother no. 1 put her head in her hands and wept. Mother no. 2 sank to her knees and clawed at the carpet.

The Officer sighed. 'Very well. I will let you keep one.'

The parents took out a ten-spiln coin. On one side was the Argonon symbol for heaven; on the other, the symbol for earth. They named the boy Solaris and the girl Terestra. Then they threw the coin in the air.

Shortly afterwards the Depopulation Enforcement Officer left with the baby Solaris tucked beneath his arm. Congratulating himself on his diplomacy, he returned to his office and filled out the necessary paperwork. He then despatched the baby to where all illegal births *were sent: down the chute to the wormhole incinerator.*

The wormhole incinerator was a transport project gone wrong. Scientists from a planet next door but one to Argonon had tried to modify a neutron star with lasers and matter-processors. The resultant wormhole was meant to provide a short cut across the universe, but, owing to miscalculations, all spacecrafts that entered were instantly compressed into anti-matter. Realizing their mistake, the scientists changed tack. The wormhole was no longer a transportation device but a dumping ground for the refuse of the solar system. This was where baby Solaris was sent.

His sister Terestra continued to grow up on their home planet. A virtuous and contented girl, she loved everything about Argonon, from its blackened skies to its arsenic-ridden soil. She learnt to love the heavy respiratory filter attached to her face as though it were her own flesh. Life on Argonon was all Terestra knew, and she had no complaints.

One day she was strolling across the manganese waste-lands when a lump of cobalt fell on her head.

'Hey!' she cried angrily, through her respiration-mask filter. She glared up at the sky, but visibility was only 0.7 metres and she saw nothing.

'Terestra, this is your brother Solaris.'

'Is this a joke?' Terestra asked suspiciously.

'No, it's not a joke. You can't see me because I am anti-matter.'

A hot gust of iron filings blustered by. Terestra bristled with irritation. She thought this joke in poor taste. 'My brother is dead,' she said coolly, 'whereas you are obviously alive, and very sick in the head to boot. Now, if you'll excuse me . . .'

'I am not dead,' the voice said indignantly. 'What you call dead, I call Argononian prejudice.'

Terestra walked on through the dense dust clouds. She hoped her tormentor would leave her alone.

Instead he pleaded: 'I want you to join me, Terestra. I

have been watching over you for the past few weeks, and I want to rescue you from this toxic lump of metal. When they tossed that coin you were the loser. Your reality thus far is nothing but a tiny impurity in an extraordinary unseen universe.'

Terestra stopped walking. Hand on hip, she said: 'OK, so how exactly do you intend to rescue me?'

The voice came back at her: 'By telling you that you must jump down the chute into the wormhole incinerator.'

Terestra laughed. 'You are a lunatic. Now get lost, you conceited piece of anti-matter.'

And to illustrate her point, Terestra scooped up a handful of manganese soil and swung her arm round, flinging it out like a toxic Catherine wheel.

Many years later, Solaris and Terestra freewheel across the cosmos. They echo wild laughter as they leapfrog asteroids and hopscotch over meteor showers.

Solaris says to Terestra: 'Remember that terrible fuss you kicked up when I first told you to jump down the chute of the wormhole incinerator?'

Terestra turns a fetching shade of pink. 'Don't remind me! I gave you such a hard time.'

Solaris shrugs. 'I barely remember . . . Hey! A supernova! Let's go and do some solar windsurfing. Last one there is an Argononian filter valve.'

Mary and Katya are sluggish as bees sunk in honey. The afternoon sun has microwaved their cerebella and their vision flickers, strobe-lit. They brush the grit stuck to their legs and roll their jeans down over the tiny craters indenting the backs of their calves. They complain that they don't want to go to work. They want to sleep while the 500 ml of alcohol they have jointly imbibed seeps through the multiple stages of catabolic breakdown. Groaning, they pull sandals over feet coated in an invisible microslime of algae and pond protozoa.

I keep my distance as they make their way down the

quiet, residential lane from the town shrine to the station. They pass three schoolboys in judo uniform who are tearing about beside a paddy-field, shucking sherbet-filled liquorice sticks. The schoolboys suspend their adolescent mayhem as Mary and Katya pass by, but when I follow 13.1 seconds later the fattest of the trio 'yeeeoww's at me and lashes out a karate chop that stops mere centimetres from my sternum. I stumble from the kerb into the road and the boys crumple up with laughter. Hypersonic enmity rays fly from my psyche. I transmit a telepathic warning to my fat aggressor: *Laugh it up while you can, Koji Subaro, because with that much cholesterol in your subclavian artery your karate-chopping days'll be over before you're thirty.* On a deep, subliminal level Koji Subaro registers my ominous message. Despite the sunshine and laughter of his playmates, he shivers long and hard at the sight of my receding back.

Eager to delay their arrival at work, Mary and Katya stop for a coffee at the Mister Donut beside the station.

I wait in the mouth of a shopping arcade, beneath the awning of a dilapidated hardware store. I watch them sit at a table with a double espresso and Americano. The happy, shiny lighting in Mister Donut's blanches all who enter into featureless zombies, but not Mary. She blows a stream of sake-sweetened breath across her coffee and heat from its caffeinated depths speeds to the surface, yearning to be borne away by this angelic breeze. The heavenly red welt of her glottis clamps shut as a sip of coffee slips down her throat. It washes over her tonsils, voluptuous their pendular caress. A soft, gaseous belch travels from Mary's stomach to her mouth, where it silently passes into the jarring, external world of Not-Mary. She seals her lips. Her lips are unlike anyone else's. Her lips are a throbbing, scarlet universe unto themselves.

Beside her the Ukrainian sourpuss frets over the number of kilocalories in a double espresso. A shop girl in bubblegum-pink uniform arranges glazed doughnuts in the counter display with metal tongs. In the shop girl's stomach is a starchy bowling ball composed of four chocolate doughnuts. Earlier she stowed fourteen cinnamon twists into her duffel bag, to distribute among the Holy Brotherhood of Leptus when she returns to the compound tonight. She knows the doughnuts will be appreciated after their long day of levitation and magical incantation.

All over the nation the working day draws to a close. Pulse rates slow to low, elephantine thuds as a tide of people wash back from the city to the suburbs. Brains switch to autopilot and internal monologues grow languid, muddled by low blood-sugar levels and a day's worth of unprocessed memory. Clothes crisp and fresh that morning are now rumpled, smudged with LaserJet ink. Fatigue stalks these work-tired souls home: a grey, monolithic entity.

Among the laggard masses I spot him straight away. His heart is a pneumatic drill on amphetamine overdrive, his pores filled with tense baubles of sweat. He wishes to be inconspicuous, yet he is the most conspicuous individual anyone has seen all day. He enters a record shop in the arcade and begins flicking through the jazz section. All customer eyes abandon the J-pop and World music compilations to focus on this man and the scar covering half his face. The disfigurement incites shock, revulsion and delight. I personally think it unremarkable. Perhaps I should remind you that in the fourth dimension all features, external and internal, exist on an equal plane, and the surface of the face is no more prominent than what lies beneath. I am no more interested in his scar than the density of his nose cartilage.

Sweat humidifies the confines of his expensive suit as he looks out of the window, rifling mechanically through the records. I have seen him before. He came to The Sayonara Bar with his boss only last week. A yakuza henchman, he has killed eighteen men and has many aliases, the most up to date of which is Red Cobra.

I hack into his optic nerve and dry-heave when I see the object of his feverish attentions: Katya. To be fair, his mental reconfiguration has elevated her onto a higher aesthetic plane; her drab complexion now has a milky opalescence, and her lank hair whispers to him, lush and inviting. His throat tightens with unspoken desire as she sips her espresso.

As the sun sinks over the tawdry retail outlets of the township, Mary and Katya leave Mister Donut's. Red Cobra moves away from the window of the record shop. He and his beloved Katya will have to part company here. His disfigurement renders him too eye-catching to pursue her further. The girls head towards the train station.

The commuter crowds are thinning out. I sneak out from behind the recycling bins as Mary and Katya buy tickets and proceed to the turnstiles. I watch as their bone marrow regenerates and lymphocytes spurt through lymphatic vessels. I access their thoughts and learn that Mary wants to doze on the train and Katya is trying to remember something. The lost memory headbutts the walls of her subconscious, bumping closer and closer to her mental foreground, until she spins 180 degrees and shrieks: 'I left my shopping at Mister Donut's!'

I freeze. The eye is drawn towards moving objects.

'Wait there!' she orders Mary. 'I will be one second.'

My heart standing still, I slink back to the recycling bins.

Mary watches Katya dash to the exit, shaking her head at what a pain she is. She smiles as a small boy with a large *kendo* stick marches past, touched by how cute and serious he looks. And then: 'Watanabe?'

The concrete floor and postered walls spin away. An abyss opens up, at the centre of which is Mary. She moves towards me with a quizzical smile.

'Hello, Watanabe! What are you doing here?'

I am here as your guardian, to protect you and guide you towards liberation . . .

'Are you OK?' she asks, her smile dissolving.

I lower the rim of my baseball hat, to shield her from the white heat of my mortification. I want to tell her that I am fine, that her concern should be saved for the rest of humanity. But not a word comes out.

12

MR SATO

I

The doorbell rang at quarter past ten this morning. *That'll be Mrs Tanaka*, I thought. Ever since Mrs Tanaka caught me returning home at dawn after my night in the bamboo forest, she has kept me under keen surveillance. In the evening time she often brings me wholesome dishes of beef and vegetable stew, convinced as she is that deficient nutrition had a role to play in my aberrant behaviour. I have told Mrs Tanaka that I am perfectly capable of cooking for myself. But she laughed at this and told me my 'namby-pamby' diet of rice and *miso* would never put any meat on my bones.

So I opened the front door, expecting to see Mrs Tanaka bearing a steaming casserole dish in those enormous red oven mitts of hers. But instead there stood a curious gentleman of about my age. He wore a moth-eaten corduroy suit and his bald head glistened in the sunshine, as though it had been lovingly massaged with glycerine before he'd left the house that morning. (Though I mustn't joke: my hairless head could be just as shiny for all I know!) The man also had a tremendous handlebar moustache, which at first glance I mistook for some comic disguise.

'May I help you?' I asked.

He was quite down-at-heel, so I expected that he had come to offer his window-cleaning services or suchlike.

'Mr Sato?' said the man. 'We spoke on the phone Thursday night. I'm Mr Onishi, head of the music department at Tsuita High School. I have come to collect the cello you have so generously donated. On behalf of the staff and students of Tsuita High, I thank you, Mr Sato.' Mr Onishi beamed and bowed twice in rapid succession.

The arrangements we had made flooded back to me: ten o'clock, Saturday morning. How had the appointment slipped my mind? I smiled and bowed, flustered by my short-term-memory loss.

'Thanks to you, Mr Sato, we are now able to offer cello lessons to our more underprivileged students. In expression of our gratitude we would like to invite you to be guest of honour at the Tsuita High School brass-band concert next Wednesday.'

Mr Onishi gave another speedy, whiplash of a bow, before smiling in expectation of a verbal contribution from me. It would have been polite at that point to invite the music teacher inside for a cup of jasmine tea, before showing him up to the cello. But I had begun to feel very strange. A clammy sweat had broken out beneath my shirt and cardigan, and I completely lacked the wherewithal to move.

At the delay, Mr Onishi's snaggle-tooth smile began to languish. 'I do not wish to intrude or be a nuisance,' he said. 'If you prefer I could return at a more convenient time . . .'

His walrusy moustache twitched as he spoke. As I have never cultivated such a moustache myself I wondered if such a thing would be an impediment at mealtimes. Would one require a special comb to remove the crumbs buried in its bristles? Mr Onishi shifted uncomfortably. To be honest, I have no idea why I said what I said next. Even hours later my incivility induces a hot flush of shame.

I cleared my throat. 'Mr Onishi,' I said, 'I am afraid that I have already given the cello away. My memory has been very unreliable of late, and I completely forgot. I can only apologize for wasting your time.'

The ease and conviction with which I lied took me aback. Where had this confidence sprung from? Obviously some devious quarter of my mind, which ought to be suppressed.

Confronted with this bad news, Mr Onishi was the height of graciousness. 'Ah, well, not to worry,' he said. 'We all make mistakes. As long as you've found the cello a good home.'

He glanced at his watch and said he had to get back to supervise brass-band practice. He told me that I was still more than welcome to attend the concert on Wednesday, that my name was down on the guest list. Then he bid me good day and set off back to school. Though Mr Onishi's corduroy suit was moth-eaten, and his moustache straggly and unkempt, I knew which one of us was the lesser man.

After he had gone I went up to the spare room and stood before the cello. There was a fine sprinkling of dust on the scroll and tuning pegs, so I removed a handkerchief from my trouser pocket and set about wiping it away. Is it true that we are all guilty of the good we haven't done? If so, then I am doubly guilty, for I drove the opportunity to do good right from my doorstep. What had possessed me to lie like this? Lies that deprive a high-school student of the chance to learn a musical instrument, no less. And the thing that upsets me the most is that to pass on the gift of music is what you would have most wanted.

I promise you I will take the cello to Tsuita High School next week, the first chance I get. I will leave it in the school reception with a note for Mr Onishi. It simply will not do to leave it idling in the spare room. It will not do at all.

II

The Public Accounts office has been lamentably short of staff for three weeks now. The endless reams of paperwork have left us all as snow-blind as Arctic explorers. Matsuyama-san says he has an enchanted in-tray: whenever he thinks he has cleared it, the tray magically refills itself. We all had a good laugh at this. But joking aside, the continued absence of Assistant Section Chief Takahara-san is of growing concern to all of us. Mid-morning I went to the office of Deputy Senior Managerial Supervisor Murakami to discuss the appropriate course of action.

Murakami-san invited me to sit in his upholstered wing-back chair and, via intercom, requested his secretary bring us a pot of coffee. Murakami-san sat at his mahogany desk. It was a morning of clear blue skies, and behind his broad shoulders metal skyscrapers ricocheted the glare of the sun.

As I voiced my concerns, Murakami-san gave deep thought to all I said; he closed his eyes and positioned his hands beneath his chin in contemplative prayer. A moment or two after I had finished saying my piece his eyes flickered open again.

'Takahara-san is most fortunate to have a colleague as considerate as yourself, Sato-san,' he said. 'But have you considered the possibility that our friend Takahara has absconded? His position is very stressful and Hawaii offers many distractions for the lonely businessman . . .' Murakami-san smiled to himself, perhaps at some private memory. 'Perhaps, rather than report him as missing, we should wait a week. He will surely contact us. Though I must say his future job prospects at Daiwa Trading are shaky.'

Well! Can you believe it? How could the Deputy Senior Managerial Supervisor be so light-minded about a matter as serious as a missing man? He lifted his coffee cup to his mouth and smiled through the steam rising from the cup. His eyes were dewy and pink, and, to be frank, could have done with some eye ointment. Though the coffee was freshly brewed and scalding, Murakami-san took a lengthy draught. When he placed the cup back in the saucer I saw that half the coffee was gone.

'With respect, Murakami-san, though I have only known Assistant Section Chief Takahara for eight months, he has impressed me greatly with his upstanding character. He would not run off without a word,' I said. 'We of the Public Accounts office would like the peace of mind of knowing he is safe and well.'

Murakami-san leant back in his leather chair. 'Very well, Mr Sato,' he said. 'I will contact the police myself this afternoon. Perhaps they will be able to organize something with the police in Honolulu . . . And for the time being I will find you a replacement for Mr Takahara.'

'Thank you,' I said, pleased Murakami-san had come round to my way of thinking.

'Now, if you'll excuse me, I have to prepare for an afternoon board meeting.'

I bowed and apologized for the intrusion. And, smiling, Murakami-san escorted me to the door.

Upon my return to the Finance Department I announced to the office that Murakami-san was to procure a replacement for Takahara-san. The news drew sighs of relief all round, and Taro, the graduate trainee, stood up and did a *banzai* victory dance. What difference it made to Taro I do not know. While the staff shortage has had the rest of us running about like headless chickens, Taro has continued in his work-shy ways. Really, the stench coming off the boy this morning could have knocked you out at twenty paces. One has to suspect he'd spent the previous night doggy-paddling about a vat of whisky, before bedding down in a giant ashtray. In the interests of public health and safety I lent the boy a flannel and a clean shirt from my locker, and sent him to the washroom, telling him not to return until he'd given himself a thorough seeing-to with the carbolic soap. We had a visitor from the Mitsubishi plant coming in at noon, and it simply would not do to have the place reeking like a brewery.

As Taro shilly-shallied about his daily assignments, I overheard him telling Miss Hatta that he had been out the night before with Murakami-san. It sounds like Taro is Murakami-san's latest protégé, to be tutored in the ways of late-night carousing. Murakami-san should know better than to take our graduate trainee out on drunken escapades at a time our office can ill afford it.

Though my work was nowhere near completion I was out of the office by eight o'clock tonight. This dereliction of duty is not my idea, but Dr Ikeda's. In my last session he instructed me to restrict my working day to eight hours. When I began to explain to Dr Ikeda what a crucial time of year it is for Daiwa Trading, he cut me short, saying that I had to reduce my daily workload to overcome my work addiction and rediscover the things of value in my life. This made me very cross. 'Addiction is not a word to take lightly,' I said. What right has he to lump me in with the alcoholics and nefarious marijuana addicts who roam the back streets of the entertainment districts? In light of Dr Ikeda's ignorance, ten hours a day is a more than reasonable compromise.

Perhaps Dr Ikeda made this personal slight out of professional bitterness. I had my second hypnotherapy session with him yesterday, and once more he was unable to 'send me under'. He says I have the most resistant mind he has ever encountered in a subject. Though he said this in complaint, I fancied I could detect a hint of awe in his voice. When I think how many thousands of patients must have passed through his musty, book-lined study over the years, I cannot help but feel secretly flattered.

That night in the bamboo forest I promised myself I would seek help. But, really, what is a man to do when his tremendous resilience of mind stymies even the doctor's efforts?

III

It is 4 a.m. and another strange day has bled into an insomniac night. I have been sitting up for hours now, summoning the courage to talk to you. My tired eyes burn through the darkness, watching the shadow puppets of my imagination dance upon the walls. I have exhausted my brain playing the incident over, reading a hundred and one meanings into her every word.

All that remains is for me to lay it down, for you to judge.

True to his word, Murakami-san sent along a replacement for Assistant Section Chief Takahara. Miss Yamamoto reported to me at eight o'clock sharp. She has a boyish haircut and sprightly laugh, and took to the job with verve and panache. For once, I was delighted with Murakami-san's choice. Miss Yamamoto is like oil to the rusty Finance Department machinery. She has a serious, intelligent approach to the work, but also an easy levity. She brought two badminton rackets into work with her, and at lunchtime invited Taro for a game in the office car park. Eating my instant noodles, I watched them from the window as, laughing, they batted the shuttlecock to and fro. Taro huffed and puffed and panted mightily. The boy seems quite smitten.

After lunch Murakami-san stopped by to check on Miss Yamamoto, and to let me know that he has informed the Kansai police of Takahara-san's disappearance. All we can do now is sit tight until they contact us with their findings.

It was a day of satisfactory progress, so I did not mind when everyone began to bow out after the five o'clock company chime. The first to go was Taro, who bounded to the door like a dog who's been cooped up indoors all day and is desperate to relieve itself in the yard. Then Matsuyama-san had to go home and look after his children while his wife taught her Tuesday evening pottery class. Miss Hatta went at six, giggling into her mobile phone to a girlfriend, and our new recruit, Miss Yamamoto, left half an hour later, with an armload of files she intended to work on at home. Such conscientiousness! I wonder if it is possible to keep her on as a replacement for Taro when Takahara-san returns.

By eight o'clock all was quiet in the Daiwa Trading building. The footsteps echoing on the stairwell and the voices calling, 'Thank you for your hard work,' became scarcer and scarcer, before vanishing altogether. Even the cleaners had ceased sloshing their mops along the corridor and gone home. Soon I was all alone, with only the dormant hum of the office computer for company.

I took advantage of the peace and quiet to get ahead with the accounts ledger. I grew peckish at some stage and considered purchasing a snack from the vending machine down the hall. But once embroiled in a project I find it a wrench to leave my desk. After a little more work I realized that I was in gross violation of the ten-hour compromise I had made with Dr Ikeda. This made me feel rather rebellious! It also gave me a peculiar satisfaction to think of my office as a solitary pocket of light in a building of darkness.

I was poring over the accounts ledger, my nose a finger's breadth from the page, when I heard the cough. The cough was crisp and feminine in timbre, and orchestrated to draw my attention. Startled, because there had been no footsteps to alert me to an intruder, my gaze flew to the door.

First glance, and my heart seized up. I mouthed your name as you stood there, holding a box wrapped in a gingham handkerchief.

'Mr Sato?' you said, and the illusion shattered. It wasn't you at all, but Mariko, the hostess.

I sprang up from my seat like a jack-in-the-box.

'Mr Sato, I—'

'*What are you doing here?*' My voice quivered with rage.

Mariko took a step back as I shakily inhaled. I was furious at Mariko because I had mistaken her for you. This was in no way a manipulation on Mariko's part, yet I reacted as though it were.

Mariko lowered her head. 'I am very sorry to have alarmed you,' she said. 'Perhaps I should leave.'

But she made no sign of departing. Her act of visiting unannounced was brazen to say the least. I recalled the telephone call she had made the other week, and was disturbed once more by her last words to me – words that filtered from the perforations in the telephone receiver, to fill me with unease.

Mariko wore a yellow sweater with a pale-blue skirt of accordion pleats. She held the gingham box with both hands, and slightly outwards, as though it contained a substance that might stain her clothes. Her hair was in a ponytail and on her feet were those red buckle shoes. How could this child, so innocuous of appearance, arouse such anger?

'What are you doing here?' My voice did not quiver this time. It hissed.

'I made a *bento* for you this afternoon. I wanted to give it to you before my shift at the hostess bar tonight. I came at five and sat on a bench in the park opposite this building and waited and waited for you to come out. By seven o'clock you still hadn't appeared. I was already late for work by then, but I just kept thinking: *Five more minutes and he'll come out; five more minutes.*'

'Why did you make me a *bento*?' I asked in disbelief.

'Because I woke this morning and felt like it.' Mariko stated this as simple fact, as if I had asked why the sky was blue. She held out the gingham box further with both hands. 'It's salmon and rice with pickled plum . . .'

Her voice trailed off nervously, and rightly so. I had my stony face on, the one I reserve for rogue builders and insurance salesmen. Four hours is a very long time to sit waiting on a wooden park bench for a person. I wondered then if Mariko entertained any fanciful romantic notions about me. I immediately dismissed this idea as ludicrous. What would a rose in the bloom of youth want from a grumpy old salaryman like me? Mariko bit her lip, eyes downcast at my fierce manners.

'Mariko,' I said, 'when you phoned me here the other

week I was *very unhappy* about it. I thought that I had made this clear to you. Well, I am unhappier still about you visiting me here in person. Your being here is highly inappropriate.'

'I made certain that most people had left before I came in. I sneaked past the security guard when he went for a cigarette break. Then I found my way to your office in the dark. I didn't knock because I wanted to be certain all your co-workers had already left.' Mariko's eyes were wide and imploring, but her stealthy pluck did not win me over one bit.

'The fact you are here when everyone else has gone makes this all even worse,' I said sternly.

'But there was no other way for me to see you,' she said. 'After I called you I thought you would stop by at The Sayonara Bar. I watched out for you every night. When you didn't come, I knew that it was up to me to visit you . . .'

'Did it occur to you that I have no desire to hear whatever you had to say?'

As you well know, this is not entirely true. And confronted with Mariko once more, the heartsick confusion of that evening I almost went to speak to her returned.

I was ready to insist that Mariko leave, when I saw that she had begun to cry. Her eyes were glossy with tears, which tumbled silently down her cheeks.

'Please . . .' she pleaded, her throat constricted with anguish.

As the tears spilt, my resolve deteriorated. I winced, ill equipped to deal with such an outburst. 'Um . . . Mariko . . . there is no need for this. Please stop that now . . .' I said.

'Since the night I first saw you,' she said, 'I have dreamt of you every night.'

It sounded as though she was reciting a romantic song lyric. I shook my head, afflicted with the overwhelming sentiment that this was wrong.

'I dream that we are walking along a white beach that

stretches for miles. We are walking, and then suddenly you keel over, screaming that someone is stabbing you. I am frightened. I think that you are dying. I try to help you up, but you are in too much pain. Our hut is further down the beach, so I run towards the hut to call for an ambulance.'

I felt the blood drain from my face. It had to be co-incidence, it just had to be.

'Then I wake up,' she said, 'and I am crying.'

'This is preposterous,' I said, in a faraway voice that seemed to filter from the air vents.

'I think I am going mad,' Mariko said. 'You are a stranger to me, and yet I think of you constantly.'

My head spun. It had been you who had run down the beach to call the ambulance. Mariko hadn't even been born then. Why would Mariko dream that she was you? This has to be a coincidence.

'You dream this every night?' I asked.

Mariko nodded.

'This is a most abnormal state of affairs,' I said. 'Who told you about the kidney stone I had in Okinawa? Who have you been speaking to?'

Though my tone was not angry or accusatory, Mariko sank to her knees in a sad, swooping motion. She threw down the *bento* box as she fell. It bounced once, and skidded beneath Miss Hatta's desk. She hid her face in her hands and wept.

'I don't know anything about your kidney stone. I don't know about Okinawa. The dreams are all I know,' she cried. 'And I don't want them. I hate them. I hate you. Every night before I sleep I pray that this will stop.'

The poor girl was truly beside herself. I leant over slightly and reached out to comfort her. My hand hovered uncertainly by her shoulder, unable to make contact with any part of her.

'Perhaps you should seek medical help,' I murmured helplessly.

'I don't really hate you,' she said.

Along the corridor a door slammed shut and we both jumped. Perhaps the door slam had been in protest against our voices, which had no doubt been raised during our exchange.

Mariko hushed her voice to a whisper. 'Sometimes, when I am still half asleep, a woman appears. She kneels by my futon and strokes my hair.' Mariko paused, to allow me time to absorb this detail of her dream world. She continued, in a voice like a wisp of smoke: 'She strokes my hair and tells me that everything will be OK. She says she will look after me. She says she knows that I am lonely and alone, but I will not have to endure this for much longer. She will guide me to safety.'

'This woman,' I said. 'What does she look like?'

All trace of tears had vanished from Mariko's face. She brushed a strand of hair from her brow and looked me dead in the eyes. 'She looks very much like me,' Mariko said, 'but she says her name is Reiko.'

We spoke no more of dreams and apparitions after that.

I saw Mariko off at the taxi rank. Then I caught the train home. Since then I have been thinking non-stop about what she said.

When Mariko spoke your name, the room fell very still, as though we were standing in the eye of a tempest. How the devil had she come by your name?

I am confounded by the riddle of Mariko's dreams. Her words echo over and over as I twist them inside out for hidden meaning, like clues to a cryptic puzzle. Maybe Mariko is lying; maybe this is an elaborate ruse. But I am not a gullible man. There was nothing disingenuous about Mariko's distress tonight. We will talk again tomorrow, when she is calmer. I have arranged to meet her at six o'clock, on the same wooden bench where she sat waiting for me today. I need to know more.

IV

At work this morning, all I could think about was the night before. My powers of concentration diminished, I caught myself staring out of the window. A skyscraper was being built half a kilometre away, and I was transfixed by the canary-yellow crane hoisting slabs of concrete thirty storeys high. Thankfully, this introspective mood did not last. There was plenty of work to do and before long I was re-immersed in the day-to-day business of the office.

Miss Yamamoto is proving herself to be quite the office star. During the night she spotted some clerical errors in the files she had taken home with her – errors that would have resulted in the monthly misallocation of over 30,000 yen of funds. If it wasn't for Miss Yamamoto's eagle eyes and acumen the Finance Department would be in very hot water come July. When I announced this to the office, no one came forward to accept the blame. I really ought to keep a closer eye on the accounts.

At quarter to six I grew restless. At three minutes to, I collected my briefcase and coat and told Matsuyama-san that I was off. The sight of me leaving earlier than him caused Matsuyama-san to look up at the clock in mild dis-orientation. '*Already?*' he asked. 'Yes,' I said. 'Don't work too hard.' Then I said goodbye and walked out of the door.

The cramped triangle of grass opposite the Daiwa Trading building scarcely merits the title 'park'. The grass is trampled and dull, and the flowerbeds are barren. You will be pleased to hear, however, that the saplings they planted in 1991 have sprung up into hale and hearty copper beeches. I sat on a bench beneath one of these sturdy specimens, my briefcase flat on my lap, as I waited for Mariko.

There were few people in the park. A man chugged about in a sweatband and jogging suit, and two high-school sweethearts stole a kiss at the park gates. The snack vendor beside my bench was packing his cart away. He caught my eye and gestured to the sky.

'It's going to be pissing down soon – you'd be best off heading home.'

It had been overcast all day, and the sky was now very dark and menacing.

'I am waiting for a friend,' I said.

'Well, your friend had better turn up soon, or she'll make a drowned rat of you.'

The vendor rolled his cart away, whistling as cans of fizzy pop rattled in the coolbox. It was now quarter past six. *It would be a shame to leave after waiting fifteen minutes and just miss her*, I thought. I was beginning to understand the logic that had kept Mariko chained to the park bench for four hours the night before.

Another twenty minutes was all it took to prove the vendor right. Without warning, the trapdoors of heaven burst wide open. Two boys with Mohawks, and chains dangling from their baggy pants, whooped and wheelied on their squat little bikes, punching the air as though there is no greater joy on earth than being soaked to one's skin. I left the park at once, muttering damnations as I held my briefcase ineffectually over my head. I proceeded to the subway station, where I joined many others seeking refuge from the rain.

Mariko's failure to appear concerned me. She had been so pleased when I agreed to the six o'clock meeting – surely she wouldn't break it without good reason. Though reluctant to do so, I decided that I had better go to the hostess bar to check that she was OK. I could be in and out in ten minutes, and thankfully it was still too early for an encounter with Murakami-san and his pesky sidekick Taro.

It had been some weeks since I had last frequented the bar. The downstairs lobby was dingier then I remembered. The floor, littered with cigarette ends, could have done with a good sweep and mop. There was also a faint urinal odour that made me not want to touch anything.

My nerves jangled all the way up in the lift. Silly, really, because I had been twice before and knew what to expect. Or so I thought.

Three American hostesses were posted at the door, foiling my plan to slip by unnoticed to the bar. 'Welcome!' they chorused and bowed. It was like being greeted by three larger-than-life mannequins. Their smiles leapt out at me, all creamy lipstick and even teeth. I shrank back towards the door.

The most Amazonian of the hostesses stepped forward in a clingy dress of emerald-green sequins. 'Good evening!' she sang in exotically accented Japanese. 'I take coat. *Wow!* You wet! Outside, strong rain. We bring towel. You come here before?' What the Amazonian lacked in fluency she made up for in volume.

'Yes, he has been here before,' another girl piped up. It was Stephanie from Florida. Her orange tresses were offset by a leopard-print dress (which in all honesty was more suited for use as a summer nightie than evening wear). 'He's a friend of Murakami-san.'

'Which one?'

Stephanie said a few words of English and the girls laughed.

'A friend of Murakami-san! Why didn't you say so?' the third girl, a blonde, oozed like treacle. 'We just adore Murakami-san here.'

'Glasses wet! We bring tissue! Wipe glasses!' shouted the Amazonian.

'Actually,' I said, 'I do not intend to stay long. I would just like a quick word with Mariko, if she is not too busy.'

I scanned the empty lounge, thinking I might spy her against the velvet maroon décor. Even without clientele or hostesses, the lounge still gave the impression of wealth and sumptuous warmth. A Japanese hostess with Cleopatra eye make-up sat at the bar, lazily picking at a salad with her chopsticks.

'Mariko?' asked Stephanie.

I nodded and the three American girls consulted each other in English, spitting foreign words as vigorously as machine-gunfire. Though I had taken two English-language modules at university, the only word I could discern was 'Mariko'. The treacly-voiced blonde looked at me, clapped her hands and shrieked with laughter. This made me rather paranoid.

Stephanie from Florida turned to me, her smile as bright and reassuring as the noonday sun. 'I'm sorry, but Mariko is not here . . . Phone us tomorrow evening and we'll let you know if she is working. That'll save you the trouble of coming all the way here.'

'Hey, why not stay?' the blonde purred, hand on hip. 'How often do you get to have three gorgeous women all to yourself?'

I gave a forced laugh of unqualified terror. 'Ha ha ha . . . I must go home now . . . thank you . . . you are, uh . . .'

I bowed and apologized, almost tripping over a potted fern in my haste to retreat.

The heavens grizzled in the aftermath of the storm. Water gurgled in the roadside drains and the streets were slick with puddles, which boomeranged light back at the store fronts. My mood was very gloomy and apathetic, and I made no attempt to avoid these puddles as I walked home from the station. I splashed through them, until my socks squelched at every step. When I realized what I had done I felt very childish and small indeed.

As I turned into our street I could hear one of the Okamura children practising 'Greensleeves' on the piano. The rhythm was clumsy and the melody was interspersed with many false notes. There was also a lengthy pause, during which I can only assume that a page was being turned. Perhaps I am getting old and sentimental, but I found the music strangely charming. Such a rag-tag of children they have in that house, how you could remember all their names I'll never know.

As I approached our front gate I saw that the light was on in Mrs Tanaka's bedroom window. The curtains were open and I could see her pacing back and forth in her royal-blue housecoat. When she spotted me she came to the window and twitched at the curtains. I remember wondering why Mrs Tanaka was so lively. As you know, from seven o'clock onwards Mrs Tanaka sits knitting and watching her favourite television programmes with Mr Tanaka. I waved to her, but she did not return my greeting. Instead she watched intently as I unlatched my front gate.

I noticed it straight away, the dark mound on our doorstep. *What could that be?* I wondered, squinting through the darkness. It looked like a bag of rubbish, or a large bundle of rags. I think I mentioned the other week about the rusty old pram someone had dumped in Mr Oe's front yard. Well, I thought a similar trick had been played on me here. I proceeded cautiously towards the mound, then stopped in my tracks. The mound moved, offering me a glimpse of something long and pale: a leg. My perspective shifted, and I saw that what I had thought was a mound was in fact a person. A girl in a skirt. Curled into a tight ball as she lay on the damp, concrete terrace.

'Mariko?' I said. 'Mariko?'

I stared for a moment longer. Then, ignoring the fanatic twitching of Mrs Tanaka's curtains, I ran to see if she was all right.

13

MARY

The Saturday morning workforce is caffeinated and deodorized, sharp of collar and mind. Lipsticked women in power suits overtake me, pinpricks of sweat breaking out on their powdered noses. Clean-shaven men jostle me aside, single-minded as salmon headed upriver to mate. I straggle in their midst, a pariah in last night's dirty clothes, sangria and stomach acid in my hair.

The strap on my sandal has broken and every few paces it flies from my foot. I chase after it, weaving among the suits and briefcases, murmuring half-hearted apologies. As I bend to retrieve it someone knocks me from behind, sending me forwards, my fingertips breaking my fall. I scowl up through the knots in my hair. These people have their commutes down to the second. They aren't going to stop for anyone, least of all a shoe-hunting foreigner with mascara smudges under her eyes. I walk on, my sandal clutched in my hand.

Next to the subway is the sunless, concrete hangar of a bus station. It takes my hungoverish brain a while to find the right stop, which has been hijacked by schoolboys duelling with badminton rackets. I stand next to a hunched old lady in a raincoat, who rocks a shopping trolley to and fro, as if the multipack of economy toilet paper it holds is a sleeping child. Next to her is a gruff old salaryman wearing a surgical mask, his brow worked into a 'nobody mess with me' frown. I want to bin my sandal, but hold onto it instead. It provides the distinction between girl with a broken shoe and mental patient on day release.

Buses chug in and out, rolling over the *kanji* signs painted in the bus lanes. A number 157 pulls up, shuddering with diesel sickness. The back door opens and an orderly queue materializes. By the time it is my turn to step up the bus is jam-packed, the ceiling straps festooned with knuckles. I shoehorn myself in and grab a ticket. On these buses you don't have to pay until the end of your journey. I could wait until then to own up about having no money, but fear of the transport police makes me shove and toe-tread my way to the driver.

'Good morning,' I say.

He blinks at me from behind his plastic partition.

'I am very sorry to trouble you,' I say, in the polite Japanese I learnt at university, 'but my purse was stolen. Would you mind taking me a few stops for free?'

This is of some interest to two old men. 'That foreigner's purse was stolen,' one remarks to the other, 'and isn't her Japanese good?'

The driver blinks again. 'For free?' he echoes. 'Ah, well, let me see . . . er . . . Sorry, no, we don't let people ride for free. Why don't you go to the police and tell them your purse was stolen?'

The driver is boyish, clean-cut, possessed of a nervous tic and the kind of scrupulous honesty the world could do with more of. Except for now.

'Oh, I don't want to trouble the police,' I say, confident my charm will wear him down yet. 'I just want to go a few stops. Thank you. Sorry for the inconvenience.'

Passengers at the back of the bus crane their necks to see what is going on. The driver gives a pained smile of genuine moral consternation. To admit me for free must go against whatever oath he had to take at Bus Driver Academy.

'Er . . . no. I am sorry,' he says. 'No one is allowed to ride this bus for free.'

'It's only a couple of stops . . .' I am not asking much. I just want to find Yuji, beat the crap out of him, then wash the vomit out of my hair.

'I am very sorry,' says the bus driver.

The exit opens with a hiss. Fine. *On your conscience be it*, I think, and step back down onto the tarmac.

Affixed to the pock-marked wall of the bus shelter is a map. I trace the route to Yuji's town and estimate it an hour's walk. I decide to follow the motorway and make a pit stop at the imitation American diner to scrub up in the bathroom. As I turn away from the map the old woman in the plastic mac hobbles towards me, her trolley trundling behind. She is hump-backed and snowy-haired. A fragile cage of osteoporosis. I see a lot of old women with mangled spines over here. Yuji says that they get like that from decades spent bent over in paddy-fields. She halts a few inches short of me.

'You need to pull down the back of that skirt. I can see your knickers,' she croaks.

'Oh.' Stupidly, I tug the back of my skirt.

My compliance only encourages her. Her mac crinkles as she prods me in the midriff. 'What's wrong with you, you mucky thing?'

I take a step back. If being ancient earns you the right to go round poking and criticizing people, then I guess old age isn't entirely without appeal.

'I lost my purse,' I say.

'You said it was stolen.'

'Lost, stolen, whatever.'

'Your Japanese is dreadful. Shall I fetch someone who can speak English to help you?'

'No, thanks. I—'

'I'll get you a policeman – they're very clever, these policemen. They'll put you right.'

'Really, I'm OK . . .'

But she's off, her trolley of economy toilet paper bouncing up the kerb behind her. I watch her go, niggled by guilt. It's a sunny day. Why the raincoat? Another number 157 pulls up, blotting her from view. I smooth down the back of my skirt and climb on board. The driver is old and grouchy, with a toothpick jutting from the corner of his mouth. When I ask if he would be kind enough to take me a few stops without charge, he grunts ambiguously and I go and find an empty seat before he changes his mind.

So far Yuji has been vague about how he is going to get the money together for us to leave Japan. My tongue is bitten to the quick from all the times I've had to stop myself from pestering him about it. Meanwhile, at The Sayonara Bar I simmer with boredom. I really can't be bothered. I forget I am supposed to be entertaining salarymen and lapse into a Zen-like state, or compose haiku in my head. I wander off while my client is in the toilet, or saying hello to another hostess, or rummaging through his wallet to pay me. Katya casts me stern, cautioning looks. 'What's come over you?' she whispers. 'You're going to get sacked.' Which, let's face it, isn't much of a threat when my hostessing career is in its death throes anyway.

Last night was one of those quiet nights that has Mamasan hissing at the silent cash register. I did little more than play a few rounds of poker and sing 'You're the One That I Want' on karaoke. I had a lot of time to think about Mariko. Mama-san called me to her office the day before to tell me Mariko had been in contact. Her father needed an emergency operation to remove his larynx and she had gone back to Fukuoka. Mama-san smoked a clove cigarette and spoke in pessimistic, funereal tones. 'Bad things happen to good people,' she said, blowing smoke from the corner of her mouth. She sent me home to pack a suitcase full of clothes to send on to Mariko. Packing up skirts and blouses in Mariko's empty room, I felt her absence very sharply. I took out my *kanji* dictionary and composed a short letter to put in her suitcase. I wrote I had enjoyed living with her, that I would miss her, that I hoped everything would be OK. Mariko lost her mother when she was a child, and now, at nineteen, she might lose her father too. Mama-san says she is going to move a new girl, an American, into Mariko's old room. She showed me a passport photo: some girl from New Jersey with overcrowded teeth and a perm. With any luck I should be gone by the time she gets here.

Yuji met me after work last night. He waited in the street outside the bar, glowering into the middle distance as though it had insulted him. He wore a window cleaner's beanie pulled down over his ears and a scruffy T-shirt and jeans. His moody profile was turned towards a dancer in front of the Big Echo who was doing some kind of cybernetic moonwalk to electronica and pulsing dental-drill samples. The dancer jerked and shifted gears like an automated device, his hair in a slippery ponytail, his face a frozen void. Shrapnel chinked into an upturned silver cap on the floor, tossed casually by one of the passing human parade.

Yuji broke into a grin when he saw me and sent his cigarette end sailing into the gutter. The first thing I thought to ask was what was happening on the money front, but I decided to choke it back for later. Instead I reached up and yanked down the front of his hat and kissed his forehead through the wool. Yuji pushed his hat back in place and kissed me, one hand on the small of my back.

'Listen. I said I'd meet some friends at a bar. Maybe you should go home – it might be boring for you,' he said.

'Your friends? Boring? Never . . .'

'Trust me, you'll be bored,' Yuji said, deaf to my gentle sarcasm.

'I don't mind.' It was stupid, but I was hurt by his not wanting me around. Seeing him was the high point of my evening. Given the agony of hindsight, I should have just gone home.

'OK, but I warned you . . .' Yuji said. 'Hey, I contacted a friend in Seoul today, a Korean I knew in high school. He said he'd put us up for a few days . . .' Something distracted him. He glanced agitatedly over my shoulder. 'Who is she staring at?'

I followed his gaze beyond the robot cabaret, to the girl leaning against the wall of the Big Echo, one leg bent, the heel of her leather boot ground into the wall. Her lips were frosted white, and she was bleached and bronzed so severely she looked like a film negative of herself. She stared at me with fight-picking eyes.

Yuji laughed nervously. 'What's her problem?' he said, and led me away.

Taku Taku was a spit-and-sawdust live house I had never ventured inside before. It was pretty much as I'd expected: black walls papered with flyers for local bands, a small stage, punk kids and hoary rockers. That Yuji's image-conscious friends would want to meet here struck me as plain weird. They're more into hiphop, if anything.

They were sitting at a table by the bar, in hooded tops and gold chains, knees as far apart as they could get them. One wore a vest that showed off his sleeves of tattoos: inky engravings of sky-blue waves, lizards and panthers, decorating arms muscled from bedroom press-ups and free weights. After a round of cool nods in my direction, they treated me like the girl who wasn't there. They had this way of shunning me with a slight tilt of the shoulders, of speaking too fast for me to keep up.

Exiled from the conversation, I passed the time lighting cigarettes from the butts of their predecessors and sinking back the drinks Yuji supplied me with (guilt cocktails – he could tell I didn't relish the role of invisible girlfriend). I people-watched too. There were some hostesses clocked off from the Copa Cabana, two pogo-ing tourists with Canadian flags conscientiously sewn onto their rucksacks, and a skinny meerkat of a boy hovering by the stage. I was bored, waiting it out until I could be alone with Yuji. People must have seen me sitting mutely and judged me a dumb blonde, unable to speak a word of Japanese. Let them, I thought.

At 3 a.m. the bar was nearly empty; perhaps we were even the last people there. I was drunk by then and as I stood up to go to the toilet I felt that strange sensation of double gravity you get climbing out of a swimming pool. As I stumbled into the toilets dozens of girls greeted me, rosy and rumpled, each in a brown A-line skirt identical to mine. My reflection bounced from every surface, the ceiling, walls and cubicle doors. I twirled and they twirled. I smoothed my skirt and they smoothed their skirts too. Then I went to unload a few cocktails.

Washing my hands, I met my gaze in the mirror above the sink. My eyes had that gently roving look and the rest of me was flushed. I was curiously ashamed, as if I had stayed in and secretly got drunk by myself. By the door was a sofa, its ripped vinyl cover patched up with duct tape. I sat down and shut my eyes, instantly plunging myself into a dark, nauseous roller-coaster ride. I opened my eyes again. It was time to go home.

The door to the Ladies had swung shut during my woozy consultation with the mirror. I went to push it open, but found it stuck fast. I pulled for a while and then stubbed my toe in a half-arsed karate kick. Realizing it was locked, I hammered with my fists, shouting to be let out. Guitar noise wailed in disheartening reply. The bar staff had begun wiping down tables and closing up the bar when I had left. They might have locked the toilets without checking they were empty first. I told myself not to panic, that Yuji would notice my absence and ask someone to go and check that I was OK. It might even have been his idea of a practical joke. I sank back down on the sofa and, against my better judgement, shut my eyes again.

Minutes later I was crouched over the toilet bowl, retching in a stomach-cramping reversal of what had made me drunk in the first place. When it was over I found my condition much improved. I went over to the basin and splashed my face, red-eyed and sobered. I cupped my hands, brought some chlorine-tasting water to my mouth and swilled it about over my teeth. Now that the room had ceased to sway, being locked in the toilets all night began to seem a depressing prospect. In the bar, the music stopped.

The barman who let me out wore a mile-wide smirk. According to him, the door hadn't even been locked. I stared past him at the empty bar. The chairs were stacked on the tables and the lights were up full. A boy in a bandanna swept around my feet. 'We're closed now,' the barman said. 'Your friends are outside.' I thanked him and walked out into a street of strangers.

I was so mad that for a while all I could do was stand and fume. Not only had Yuji left me, he had taken my purse as well. How was I meant to get home? I roamed the nearby streets, looking in the windows of bars and noodle shops for his stupid window cleaner's hat. Had he assumed I had gone home and taken my purse for safe-keeping? Had the bar staff told him I had gone? Either way I was going to give him hell when I caught up with him. After an hour of wandering I went and sat in the subway, intending to wait it out until the buses started running. I woke three hours later to stampeding masses and a murderous crick in my shoulder. I was furious. Yuji's reasons for leaving without me had better be watertight, or I will have to seriously rethink the whole leaving Japan thing. I can't let him treat me this way.

The bus stops near the bottom of the hill leading to Yuji's apartment. I thank the driver and step down into the sunshine. The hill Yuji lives on is so steep it can only be tackled with a clownish, forward-leaning gait. Cyclists have to dismount and push their bikes uphill, and when cars drive by I worry that gravity will overpower the grip of their tyres and send them screeching out-of-control. I set forth, wincing as roadside scree studs my bare foot. Developers have dug wide stepped terraces into the hillside for apartments and houses, and each terrace is bridged by sloping bamboo groves, buzzing with mosquitoes and other invisible predators. By the time I reach Yuji's apartment building my skin is slick with the poisons of the night before. I pause in the lobby, waiting for my breathing to return to normal, licking the salty layer of perspiration from my upper lip.

It has been weeks since I last visited Yuji's flat. We don't spend much time there – none at all since the break-in. I prefer to crash at mine, where the futon isn't the catchment area for dirty plates, and every concave surface doesn't automatically double as an ashtray. I am amazed he actually noticed the break-in the other week, the place is such a mess. A mad slew of clothes and junk cover the floor, as if demoniac forces came and deranged the room and its contents. In the apartment's tranquil moments the rustling of cockroaches can be heard as they excavate the landfill site for crumbs. The only decorative touch is a photograph of a mean-looking ex called Yukie on the fridge. She ran away to Tokyo to become a model and hasn't been heard of since. Katya met her once, way back when. She tells me she was a complete headcase.

I ring the buzzer in the entryway, prepared for a two-minute delay while Yuji drags himself to the door. The intercom clicks wordlessly, and the door opens. Weird. I go inside and walk upstairs, past the mosquito-netted window and the poster with the talking recycling bin. Yuji never locks his door, so I walk right in.

'Where did you get to last night?!' I say. I raise my arm, ready to throw my broken sandal at his head.

I get to the living room and scream. A man is pointing a gun at me.

'Jesus. Shut the fuck up,' he says with a roll of the eyes.

I shut the fuck up. My legs want to buckle and I will them not to. I have never been this close to a gun before. He is going to squeeze the trigger and shoot me. I know it. I am coursing with adrenalin. Too scared even to blink.

'That's better,' he says.

He puts it away, into a holster inside his suit, and the crashing of the room subsides. The man regards me in the half-light of the slatted blinds, bemused by my mute terror. There is something wrong with him. One side of his face is hideously scarred. Melted out of shape, like plastic left too close to the fire. The eyebrow is gone and his eyelid is a misshapen slit. I realize that I know him, that the last time I saw him he wore white bandages on his face. He was in the karaoke room that time with Yamagawa-san. The prodigal son.

'Mary, isn't it?'

I nod. He has a name too, but I can't remember it.

'You speak Japanese, yeah?'

Another nod.

'I'm not going to hurt you,' he says.

I stare at his jacket, where his gun rests against his chest. He looks too intimate with the giving and receiving of pain for me to take him at his word. Instinct tells me to stay quiet, but anxiety overrides it.

'Where's Yuji?'

'I don't know,' he says. 'I am waiting for him here – though, to be honest, I don't expect him to show up.'

The air is dank and heavy, as though stale laundry and the futon have been respiring, breathing out their rankness. The mutilated gunman stands on a broken minidisc-player and a torn *manga* comic.

'Why are you waiting for him?' I think of the gun and feel a queasy kick in my guts.

The prodigal son gives a crooked smile, all expression concentrated on the good side of his face. 'What do you think he has done?'

'He took some money,' I say. This is the first thing that comes to mind. He said he would raise the cash we needed to leave the country and must have got himself in trouble doing it. Poor, stupid Yuji.

The prodigal son flashes another crooked smile. 'He told you?'

'No.'

'Lucky guess, then. He embezzled some business-loan repayments collected on Yamagawa-san's behalf. He made it look as though the borrowers were shirking on repayments.'

He makes no attempt to simplify his language. I stall on a couple of words and it takes a while to understand what he is saying. Comprehension is met with fierce scepticism. I know about the loan-collection business. Yuji feels bad enough about harassing these people already without landing them in more shit. He wouldn't cheat ordinary people. Once we left a restaurant in Kyoto and forgot to settle our bill. Halfway across Gion, Yuji realized and got our taxi to turn round. I was all for keeping the money, but Yuji was adamant. He said he knows how small businesses struggle.

'It wasn't the amount he took,' the gunman says, 'it was the theft itself that ticked Yamagawa-san off. He expects loyalty from his employees. Under ordinary circumstances Yuji would be . . .' he slashes a finger across his throat '. . . but Yamagawa-san and his mother go back decades.'

'So you're not going to hurt him, then?'

He laughs. 'The loan thing wasn't his only scam. Some drugs went missing as well. We turned this place over straight away. Didn't find anything but knew it was just a matter of time. Sure enough, yesterday Yamagawa-san was informed of negotiations made to sell the drugs behind his back. Yuji had approached a long-term client of Yamagawa-san, thinking that a discount would buy his silence.' He winces, as if witnessing a clumsy and painful accident. 'Do you have any idea where your boyfriend got his sudden death wish from?'

As he speaks, the chronology falls into place. If this is true, then Yuji's crimes go back way before this flat was broken into, before he decided to leave Japan. For what other reason would he take such a risk? Whoever informed on him must be lying. I have to find Yuji and speak to him.

'What are you going to do to him?' I ask.

Across the room the gunman's eyes flash darkly. He moves towards me, Yuji's possessions crunching underfoot. As the distance closes between us his scar is all I can look at. I hear the blood roar in my ears.

'Look at me,' he orders. 'Take a good look at what they did to me. Can you guess how they did it?'

Anger pulls the muscles of his face into a near snarl. Not a finger is laid on me, but his nearness is suffocating. I twist my head away from him. He grabs my face and, fingers gouging my chin, twists it back.

'With acid,' he says. 'It ate through my face. If I have anything to do with it, *that* is what they will do to Yuji.'

He lets go of me and takes a step back. He is sick: a psychopath who belongs in a secure unit. I will go to the police and tell them about Yamagawa-san and they'll go round and arrest them all. *Drugs*, that is all I have to say. They will come tumbling down like a house of cards.

'Where are you from, Mary?' he asks.

'England.' The word is a spike in my throat. The last thing I want to do is to engage in small talk.

'England,' he echoes. 'What you must do, Mary, is go back to your England. Don't bother about Yuji any more.'

I want to damage him with the closest thing to hand. Tears smart my eyes. 'How can you be sure it was Yuji who did all that stuff?'

His brow thickens at this provocation. 'Listen, Mary. How well do you know Yuji? Has he really managed to convince you he's the loving boyfriend? That he's not screwing other women every other night of the week? I was exiled from Osaka because of him. Because of your boyfriend they threw acid in my face and sent me away for something I didn't do. I had to leave my fiancée behind. They told me if I tried to contact her they would force her back into the brothel that I rescued her from. The night I was sent away she got back from work to find Yuji waiting to tell her I was dead. It was months before I got word to her that I was alive. Months.'

Outside, a tofu van rolls by. With the aid of a loud-speaker the tofu-seller alerts the neighbourhood of his wares. My nausea of the night before resurfaces. The man standing in front of me will only be at peace once he has made a trophy of Yuji's scalp.

'Go home, Mary,' he says. 'Go back to England. I hear that you're a nice girl. Go away and stay out of trouble. And I wouldn't bother with the police. They are not going to help you. Unless you get lucky and they deport you.'

Granted permission to leave, I turn and make for the door. I am trembling, shaking all over. I have to get away from here. I have to get to Yuji and make sure that he is OK. In the doorway I hear his voice behind me.

'Wait.'

I stop but don't turn round. In my head I see the gun. Steel chamber of possible death. Aimed at my back.

'When you see your boyfriend,' he says, 'tell him Hiro is back.'

My back to him still, I nod and step out into the cool air of the corridor.

14

WATANABE

Yuji tears at the planks nailed across the door, splinters piercing his hands. Knuckle weals on his cheekbones throb and bacteria graze upon his many cuts. Planks cast aside, he rams against the door. *I'm done for*, he thinks, clutching his battered ribs. The door breaks open and he reels inside. I sit and watch, cushioned on the mossy bank of the railway tracks 19.2 metres away, plaque drilling my tooth enamel as a vitamin C tablet dissolves on my tongue. My hand wanders to the petrol can by my side. *Indeed you are*, I think, *indeed you are*.

The shroud of night drapes the globe. Its dark border advances now, across the mountain ranges of Peru, the glaciers of the Arctic circle. The stars recede, echoing red light, and a ghost galaxy twinkles 100 million years in the afterlife. Aeroplane tail-lights blink by, and I spot the famous sumo wrestler Chiyonufuji sitting in business class, eating soya-bean curd in his Playtex trainer bra. I return to the earth and tunnel down, beneath the thousands of squirming annelids, beneath the maggots suckling on the remains of dead cat. I burrow 502.3 metres deep into a strata of Cretaceous-era rock, where the fossil of a mega-lonyx thrusts forth its mighty tusks and claws, the stunned and terminal expression on its face relaying the exact moment the meteor struck.

In the dark, run-down interior of the Lotus Bar Yuji tumbles into a wooden booth, his exhausted head thudding against the wall. He scarcely recognizes the decaying bar of his youth. Once a thriving den of iniquity, inhabited by sashaying hostesses and wealthy businessmen, the Lotus Bar is now host to a thousand industrious ecosystems: field-mice feasting on seat covers, cockroaches nibbling the peeling wallpaper, vipers in search of furry mammals in which to sink their fangs. Mama-san sent me here once, six and a quarter moon cycles ago, to reinforce the planks nailed across the back door. I found the hammer and nails where she told me I would, corroding in a drawer, glistening with rat urine.

Seven lonely years have gone by since Mama-san was proprietess of the Lotus Bar. It was a business venture doomed to failure. Shortly after the grand opening (which saw hostesses in showgirl costumes handing out free glasses of champagne), Mama-san received a letter informing her that construction of the Kansai line extension was due to begin within literal spitting distance. Despite the lengths Mama-san went to to stop the construction from going ahead (petitioning rail executives, plying them with wine and women, lying prostrate in the path of a bulldozer), within eighteen months bullet trains were whizzing by, a dozen every hour. Each train delivered a miniature blitzkrieg, a seizure that shook the walls and displaced customers from the bar stools. For eleven months Mama-san smiled through the violent intrusions, nimbly catching objects that fell from the shelves, and reassuring customers. But litigation proceedings made by a salaryman knocked cold by a falling bottle of Old Navy rum was the straw that broke the donkey's back. Mama-san put the Lotus Bar up for sale. It remains on the market to this day.

Though his mother's nerves were shredded to confetti, Yuji's time at the Lotus Bar was his halcyon days. The hostesses doted on the prepubescent Yuji like a midget customer, constantly telling him how cute he was, how adorable. Slumped in a fog of pain Yuji rewinds to these happy days. Tiny beetles scamper over the bar top where he used to sit and pretend to do his homework, as hostess Yoko praised his cleverness in her silken tones. The stingray of agony delivers another internal lashing. Yuji moans, half in pain, half in bittersweet nostalgia. He runs his tongue along a fractured edge of tooth and he moans once more.

In shivering confusion, Mary walks the streets 8.3 km southwest. It tore me apart to leave her stranded, it really did. But fate reared up, forked like the tongue of a snake, urging me to make a choice. I desperately wanted to rescue her, to send her home in a Cinderella carriage. But that would only solve her problems in the short term. The petrol will solve them in the long term.

An empty train blasts by, inches from my nose, a trainee driver at the helm. The venetian blinds of the Lotus Bar dance crazily and Yuji's cranium rattles against the walls. Chairs and tables jump and jive across the floorboards, and the chandelier rocks. The train passes into the distance and the mad oscillations diminish. On the other side of the railway tracks an abandoned refrigerator watches me, a Venus child-trap in waiting, oozing chlorofluorocarbons into the ozone.

I knew that something was afoot tonight. I could sense it in the luminiferous ether of the universe. After work I followed Mary and Yuji through Shinsaibashi. I shadowed them through a covered arcade, past the Citibank tower, past the holy ground of an urban shrine. Though Yuji held the hand of his golden trophy, the corpulent thighs of a prostitute walking in front of them snared his gaze. How could he be so ungrateful of his proximity to Mary, when I am envious of the microscopic mites that live in her eyelashes and the waxy deposits in her ears? When Mary transcends I will ensure she is never neglected again.

Yuji's friends were waiting for him in a bar. The bar was a real cloven-hoofed pit, awash with anarchist transsexuals and Satan worshippers. My pity went out to these poor, misguided fools. If they ever evolved the hypersense to see what a sad figure Lucifer really is, they would flee the occult scene in a heartbeat. Reduced to being a nether-worldly C-lister, nowadays the Devil ekes out a living making guest appearances at black mass and Belgian metal concerts. Enough to make anyone think twice about drinking goat's blood.

The Satanists did not intimidate me. They were mewling kittens compared with Yuji's lantern-jawed yakuza friends. As soon as I saw them I knew that they intended to do real and lasting damage to Yuji. 'Judas will get what's coming to him,' one of them muttered as the Judas in question made his entrance.

Panic seared down my neural expressways. Though I have nothing against Yuji being beaten up, Mary would be present. And these guys would sooner knock Mary into a coma than endure her frightened, screaming demands. The three yakuza sat in a testosterone stupor, a colostomy bag of society's ills where their morality should be. Kenji, the one with the gold caps and double-Y chromosomes, once put his Rottweiler in the bath and threw an electric toaster in. Trixie's death throes proved so hilarious, Kenji immediately went out in search of more dogs. And Shingo and Toru take it in turns to strangle each other in their basement flat, squeezing until the whites of their eyes roll round. Even in public they are unable to rein it in, blistering each other under the table with cigarette lighters.

While predator and prey exchanged greetings at the table, I slunk away to commune with the shadows. Once seated, Yuji and his friends began to talk, ostracizing Mary.

The hands of the clock moved. Beneath the mantle of Japan, convection currents heaved the land mass by a quarter of a millimetre. Lucifer's army fed 100-yen coins into the bar jukebox, ensuring back-to-back death metal.

Mary drank cocktail after cocktail. She drank to asphyxiate the vines of tedium twisting through her mind, and to stave off the humiliation of being treated like an inanimate blow-up doll. Once Mary discovers the portal into hyperspace she will never be bored again. Dimensional transcendence is weed-killer to boredom. Until then I can only observe in sad torment.

Blind to the change in his friends, Yuji was his usual egotistical self. They tolerated his verbal dominance with ease, salivating in anticipation of his violent demise. They had a secret code of smirks and nostril flares, rising in frequency as the night-club crowd thinned out. I deciphered this primitive code to learn that the signal to attack was the departure of the last customer. As the numbers shrank, six yellow eyes were drawn to a stubborn, unmoving figure in the shadows. Me.

The creature of the shadows watched them back, his hyper-intellect thrumming. When the thugs saw I was in no hurry to leave, they grew agitated. The temptation to disobey Yamagawa-san's instructions was almost too much for them. The bar staff were also agitated – the faster the thugs made their kill, the faster they could clean up the spilt blood and go home. But I was not to be the first domino in the chain. Not me. During my two hours in the shadows I had come up with a plan. All hinged on Mary's bladder.

I had been monitoring Mary's waste-elimination system from the moment she sat down. She had urinated twice that night, once at 21.46 hours and again before meeting Yuji at 00.59. By 03.04 hours the tender, springy pillow of her bladder had swollen once more. In the nephrons of her kidneys waste molecules filtered from her plasma. Broken fragments of haemoglobin and five-month-old aspirin trickled through her convoluted tubule. I watched, on tenterhooks to see if she would obey its tug before the patience of the yakuza thugs gave out.

I shuddered with relief as Mary's daydreams were cut short by a fluctuation in electro-potential relaying her need to urinate. She rose and swayed across the bar, then down the short corridor leading to the women's toilets. I got up and followed. The door to the Ladies was open. I pulled it shut. Then I clung to the handle for all I was worth.

Meanwhile, in the bar, Toru's resentment had arrived at critical mass. The last customer was out of sight. That was good enough for him. He stood and swung his arm round like a tattooed scythe, knocking the ashtray and empty glasses to the floor. Veins boiled in his temples as he smashed his anvil fist into Yuji's face.

'Traitor!'

The bar staff watched Yuji sail backwards in his chair, wincing at the sound of splintering carpentry. Yuji coughed up the blood seeping into his throat. Shingo and Kenji went next, their faces viciously contorted as they kicked his ribs and arms. At every kick Yuji jerked as if electrocuted.

'*Where* . . .' Kick. '*Is* . . .' Kick. '*It* . . . ?'

Demented with pain, laughter gurgled through Yuji's blood-sluiced throat. '*Mary has it . . . Get Mary!*'

Tranquillity restored to her bladder, Mary headed for the toilet door. Despite her low muscle bulk and state of inebriation, Mary managed to exert a force of 103.1 Newtons on the door handle, increasing in proportion to her panic to a stalwart 312. I put the sole of my foot against the door jamb and leant back as the door jimmied and shook.

Out in the bar the thrashing ceased as Toru knelt beside Yuji.

'*What did you say?*'

'*Mary has it . . . Get her!*'

My heart roared in anger. Fortunately, Yuji's throat was so choked with blood and mucus he was unintelligible. He brayed another geyser of bloody laughter. Toru spat in his face. Yuji was then hauled to his feet and pushed, with his arm twisted behind his back, towards the delivery entrance of the club. The bar staff bowed and waved good-bye to the blood-spattered procession.

Mary and I continued to fight over the door. She hollered: *Hello, can someone let me out!?* seven times, before turning away in drunken surrender.

I sprinted out into the bar. The bartender sweeping up the shards of broken glass jumped as I rushed past him, my trainers crunching silicon dioxide into the floor, smearing the scattered petals of Yuji's blood.

Outside, Kenji, Shingo and Toru stood in the flashing blue lights of a patrol car, venting sulphurous emissions as a policeman took down their details in a notebook.

A street away, Yuji hopped towards a vacant taxi, a bird with a broken wing.

Inside my petrol can claustrophobic hydrocarbons ram each other, writhing angrily, ready to combust. These molecules were once Jurassic rainforests and dinosaurs, which dominated this Earth without the slightest inkling they would be squashed for many millennia between sedimentary rock, then siphoned off in oil refineries of the future. I can understand the frustration such a demotion would induce.

On the other side of the railway tracks, Yuji strikes a match. The phosphorus reactive tip flares in the dark of the Lotus Bar, and he watches it burn down before lighting another. Perhaps you have guessed what my petrol can is for – that I intend to do to Yuji exactly what he just did to that match. I expect the morally conscientious among you are appalled, think me a reprehensible monster. But let us try to think rationally for a moment. Extinguish Yuji and the total sum of suffering in the world will be reduced. Allow him to continue to contaminate the Earth with his existence and he will endanger not only Mary's life but the life of anyone who crosses him in the future. This is not a decision made from the fiery seat of passion; it is a practical one. This is not murder; it is the simple conversion of human flesh into carbon dust and energy. The total sum of matter in the universe will remain constant, and nothing of real significance will be lost. Even his soul will trans-migrate into the nearest thing being born. A housefly larva or a hatching nit. Like I said, I have no qualms about this.

In his wooden booth Yuji claws his brain for a way out, unaware that the deus ex machina has already descended. Not once does he regret his attempt to implicate Mary in his crimes. Instead he wonders if he can persuade her to provide an alibi for him, or take some of the blame for his wrongdoings.

An owl spreads its wings in the translunar light. An ice floe the size of China drifts down a Martian canal. A cat prowls the Lotus Bar roof, the green patina of its irises glowing through the dark. I rise to my feet and the cat springs to the ground and pads away, mindful of its remain-ing three lives. The petrol sloshing at my side, I run across the railway tracks. I scramble up the mossy bank to the hostess bar. For all its ramshackle appearance there are 7.9 trillion kilojoules of energy in this wooden building, just waiting to be exploited.

The Lotus Bar is more than just a thriving ecosphere, re-possessed by nature, or a hideaway for fugitive yakuza. It is an archive of hostesses past. Ghostly wisps of them linger in the dark, forgotten moments relived for the benefit of no one. I see the enchantress Kiyoka, who sneaked into Yuji's bedroom at night to perform tantalizing belly dances for the wide-eyed eleven-year-old; the fun-loving Shizuko, who liked to insert her glass eye into her mouth, a light-hearted joke that redefined eroticism for many; and a younger Mama-san, quite the temptress without that extra layer of subcutaneous fat . . . Mama-san will be quite devastated by her son's death. Mr Bojangles will have his work cut out consoling her. Mary will also be among the number who will grieve for him. But her sense of loss will quickly vanish once she has transcended.

I tip the can and begin to pour. I walk the circumference of the bar, inhaling the scent of anarchy as the flammable liquid trickles over the weeds. The acrid odour tickles Yuji's nostrils as well, but he is too captive to self-pity to wonder what it is or where it has come from. Once Yuji is out of the way, Mary's transformation into a hyper-being will progress at an exponential rate. It unnerves me to think that I will soon be as transparent to Mary as she is to me. That she will soon see the ribosomes zipping about my cytoplasm like lightning; the verruca on my foot and my wonky appendix; the curse of my upbringing and the shadow of my father haunting my soul. At least Mary will know not to expect any cosy family dinners. My father has always strongly opposed my having relations with the opposite sex. Since childhood he has made it clear to me that women are forbidden until I have completed my Ph.D. in economics and have a job in the Ministry of Finance. Only then will he find me a suitable marriage partner.

For most of my high-school years my father's instructions were easy to heed. I never really liked girls back then. Not for any misogynistic reasons; it was just that I thought them very stupid and dull. In my senior year, however, one girl came into my life and changed my opinion of women for ever.

There were six of us in accelerated maths: Tetsuya, my ardent ping-pong-player friend; Hide and Jun, genius siblings who never communicated with anyone except each other, and then only in ancient Latin; Yuu Kano, a modestly popular basketball-player who told us that he would rip out our tongues if word got out that he was taking a class with us freaks; and Ai Inoue.

Ai was well known by everyone in our school for two reasons. First, her father was the high-school janitor and they lived together in a wooden shack at the end of the playing fields. Second, from the age of twelve she had worn a hulking metal brace on her back to correct her juvenile scoliosis. It goes without saying her handicap made her something of a scapegoat for bullies. Girls would bring in fridge magnets to stick to her brace, and the boys used to shout, 'Hey! Iron Maiden!' when they saw her coming and everyone would fall about, laughing. High-school life for Ai Inoue was hell.

Unlike the rest of the school population Ai did not belong to any clubs or attend a private cram school. After classes she would help her father scrape the chewing gum from under the desks, or wander alone through the bamboo forest, her metal brace clanking a warning to the birds. My most potent memory of Ai is during a typhoon in the autumn term of our senior year. Classes had been cancelled that day due to the hazardous weather conditions, but, braving the gale-force winds, I went in. I was eager to complete my project on electromagnetic induction and my physics teacher, Mr Kazaguchi, had said I could use the laboratory. By mid-morning I had my experiment set up and was busy taking readings from the voltmeter, when something out of the window caught my eye. It was Ai Inoue, standing alone on the roof of the school gymnasium. Her school uniform was drenched and the wind tore at her hair. The rain lashed at her as she stood with her arms outstretched, like the majestic figurehead of a ship on stormy seas. I will never forget the look in her eyes: wild, heroic and insane. I noticed she was not wearing her brace.

From that moment on, I was intrigued. But, like I said, Ai was very unpopular, and I was reluctant to be tarred with the same brush. Two unpopular people closely associated would become the laughing stock of the whole school. Our lonely sufferings would be greatly amplified.

The first time we ever spoke was some months after the typhoon, when she came across me lying face down in the bamboo forest one afternoon. I had just received a vicious beating from the twin bullies Michio and Kazuo Kaku, who'd been enthusiastic to test out their new mail-order numchucks on me. Hearing the approaching clank of metal, I looked up to find myself lying in the inquisitive shadow of Ai Inoue. She leant over at the slight angle her brace would permit.

'Do you mind?' she said. 'You are lying on a rare species of herbaceous flora. You really should show some respect.'

I shifted sideways, then sank my face back in the mud, expecting her to go away.

'Y'know, Watanabe, the Kaku twins have waited for you in the same place at the same time every month since fourth grade. Why don't you just take a different route home from school?' she asked.

I looked up again and told her that to avoid them would be to deprive myself of a valuable learning experience. The look in her eyes told me she thought I was a loon, but she held out her hand anyway and helped me to my feet.

From that day on we were friends. And, as expected, the opprobrium of our peers rocketed. We were told we should run away and join the circus together. My glasses were repeatedly stolen and the lenses smeared with glue. Even in the staff room the teachers joked that at least there was no risk of teen pregnancy with Ai wearing that oversized chastity belt all the time. But, to my delight and surprise, none of this mattered to me. I began to skip cram school and spent many a happy hour helping Ai collect botany samples from the forest, or calculating prime numbers and listening to the Russian opera station her brace picked up on clear evenings. We never spoke much. Owing to our solitary childhoods and social exclusion from the high-school community, neither of us were well versed in the art of conversation. We were content just being in each other's company. Our persecutors succeeded only in strengthening this bond.

My second most potent memory of Ai was made on the penultimate day of our friendship. We were walking together in town when we spotted some schoolyard tormentors coming towards us. Anxious to avoid them, Ai took me by the hand and pulled me into the alleyway beside the KFC. We each held our breath as the rowdy gang scuffled past, pushing and shoving and crudely denigrating each other. Perhaps it was the risk and excitement of being caught. Perhaps it was the stench of burning chicken fat. Whatever it was, to this day I cannot pass a KFC without remembering that moment Ai pulled me towards her and put her lips to mine.

That night I walked home upon cushions of air. I sat at the kitchen table and ate without tasting a single mouthful the food my mother had set out for me. I then floated up to my bedroom, and sat leafing dreamily through a section in my physics textbook on Faraday's Law. Within minutes the bedroom door opened and my father walked in, his stern grey expression shattering my blissful mood. He strolled over to my desk and adjusted my anglepoise lamp so it shone directly in my face.

'Watanabe,' he said, eerily calm, 'your private cram school telephoned today. They said you haven't attended any classes for the last two weeks.'

Terrified, I tried to blink away the vivid sunspots and spectral bulb filaments drifting across my retinas.

'Now, Watanabe, tell me the name of this vile slut you have been seeing.'

I hung my head, cringing beneath the intensity of his gaze. Then, in a devastated whisper, I told him.

I rushed through the school gates the next day, pale and nervous after a night of sleepless dread. I was desperate to speak to Ai, to warn her of my father's wrath. At morning recess, I picked out her unwieldy metal gait lumbering down the corridor.

'Ai-chan,' I called. 'Ai-chan.'

She spun round, her red chemistry folder clutched to her chest.

I ran up to her and put my hand on her shoulder. 'Why weren't you in accelerated maths this morning?' I asked.

She looked me up and down, her nondescript beauty un-tarnished by the spit-balls flecking her hair. How I longed to take her aside and lovingly pluck them out.

'Why wasn't I in accelerated maths?' she repeated. 'Because I was in the principal's office denying the charges of sexual harassment your father has lodged against me on your behalf. Now, would you please remove your hand from my shoulder. I would hate this to be misconstrued.'

Then, her eyes flashing with fury, she turned on her heel and marched away.

I was sad for a long time afterwards. But I truly believe that what happened was for the best. From time to time I like to sail across the oceans of hyperspace and look in on Ai Inoue. After her first year of college Ai took her new poker-straight spine over to America, where she had won a scholarship to study botany at Stanford University. Though Ai Inoue will never know the fourth dimension, I have to concede that she has done quite well for herself. She even has a new American boyfriend, Chip Fontaine. I was jealous of him at first, but then I reminded myself of the stellar heights I have ascended to since my days of the third dimension. And the jealousy goes away.

The circle of petrol is complete. All that is needed now is a naked flame. Intuiting his imminent death, Yuji has crawled to the middle of the bar. Saline leaks through his tear ducts. Perhaps I should allow him five minutes to marinate in his misery before the roasting.

Why me? I belong at the top of the food chain, not here, bleeding to death on my hands and knees. Look at what I have become . . .

I really should get a move on. I have wasted enough time outside this hovel already. The sooner I get this over with, the sooner my reunion with Mary.

This pain is killing me. I must be dying. Please, God, I swear I will believe in you if you let me live. I will lead a holy and devout life, just please don't let me die alone . . . I am so alone . . .

Existential horror seizes Yuji by the throat. The dark truth of the fundamental solitude of man has lurked in his mind since childhood, but Yuji has always hounded it out in his lonelier moments with hiphop, video games and

Internet porn. And for the record, Yuji is not dying. He is a crude insult to the 15.2 citizens of Osaka actually gasping their last at this precise moment. I think it is my duty to teach this oversized baby what dying is really about.

My fingers close round the plastic lighter in my pocket. Then I hear it. A broken whimper, so thin and babyish that, were I not omniscient, I would mistake for a girl scout lost in the woods. Disgusted, I take my hyper-scalpel and make an incision into the fugitive's head. As I suspected, his expulsion and persecution by his gang has left him bereft of sanity. It will take him months to recuperate.

I hurl the cigarette lighter high in the air. It lands on the other side of the railway tracks with a flimsy thud. To spark the bonfire now would be a gesture of goodwill, a *coup de grâce*. Why bother?

For the time being, humanity is safe.

15

MR SATO

You always used to joke that a rainstorm was the way the sky cleared its sinuses. Not the most charming of images, but when I left the house this morning and breathed in the crisp, new-born air it felt remarkably apt. Eight yellow hats bobbed by our front gate as a procession of neighbourhood children made their way to elementary school. They halted outside number 47 and waited for a little girl with pigtails to emerge from the front door. She skipped towards them and tagged onto the end of the group, which had begun to move off again. They each had identical yellow satchels, and reminded me of jaunty little ducklings waddling down to the pond.

When I saw that there was no one at the mailbox I hurried down the path post-haste. But I should have known my expeditiousness was in vain. As I unlatched the gate I heard Mrs Tanaka's front door open and her signature call: 'Cooeee, Mr Sato!'

I turned and watched Mrs Tanaka traverse the lawn as though in possession of seven-league boots. Her will to pry obviously lends her powers beyond those of an ordinary pensioner with an artificial hip.

'Good morning, Mrs Tanaka,' I said.

'Mr Sato,' Mrs Tanaka said, catching her breath.

'That rainstorm cleared the skies nicely, didn't it?'

'Hmmm . . .' Mrs Tanaka replied, impatient with frivolities such as the weather when there was busybodying to be done.

In her rush to catch me Mrs Tanaka had donned her pink quilted housecoat in a slapdash manner, resulting in buttons being secured in the wrong buttonholes. Her grey hair was still bound in curlers and encased within a gauze hairnet. She crossed her arms and eyed me in a shrewish manner. I was about to make my usual remark about the 7.45 express being unsympathetic to the plight of the tardy, when Mrs Tanaka said: 'Well, Mr Sato, aren't you the dark horse.'

'Am I?' I said, though I knew perfectly well why she would think this.

'Yes, you are! Imagine my surprise when I stepped out last night, to put the rubbish out for collection, and saw a young girl on your doorstep.' Mrs Tanaka was mildly affronted in tone, as though the girl had been put there on purpose, to provoke her.

I smiled politely. As you know, rubbish-collection day is not until Monday.

'She gave me quite a fright!' Mrs Tanaka continued, pressing her hand to her chest as if to quell the lingering shock. 'Who is she? A friend of yours?'

'No . . . A colleague from work.'

'A colleague from work!' Mrs Tanaka cried, widening her eyes. 'I thought she was a schoolgirl who had lost her way.'

My smile came unstuck at the edges. 'She did not stay for long,' I fibbed. 'She left very soon after I returned home. She just wanted to speak to me about some . . . work matters.'

'I didn't hear your front door slam,' Mrs Tanaka said, not one to miss a trick.

'I closed the front door very quietly so as not to disturb you.'

'And you let her walk home alone, did you?' Mrs Tanaka persisted.

'No. I called a taxi for her . . .'

'The only car I heard in our street last night was Mr Okamura's, when he returned home from work at quarter past ten.'

An excruciating liar's blush rose upon my cheeks. Mrs Tanaka is the eyes and ears of the neighbourhood, and near impossible to deceive. I felt like the boy who swore blind he hadn't touched the red bean cake when his mouth and fingers were smeared with its paste.

'How odd,' I remarked weakly.

My burning cheeks must have been vanquishment enough for Mrs Tanaka. She pushed on to the next thing she had to say. 'Very strange girl, your work colleague,' she said.

'Really?'

'Yes,' Mrs Tanaka continued. 'She was sitting on your front stoop, in the dark, quiet as a church mouse. I went up to her and asked if she was waiting for you. I thought she might have got the wrong house. Well, the girl looked right through me, Mr Sato, as if I were thin air.'

'She was a little unwell, I think,' I said.

'Hmmm . . .' said Mrs Tanaka. 'I thought perhaps she was slightly deaf, so I moved a few steps closer to her and asked her again, in a very loud, clear voice, if she was waiting for you. Then I told her that you often work late, and if she would prefer she could come and sit in my nice warm living room and wait for you there.'

'What did she say?' I asked.

'Not a word,' Mrs Tanaka said. 'But this time she looked right at me, and there was no mistaking that she had heard precisely what I had said.'

'Perhaps she is a little shy with strangers.'

'Shy with strangers!' Mrs Tanaka scoffed. 'She was quite the opposite of shy, Mr Sato. She looked right at me and grinned. I thought to myself, *Who does this saucy madam think she is, grinning at me like that?* Then she began to laugh at me, as though I was an idiot or a circus clown. I asked her what on earth was the matter, and the girl laughed even harder. Well, after that I left her sitting in the cold and wet, laughing to herself like a loon. I refuse to waste my hospitality on such an ill-bred young lady.'

'I can only apologize on my colleague's behalf,' I said, though I suspected that there wasn't really any misdemeanour to atone for. Mrs Tanaka is prone to exaggeration and Mariko was probably too ill to be coherent. 'I am sure there is a rational explanation behind her behaviour.'

Mrs Tanaka reacted to my apology as one would a personal slight. She pursed her lips and a frown commandeered her brow into a barricade of wrinkles. She gazed up at our bedroom window as if Mariko's mischievous face might peep out from the curtains, in mockery of her.

'You have left your curtains closed today,' Mrs Tanaka said.

I open those curtains every morning without fail. What further proof does Mrs Tanaka need that the room is occupied?

'How forgetful I am,' I said, unconvincingly.

'Well, Mr Sato,' Mrs Tanaka huffed, 'I would hate to make you late for your train.'

This was her sure-fire way of letting me know how cross she was. Most mornings she will natter merrily on, utterly indifferent to my having a train to catch. Now she bade me good day and shuffled indignantly back to her house. This made me quite sad. Even though I am entitled to my privacy, I could not help but feel I had let Mrs Tanaka down.

I spent last night on the futon in the spare room, drifting at the cusp of sleep. Ten times an hour I jerked awake, at the gurgling of pipes, the caterwauling of amorous cats, at every creak and sigh our house made as it settled on its plot of land. I stared into the dark, stirring the shadows until the bookcase and cello took on new and sinister forms. Unaccustomed now to another living, breathing presence in the house, I listened as Mariko tossed and turned in her sleep, grief rampaging through her dreams. I did not know what to do. I spent the night on stand-by, waiting for her distress to break the surface, as she lay a room away, restless as a ticking bomb.

My briefcase fell upon the wet lawn when I saw her. I ran over, my heart thumping in fright. 'Mariko,' I called. She was as unresponsive as a pile of wet leaves. I dropped to my knees and shook her by the shoulder. 'Mariko.'

There was a limp lifelessness about her that terrified me. For one macabre moment I thought she was dead, and our doorstep a mortuary slab. She was on her side, her knees drawn up to her chest, her hands over her face, as though she had curled up as tight as could be to protect herself from an invisible predator. I took her wrist and my heart plummeted at her inertness of pulse. I pushed the hair from her face. A few strands remained stuck to her forehead, which was damp with a feverish sheen. Seeing that her lips were parted, I put my hand in front of her mouth to check she was breathing. I shook her again. 'Mariko!'

One hand securing her head, the other her shoulders, I heaved Mariko upright. She remained limp and insensible, her head rolling back to expose her swan-like neck, a damsel fainting in the arms of a vampire.

'Mariko. Now, listen here. I am going to phone for an ambulance. I have got to get you to hospital.'

From between the parting in her lips came a murmur of resistance.

'Mariko, wake up. Try to sit up properly. I am going to phone for an ambulance for you.'

I lifted her head upright. Her eyes opened a fraction and she looked at me from beneath the fronds of her lashes.

'No,' she demurred, in an empty husk of a whisper.

'Mariko, I am going to leave you here for a minute while I quickly go inside and phone them.'

Her eyes opened wider. I felt some weight leave my arms as she strained to support herself.

'No, please.'

'Mariko, you need to go to hospital.'

'No! I have to go . . .' Fear had jerked her into panicky sentience. Her eyes darted all over the place.

'You are very ill. Now, I am going to help you inside,' I said. 'Can you stand up?'

Mariko nodded.

I unlocked the front door and then, clasping her by the upper arms, lifted her to her feet. Taking a deep breath, I scooped her up into my arms. She was even lighter than I had anticipated, and my lower back withstood the journey to the living room without a stitch of lumbago. Panic made me clumsy, though. Twice Mariko winced in pain as her crown knocked the door frame. Having taken care to enter the living room sideways, I deposited Mariko on the sofa. The plastic dust-cover crackled slightly as I moved her so her head was elevated by the armrest.

'Thank you,' she said.

'That's quite all right,' I said.

I turned on the light and had a good look at her. She wore a peach cardigan with pearl buttons and a pleated skirt with grass stains on it. Her cheeks blazed against a candescent pallor that had settled upon the contours of her face like snow. Her eyelids fluttered shut again, and I heard her breathing, light and irregular. I went and pulled the heavy red curtains to, wary of neighbourhood spies.

'Mariko,' I said, 'do you want me to take you to hospital?'

Without opening her eyes, Mariko shook her head.

I paced the stretch of carpet in front of the mantelpiece. 'Mariko,' I said, 'you look very ill. Perhaps I should call my doctor. It would be foolhardy to do otherwise.'

'I just want to sleep,' Mariko said, her voice so insubstantial it was almost drowned out by the ticking of the mantelpiece clock.

'But you could be seriously ill.'

'I just need to sleep it off.'

'Sleep what off? Have you taken any medication or drugs?'

Mariko roused at this, visibly anguished that I would suspect her of this highly prohibited activity. 'No, no!'

I went to get the first-aid box from the cupboard under the stairs. I took out the thermometer, wiped it with a sterile swab and returned to the living room. 'Mariko, I want to check your temperature,' I said.

I inserted the thermometer beneath her tongue, then rolled up my shirtsleeve and timed one minute on my wristwatch. When the minute was up, I inspected the thermometer. It was a fraction of a degree above 37. But taking into account the margin of error in the thermometer's calibration, Mariko's temperature was probably normal. I looked at her in confusion. Against the opalescence of her face her cheeks glowed like embers, as though she was burning up deep inside.

'You haven't got a high temperature,' I told her. 'Do you have any idea what is wrong with you?'

The mantelpiece clock ticked. The hot-water timer clicked on and the pipes rumbled as water began to circulate. Mariko lay still, her arms and legs lifeless, as though excommunicated from the rest of her. Tears welled in her eyes.

'My father is dead,' came her reply.

I climbed the stairs with slow and heavy footfalls, Mariko asleep in my arms. Now I am no psychologist, but if I had to guess what Mariko was suffering from I would have to say grief. I was still in a quandary about whether to call a doctor, though. In the end I decided there was no point in disturbing Dr Sono in the evening time if Mariko was not running a high temperature. It was better to wait until the next day. I laid Mariko down on the bedspread and, averting my eyes, pulled down the hem of her skirt, which had ridden up slightly. I unfastened her red buckle shoes and put them by the bed. I debated whether to remove her socks, as sleeping in your socks can give rise to all manner of fungal infections. But fearing it might cause her embarrassment to wake and find her feet denuded, I decided that one night wouldn't cause any irreparable fungal damage. I took one of your handmade patchwork quilts from the linen cupboard, shook it out on top of her and drew it up to her shoulders. She still had a pale, consumptive look about her, but her expression was peaceful now, like that of a sleeping child. Her lips were dry and cracked, and I wanted to apply some moisturizing lotion, but thought it would be wrong to do this without her consent.

As I watched her sleep I was conflicted with tenderness and anger. Part of me wanted to shake her awake and demand to know what she was playing at. Why *my* doorstep? Why not the doorstep of an acquaintance proper? You will be glad to hear that this selfishness was short-lived, though. How deplorable to think only of the inconvenience to myself when Mariko has endured such loss. I resolved to speak to her the next day. In the meantime she needed to rest.

As I pulled the curtains shut I heard Mariko whimper softly. I turned to where she lay and watched her until guilt at my voyeurism made me turn away. As I left the room I remembered the strange confession she had made the night before, and for a moment I wished I could trespass into her dreamworld. It was the only way to see if what she had said was true.

Owing to Mrs Tanaka's bad mood I arrived at work in good time this morning. Miss Hatta, the office assistant, and Miss Yamamoto, Mr Takahara's temporary replacement, were already there. Miss Hatta was humming to herself and putting a fresh filter in the coffee-making machine. Miss Yamamoto was already logged into the computer system, checking the email account enquiries. We exchanged our morning greetings and I was just getting settled at my desk when Matsuyama-san burst in, waving about a sheet of white paper.

'Deputy Senior Managerial Supervisor Murakami just stopped me in the corridor. He gave me this letter. Takahara-san faxed it from a 7–11 in Hawaii last night.'

'No!' Miss Hatta gasped.

'Good Lord!' I exclaimed.

I rushed from behind my desk and snatched the fax from Matsuyama-san. Miss Hatta and Miss Yamamoto came and stood by me as I read the handwritten note, shaking my head in disbelief. I read it twice to myself. The third time I read it aloud in the hope that the sound of my words rebounding from the filing cabinets might help the contents of the fax to sink in.

'*Dear Finance Department,*

'*I hope this fax finds you all in good health. I am well, though I have a little food poisoning after eating some undercooked swordfish. Apologies for going AWOL on you all. There is no excuse for what I did.*

'*I expect you are all wondering what has happened to me. I also, from time to time, wonder what has happened to me. The simple answer is: the most ordinary, yet extraordinary thing that can happen to a man: a woman. A beautiful Hawaiian lady called Leilani. She cannot speak Japanese and I can only say "Hello, I am a citizen of Japan" in Leilani's mother tongue. But our love soars beyond vocabulary. It is astonishing how much can be said without words.*

'*We married last week in a beach ceremony, and barbecued a small hog at the reception afterwards. I know that my career at Daiwa Trading is for ever*

*ruined. But that's OK. I never enjoyed the life of a
salaryman anyway. I collect shells now and fashion
them into trinkets to sell to tourists. Please, do not
worry about me. As I breathe in the tropical sea
breeze I feel nothing but gratitude for the good
fortune that has befallen me. I intend to live out the
rest of my days in Leilani's Honolulu trailer, helping
her to raise her five children from a previous marriage.
Good people of the Finance Department, I only hope
that one day you will all be as happy as I am now.*
   'Goodbye and good luck.
   'Ex-Assistant Section Chief Takahara'

The shocking news drew us into a tight, sombre circle.
Our crowns touched as we rescanned the letter. It was as
though we had been delivered news of Takahara-san's
death.

Matsuyama-san tutted. 'His wife can't even speak
Japanese, eh? What kind of marriage is that?'

'But he hates the beach,' Miss Hatta cried. 'Before he
went he said he had a sun allergy.'

Miss Yamamoto, who had known Assistant Section
Chief Takahara-san only by sight, said: 'Well, at least he
hasn't been eaten by sharks.'

Taro tap-danced in, wafting into the office the
carnivorous stink of the McDonald's breakfast muffin he
was eating. When he asked what was going on, I
despondently handed him the fax and watched as he read
it, his lips silently forming the shape of each syllable.

'Way to go, Takahara!' he cheered upon reaching the
letter's conclusion. Humming off-key, he did a little
Polynesian hula dance about the photocopying machine.

Miss Hatta went to the coffee-pot to pour a cup for
Matsuyama-san, who had announced his need of a stiff
drink. Miss Yamamoto returned to the emails. I excused
myself and went to the bathroom to splash my face with
cold water. Since moving to the Finance Department eight

months ago I have worked with Mr Takahara nearly every day. During that time his fastidious character has impressed itself upon me greatly. He was a first-rate accountant and head of the Daiwa Trading Tea Ceremony Society. When a brief mania for ambient-nodding Moomins swept over the desks of junior employees, Takahara-san successfully petitioned for a company-wide ban. Had he really abandoned his position as Assistant Section Chief for the life of a hapless beach-bum? I could not help but suspect foul play. Or a blow to the head, instigating a serious personality disorder.

All day today I had trouble concentrating on my work. As I negotiated contracts with clients over the phone, my thoughts stole back to Mariko, lying beneath your patchwork quilt. As I proofread the Hitachi report my mind swam with the previous evening. It has been years since happenings in my own life have consumed me so.

Mid-morning, Miss Hatta came to my desk with a cup of honey-laced camomile tea. As I burnt my tongue on the hot liquid I began to worry, somewhat irrationally, that my colleagues would find out that I had a young hostess in my bed. The news is so full of monstrous salarymen enticing schoolgirls to love hotels with the promise of designer clothes and jewellery, people would automatically assume something of a sexual nature had occurred between us. How their estimation of me would sink! At least I can trust Mrs Tanaka to have the good sense to know otherwise.

Alone in the office at lunch-time I ate a boxed meal of rice and salmon that I ordered from the canteen and reflected further upon Mariko. Was she awake? Had she found the note I had left her? The bread and jam I had put out for her? I was tempted to phone the house to check she was all right, but I did not want to wake her if she was still sleeping. Laughter drifting up from the sunny car park distracted me. I took my lunch over to the window and saw

Taro and Miss Yamamoto amusing themselves with a badminton rally. Miss Hatta and Miss Akashi from the Delivery Department had joined them also, giggling as they stretched a long roll of accounting paper out between them as a makeshift net. In mischievous spirits, the girls raised the net when Taro batted the shuttlecock, blocking its path to Miss Yamamoto. Taro waved his racket about, gesticulating in a wild show of frustration. Anyone could see he was in seventh heaven to be in the company of such pretty girls. I chuckled to myself.

A deep voice boomed behind me: 'Ah! Children at play . . .'

The voice gave me a fright. I turned from the window and saw the silvery crest of hair and imposing shoulders of Deputy Senior Managerial Supervisor Murakami blocking the doorway. He greeted me with a nicotine-ravaged smile.

'Indeed,' I said. 'I thoroughly approve of a little physical exertion at lunch-time. It kickstarts the metabolism . . . Banishes the usual afternoon lethargy.'

Murakami-san crossed the room to join me. 'And yourself, Mr Sato? Have you had much physical exertion lately?'

'Just my daily walk to and from the train station. That's twenty minutes a day – what the medical board recommends for a man of my age.'

'I'm sure you could get away with much more than that. I like to take as much exercise as possible . . . keep the old motor running.'

Murakami-san gave me an infuriating wink. He may be a keen golfer but that is no reason to assume he is in better shape than I am. I wanted to tell him of my weekend DIY, but it struck me as absurd to defend one's health before an alcoholic chain-smoker. I dug some rice up with my chopsticks and put it in my mouth. In the car park Taro acted out a buffoonish pratfall as a shuttlecock hit him on the head. The girls pealed with laughter, the net collapsing in their mirth.

'See how Taro strives to impress Miss Yamamoto,' Murakami-san remarked indulgently. 'It must be love.'

I chewed and *hmmmed* non-committally.

'And look at old Takahara-san and his Hawaiian missus. Who would have thought it, eh? The love bug has bitten everyone lately.'

'Yes. I was going to speak to you about Takahara-san,' I said solemnly. 'I think that someone ought to track him down and speak to him directly. The whole thing is so out of character I cannot help but suspect he is suffering from some kind of mental affliction.'

Murakami-san chortled. 'Ah, Sato-san, ever the cynic! Well, I will definitely be contacting him in the near future to rebate his pension payments. Until then, you'd better give him the benefit of the doubt. Is it so hard to believe the man has given it all up for love?'

I *hmmmed* once more. Down in the car park Miss Hatta and Miss Akashi were rolling up the improvised badminton net and Miss Yamamoto was caught in a post-match hand-shake with Taro. He grinned adoringly at her, unwilling to relinquish her hand.

'I must get back,' Murakami-san said. 'I have to show round a few officials from City Hall this afternoon. I am still worn out from entertaining our guests from the Taiwan office last night!'

'What a busy schedule you keep,' I remarked.

I observed Murakami-san's profile as he unleashed an extravagant yawn. The broken veins in his nose and cheeks wriggled like tiny worms, elongating as his face did. In the breath expelled by his yawn I detected whisky and breath mints.

'See you later, Sato-san,' he said, giving me a hearty slap on the back. 'And try not to be too hard on old Takahara-san. You never know, the love bug might bite you next!'

His crow's-feet proliferated in another crafty wink. Then he was gone, pounding down the corridors of Daiwa Trading as the company chime sounded for the end of lunch.

*

Around five o'clock I became very fidgety and could barely sit still. I was gathering loose paper-clips and straightening up my in-tray when Miss Yamamoto came to speak to me. She looked as fresh as she had been at the 8.30 chime, smart in her white shirt and pinafore dress. She asked my permission to begin the Nakamura credit check – a lengthy undertaking that required my supervision and would consume many hours. Reluctantly I assented and, before I could restrain myself, let out a weary sigh. As you know, I try not to sigh. Too many sighs can negatively charge the office, creating an atmosphere unconducive to work.

Quick to register my lack of enthusiasm, Miss Yamamoto said: 'There is no need for you to stay and supervise, Mr Sato! You have worked so hard today. I can manage perfectly well by myself . . . In fact, *I insist* you go home.' She spoke with such gusto and determination I had to smile.

'Very well, then, Miss Yamamoto,' I said, 'it's all yours.'

'You can count on me, sir!' Miss Yamamoto replied, and gave me a witty salute.

When I alighted from my express train at Osakako the weather had turned quite blustery. The wind boxed at my ears and tore at my jacket lapels. My necktie flew out in front of me, pulling this way and that like a leash. As I turned into our street I saw two of the Okamura children flying a kite fashioned from a plastic carrier bag and string. They both held tight, shouting as the wind threatened to wrestle their economy kite away from them. When I reached our house I was pleased to see the bedroom curtains wide open and the windows narrowly opened to encourage ventilation. This meant Mariko was up and about. I put my key in the front door and found it had been left on the latch. 'Mariko?' I called.

The house was silent as a grave. I kicked off my loafers in the entryway and put down my briefcase. I jogged up the stairs and knocked on the bedroom door. When there was no reply, I listened with my ear pressed to the panelling for a few seconds before peeping inside. The patchwork quilt had been carefully folded and the red buckle shoes were gone. I turned back down the corridor.

The bathroom door was open a crack. I rapped gently on its surface. 'Mariko?'

I slid open the bathroom door and stepped into an embrace of moist warmth. Bath-water vapours misted my spectacles and condensation speckled the wall tiles. Mariko must have bathed quite recently. I could smell my supermarket-brand anti-dandruff shampoo (I have had the same bottle for over a year now, so low are the shampoo requirements of my balding pate) but the chemical fragrance was tainted with something else, something sweet and musky, like honeydew. I wiped my spectacles on my shirt, and as I replaced them something unusual caught my eye. On the mirror of the bathroom cabinet the word '*FATE*' had been etched in the condensation. The tapering of the strokes was just so, making it appear to have been drawn with a calligraphy brush. A towel was draped on the rail. I reached out and touched the dampness of its fibres, before going back downstairs.

In the kitchen the bread and jam were gone, and the plate and knife had been washed and placed on the draining board. The note I had left Mariko had been folded into an origami lotus flower. I surveyed the empty kitchen in disappointment. 'Fate,' I said aloud. 'What a funny word to write on a mirror.' Then I heard the front door click open.

I waited, listening as Mariko exchanged her shoes for a pair of indoor slippers and padded towards the kitchen.

'Mariko . . .' I said, as she came into view.

She stopped in the doorway and looked at me, her eyes burning with shame and gratitude. Her clothes were sleep-rumpled, the pleats of her skirt flattened. One sock was drawn up to her knee, the other bunched up around her ankle. I was relieved to see that the peaches-and-cream of her complexion had been restored. Your old wicker

225

shopping basket, long banished to a distant corner of the kitchen, had been dusted off and hooked over her arm. Her damp hair was a fright, mauled and matted by the wind. I thought it unwise of her to venture outside with wet hair.

'I . . . I want to apologize for my behaviour last night,' she began.

I cleared my throat. 'Are you feeling better now?'

Mariko met my gaze with a lucidity she had been incapable of the night before. Her cheeks coloured. 'Yes, thank you. Thank you for taking care of me. I feel terrible about turning up on your doorstep and . . . and burdening you like that.'

Why me? I wanted to ask. *Why my doorstep?* But I knew this question held back a whole avalanche of questions. I told myself to at least let the poor girl sit down first.

'I am glad to see you have recovered,' I said.

'I found the bread and jam. Thank you. I was so hungry I finished all of the bread. When I saw you had no more food in the fridge I went to the market for you . . .' Mariko raised the wicker basket, then lowered it again, her gaze askance, perhaps out of fear I would think her kind gesture presumptuous.

'That is very thoughtful of you, Mariko. I seldom have the time to go shopping myself.'

Mariko smiled. The kitchen was dim with the crepuscular shadow of dusk. I usually snap the light on right away, to avoid eye strain, but tonight I let the shadows harvest.

'I would like to cook dinner for you before I go,' she said. 'To say thank you for your help last night. It's the least I can do.'

'Really, there is no need . . .' I protested.

'But I would feel so much better if I did something to repay you for your kindness . . .' Mariko touched her fingers to her damp hair. 'And I think I owe you an explanation. Shall we sit down?'

Mariko set the wicker shopping basket down on the

floor and we each pulled back a chair. In the semi-darkness the salt and pepper mills and milk jug sat in a runic circle on the table-top. Yesterday's newspaper lay beside the pot plant, only main headlines legible. Mariko's smile swept over these objects, towards me, like a wave crashing against a shore.

'I woke quite soon after you left for work,' she began, 'so I have had all day to sit and think about my situation and what I must do. Firstly, let me explain what was wrong with me last night. Sometimes, when I am very unhappy or distressed, I fall into a deep sleep. It is a medical condition I have suffered from since childhood. I suppose it is a kind of narcolepsy. It does not prevent me from leading a normal life, but sometimes an episode will catch me unawares, like last night.' Mariko spoke with a matter-of-fact fluidity, as if she had delivered this explanation so many times she had learnt all the words by heart.

'I am very sorry to hear this, Mariko,' I said.

Mariko laughed, perhaps to set me at ease. 'It is quite funny when you think about it. When I was naughty at elementary school my teacher would send me to the head-mistress. More often than not, the headmistress would find me fast asleep on the chair outside her office.'

'I have seen a documentary about this condition,' I said.

Mariko smiled. 'It is very rare. Exams, emotional upset, earthquakes: all of these things will send me into the deepest slumber.'

Darkness had filled the kitchen like a swarm of silent bees. Across the table Mariko looked much older than her years.

'I expect it must be very frightening for you,' I said.

'Not really. I try to control it sometimes, by tricking my mind into thinking it is relaxed. But it doesn't always work. Last night I received some bad news and . . . well, there was nothing I could do to prevent another episode.'

The bad news must have been the death of her father. I wondered if she remembered telling me about it. I decided not to mention it for fear of her losing consciousness again.

'Is there any medication you can take to control it?'

Mariko shook her head. 'Not even a packet of caffeine tablets can keep me awake.'

'How awful.'

'You get used to it.' The warmth of her smile showed me that she had made peace with her unfortunate condition. 'Shall I turn on the light?'

Mariko rose from the table and before I knew it the room had sprung into brightness. I sat flinching as she lifted the shopping basket from the floor and moved to the counter.

'Well, I must hurry up and cook for you. You must be hungry.'

'Perhaps *I* should cook, Mariko,' I said. 'You are the guest, after all.'

'Ah, but I have a special recipe I want you to try,' Mariko breezily insisted.

It was then that I realized she still hadn't told me why she had come to our house. I went to the fridge and took out a pitcher of barley tea. I watched Mariko empty the contents of the shopping basket onto the counter. Despite it being late in the day for the market, everything looked of excellent quality: fresh buckwheat noodles, shiitake mush-rooms, peppers, onions and chicken breasts. She put on the checkered apron and secured the strings tightly behind her back. Then she took the wooden chopping board from the drying rack and selected a long, slender knife.

'Perfect,' she said, admiring the blade. She began to rinse the vegetables under the tap.

'Mariko,' I said, 'how did you find your way to our house?'

When she heard the question she turned the tap off. She did not turn round. Instead she stood with her back to me, perfectly still. 'I wish I could remember,' she said softly. 'But I can't.'

16

MARY

The blue pick-up slows as it approaches me in my hitch-hiking stance. Two builders sit in the front, rough-hewn of face and leathery of skin. Relieved, I lower my thumb, but see they only want to rubberneck. The driver leans out of the window. 'Hey, blondie!' he shouts, and his sidekick hoots with laughter. The truck bumps off into the distance, a loose corner of the tarpaulin in the back fluttering me a goodbye wave. I move to the middle of the road and give them the finger. I normally conduct myself with more decorum, but I am having a bad day.

I feel like I've been walking on this road for ever. I swear, the next car that doesn't stop will get a rock thrown at its tail-lights. I am sick of the sight of paddy-fields and this sun blistering my skin. The need to see Yuji is a powerful, physical ache. It's the only thing that stops me from lying down in the ditch and having a good cry.

A travelling salesman picks me up. He is peddling pet toilets and gives me the spiel about them all the way to Shinsaibashi (he says it takes only three days to teach an average dog how to use the flush; an intelligent cat you can teach in an hour). I like him, mainly because he is cheerfully oblivious to the fact I look like I've spent the night in a hedge. Also, his sales-pitch nonsense is soothing as white noise. When he drops me off I take his card and promise to spread the pet-toilet gospel.

Amerika-mura is dense with people. Shoppers, pamphleteers, and surly microcosms of Goths and skaters. I slip into a noisy side street, where every shop blasts out its own soundtrack to shop by. Sugary pop anthems lure teenage girls into 100-yen shops, Serge Gainsbourg croons from a vintage-clothing store. Among the fashion emporiums sits a love hotel, about as discreet as a rabid dog. The Statue of Liberty towers over the entrance, torch aloft, as she doles out mechanical winks to passers-by. Yuji and I once spent the night there, in the Rock 'n' Roll suite. A statuette of Elvis came out of the wall and sang 'Love Me Tender' every time you sat on the bed.

I cut through the alley behind Mos Burger, to the bar strip. Everywhere you look, rubbish stews in black bags, listlessly awaiting collection. The strip is dismal by day, just killing time till dusk, when it is reanimated by neon and bar-crawlers. The only living creature I see, other than the rats, is the grilled-eel-restaurant chef. Stooped in the doorway, he sucks his cigarette and watches me through his sow eyes. Lacking the will to mime cheer, our stares clash vacantly. His apron is splotched with rust-coloured stains, as though he spent the morning in an abattoir.

Mama-san stands in the doorway, in a robe of red silk. I have never seen the grande dame without her make-up before – without the illusory aid of lipstick her lips are barely there. She looks nice, though, like a woman on the bus; older but more dignified. In her arms Mr Bojangles yawns hugely, his fur matted and in need of a groom.

'I phoned your flat this morning,' Mama-san says. 'When no one answered, I expected you'd be on your way here.'

'Is Yuji OK? Where is he? Is he here?'

Mama-san laughs softly. 'Look at you! You look as

though you've been chased by the devil himself . . . Yuji is not here. But he's in a safe place, don't worry. I will take you to him later.'

Each word is a tiny tranquillizer dart of relief. I shudder with a pent-up sob.

'I went to his flat this morning and there was a man there with a gun. He said he was waiting for Yuji . . . He said . . .' The rest of what I say is unintelligible. I feel stupid crying like this in front of Mama-san, but it is beyond my control. The tears are coming out faster than I can wipe them away.

'I know,' Mama-san says. 'I am sorry. There was no way I could warn you.' Her hand descends onto my shoulder and I look up in surprise. Blinkered by tears I cannot read the expression on her face. 'There's no need to cry,' she says. 'The worst is over now.' She rubs my shoulder-blade to comfort me.

I tell myself to get a grip. I tell myself that Mama-san wouldn't be acting like the high priestess of calm if her son wasn't safe. I take a deep, shaky breath. 'Yuji is in a lot of trouble, isn't he?'

'Yes. A lot,' Mama-san says. 'But you have nothing to worry about. I will see that everything is taken care of.'

I wipe away the last of my tears. The skin around my eyes is raw and inflamed. In all my time in Japan I have not once let go like that. I had forgotten how good it can feel.

Mr Bojangles closes his eyes as Mama-san's ruby nails scratch the fur behind his ears. 'Come and drink tea with us,' she says.

I step into the nocturne of the bar. The tables bask in sallow lamp glow, and the silver mirror-ball revolves, sifting moonbeams over the dance floor. Beyond the reach of sunlight, this place is a timeless vacuum. Only the quietude and Mama-san's clear want of glamour hint at the time of day. I notice a woman sitting at the bar top and realize, with a murmur of shame, that she has been watching me all this time. Beside her a cherubic toddler sleeps in a pushchair. The woman is well dressed and very pretty, her silky black hair framing a face that seems to effloresce through the gloom. On the bar top sit three earthenware cups and a teapot with steam rising from the spout.

'Introductions,' Mama-san says: 'Aya, Mary. Mary, Aya.'

Mama-san bends over and deposits Mr Bojangles on the floor. He springs away on his little legs behind the bar, then back out again, in pursuit of phantom prey. Mama-san pours green tea into one of the handleless cups and passes it to me.

'Aya used to work here,' Mama-san says. 'But I had to fire her. She is the worst hostess I have ever employed.'

'I hated every minute of it,' Aya says. 'Salarymen and their bad breath. Yuck.' She pulls a face and we smile at each other. The child sleeps on. This is the first time I have seen Mama-san socializing without any evidence of financial lubrication. I take a sip of green tea, which tastes like dishwater laced with arsenic. Mama-san kneels by the pushchair and strokes the brow of the sleeping toddler, brushing aside a tiny kiss curl. Aya dips her hand into her handbag – the same leather Gucci number a client gave me once – and pulls out a vial of pills.

'Valium?' she says.

'Er, no. I'm OK now, thanks,' I say.

She shrugs and puts them back. 'They are very mild,' she says. 'They came in handy when I worked here. Now I only need them in emergencies.'

Her child murmurs in its sleep. Aya tilts her head and regards my blotchy face with unconcealed pity. 'No, I don't miss being a hostess one bit,' she says.

Mama-san and Mr Bojangles lead me through a door I have been curious about for a long time. I follow them up a stairwell, holding onto the banister rail, unsure of my footing in the dark. At the top of the stairs Mama-san extracts a key. I hear it twist in the lock, then the dirge of warped wood. I pursue her dark silhouette into the widening shaft of light.

Her living quarters are traditional, minimal Japanese – not what I expected from her at all. Her flamboyant dress sense promised fun and high camp: florid pink décor and dreamy black-and-white photographs of Mama-san in her hostessing heyday. Instead there is tatami, floor cushions, and a tasteful dragon wall scroll. Incense and furniture polish scent the air of what could easily pass for the home of a suburban housewife. As with the bar downstairs, there is not a window in sight.

Mama-san registers my confusion with an arched eyebrow. 'Do your surroundings disagree with you?' she asks drily.

'No, not at all . . . I wanted to ask downstairs, what happened to Yuji last night? We were in this bar, and I went to the toilet, and when I came out again he had—'

'Patience,' Mama-san says. 'I told you I would take you to him later. It is better that he explains to you himself.'

She sets Mr Bojangles down and opens a sliding-wall compartment. She pulls out a plain cotton bathrobe and hands it to me. It has been laundered and starched stiff as cardboard.

'There is bath water ready,' Mama-san says. 'I had intended to take a bath, but you go ahead of me . . .' She looks me up and down. 'You need it more than I do.' Gently she touches my arm, a shadow of the bitchy tyrant I have known all these months. 'I must go back down and say goodbye to Aya. The poor girl hasn't a clue what is going on. Today was a bad day for her to visit.'

In the bathroom a single bulb glows through the steam. As I enter, a spider scuttles a few inches across the ceiling, then freezes, as if playing an imaginary game of statues. I lift the bamboo covering from the metal tub and skim my fingers through the water. Hot enough to poach an egg. I strip off my clothes and throw them in a dirty heap on the floor. I remember to shower first, as is requisite here. I sit on the plastic stool beneath the waist-high shower, soap and scrub myself, then lather my hair with Mama-san's apricot shampoo. I watch with satisfaction as dirt and nicotine spiral down the plug hole. When I have rinsed away every last trace of soap, I lower myself into the bath, my flesh protesting, inch by inch, as it is introduced to the scalding heat. Mariko used to be appalled by my Western bathing habits at the flat. 'How can you wallow in your own dirty water?' she used to ask. I told her that I prefer my own dirt to other people's. Over here entire families share the same bath water, reheating it day after day, for weeks on end. And no matter how thoroughly you wash beforehand, fragments of yourself are bound to work themselves loose in the water. In illustration of this point I can see two short black hairs, buoyed by surface tension, that definitely do not belong to me. Not very pleasant, but I let it go in the name of cultural relativism.

In the water my hair swishes like seaweed and heat blasts the ache from my limbs. I stretch my legs, placing my feet on the metal rim of the bath. I notice two mystery bruises, one on my ankle and one on my collar-bone, and try to remember how they got there. I shut my eyes and slide down, submerging my head. There is an underwater rush in my ears as everything changes to a subterranean pitch. Why won't Mama-san tell me what happened with Yuji? What difference would it make? I hope I am taken to him soon. I lift my head from the water. Rubbing my eyes, I hear the bathroom door sliding open.

Mama-san enters in a breeze of red silk. I straighten up in alarm, drawing my knees up, sloshing water over the side of the tub as I fold my arms over my breasts.

At my embarrassment, Mama-san gives a soft, unapologetic laugh. 'So modest!' she exclaims, sliding the door shut behind her. 'I am sure you have nothing I haven't seen a thousand times before . . . Or have you . . . ?'

She sits down on the plastic shower stool, though the seat is wet and sudsy and will soak through her robe. Her hem trails on the floor, and the silk darkens as it drinks from a puddle at her feet. Mama-san smiles through the bath-water haze. The smile tells me she finds me comical and prudish. I want to tell her to get out – not because I am ashamed of my body: I just like to have some say in who gets to look at it.

'You Westerners are so shy,' Mama-san says. 'We Japanese spend a lot of time at hot springs, bathing in the company of strangers.'

I fail to return her smile. I don't care how many strangers she's bathed in the company of. Maybe this is some kind of weird maternal voyeurism; maybe she wants to see what her son has seen. I stretch out again, trying to shed my self-consciousness.

'Feel better now?' she asks.

'I feel cleaner now.'

'Well, that's something,' Mama-san says. 'You have shadows under your eyes. You look as though you haven't slept.'

'I haven't really. But I'm not tired, though.'

'You are shaken-up. An encounter with Hiro will do that to anyone.'

'Hiro? You mean the guy with the burnt face?' My stomach flips at the memory, even though he and his loaded gun are miles away.

Mama-san is in no hurry to answer my question. She rises from the shower stool and turns to the tiled ledge, wet silk clinging to her ample backside. She selects a jar of cream and sits down again. She unscrews the lid and begins to smear cream on her neck, in lavish upward strokes.

'He was Yuji's childhood friend,' she says. 'His mother was an alcoholic and didn't look after him very well, so he stayed with us a lot. He has bathed in that tub, where you are now, a hundred times or more. He and Yuji were like brothers.'

'Brothers? He hates Yuji! He said that Yuji got him sent away from Osaka, and that he deserves to have acid thrown in his face.'

Mama-san stops smoothing cream on her neck and puts down the jar. Misted by the vapours that hang between us, her face reminds me of a pale moon. She sighs a protracted sigh, as if watching children squabble in the playground.

'Is it true that he stole drugs from Yamagawa-san?' I ask.

'So they tell me,' Mama-san says. 'I have offered to pay Yamagawa-san back, but he is being awkward. Fortunately, I am influential enough to help Yuji out of this . . .' Mama-san squares her shoulders as she says the word 'influential'. She notices me noticing this and laughs. 'I bet you are thinking, *How can this old hag be influential?*'

'Not at all,' I say, impressed by her mind-reading powers.

'How do you think this hostess bar has managed to stay open for so many years, despite the fact there is not a single valid work visa on the premises?'

In all the time I have worked here I had never given this much thought.

Mama-san smiles briefly. 'My son is no longer safe in Osaka. This breaks my heart because Osaka is our home. But even after things are cleared up with Yamagawa-san, Yuji cannot stay here – not as long as there are idiots like Hiro who want to throw acid in his face. He told me about your plans to go abroad, and I think this is a very good idea. I can help you leave for Seoul tonight . . . if you are still willing, of course.'

My heart leaps. I am very willing. 'Yes, I am.'

Mama-san nods. 'I thought so.'

From the folds of her red silk dressing gown she takes out a slim packet of cigarettes. She reaches behind her and pulls forward a metal ashtray on a table-high stand. Then she lights a thin, brown cigarette and holds it out to me. I accept with damp fingers. It is a gourmet cigarette, rich and slow-burning, tasting of cloves and bank rolls. I spot an extractor fan above the bathroom cabinet and wonder why Mama-san does not turn it on. All the steam makes it seem as though we are in the middle of a cloud, a ceramic-tiled heaven. Together we funnel blue smoke through the haze.

There is an air of ceremony between us, an intimacy in the ashes tapped into the damp ashtray. I decide that Mama-san isn't so bad after all. It took the whole duration of my time in Japan for us to reach this truce, but better late than never.

Maybe Mama-san is thinking the same thing because she says: 'How long have you been in Japan now, Mary?'

'Eight, nine, months.'

'That is a long time for a girl so young. Do you miss your family in England?'

'I don't really have a family in England. Just an uncle.'

Mama-san raises her eyebrows at this. 'Where do your parents live, then?'

'My father died when I was a child. My mother lives in Spain with her boyfriend. They moved out there about five or six years ago, to run a bar at a holiday resort.'

'Spain, eh? I saw a travel programme about Spain once. It looks beautiful. You must really enjoy going to visit them.'

I give an underwater shrug and blow clove-scented smoke up towards the spider on the ceiling. 'I haven't been out there.'

'So your mother visits you in England, then?'

'No . . . She likes to stay in Spain.'

I meant this to sound breezy, but it comes out hard and bitter. I don't like talking about my mother. People act like I was abandoned or something when I tell them she went off to live in Spain while I was still at school. She did invite me to come along but I really didn't want to go. My mum never took to motherhood anyway. When I was a kid she used to go on about the seven pints of blood she lost when she gave birth to me, as though those seven pints compensated for the lack of effort thereafter. Sometimes she'd up the number of pints to eight or nine if I hadn't done the washing-up or whatever. We used to talk on the phone once in a while, but now I don't even know her number any more. I just send her cards on birthdays and at Christmas, and hope she is still living at the same address.

'Yuji grew up without a father too.'

'He said.'

Our smoke twists up to the ceiling. I still have a good inch of cigarette to go but the novelty has worn off. I grind it out in the ashtray. The skin of my fingers is wrinkled, the top layer translucent white.

'I've heard there are a lot of single mothers in England,' Mama-san says.

'Yeah. More people get divorced.'

'Over here, people act as though single mothers have something wrong with them. And a single mother who works in a hostess bar, well, God help you, you may as well be a leper. It's the other mothers who are the worst. I had to move Yuji to a school far away from the neighbourhood we lived in, just so he wouldn't be bullied because of my job.'

'Elena was telling me how bad it is. What have they got against hostesses?'

Mama-san's lips curl into a wicked smile. 'Where do you think their husbands disappear to night after night? They can't stop me from making a living. But they can encourage their kids to pick on my son. They will always see me as a low-life, never mind that I provided for Yuji just as well, if not better, than two parents. I used the contacts I made hostessing to get him a place in a private elementary school, and a private junior high after that. The junior high school he went to was the best in Kansai, connected to all the best universities. His classmates were the sons of politicians and company chairmen.'

'Really? The best in Kansai?'

Yuji went to private school. I almost laugh out loud. He always presents himself as if he were straight from the streets. His walk, his thick Osaka drawl, his tough, mistrustful way of sizing people up. And Mama-san has surprised me too. She always seemed to possess a self-made woman's contempt for education.

'One of the top five middle schools in the country. Don't

ask me how I got him in; his grades at elementary school were average, and he had already begun to make a reputation for himself as the class trouble-maker. I pulled many strings and flattered many toads. I thought a good school would set him on the right path. But that was where his troubles began.'

The avocado wall tiles sweat condensation. A droplet of water quivers on the shower head, ready to drip. I lean closer to Mama-san, one arm slung over the edge of the bath. Yuji never talks about his childhood or early teens. He acts as though he came into the world a hard-boiled twenty-one-year-old. Unfortunately for him, though, his mother doesn't share this pretence.

'It was the kind of school where background matters. I briefed Yuji before his first day. If anyone asked about his father, he was to say he died in a car crash. And if they asked about me, he was to say I am a businesswoman. I wanted to protect Yuji from the snobbery and cruelty you get in these elitist schools.'

The best protection against snobbery would have been to not send him to an elitist school in the first place. Mama-san practically *taught* him to hide and be ashamed of who he is.

'Is that what went wrong?' I ask. 'They found out you were a hostess?'

Mama-san shakes her head. 'They found out that I am a Burakumin.'

'Burakumin?'

She looks very uncomfortable. I went to a museum exhibition on Burakumin once. They are a lower caste that evolved from people whose work was seen as being contaminated by death – stuff like slaughtering animals and digging graves. But that was generations ago. It's illegal to discriminate against them now, and I never hear anyone talking about it.

'I was born in a Burakumin ghetto outside Osaka. A slum run by gangsters and corrupt policemen. Lots of crime and poverty. It has improved since I was a child, but you would still have difficulty persuading a taxi driver to stop there. The chances of getting a decent education and a job there are slim.'

I nod. Listening to Mama-san talk like this makes me ill at ease. We were never friends before today. Her intimacy feels forced.

'I didn't know you had ghettos in Japan.'

'You're a foreigner – of course you wouldn't. Even educated Japanese know little about these places. Who wants to acknowledge slums and misery in this clean and efficient land? I got out when I was fifteen.'

'When you were only fifteen?'

'I got a job in a restaurant kitchen. I grew up fast.'

'Do you ever go back?'

'Not for many years. I sent money to my parents once in a while. I had no illusions of improving their quality of life – the quality of liquor they drank, more like. My mother died a decade ago; my father four years after her. It was because of my father that Yuji had problems at school. My father's liver and kidneys had been failing him for a long time, and before he died I paid to have him moved to a private hospital. While I was there one of the hospital specialists recognized me – he had a son in Yuji's class at school. He was friendly until he saw my father bawling and pissing on the hospital sheets. He told me they had to move my father to another room, that they'd had complaints from the other patients.

'Two things happened the next day: my father died, and Yuji was sent home from school for fighting. Yuji was a mess, with one eye so swollen he couldn't see out of it. He went straight to his room without a word. Not a word. But I knew what had happened. I sent some friends round to the doctor's house that night, to teach him some respect for a patient's right to privacy. But by then it was too late. Yuji wasn't going to school any more. How could he when even the teachers would treat him like dirt?'

'He left for good?'

'He was fifteen, the same age I was when I left.' Mama-san laughs to herself. 'Fate doesn't care how much money you throw at it. It will always do what it wants to do in the end.'

The shower head expels another drip. The water is cooling now and my wet hair chills my scalp. I think I understand now why Yuji set his ambitions so low.

'Why are you telling me all this?' I ask. Just last night she was correcting my posture and ordering me around, so why now, hours later, is she telling me the secrets of her past?

'Because it is important you know who Yuji is . . . who we are. Can I be honest with you, Mary? I never liked you much . . .'

I break eye contact. It's always been as plain as the dye in her hair, but it hurts to hear it out loud.

'You have a good heart, Mary – anyone can see that. But a good heart doesn't stop prejudice against mixed-race couples.'

I knew it. I watch the rise and fall of the bath water harmonize with my breathing. What prejudice? She is the only person to have shown hostility to me because I am white.

Seeing I have taken offence, she swoops in to limit the damage. 'But here you are, months later, standing by him. I see now I was wrong to be concerned by something so trivial. You love my son, I can see that now.'

I do love him. But did everything have to go to shit before she accepted me? Mama-san smiles and I see that this is her botched attempt at an apology. I force myself to smile back.

Mama-san stands and pulls a towel from the rack on the wall. 'The water must be getting cold,' she says. 'Dry yourself off while I make up a bed for you in the spare room.'

'I don't need to sleep. I'm not tired. I would rather go and see Yuji.'

'You can't see him until tonight. There are things I need

to sort out first. I want you to rest until then. Trust me: you need sleep.'

I wake in darkness, from a dream of Yuji. In the dream we rutted like animals, lost to everything but the touch and taste of each other's flesh. How long this delirium lasted I'm not sure, but it ended when I noticed, over his shoulder, his mother sitting in the corner of the room, watching us. That woke me up like a shot, killing dead any excited nerve endings into the bargain. My subconscious has a really sick sense of humour. But at least it is uncomplicated. It doesn't take a psychoanalyst to guess what is going on here.

I lie on the futon, listening to my stomach grizzle between the sheets. This room is so dark. There's not even a sliver of light beneath the door. According to my mental clock it is just after seven. My mental clock is usually pretty good, so I am sure it's not that far off.

I stand and walk with my arms outstretched until they hit a wall. Then I sweep my hands back and forth in search of the light switch. When the room is illuminated I see the clothes I had discarded in the bathroom neatly folded at the end of my futon. I pick up my shirt, hold it to my nose and breathe deeply. Fabric-conditioned to alpine freshness. The same goes for the rest of my stuff; even my knickers look as though they have been ironed. I shed the bathrobe and quickly dress, impatient to get out of here and see Yuji. My hair is a mass of knots, so I try and finger-comb it back to respectability.

By the wall is a low table with a large wicker cage on it, the kind used to keep flies off food. I lift the cage and see a plate of rice balls and a can of barley tea underneath. Ravenous, I take a rice ball and bite into it, my teeth sinking through the crisp seaweed. In the middle of the rice ball is tuna mayonnaise. Seaweed, rice and tuna mayonnaise: never has the combination tasted so good. I am washing down my third rice ball with tea when the door opens. Mama-san enters, wearing full make-up, a Hermès scarf, and a short black dress that shows off her dimpled knees. Mr Bojangles is cradled in her arms. His ruff has been groomed so it stands out like a fluted collar.

'How did you sleep?' she asks.

'OK. Thanks for washing my clothes.'

'I have a car waiting for you on Nagahori street. Do you know how to get there?'

I nod. 'Will it take me to Yuji?'

'Yes. You will have to leave the building by the fire exit. None of the girls must see you.'

I had forgotten that the hostess bar is just downstairs. Most of the girls will be on the first gin and tonic of the evening by now. I think of the sad, smoky world I am leaving behind, the friendships and rivalries, the boredom and shift-swap negotiations. Katya is the only one I will miss. It seems like days since I last thought about her.

'Is Katya here yet?'

'Yes. Late as usual.'

'Is there any chance I could speak to her?'

'That's not a good idea, Mary. We are in a rush and it is better that no one knows you are here, not even Katya.'

'It will only take two minutes . . .'

'No.'

Why not? I want to shout. Then I remember she is taking me to see Yuji. 'Well, could you pass on a message to her . . . ? Could you tell her that I will miss her?'

Mama-san nods, her face softening. 'I will,' she says. 'Come on then, Mary. It's time to go.'

17

WATANABE

I wake to an instantaneous guilt flash as the carriage rocks between Noda and Fukushima. I boarded the train at 05.16, just as daylight began to douse the fiery furnaces of the stars. Now it is 10.16 and the train has made 17.3 circuits of the JR loop line. The plan had been to join Mary at Umeda station, to be on hand as her loyal, invisible human shield. But two days without sleep proved too much for the hyper-sensorium of my mind. It shut down against my will. I may be transcendent, but my brain is sadly organic and requires neurone regenesis. Torn by guilt and separation anxiety, I swoop over the rooftops of non-Euclidean space. I find my tattered, tear-stained angel and shudder when I see what I could have prevented had I not fallen asleep.

I straighten my baseball cap and prepare to alight at the next stop. It is time to reunite with Mary, to compensate for my neglect.

Outside the hostess bar I have the joyful premonition that I am darkening its doors for the last time. Night after night I have watched this place suck the human spirit dry. Mementoes of these slain souls are everywhere.

Dark chimeras float in the lounge, writhing in discontent. Broken egos weave among the chair legs and hide in the drawers of the cigarette machine. These poor salarymen and their poor, squinting souls. When will they learn that the over-priced whisky, a curve of breast here, a bulge of thigh there, will never cure them of their desperate malaise? Escape is to throw off the chains of third-dimensional incarceration, not to intoxicate yourself to the point of forgetting they are there.

Four hearts pump at the bar. Semi-lunar valves open and close, channelling litres of blood through cardiac cycles. One heart belongs to Mama-san (61 bpm), another to Aya (68 bpm), an ex-hostess Yuji knocked up three years ago. The demon progeny is also present, visiting grandma. Like an oestrogen-rich pigeon, Mama-san coos over Katsu (84 bpm), asleep in his pushchair throne. Mr Bojangles (131 bpm) watches jealously. To him the baby is an impostor, and an inferior one at that, with his subservient pack scent and non-existent coat of fur. Mama-san rises and heaves herself onto the stool next to Aya, lifting the folds of her red silk robe.

I choose this moment to push through the doors. Mama-san is pouring tea. She looks up from the stream of water molecules and tannin compounds arching from the spout of her teapot.

'Watanabe,' she says. 'To what do I owe this dubious pleasure?'

Aya smiles. She is in a good mood because her imaginary husband has accompanied her to the bar. He stands behind her, 180 cm tall, taut and rippling of muscle, his nebulous face reforming, harmonizing with the face of the model from the razor ad she saw on TV that morning.

'Erm . . . I've come to work,' I say.

Mama-san draws out a long silence, allowing me to feel the intensity of her disdain. Finally she says: 'Watanabe, your shift doesn't start for another eight hours. If you think that I am going to pay you before seven o'clock I would like to shatter that fantasy right now.'

'OK,' I say.

'Good,' Mama-san replies. 'Did you have any particular task in mind?'

'Er . . .'

'Well, you can dismantle and clean the pizza oven.'

'OK.' I shuffle past the bar and into the kitchen.

Mama-san shakes her head, thinking, *The boy may be a simpleton, but at least the pizza oven gets a clean.* Aya smiles, bemused. *Where was this one when they were handing out the brains?* she remarks to her imaginary husband.

It is impossible to take offence. Let them think me a simpleton. How are they to know that I am situated like a god; immanent in the world yet transcendent of it? That I can calculate pi to a million decimal places? That I can read the mind of a lichen clinging to the side of an underwater cave a thousand kilometres away? Exiled by my higher dimensional expeditions I am an iconoclast, a heretic . . . But I digress.

In the kitchen I clatter the pizza-cutter against the oven to make it sound like I have begun work.

At the bar Aya leans towards Mama-san, eager to resume the conversation I interrupted. 'Is she pretty?' she asks.

Mama-san scrunches her lips. 'She is abnormally tall. Her mouth and hips are too wide, and her nose has a bump in it. Her one saving grace is her hair, because it is blond.'

I seethe like a pan of boiling milk. What does Mama-san know? The woman suffers from ultra-subjectivism. When everyone sees an apple, she sees a banana. When everyone sees a banana, she sees a runner bean. But that is neither here nor there. Mama-san can only perceive the external Mary. She is blind to the beautiful infinitude beneath.

'Will she be here soon?' Aya asks.

'In the next hour or so. Mizutani called me. He drove past her trying to hitch a lift back in Amagasaki, near Yuji's place. He says she had no shoes on!'

'And he just drove past her? He didn't offer her a ride?' Aya laughs. 'That Mizutani is a real gentleman! Do you think Mary had a run-in with whoever Yamagawa-san had watching the apartment?'

'Mizutani said he heard Hiro scared her away with his gun.'

The myofibrils of my hand contract, causing the pizza tray I am holding to clatter to the floor. Strange how one's body can recoil in shock when one's mind is already acquainted with the facts.

'Watanabe, be *careful* in there!' Mama-san rolls her bloodhound eyes. 'Why do I let that cretin loose in my kitchen?' she asks Aya.

Aya smiles. 'What will you do with Mary when she gets here?'

'Send her on to Yuji. He needs a woman at a time like this . . .'

My mind goes blank with rage. How dare she treat Mary as a comfort woman, a pleasure receptacle to be sent to Yuji in his rotting lair!

'. . . But I have to wait for Yamagawa-san to call before I can do anything. He knows, and I know that he will let Yuji go free, but he needs the illusion of power and control. Just like a man. How many times have I supplied him with women? How many times have I loaned out my best hostesses to spy for him? I lost one of my best girls because of his carelessness. And after everything I have done for him he still wants to keep me in suspense.'

Aya nods. 'He just doesn't want to look like a pushover for letting Yuji off the hook too quickly. Does Mary know what is going on?'

'I doubt it. These stupid Caucasian girls rarely do. What do I care? I do what is best for my son.'

Mama-san inspects her scarlet talons. Evil is the product of human will. And there is no greater evil than a mother's will to override all moral agency to save the neck of her criminal son.

Aya knows this, she was once part of this world too. She nods and smiles.

*

I glide 7.3 kilometres due west to where Mary stumbles at the outskirts of town, trying to hitch a lift. Mary is in a state of shock. Her confrontation with the cold steel barrel of an automatic is the single most harrowing event in her twenty-two years, marking a rupture in her personal identity. Trailing behind Mary is her discarded self of one hour ago. An optimistic and happy-go-lucky Mary, displaced from its incarnation by a hardened, wiser version. The Mary of one hour ago has no choice now but to tag along behind with the thousands of other selves Mary has discarded throughout her life, such as the Mary-who-has-never-been-kissed and the Mary-who-wets-the-bed. Most of them it was necessary to discard, in order to progress into adulthood. But the self who-has-never-been-threatened-by-a-gun is one self you hope to hang on to all life long.

Her suffering makes my extremities numb with fear. I swear I will never let this happen again.

At the bar Mama-san fusses over little Katsu. Mama-san enjoys these visits from her two-year-old grandson. Now Yuji's career has gone belly-up, she needs a substitute vehicle upon whom to project her dreams of conquering the criminal underworld.

Let me tell you about Aya. Meeting the Aya of today it is difficult to believe that she was once a vicious nympholeptic, prone to violent fits of rage. Many men found her kamikaze spirit alluring, including the teenage Yuji, who impregnated then dumped her (resulting in the 117 stitches needed to reattach his upper ear). Yet from this devil-spiked chrysalis emerged the loving mother of today.

It wasn't motherhood that transformed Aya. Early motherhood saw her at her lowest ebb, clawing the walls of her bedsit, waking from dreams of mixing meths into the baby formula. The transformation occurred one afternoon as she sat watching TV with the volume up loud enough to drown out her baby's cries. Through her medicated haze she saw a young actor on the screen. Admiring his chiselled good looks, she thought how perfect it would be if he could climb out of the TV set and become her husband. She imagined their wedding day and to her surprise found herself consoled by the fantasy. This calmed her enough to take Katsu for a stroll – for the first time ever in his six months outside the womb. That night as she ate her noodles she imagined that it was a special dish prepared by her new husband. And so it went on. Each day her fantasies grew, and before long she was spending every moment with her imaginary husband. And who can blame her? He is thoughtful, compliant to her emotional needs, and offers blessed retreat from her cultural demographic as a single mother. He makes Aya happy. Reality is cold and stale in comparison. Even now, sitting at the bar with Mama-san, she is impatient to be alone with him again.

To witness such self-delusion, such endeavour to negate reality, chokes me with terror. It is dangerous to take such undisciplined flight into the realms of fantasy. The only good thing that can be said about it is that at least it keeps in check Aya's infanticidal streak.

Thirty-two of those arbitrary sub-units of time called minutes pass by. I dismantle the pizza oven and follow Mary as she moves through the concrete maze towards The Sayonara Bar. I sweep through her, again and again, whispering, 'Turn away, turn away, turn away.' But it is no good. Mary is a totalitarian state governed by the desire to see Yuji. She will not turn back.

At the urgent knocking at the door Mama-san dismounts the bar stool and scoops Mr Bojangles into her arms. She likes to feel his tiny bestial heart beating next to hers. She looks at Aya and a poison smile slips between them.

Mama-san pulls open the door and Mary spills in.

'Is Yuji OK? Where is he? Is he here?' Her hair looks like it has been backcombed with steel wool and her eyes are bright and frantic.

Mama-san soaks up Mary's anguish like manna, or life-giving corpuscles of sun. With a kindly, motherly laugh she says: 'Calm down. Yuji is not here. But he's in a safe place, don't worry. I will take you to him later.'

Mary is so relieved she wants to smother Mama-san with kisses. Her diaphragm contracts in a sob. Mama-san grits her back teeth. The last time Mama-san cried was when she was eight, and her brother had just decapitated her pet kitten by holding it up to the ceiling fan.

'I went to his flat. There was a man there with a gun. He said he was waiting for Yuji. He said . . .'

Mary's tear glands haemorrhage, expelling the trauma, drip by salty drip. Mama-san taps her foot irascibly. Aya smirks. How I wish that Mary and I could transcend together. Up to where Mama-san is scattered into a million ugly shards. Together we would raid her memory bank and laugh at how she dances with her reflection in the mirror when she is lonely and drunk. But Mary cries on.

Before long Mama-san invites Mary upstairs for a bath, leaving Aya to indulge her personality disorder and rock Katsu in his pushchair. I pace the kitchen, trying to determine the best course of action.

Last night I made a terrible error of judgement. Though I was correct in interpreting Yuji's sanity to be cracked, my assumption that he is no longer a threat to Mary was wrong. I totally misread his n-dimensional neural geometries. During the hours I slept on the train the threat to Mary reappeared. I should have incinerated him at the Lotus Bar when I had the chance.

I pan back in hyperspace, to view four locations at once: Mary upstairs with Mama-san; Yuji sprawled at the Lotus Bar; the gunman doing one-handed press-ups in Yuji's apartment; yakuza boss Yamagawa-san hanging upside down in his wardrobe, like a bat.

Yamagawa-san's dopamine levels indicate that he will be asleep for several hours. Mama-san will not do anything until he wakes and phones her, so Mary is safe for the time being. The gunman, code name Red Cobra, is bored from empty hours of waiting. Trained to wound and maim, he itches to take Yuji out. At once I see a way to get Yuji while absolving myself of the dirty work. And all I have to do is superimpose Red Cobra's spatial co-ordinates with the Lotus Bar.

Inspired, I sprint out of the kitchen, just as Mama-san emerges from the door leading up to her apartment.

'Watanabe,' she says. 'One of the toilets needs unblocking. Get a wire coat hanger from the changing room and see if you can fix it.'

I stop for a moment and watch the caffeine molecules from her tea excite her postsynaptic membranes. I see myself, carried along by fragments of light, sifting miniaturized and inverted through four scrutineering optic lenses. They hold me in high regard, Mama-san and her dog: right now, they are thinking I have no higher purpose in life other than to unplug their toilet.

'What are you waiting for?' Mama-san asks.

Good question. What exactly am I waiting for? Ignoring Mama-san, I run towards the double doors, accidentally kicking over the potted fern by the cash register. Soil and fertilizer nitrates spill over the carpet, but I don't have time to clean it up. I have a bus to catch.

I climb the hill to Yuji's apartment. The clouds part and the hill is flooded with ultraviolet light. In their hillside homes housewives gossip and eat tiramisu. Toddlers watch adults in fuzzy romper-suits caper about on TV. Most people would be scared if they were on their way to talk to an armed yakuza henchman. Not me. Once Red Cobra learns of our shared objective we will be fast friends. I am sure of it. I am not afraid. It would be nice to call my autonomic nervous system to heel, though. The shaking and cold sweats are really becoming distracting.

I vault back to the hostess bar. Back to Mary, naked in

the bath. Her blood vessels dilate as she lies steeping in hydrophilic content. I watch her in this fragile quietude, and for a second I wish that it could last for ever; that she and I will never be exposed to the unknown future. Then I unwish it. Time must run forwards if she is to reach the promised land. And until then I must toil behind the scenes, in the hope of easing her passage.

I reach the apartment lobby, light-headed with altitude sickness. In the grip of a nervous fever, my body has turned fugitive against my mind. It quakes and perspires, my biorhythms subject to fits and starts. Fortunately my mind is steady as a rock.

I penetrate the intercom system and trace the emergency-access code. I enter the three-digit code and press the hash key. Nothing. Tricksy things, these electronic codes. I try again, substituting the star key for the hash. The doorbell of apartment 227 begins to buzz. *Shit*. I will have to pretend I am the TV-licence inspector.

There is a click as Naomi Takishima in number 227 picks up and shrills: 'About time! You should know better than to keep a hot piece of ass like me waiting, you stupid man. Get up here *now*!'

The receiver is slammed down and Naomi Takishima of room 227 releases the door without so much as checking my identity.

I slip down the corridor to Yuji's apartment, dissecting the plasterboard to see Red Cobra, gun in hand, stiffen at the sound of my footsteps. For one awful moment outside the door my stomach feels ready to void in both directions. But the moment passes and I knock, twist the handle and enter. All the blinds are lowered against the afternoon sun. Red Cobra is behind the living-room door, his gun cocked, reflexes sharpened. This is a delicate situation. I had better announce myself and let him know I am not a marauder, or he will shoot me in the head.

'Er . . . hello,' I call into the dark, malodorous living quarters of Yuji Oyagi.

Red Cobra remains silent, waiting to see what I will do. 'Hello,' I repeat. 'Er . . . I am safe.'

Still no reply. Behind the living-room door Red Cobra is on intruder alert. I pause in the doorway, Red Cobra only an eighth of a metre away. Once I introduce myself his defences will ease off. Then we can discuss, man to man, a strategy for annihilating Yuji Oyagi. I walk into the room . . .

. . . And with a subsonic crack a .22-calibre bullet zips past me at 137 km per hour and buries itself in the plaster by the window. I belly-flop to the floor, the sound of gunpowder ringing in my ears. The fifty-four stay-at-home inhabitants of the apartment building stop what they are doing and look about themselves, trying to discern the source of the noise. A car backfiring? An exploding boiler? Instinct tells me to squeeze my eyes shut tight and press my forehead against the pine laminate floor.

Red Cobra rubs his right shoulder, aching slightly from the recoil kick of his Glock 18. He looks down at my quivering, floor-hugging form. He sizes me up, drinking in my dirty non-designer jeans and my baseball cap. He scratches the premature five o'clock shadow thrusting through the epidermal layer of his chin.

'Sorry. I could have sworn you were Ace Ishino of the Yamaguchi gang, skinny runt that he is.'

He is a liar with a poor sense of humour. Three footfalls bring him closer.

'I hope no one has called the police . . . Ah well, too late to worry about it now. Who are you anyway? Get up.'

My automative response unit has a malfunction. My muscles are paralysed into this position and I cannot move.

Red Cobra kicks me in the ribs. 'Turn around so I can see your face,' he growls impatiently. 'If you can't show me that you're not Ace Ishino, I'll just have to assume you are and shoot you.'

Cured of my paralysis, I turn my head sideways.

Red Cobra's scar tissue robs his face of expression, but

inside he shivers with awe. He senses that I am different. 'Work at the hostess bar, don't you? The Mama-san sent you to see who was here, didn't she?'

I shake my head, offended by this crude assumption.

'Well, speak, then. What are you doing here?'

I clear my throat. My emergent voice is strangely castrato. 'I want to show you where Yuji is.'

The magic words. A change comes over Red Cobra. He turns away to hide the naked want in his face. Never have I seen such coition of exhilaration and hatred. Revenge beats in him like a second pulse.

'Where?'

'He is hiding in an abandoned bar in Amagasaki.'

'The Lotus Bar?'

I nod.

Though Red Cobra senses my genius, his yakuza training warns him to be vigilant. He takes a step back. 'Mama-san sent you to tell me Yuji is hiding out at the Lotus Bar so I'll go and get jumped by whatever she has set up for me. Correct?'

'No. She wants Yamagawa-san to let Yuji go free. She isn't going to make trouble . . .' My voice fissures, unused to producing so many words in a row.

Red Cobra is stony with hate. He would rather commit hara-kiri than watch Yuji go free. He will not let it happen. He would sooner violate gang rules and take matters into his own hands.

'If someone is waiting for me at the Lotus Bar you'd better spit it out now, 'cause if there is you'll be the first to get it.' Beneath his tailored suit his Glock 18 pulses darkly. He is deadly serious.

'There is no one there but Yuji.'

'OK. Get up off the floor. You are coming with me.'

Red Cobra parks his Mercedes in the junk yard, 48.3 metres due east from the Lotus Bar. I scythe through the Lotus Bar walls. Yuji lies on his back in the middle of the floor. Other than paying a quick visit to a phone booth to call his mother, Yuji has spent the whole day in the dank, decaying bar. Lucky for him his mind is broken: time passes quickly for the insane.

Red Cobra takes a packet of Winston from the dashboard and taps one cigarette free. He lights it and smokes in silence. Just as he drove here in silence. The bond we share need not be sustained by words. The interior of the car hums with amity and cigarette smoke.

'He'd better be in there,' Red Cobra mutters.

I say nothing. He will see for himself soon enough. I study his yakuza cognitive life, bland and unimaginative but for his revenge fantasies. I watch a reel out of interest. It is quality viewing, all brutal choreographed violence, culminating in the gleaming tip of a samurai sword entering Yuji's throat.

Red Cobra blows a nervy smoke ring. He is stalling. He has yearned so long for retribution that, confronted with the real thing, he has stage fright. If I don't speak up he will stall for hours.

'What are you waiting for?' I ask.

Red Cobra stares ahead. Smoke exits his nostrils. 'I am watching,' he says.

This calls for a man-to-man pep talk. I think of telling him that killing Yuji is a pre-emptive strike on the behalf of humanity. Instead I watch the magic tree hanging from the rear-view mirror release aromatic molecules.

Red Cobra grinds his cigarette into the ashtray. 'Why have you brought me here, kitchen boy?' he asks. 'What's your beef with Yuji?'

Thermogenesis pinkens my cheeks. He will never understand. I might as well crouch down in the junk yard and tell it to an ant. 'Mary,' I say.

Red Cobra's scar tissue creases into a smile. 'Mary,' he echoes. 'I see . . . Well, let's go and get him then.'

I nod. This is exactly what I have been waiting to hear.

*

255

We trample over withered grass towards the Lotus Bar. A bullet train streaks by, sending a deep rumble underfoot. We make a formidable team, Red Cobra and I: Red Cobra of the muscle and menacing scars; Watanabe of the hyper-intellect. The Lotus Bar quivers at our approach. Field-mice halt their creaturely business and rise up on their hind legs. Cockroaches turn their listening ventricles towards us. Even Yuji senses something.

At the door, Red Cobra takes one final opportunity to mutter: 'If this is a trick, I swear to God I'll pump you full of lead.'

He creaks the door open and sunshine trickles in, inter-rupting the constant murk. Dust motes dance, rejoicing in the rays of light. Elsewhere the darkness pants in expect-ation. As he heard the door open Yuji crawled beneath a table, his heart pounding, waiting to see who we are. Red Cobra squints into the dark, his stage fright slain and dying in the wings. Squinting does not help Red Cobra see, though – the photosensitive pigment of his retina is still night blind. Yuji has one advantage over him: invisibility. Fortunately for Red Cobra I have no need of photosensitive pigments.

'Watch out!' I shout. I grab Red Cobra's arm and pull him sideways.

A fire extinguisher clips his shoulder before slamming into the rotting floorboards. If it weren't for my quick thinking the extinguisher would have staved in his skull. Red Cobra has no time to thank me for saving his life. He fires a shot into the dark.

'Come out from under the table,' he says.

Yuji stays where he is, like a sulking child.

Our eardrums recoil as another kinetic pulse is fired from the Glock 18. The .22-calibre slug punctures the table top, leaving an 11-cm-diameter exit wound. The bullet has missed Yuji by a gap of .32 metres, but Yuji imagines it bristled the hairs of his cheek. He scoots out from under the table with his hands up. In the half-light he picks out

Red Cobra's grotesque scar. His gall bladder hums with satisfaction.

'Long time no see,' he says.

Keeping his gun aimed at Yuji, Red Cobra lifts the fire extinguisher from the floor. 'Meant for me, eh?' he says.

He hurls it, one-handed, over the bar. It collides with the chandelier and sets it swinging.

Yuji does not cower or beg for his life or protest his innocence. He is motionless. The room reeks of imminent death, but Yuji is unafraid. His mind is broken and his fear responses muted.

'Did you lay a finger on her while I was away?' Red Cobra growls.

Yuji shakes his head. 'I can't speak for everyone else, though.'

Red Cobra is upon him. His fist sends Yuji to the floor. Yuji half laughs in deep, painful regret. The snout of the Glock 18 is pressed tight against his pounding temple. Towering over Yuji, the muzzle of his gun exactly where he wants it, Red Cobra is intoxicated, phantasmagoric with power.

'Listen carefully,' he says in a low whisper. 'I am going to shoot a hole in your face. But first I am going to give you the choice that I never had. I want you to pick a side: left or right. That will be the side I shoot.'

Finally Yuji feels something more than numbness. The route to his heart is through his vanity. To Yuji, ugliness is a fate worse than death.

'Hurry up. Or I'll get kitchen boy here to choose for you.'

Yuji looks at me in speechless recognition. He laughs feebly. 'Left,' he says.

'Put your head back and open your mouth wide,' Red Cobra instructs.

Yuji is shaking so much he can barely open his mouth. Red Cobra positions the gun between Yuji's teeth, ready to shoot through his cheek. My advance ballistics calculations tell me that the Glock 18 is too close-range. By pulling the trigger he will kill Yuji. I hold my breath. Mouth around the gun nozzle, Yuji squeezes his eyes tight shut. I can hear muscle fibres in Red Cobra's hand contract one by one as the trigger is squeezed.

'Wait!' I shout.

Red Cobra jerks and turns in surprise. 'What?' he asks. 'What is it?'

My mouth falls open. Red Cobra's mobile phone rings. We each leap out of our skins, all of us mistaking the first note as the misfire of the gun. Instead a shrill J-pop melody fills the crumbling ruins.

'What the fuck?' Red Cobra spits. He is breathing hard and fast.

The caller identity is concealed, so I follow the mobile phone signal back to the source.

'Don't answer that!' I say.

But it is too late; he has the phone at his ear.

'Red Cobra,' Yamagawa-san oozes through the earpiece. 'Put your gun down and step away from Mr Oyagi. He is not to be harmed. Do you understand? *He is not to be harmed.*'

18

MR SATO

I

The stars are out for my midnight jaunt, shining through the canopy of bamboo leaves. The air is balmy, perfumed by the rising sap and the fertile peat beneath my moccasins. I must look as though I am heading off to a woodland pyjama party, for I slipped out of the house tonight without my jacket or overcoat. Toads serenade me with their throaty song, the machinery of a nearby canning factory clanking in percussion. It does me good to breathe this air, to displace the traffic fumes and heaven knows what else from my lungs. Health benefits aside, though, I cannot help but think it a dismal state of affairs that I have had to walk all the way out here just to talk to you.

I endeavoured to reach you at the kitchen table, where I sat drinking a mug of hot cocoa after Mariko had gone up to bed. But I could not concentrate. I kept imagining the creak of bedsprings, the dull thud of a pillow being pumped, long after Mariko had, in all probability, fallen asleep. All these non-existent sounds conspired to remind me that for the third night in a row I had a visitor. I suppose other people might take the event of an overnight guest in their stride, but I am not yet used to having another living, breathing presence in the house. I washed up my

259

cocoa mug and opened the kitchen window. A light breeze swept in, bearing with it the forest air, fresh and alive. I went and put on my shoes at once, and let it guide me to the woods, like an enchanted melody from the Pied Piper's pipe.

I know that inviting Mariko to stay was the right thing to do. Newly orphaned and abandoned by her brothers as she was, the only place she had to go was back to the shady world of hostessing. A world where they prey on the young and vulnerable. When Mariko told me how desperate she was to leave the profession, my duty was evident at once. Nevertheless, it took me an hour or two to propose to Mariko that she stay in our house. As you know, my generosity lacks the natural spontaneity of yours. I am glad I did eventually, though. The worst thing Mariko could do at this unhappy time in her life is to return to that smoky, insalubrious hostess bar. Especially with her precarious medical condition.

Hearing the soil squelch underfoot brings me childish pleasure. From somewhere nearby comes the garrulous tinkling of a stream, though its exact whereabouts are a mystery to me. The breeze has lulled, yet all the leaves seem to whisper me on my way. I shall walk a little farther before I turn back.

I wish I knew how to counsel Mariko through her grief. I never know what she is thinking or feeling. Her emotions are kept hidden, and only surface when she thinks my attention is diverted elsewhere. Last night, for instance, as I took the rubbish out into the back yard I glanced back at the kitchen window, where Mariko stood drying a saucepan, and saw a solitary tear roll down her cheek. Yet in my company she is cheerful and studiously avoids the topic of her father. Instead we talk about the marigolds, or the best colour to paint the banister. If only you were here. You would know exactly what to say.

This morning I heard Mariko rise before me and go

down into the kitchen. The frying pan clanged on the hob, and drawers opened and closed as if troubled by a restless poltergeist. Though tempted to investigate, I did not want to miss my radio callisthenics broadcast. I contained my curiosity long enough to do my morning exercises, then shave and change into my suit and tie. As I left the bathroom, delicious cooking aromas climbed the stairs to greet me, possessing my nostrils with a rabbity twitch.

'Mariko!' I chided upon entering the kitchen. 'Really, there is no need for all this.'

Mariko turned from the stove where she was frying prawn *tempura*. The brightness of her smile more than compensated for the absent sun. 'Good morning, Mr Sato! I have made breakfast for you.'

Laid out for me on the table was a traditional feast of rice, *miso* soup, pickles, fermented bean paste and grilled fish.

'Good Lord, Mariko! I usually have just toast and jam,' I said.

Mariko laughed and gestured that I sit and eat. She did not join me, but busied herself preparing me a *bento*. I ate at a leisurely pace, listening to the parliamentary report on the radio as though it were a Saturday. At 7.35 Mariko gently reminded me that if I didn't hurry I would be late for work. She placed my *bento*, bound in a lace-edged handkerchief, in a bag for me to carry. I took one last swallow of coffee and rose from the table.

'Would you mind accompanying me into the garden, Mariko?' I said. 'There is a person I would like you to meet.'

Mariko glanced down at her muslin peasant blouse and blue skirt. She touched her hands self-consciously to her head, where her hair was tucked away beneath a yellow headscarf. She seemed quite dismayed. 'But, Mr Sato, look at what I am wearing. I am a mess!'

Her eyes darted to the ceiling, betraying her desire to dash upstairs and pick out something smarter from the tiny suitcase of clothes and toiletries she brought to the house yesterday.

'Really, Mariko, you look quite presentable. I only intend to introduce you to the lady you saw snooping about yesterday morning. Otherwise she will be at it again the minute I am gone. You will never get a moment's peace.'

Mariko bit her lip. I could appreciate her reservations. For a good forty-five minutes yesterday morning Mrs Tanaka had circled the house, peering through all the windows, while pretending to water our rhododendrons. This made Mariko quite afraid to venture downstairs. I had also told Mariko Mrs Tanaka's tale of their encounter at the front porch. Unsurprisingly she has no recollection of this.

'OK,' said Mariko, relenting gracefully.

The sky this morning was drab and dish-water grey. Birds lunged across its blank expanse like thrown stones. We stood side by side on the front lawn, facing the Tanaka residence. Armed with my *bento* and briefcase I felt rather confident, but Mariko nervously twisted the fabric of her skirt. I assured myself that once Mrs Tanaka sees what a sweet-natured girl Mariko is the pair will get along famously. Though separated by two generations I believe they had much in common, such as a mutual love of domestic duty and headscarves.

'Mrs Tanaka won't be long now,' I promised.

Mr Ue marched by on his way to catch the 7.45 express, his briefcase in a high pendular swing. When he saw Mariko standing on my lawn, toying with the fabric of her skirt, he spluttered on his can of Hercules Extra Strength coffee. Determined to conduct myself in an open, nothing-to-be-ashamed-of manner, I bid Mr Ue a lusty good morning. Mariko smiled coyly. As he progressed further up the street, Mr Ue nearly dislocated his neck twisting it to look back at her.

Mrs Tanaka kept Mariko and me waiting for a good long while. Just as my patience was about to give out, her front door opened. Out she stepped in her claret quilted house-coat, her curlers encased by a turquoise turban. I recognized this particular ensemble as the one she wore in hospital after her hip-replacement operation. I could not fathom her reasons for wearing it this morning. As she approached us she stopped to fuss over some skid marks Mr Tanaka's wheelchair tyres had left on the lawn, tutting to herself in annoyance. As you know, Mrs Tanaka's will to pry is all-consuming. It must have cost her a great effort to affect such apathy.

'Good morning, Mrs Tanaka.'

'Mr Sato. Good morning. I see you have a friend.' Mrs Tanaka smiled thinly, her eyes keenly devouring every detail of Mariko's dress and deportment. 'I believe we have met before,' she said.

Mariko rushed in breathlessly: 'Yes, I am so very sorry for my rudeness. I was unwell at the time, you see, and not my usual self.' Mariko bowed, her face luminous with apology. I could see Mrs Tanaka begin to thaw at the edges. 'My name is Mariko and I am very pleased to meet you.'

'Mrs Tanaka,' Mrs Tanaka said, tersely.

Mariko gave another generous bow, which Mrs Tanaka met with a parsimonious dip of the head.

'Mariko is staying with me for a while,' I said. 'She was made redundant from Daiwa Trading the other week and I have offered her a place to stay while she seeks employment elsewhere. Her family live in Fukuoka, you see, but her job prospects are better here in Osaka.'

I scratched at an itch that felt like a tiny ant crawling over the bridge of my nose. That Mariko should pretend to be an employee of Daiwa Trading was an idea I had the night before whilst assisting her with the dishes. Though the topic of hostesses has never arisen in conversation between myself and Mrs Tanaka, I am certain that she frowns upon the profession.

'Such a shame you were made redundant,' Mrs Tanaka said, in a distinctly unsympathetic tone of voice. 'You should count your blessings that Mr Sato has been so good to you.'

'I am indebted to Mr Sato for his kindness,' Mariko declared. 'My father recently passed away, and . . . and I wasn't sure what I was going to do, I mean . . .' Mariko flushed, her gaze fluttering down to the grass.

'In which department did you work when you were at Daiwa Trading?' asked Mrs Tanaka.

At this remarkably cold-hearted change of subject my stomach did a pancake flip. I had not briefed Mariko on the details of her pretend job and I doubted her knowledge of business and commerce would be enough to convince Mrs Tanaka.

'I worked for the Public Accounts office,' Mariko said.

'The Public Accounts office,' Mrs Tanaka parroted. 'What did you do there?'

'Oh, I was just an office lady,' Mariko replied. 'I am afraid I am not very clever when it comes to numbers and accounts.'

'Well, let's hope that you find another job quickly. I am sure you don't want to be taking advantage of Mr Sato's hospitality for too long,' Mrs Tanaka said briskly.

Mrs Tanaka's rudeness knocked me for six. Did she not hear Mariko say her father had just passed away? Mariko trembled with shame.

Determined that she should not pay any attention to Mrs Tanaka, I said: 'Nonsense. Let's not hear any talk of "taking advantage". Mariko, you are welcome to stay for as long as you like. It is important you find yourself a decent, well-paid job. You mustn't rush into anything unsuitable. Towards this end my hospitality is unlimited.' A generous declaration indeed, provoked in part by my anger at Mrs Tanaka, who sniffed in a put-out manner, and patted the ruche of her turquoise turban. Mariko smiled weakly, flinching still from Mrs Tanaka's remark.

At this inopportune moment it occurred to me that I had missed two trains and would be late for work. Though reluctant to leave Mariko in Mrs Tanaka's interfering clutches, I had little choice. As Section Chief of the Finance Department it would not do to be unpunctual. I bid them both farewell and left them on the lawn, praying, as I proceeded to the station, that the mysterious alchemy of female bonding would occur in my absence.

At my late arrival Matsuyama-san's eyebrows lifted over the rim of the cup of coffee he was drinking. Taro winked and greeted me with a chirpy 'Good evening, Mr Sato!' I apologized to my colleagues and confessed that I had carelessly lost track of time. Then I went to my desk, where Miss Yamamoto was busy examining the contents of my in-tray. Though she had stayed late the night before to finish the Hashimoto file, Miss Yamamoto was bright-eyed and perky, not to mention stylish in her white blouse and pin-striped skirt.

'Mr Sato. Good morning. I was just checking your mail – I hope you don't mind.'

Guilt stirred like a nest of snakes. Had I been on time Miss Yamamoto would not have felt obliged to check my mail for me. I hung up my coat and laid my briefcase on the desk.

'Of course not. Thank you, Miss Yamamoto. Anything important for me today?'

'Just an email from Murakami-san reminding you the budget dissemination for the export department is overdue.'

I sighed. My memory has been as effective as a sieve of late.

'I can do it if you want,' Miss Yamamoto volunteered, with her usual eagerness.

'No. I should do it. It is very important and there cannot be any mistakes.'

'Well, why don't I take care of some of your accounts, then?' Miss Yamamoto said.

As a rule I do not give out assignments entrusted to me,

but Miss Yamamoto is more than competent, and there is no harm in a little delegation now and again. I handed her the files and she smiled and told me she would do her best, before trotting back to her desk with them, pleased as a dog with a frisbee in its jaws.

At lunch-time I untied the lace-edged handkerchief and opened up my *bento*. Matsuyama-san was quite envious when he saw my high-quality lunch box. His wife had given him cold meatballs in tomato sauce and rice. Mariko had given me rice with bamboo shoots, prawn *tempura*, grilled eel, carved radishes and a variety of other gourmet treats.

'Nice lunch, Sato-san,' he said. 'Make it yourself?'

I gave a half-nod and took out my chopsticks.

'Not bad. I haven't seen you with a fancy lunch like that for a long time, not since we worked in Transport and—' Matsuyama-san broke off quickly and looked down at his cold meatballs. 'Ugh,' he groaned. 'She means to poison me.'

After polishing off the last of my rice I put my lunch box away and picked up the latest issue of *Kansai Jobs*. I thought Mariko might appreciate some help job hunting, as it is quite hard to motivate oneself after the loss of a loved one. The task was harder than I had anticipated, as Mariko has little more than a high-school diploma to her name. Most office work, even clerical jobs, require further qualifications. After a good twenty minutes of disillusioned scanning I struck upon a suitable position. A fishmonger's in Namba required an apprentice. The pay was low but they offered benefits, a pension scheme and the prospect of promotion. I circled the ad in red and felt very pleased with myself. I wanted to rush home and tell Mariko straight away.

The remainder of the day went by quickly. I should have worked into overtime to finish redrafting the budget plan, but I wanted to get back to Mariko, who was probably awaiting my return after so many hours spent alone. At five minutes to five I found myself sitting at my desk with my briefcase packed, ready to leave before the company chime. It was a scenario that less than a week ago would have been unheard of. Also waiting to leave was Taro, his parka zipped up over his suit as he sat grinning out from the depths of its fur-lined hood. At the chime we said goodbye, and excuse-me-for-leaving-early, and left the office together. I was quite ashamed by my premature departure, but Taro seemed rather jolly. Outside the office he snapped his heels together and began gyrating his hips and clicking his fingers as though he were no longer a graduate trainee from the Public Accounts office, but John Travolta in *Saturday Night Fever*.

'Hey, Mr Sato. I'm meeting Ace Ishino at the bar opposite City Hall for some drinks. D'you want to come?'

Ace Ishino is a motorcycle courier for Daiwa Trading, whose greatest joy is near-fatal traffic accidents. Whenever he comes to our office he recounts them for Taro with the same dreamy nostalgia others use to hark back to exotic holiday destinations. Once Ace was thrown clear of a pile-up on his way to deliver a contract for the Finance Department. After twenty minutes of treatment for concussion in Osaka hospital Accident and Emergency Ace detached himself from his drip and went to fetch his bike, in order to finish delivering our contract before the four o'clock deadline.

'Are you joking, Taro?' I asked suspiciously.

Taro was side-tracked for a moment as he waved to Miss Akita from Marketing, who passed us by with a clippety-clip of heels and a lipsticked smile.

'Yeah, I'm joking,' Taro admitted with a grin. 'I know you can't make it anyway. Got a hot date, haven't you? What's her name again? Michiko or something, isn't it?'

I staggered a step, queasy with shock. The fiery itch of shame spread across my face. How did Taro know about Mariko?

'What did you say?' I replied, in a strangled voice.

'Ha! Knew I was right. Who is she? It's Miss Kano

at reception, isn't it? Taking her out somewhere swanky? Octopus Hut? The Big Echo?'

Relief came in a huge wave. Taro was only teasing me, clowning around as usual.

'Yes, that's right, Taro,' I said drily as we drew towards the stairway. 'I am taking Miss Kano from reception out to Octopus Hut. Never mind the fact she is married, in the third trimester of her pregnancy, and I am easily twice her age.'

Taro winked and gave me a thumbs-up. 'Nice,' he complimented. 'The Deputy Senior Managerial Supervisor doesn't let that kind of detail get in the way either.'

'Quite,' I said.

Taro bounded down the stairs two at a time, then waited for me at the bottom. Together we turned into the lobby. Behind the reception desk, talking into her phone headset, was Miss Kano, looking very weary and bruised around the eyes, her bump clearly visible beneath the maternity pleats in her blouse. Taro sniggered to himself.

'Well, Taro,' I said, 'I have to go and remind Miss Kano that we are expecting a visitor from Kyoto bank on Monday. I hope you and your friend Ace have a pleasant evening.'

'Heheheheh,' Taro said, stroking his chin. 'Won't be as pleasant as yours, I bet.' He turned and dived into the revolving doors. 'You'd better watch out, Section Chief Sato,' he heckled over his shoulder as the doors revolved him mercifully away from me. 'Michiko might be the jealous type.'

After briefing Miss Kano on the Monday-morning inspection I rushed down to the station in time for the five fifteen. Shortly after six I turned onto our street. A half-circle of Okamura children were standing in the early dusk, conducting a spinning-top tournament. The tops they used were not the wooden type of our childhood but streamlined, hi-tech aluminium-looking things. They respectfully interrupted their game as I went by, removing the spinning contraptions from my path. Just outside our house the two youngest Okamura children were crouched down, making two naked plastic dolls swim in the gutter dirt. They both had pageboy haircuts and wore dungarees, leaving me clueless as to their gender.

'You shouldn't play there,' I told them. 'It's not clean.'

They looked at me with blank eyes, which made me wonder if they had yet been taught to talk. They were both very young.

A movement to the right of our house caught my eye. It was Mrs Tanaka, peering out at me from her bedroom window. Beneath the turquoise turban her face was stern and forbidding. As I waved to her she began to close her bedroom curtains in a deliberate snub. The message was loud and clear: she did not approve of Mariko. A terrible sadness welled up inside me. Not for me, or even for Mariko, but for our good friend and next-door neighbour. As we both know, Mrs Tanaka can be pushy, tactless, nosy and indiscreet. But never cruel. And to be more concerned about the tone of the neighbourhood than poor Mariko's orphaned plight is very cruel of her indeed. I started towards the front door, disappointment bearing down on my heart.

As I inserted the key in the lock something felt different. I twisted the key and pushed the door open.

'I'm back!' I called.

I kicked off my shoes and unbuttoned my overcoat, intending to go and put the kettle on for tea. But I did not make it as far as the kitchen. Instead I froze at the foot of the stairs, clutching the banister rail, my chest drawn tight as a drum.

The mournful bray of the cello filled the house. Note followed note, bringing on an ache in my bones. I climbed the stairs as though I were sleepwalking. The cello was out of tune, and the bow so in need of rosin that each note rasped like an old man on a ventilator. Yet the music touched me with its nameless, unspeakable beauty.

Through the open door of the spare room I saw that the cellist was Mariko. She sat on a stool in the middle of the room, the cello between her parted knees. Staring intently at the yellowed sheets spread out on the music stand, Mariko did not notice me standing in the doorway two metres away. She wore an expression of fierce concentration as she manipulated fingers and bow to match the sequence of notes on the score. Mariko's execution was shaky, her performance all elbows and clenched determination: almost the opposite of how you used to be mid-recital – so fluid and passionate, the sway of your head mirroring the pull of the bow. Mariko had selected the Elgar you performed at the end-of-term concert at college. We had only been courting for six weeks back then and were still quite shy of each other. Up on stage that night, in your black velvet dress, you played with such beauty that the entire auditorium held its breath.

I cleared my throat.

The melody ended mid-note as the bow came to a chafing halt. Mariko lifted her head and blushed hotly. 'Mr Sato, I . . .' She scrambled to her feet, one hand holding the neck of the cello, the other hiding the bow behind her back. 'I . . . I didn't expect you back until six,' she stammered. 'I will put this away at once!'

Mariko quickly turned and leant the cello back against the bookcase, knocking the scroll in her haste. She began to tidy away the sheet music.

'I am so very sorry, Mr Sato. This is so terrible of me! You probably think I have no respect for your privacy . . .' Her voice was fraught. '. . . It's just that I thought, well . . . I heard something, some footsteps, coming from this room earlier today. It was nothing, of course, nothing but my silly imagination . . . but when I came to have a look I saw the cello. I played it in high school, you see, and it has been almost two years since I . . . Anyway, all day I was itching to play it, but I wanted to do the proper thing and wait until you returned to ask your permission.'

Mariko sighed heavily. 'I'm afraid my will-power gave out.'

I smiled limply. The sight of Mariko's young fingers dancing up and down the neck of the cello had left me rather dazed. Years had passed since notes had been drawn from its ageing strings.

'Your face is so pale, Mr Sato . . . I have upset you, haven't I?' Mariko's chin quivered. 'I am sorry. I promise never to touch the cello again.'

She plucked at the skirt of the yellow dress she had changed into. The headscarf was gone and she had tied her hair in two simple plaits. It made her face seem rounder, sweeter.

My tongue stumbled out of hibernation. 'I am not upset,' I told Mariko. This was true. The word 'upset' did not correspond to how I felt. 'You are welcome to play the cello. It is important you practise every day or you will forget what you learnt in high school. I would prefer it, though . . .' I paused and Mariko waited on tenterhooks '. . . if you did not play while I am here.'

As I said this I knew that you would disapprove of this irrational request. I am not sure I approve myself. All I know is that hearing the cello is not good for me, just as the sound of siren song is not good for a sailor at sea. Mariko nodded and did not ask why. She gathered the sheet music and put the stand away.

For dinner Mariko made a very flavoursome lamb stew, followed by an apricot pie baked in accordance with your secret family recipe. After the washing-up was done we played Monopoly, which I won three times in a row. Lacking in general knowledge and uncompetitive by nature, Mariko was a very weak opponent. But she laughed a lot and enjoyed herself nonetheless. After her third loss she congratulated me and declared me to be the cleverest person that she knows. I told her if that was the case then she really ought to widen her social circle. Mariko laughed at this and said: 'Mr Sato, *you* are my social circle!' She was very happy when I told her about the job vacancy I had found that lunch-time. One of her elder brothers was a fishmonger, she said, and as a schoolgirl she used to enjoy watching him at his shop.

Ah! I have stumbled on the stream at last, or rather my newly soaked feet have! It trickles over rounded pebbles and sand, silvery with the glint of the moon. It is very late now, and I really should make my way back. Even though tomorrow is a Saturday I want to be up bright and early to assist Mariko with her job hunting. I am optimistic that under my careful supervision things will turn out well for her. For the time being she is happy pottering about our home. She has unearthed all your old cookery books and has been trying out your family recipes. As you once said yourself, recipes ought to be passed down from generation to generation, to keep them alive . . .

How chill the forest air has turned. Such a sharp drop in temperature! I shall have to walk fast to keep myself warm. It shouldn't take me long, though. Not when I have the stars to guide me. See how they twinkle, like Cat's-eyes for wandering insomniacs.

II

I awoke this morning to the sizzle of bacon. The time was nine o'clock, which meant I had overslept by two and a half hours and missed the morning callisthenics broadcast. I picked up my clock in confusion, as one would have to be stone deaf to sleep through the shrill of my alarm. The alarm had been switched off – I must have done it by accident. I threw back my quilt, went to the window and opened the curtains. The morning light revealed that much of the bamboo forest had accompanied me home, in the form of twigs and stray leaves clinging to my pyjama bottoms. I stood at the window for a moment and watched as Mr and Mrs Ue went by in their matching tracksuits, dragged along by their yappy fleet of dachshunds.

I washed and shaved, and changed into my shirt, tank-top and corduroy slacks. Downstairs in the kitchen a pitcher of orange juice and a rack of toast sat on the table. Mariko was at the stove, spatula in hand, transferring bacon from the frying pan onto a plate. She wore a floral dress, long socks and a beige cardigan. When she saw me her cheeks dimpled in a smile.

'Good morning!' she said. 'I hope you like bacon.'

Well, as you know, I like bacon very much and I ended up polishing off seven strips, as well as plenty of toast and marmalade. Mariko had a glass of hot water and half a grapefruit. Afterwards I patted my stomach and joked that my cholesterol level was now so high I would fail my yearly medical examination.

Mariko shook her head at me and said: 'Really, Mr Sato, you are as fit and trim as a man half your age. I am sure you have nothing to worry about.'

Over coffee I told Mariko that we should take full advantage of the day ahead and see about the position in the fishmonger's. Mariko was very enthusiastic about this and suggested we type out a resumé to distribute among local shops and restaurants. I thought this was an excellent idea and went upstairs to fetch the typewriter. I put it on the kitchen table as Mariko finished the washing-up.

'Why don't you leave that now, Mariko?' I said. 'Why don't you come and make a start on your resumé? I will put the dishes away for you.'

'But I do not know how to type,' Mariko said.

It was decided that Mariko should dictate her details and I would type them. We did not get very far – one line, to be precise: *Name: Mariko Wada. Date of birth: 20 May 1986.*

As the typewriter keys clattered out her date of birth I looked up at Mariko in surprise. 'Why, Mariko,' I said, 'that's today.'

*

As you know, my own birthdays in recent years have passed very quietly. I seldom mention the day to my colleagues, so the only person who ever remembers is Mrs Tanaka, who always bakes a king-size cake and wheels it round in Mr Tanaka's wheelchair. Do you remember the cake she made me last year? How she decorated it with so many candles it took nearly a dozen attempts to put out the blaze? At my age the whole business of birthdays is rather embarrassing. But Mariko is too young to be as jaded as I. After her loss and hardship I thought a birthday celebration might be just the thing to cheer her up. I pushed the typewriter aside and told her that we would spend the day doing whatever she wanted.

At this proposal Mariko grew very shy: 'Really . . . I don't want to do anything special – I mean, not this year . . .'

'It doesn't have to be special,' I said. 'Just whatever you feel like doing.'

Mariko tucked a strand of hair behind her ear, turned to the window and examined the clear blue sky. 'Well, we could go for a picnic,' she said.

So together we prepared a hamper of seaweed rice balls and a flask of oolong tea. Then we set off to the train station to buy two day returns to Arashiyama.

How many times have you and I been to Arashiyama? It must be a hundred or more! I can think of no better place to admire the cherry blossom and maple leaves, and the other beautiful effects of seasonal change, than Arashiyama. However, I think that you will be disappointed by the district's decline in recent years. The vending machines and tourists have quadrupled, and one cannot turn a corner without running into a stall selling green-tea ice cream or tacky souvenirs. Yet despite this, Arashiyama still manages to cling to some of its rustic charm. It was Mariko's first ever visit and the mountain forests and glistening lake had her in transports of delight.

Before lunch we trekked up Monkey Mountain to visit the monkeys that live there. What a mean and savage bunch they were! At the top we went inside the feeding cage and passed them pumpkin slices through the chicken wire. They snatched violently, red-eyed and Einstein coiffed, man-handling and swiping at each other to get at the food. The children enjoyed the full-scale monkey riot very much indeed, taunting them further with potato crisps. But Mariko shuddered and emptied out her bag of pumpkin slices all at once, just to get it over with.

After lunch we hired a small boat and took it in turns to row ourselves about the lake. For someone with such thin arms Mariko proved to be a competent little rower. Above the mountains encircling the lake the sky shone forget-me-not blue, and the tranquil waters shimmered, made iridescent by the touch of the sun. Laughter drifted from nearby boats as children and couples frolicked. Tourist rickshaws drawn along by sturdy young men rattled over the bridge in the distance. After a while we gave the oars a rest and let ourselves drift. Not much was said as the boat gently rocked; only a few words of praise for the idyllic scenery, or the occasional accolade to the fine weather.

That evening when we returned to Osakako station I gave Mariko the house keys and sent her home ahead of me with strict orders not to do any cooking. Holding the empty picnic hamper, Mariko shook her head and smiled, insist-ing that I was not to go to any trouble. After she left I hurried into the supermarket before it closed and bought a birthday cake, a gourmet box of sushi and a large, expensive bottle of sake. As I picked out the sake I wondered if it was necessary, as I am a teetotaller, and I had yet to hear Mariko profess a liking for alcohol. But I decided the occasion called for it. After all, Mariko had just reached the legal drinking age of twenty.

When I got back, shopping bags hanging at my side, I was surprised to see the front door wide open and Mariko standing on the lawn, hugging herself against the chilly night air. It struck me as very odd that she should be standing by herself in the dark.

'Mariko?' I said. 'What are you doing out here? Are you OK?'

'Yes, I am fine . . .' She wore a perplexed expression. 'I heard a noise, like someone was scraping the wall at the side of the house. I came out to have a look. But there is no one there.'

I peered down the narrow gully between the Tanaka residence and mine. It was dark and empty. All the lights in the Tanaka residence were out, suggesting that they had already left for their Saturday night mah-jong at the community centre.

'It must have been the Murasaki cat,' I said, hungry and unconcerned. 'It often goes on the prowl after dark. Why don't we go inside now. I have a treat for you.'

To mark the festive occasion I covered the kitchen table with a white cloth and took out our best china and sake cups. Then I folded some red napkins into swans. The sushi was ready made, so all I had to do was remove the lid of the box to reveal the mouth-watering platter of yellowtail, octopus and cod roe beneath. Once prepared, I sat and waited for Mariko to finish her bath.

She was very swift, and before long the excited patter of bare feet came down the stairs. She slowed with ladylike restraint before she entered the kitchen, the damp patches on the shoulders of her dress indicating she had been too impatient to towel-dry her hair properly.

'Mr Sato! I thought I told you not to go to any trouble.'

Her face was vivid with delight. How little it takes to make her happy! I pulled out her chair and she sat, reaching out to admire one of the swan napkins. We put our hands together and said thanks, then began to eat, dipping our sushi in soya, and squeezing pickled ginger from the sachets. Mariko poured us both sake and did a funny impersonation of Deputy Senior Managerial Supervisor

Murakami when he is drunk. It really made me chuckle. She has a very sharp wit for a girl so young.

When we had had our fill of sushi I threw the box away and made Mariko cover her eyes while I took out the birthday cake and decorated it with twenty candles. I lit the candles and turned out the light. I think I might have already been a little tipsy from the sake, for I began to sing, 'Happy birthday to you, Happy birthday to you . . .' in very bad English. Mariko opened her eyes, and laughed and clapped her hands. When I asked her to make a wish she closed her eyes tightly and blew at the candles with all her might.

Later we sat at the kitchen table with the gooey, chocolatey remains of our cake, joking that our stomachs were ready to burst at the seams. A third of the sake was already gone, for working in a hostess bar had taught Mariko to keep the drinks replenished. I tuned the radio into a golden oldies station, with lots of lovely tunes by the Beatles and Simon and Garfunkel and suchlike. As we sat drinking I told Mariko about the folk clubs we used to go to in Tokyo, the sweet clouds of patchouli incense, and the cosy nooks lit by candles in Chianti bottles. I told Mariko about the faded bell-bottoms I once wore, and the waist-coat embroidered with a rainbow. At this Mariko giggled until she nearly fell sideways off her chair.

'I bet your university days were really fun. I wish I could have been there in the Sixties.'

'The Seventies, Mariko. I was just a schoolboy in the Sixties.'

Later, when the level of the sake bottle had sunk even further down, Mariko said: 'Thank you, Mr Sato.'

'Really, Mariko, you keep on saying that! There is no need. Once is enough.'

'I could thank you until the end of time and it still wouldn't be enough.'

'If you thanked me until the end of time I would sorely regret ever having helped you.'

Mariko's laughter tinkled like a bell above a shop door. Sensing the onset of a headache I closed my eyes and rubbed my temples, my elbows on the table like a sloppy teenager. Owing to my alcohol intolerance my face had grown unbearably hot. I was relieved when Mariko brought in a small table lamp from the living room to use in place of the harsh kitchen light. I was sure that my cheeks had turned an unsightly shade of red.

My drunkenness confounded me. For years I had been very careful not to drink too much at work-related functions, and was constantly turning down invitations to after-hours drinking parties. Yet here I was at my own kitchen table, watching the jars in the spice rack revolve as if they were on a carousel. The irony did not escape me.

Headache aside, I began to enjoy the floating sensation of being drunk. Mariko was happy, talkative, and a pleasure to be with. Instead of paying attention to the words she said, I found myself admiring her pretty face and thinking what a fine young woman she will turn out to be. Back-lit by the table lamp, her features were charmingly sphinx-like, and every time she smiled her even white teeth gleamed. For hours we filled the kitchen with our senseless chatter, laughing for laughter's sake as golden oldies played in the background. The sake seemed to dissolve the filter between my mind and mouth. A question I had previously thought too intrusive to ask slipped out.

'When will you go back to Fukuoka?' I said to Mariko. 'Do you intend to return to your family there?'

Mariko held her gaze clear and steady and said: 'No, Mr Sato, I do not. Fallen blossoms do not return to branches.'

Mariko spoke as if this silly proverb were an eternal truth. I thought this very sad indeed and tried to persuade her otherwise.

'Blossoms are one thing, Mariko,' I said, 'and families another.'

Mariko fell quiet and thoughtful.

'And you are not a fallen blossom,' I added.

At this, Mariko looked up at me. 'Thank you, Mr Sato, but you speak of what you do not know.'

She laughed softly in embarrassment, making me regret my breach of manners. I did not want to put Mariko into a melancholy mood – after all, this was supposed to be her birthday celebration. Mariko picked up the much diminished sake and poured some more into my cup. Though I had found it disagreeable at the start of the evening, the sake now went down like sugar water. The radio was playing 'Puff the Magic Dragon'. I closed my eyes and imagined a beautiful jade- and emerald-scaled dragon swooping over the hills of Arashiyama.

'I like it here. I am very happy,' I heard Mariko say.

I opened my eyes, relieved to abandon the dragon, whose ambitious loop-the-loops had begun to make me queasy. 'I am glad to hear it, Mariko,' I said.

'I have never known anyone as kind as you, Mr Sato. The way you have welcomed me into your home . . .'

'Really, Mariko, in a week or two you will be dying to escape my boring, fusty old ways. You must think of this house as the place where time stands still.'

Mariko was quiet for a moment, then she smiled and said: 'I wish it would stand still for ever.'

The alcohol had made me drowsy, so we retired at ten o'clock. I stood before the bathroom mirror, watching my reflection sway as I haphazardly brushed my teeth. The jukebox in my head was stuck on a remembered snatch of Simon and Garfunkel, a jumble of foreign syllables, meaningless to me. I soaped and rinsed my face with cold water, then I stumbled into the spare room and undressed, tossing my discarded clothes all over the floor. I pulled on clean pyjamas and unrolled my futon. Within a few seconds I had sunk into sweet oblivion.

I woke not much later, sensing that I had not been asleep long. I had been dreaming of you. In the dream we were in a boat, in the middle of an empty lake. You were afraid of the water and begged to be taken to the shore. So I began to row to the jetty. But as is always the case in these dreams, the harder I rowed, the further away the jetty seemed to be. Though I was dreaming I understood this paradox, but could not bring myself to stop rowing. It was a very powerful dream and I woke disorientated, wondering how the devil I had managed to row the boat into the spare room.

A figure was standing at the end of my futon. It was Mariko in a long white nightdress. Behind her the curtains were open, and yellow light streamed in from a neighbouring house. Raindrops, falling at a slant, tapped lightly at the windowpane.

'Mariko?' I said. 'What is the matter?'

I sat upright. With her back to the window, Mariko's face was in darkness, her hair loose about her shoulders.

'I had a dream,' she whispered.

'A nightmare?'

The outside light shone through the thin cotton of Mariko's nightdress, drawing my attention to the silhouette of her legs. This shadowy intimacy was most disconcerting and I wanted to get up and switch on the light.

'No, not a nightmare. And maybe not a dream either. I heard a voice – the same voice that urged me to take up that cello yesterday. The same voice that told me to go to your office.'

Her whispers lifted the hairs on the back of my neck. I wanted to hear more, but I was concerned by how inappropriate it was for Mariko to come to me in the dark, in only her nightdress.

'She said that I mustn't let you live alone any more,' Mariko said.

Her shadowy face was deathly serious. I remembered her tale of the woman who knelt by her bed and spoke to her. The woman with your name. The air beneath my duvet became clammy.

'I am quite happy living alone,' I said, hoping my

brisk tone of voice would drive out the eerie atmosphere.

Mariko stood quietly, waiting to hear more. The drawstring at the neck of her nightdress was untied, exposing the ivory wings of her collar-bone.

'I am sorry that you had a bad dream, Mariko, but I think you ought to go back to bed. We can talk about this in the morning.'

'What I have to say cannot be said in the morning,' Mariko said.

'Well, if it cannot be said in the morning, then perhaps it shouldn't be said at all. I think you had too much sake and need to go and sleep it off.'

'I barely had a drop.'

'Please go now, Mariko. We will talk tomorrow.'

'If you think I have a choice whether or not to be here, Mr Sato, you are mistaken. I chose to be here no more than you chose to walk into the bar that night.'

'Really, Mariko, you are making no sense.'

'We were led to each other. Don't you see?'

It made me light-headed to hear this secret intuition of mine spoken out loud. An intuition I have had since the night she stole into my office. Perhaps you have known of it all along. As I sat dumbstruck, Mariko took the opportunity to lift up the skirt of her nightdress. Before I had time to realize what she was up to, she had pulled the dress over her head. It fell to the floor beside the cello in a sinking cloud of whiteness.

'Mariko!' I said. I threw back my duvet and leapt up. I twisted my head away, as if Mariko were Medusa and one glance might turn me to stone. 'What on earth are you doing?' I was shocked. Had she been driven mad by grief?

'Why are you afraid to look at me, Mr Sato?' she asked calmly, as though I were the aberrant one.

I turned my eyes back to her, to where she stood in only her knickers. Everything about her, from her narrow hips to her slight bosom, screamed with obscene youth. She looked at me steadily, as serene and unabashed as Eve before the fall. I switched my gaze to the cello to banish her from my field of vision. I would not let my body respond. I would not.

'Mariko,' I said, 'I am going outside for a walk. When I return I want you to be back in your own room. Do you understand?' My hands were shaking as though I had some disorder of the nervous system.

'OK,' Mariko replied. 'I promise to go and leave you alone. But first, you must look at me again.'

'No,' I said.

'I promise you. Look once and if you still want me to go away and leave you alone I will. For ever, if that is what you want.'

Who was this changeling who had possessed Mariko and cornered me in my own home? I wanted to bolt for the door, but was nervous she would block my path. My eyes roved desperately along the dark spines in the bookcase.

'Why are you doing this?' I asked.

'Why do you think?' she whispered.

'I think you have taken leave of your senses!'

'She says she is sorry for what she did. That you were a good husband, but she could not go on in this world . . .'

Well, I was livid. Never have I wanted to hit a woman as I wanted to hit Mariko right then. But it passed, thank God. I turned my head and looked her straight in the eye. Her nudity had lost all its power.

'My wife did not kill herself,' I said. 'You do not have the slightest idea what you are talking about. I do not know who has been visiting you from the spirit world, but let me tell you this: it certainly isn't my wife.'

Mariko's confidence did not falter. She stood there bold as can be. Either she was truly convinced, or lying through her teeth. It did not matter. Her integrity had vanished in my eyes.

'She told me that you would not believe me at first. She told me that I must give you time.'

'Why are you doing this, Mariko?'

'You mustn't resist the truth.'

'Who are you?' I asked. I truly did not know any more. Everything she had told me was suddenly cast into doubt. Why was she making up these lies? What end did it serve?

Mariko began to move towards me, but stopped at the chime of the doorbell. The doorbell never rings at night, and the intrusion felt surreal. Mariko looked behind her and back again, uncertainty flickering in her eyes. 'Leave it,' she said.

But I had already sprinted from the room.

Outside, the flashing lights of an ambulance bathed our lawn. At the door, beneath a large, rain-drummed umbrella, stood Mrs Tanaka's niece Naoko with Mr Tanaka in his wheelchair. So unexpected was the sight of the ambulance I wondered if I had opened the front door into a parallel universe. Had the sinister melodrama upstairs really managed to distract me from all this? Across the road Mr and Mrs Ue were at their living-room window, noses pressed to the glass.

'Naoko!' I exclaimed. 'What is going on?'

'My aunt is in that ambulance,' Naoko said gravely. 'She fell and knocked herself unconscious in the garden this afternoon. She had been lying there for several hours before my uncle telephoned for help.'

'Oh, no!' The news winded me like a punch in the stomach.

Mr Tanaka grimaced, his lips like slippery eels. He looked very disgruntled to be out in the cold and wet so long after his bedtime.

'They say she is in a coma,' Naoko continued.

The ambulance began to pull away, the siren wail starting up.

'They are taking her to Casualty . . .'

A lump of sorrow caught in my throat. 'Are you going there too?' I asked.

Naoko nodded. 'We are leaving now.'

'OK,' I said. 'Wait one minute. I just have to change my clothes.'

III

Mrs Tanaka has been transferred to a private room in the head injuries ward. They have just let us see her. Oh, it was awful! She has an oxygen mask on her face and tubes coming from everywhere. Weighted by the cruel hands of gravity, the flesh of her face hung slack and sallow. The doctor came and spoke to Naoko and me. He said that her condition is stable and there is a good chance of her pulling through. Naoko wept very hard when the doctor told us this, even though it is good news. I patted Naoko's shoulder, then I excused myself to go to the bathroom, where I splashed my face with cold water. Afterwards I went to the hospital pay phone, inserted some change and dialled our home telephone number. The phone was picked up after the first ring.

'Yes?' Mariko said.

She sounded wide awake though it was nearly two o'clock.

'Mariko,' I said, 'I am staying at the hospital tonight. I want you to know that you are welcome to stay at my house. But first you have to tell me what is going on. And why you lied to me the way you did.'

I waited. From the other end of the line came a hesitant silence. Then a deep breath and a sob as Mariko began to cry.

19

MARY

The car gutter-crawls through the grid of streets, modifying its course now and then, like the line of an Etch-a-sketch. We drive by the Umeda ferris wheel and the flashing arcades. Everyone seems caught in a mood of excited abandon, the neon buzz as heady an aphrodisiac as the full moon. Girls emerge from print-club booths to giggle over their pictures, their cutesy poses and love-heart motifs. A new tribe of male bar hosts, slick in Comme des Garçons suits, sweet-talk passing women into their clubs for champagne and exorbitant tête-à-têtes. I am uneasy about being chauffeured like this, like some imitation VIP. At the traffic lights we purr in challenge to the other cars, quietly confident of our superiority. I want to tap on the partition between me and the driver and ask where we are going, but the partition must be up to avoid just that. I twist my neck round as we pass over the Yodo river, discomfited to see the Osaka I am familiar with slipping away. We join a motorway and I read the *kanji* signs listing the exits for commuter satellite towns: Amagasaki 5 km, Tarakazuka 9 km. Is this where we are headed? My chest is tight, my stomach an aviary of fluttery birds. The last time I had a case of nerves like this was when I first arrived in Japan, jet-lagged and culture-shocked. I ease the slippers lent by Mama-san off my feet and massage the pinched flesh above my toes. None of Mama-san's shoes fit me and she was in too much of a rush to go down to the dressing room to find something in my size. So she gave me her toilet slippers – the very same pair she slides her dainty feet into before squatting atop the porcelain shrine. They were the only things she had that could accommodate my *gaijin* feet. If I was Japanese I would be mortified to be breaking the sacred taboo 'thou shalt not wear toilet slippers in public'. But I'm not, so the cultural stigma is at one remove. Let others be mortified on my behalf.

The BMW rolls into the outskirts of a small town, shunning the township lights, and turning onto a dirt track parallel to the railway lines. The area is desolate and lonely, the only buildings haunted-looking shacks. The car bounces along, the suspension jolted by the stones and potholes. What would Yuji be doing out here? Is the driver taking me to the right place? I try to remember what he looks like behind that partition: tall, broad, wearing a uniform and chauffeur's cap. Was it my imagination or was that a homicidal glint I saw in his eye as he opened the door for me? The headlights are the only source of light now, illuminating a few metres either side of the car, rendering visible bamboo thickets, a rusting bicycle, an abandoned refrigerator, its door hanging from the hinges like a dislocated jaw.

The engine drone shifts in pitch as we turn into a decaying yard, at the end of which sits a house with windows behind wooden shutters. We stop and the driver's door clicks open. A moment later mine does too.

'This is it,' he announces.

I climb out onto the hard-packed earth. There are stars in the sky and a distant bonfire smell.

'What is this place? Is Yuji here?'

The driver gives a shrug of indifference, impatient to

drive away and leave me outside this derelict house, the kind dumb teenagers in slasher movies use for games of hide-and-seek. The glare of the headlights picks out the busted neon sign above the porch: *LOTUS BAR*. More neon tubing is attached to the wall, twisted into the likeness of a curvy, hour-glass woman; classy. By the door an upturned paint can sits in a puddle of green emulsion. A vandal has splashed green paint along the bottom of the wall and all across the doorway. In the headlights I can see the paint has been splashed right round the corners, to encircle the building in a ring of green. I remember something I learnt in a history lesson, half a lifetime ago, about the red crosses they painted on doors to mark out households with the plague.

I turn to the driver with pleading eyes. 'Can you wait with me while I check whether Yuji is in there?'

But he is already reopening his door, ducking down so his chauffeur's cap doesn't get knocked off by the door frame.

'Please . . . just for a minute or two.'

The driver slams the car door and fires the ignition. Jesus, he's going to leave me here. I want to thump the windscreen but instead I watch him go. The headlights vanish back down the dirt track and the yard is devoured by darkness, leaving me with nothing left to do but venture inside.

There is no doorbell, but the lock is broken. The first thing I see when I swing open the door are the candles, dozens and dozens of them, everywhere. Stout candles without holders, dripping wax on the tables, over the bar. Everything is bathed in their cathedral glow. The walls are alive with flickering shadow, the cobwebs in high corners transformed into a gossamer canopy. Beneath the deceptive gilt of the candles I can see the bar top has been eaten away by mildew, gangrenous with decay.

'Mary.' Yuji is behind me in the doorway. He must have hidden outside when he heard the car coming. For a split second I think that he is wearing a mask, his face is so disfigured by swellings and blood.

In English I murmur: 'Jesus, Yuji . . .'

I rush over and hug him, half crying. He must hurt so much.

'I know. I look like shit.'

The front of his T-shirt is stiff with dried blood. I hug him again and Yuji sucks in his breath as my arms crush something damaged. I pull back and touch his face, sticky with congealed blood. His forehead bears a two-inch gash, like someone tried to hack a second mouth below his hairline.

'Oh God. You need to go to the hospital, you need to get . . .' I don't know the word for 'stitches'. '. . . You need to get sewn up.'

'It'll heal by itself.'

'But it must hurt.'

'I've got used to it.'

'Where are we? What is this place?'

'Some old bar. It's safe here.'

'Your nose looks strange. Is it broken?'

'I don't think so. They broke my tooth, though.'

'Who broke your tooth? Who are "they"?'

'Masked assassins. Ninjas. They came down from the sky on ropes. Twelve of them. They've learnt their lesson, though. They won't be coming back round here for a while.'

A loud reverberation comes up through the ground, shaking the building like an epileptic fit. The candle flames quiver wildly and the venetian blinds chatter.

'They're back,' he says solemnly, 'to finish the job.'

The train rumbles off into the distance and I smile and slap him lightly on the shoulder, embarrassed. He grins back and I see the chip missing from his tooth.

'My mother told me what happened. I'm sorry.' Yuji cups my face in his hands. 'It's my fault you went through all that. I don't know how I can ever make it up to you . . .'

'Please, it's not your fault. Nothing happened to me, nothing compared with what they have done to you. I don't care about . . .'

He kisses me, tentatively at first, careful of his split lip. But then harder, so I taste the metal of his blood. Another train sends the bar into seizure, rattling the loose slats on the walls, the dusty glasses behind the bar. We drop to our knees and Yuji pushes me down onto the floor. I run my hands beneath his T-shirt, helping him pull it over his head. He fumbles at the buttons of my shirt and I help him with those as well. I pull him down close, whispering that I want him, lifting my hips so his hands can slide underneath. His mouth traces an invisible trail, over my collar-bone and breasts, down to my navel. I run my thumb beneath the cut in his forehead before I tug him back up to feel his mouth on mine again. He pulls away, looks away, says he looks fucking awful. I shake my head and tell him, no, he looks fantastic, always does. He laughs and calls me a liar. So we roll onto his back, and I hitch up my skirt and lift myself astride him, to see if I can't prove him wrong.

In the midst of the ruins, the candles are burning themselves down, extinguishing one by one in a puff of darkness. I sit in my knickers and underwired bra, my skirt and blouse cast aside, defiled by grime and fingerprints. Yuji is lying down, shirtless, staring at the damp sunken ceiling. He smokes a Marlboro from the packet I brought, and after twenty-four hours' abstinence is heavy-lidded with near-narcotic delight. Cross-legged beside him, I dab at the gash on his ribs with some cotton soaked in antiseptic. Yuji winces and sucks air through his teeth. 'Keep still,' I say: 'it's for your own good.' We grin at each other, because I sound like the school nurse. Every so often the patter of tiny paws can be heard, as dark shapes dart from one side of the room to the other, wary of the rise and fall of our voices. The mobile phone Mama-san gave me lies dormant on the floor beside us, waiting to be rung.

'I can't believe my mother gave you her toilet slippers,' Yuji drawls.

'You spend the night soaked in your own blood and still you find fault with my shoes.'

'*Toilet slippers* . . . There's a big difference . . . Ouch.'

I apologize, and blow across the graze to take the sting away. Then kiss him on the forehead again, because tonight I can't seem to stop kissing him.

He lifts back the tent my hair has made over his face. 'Your hair is tickling my cuts.'

I pull it back over my shoulders. The hand not holding the cigarette rubs my lower back, probing beneath my knicker elastic. Another bullet train shoots by, shaking the walls. The clock on the phone says it is exactly ten. I trace the ridge of hair, the tufts and whorls leading down from his belly button to the waistband of his Levi's.

'Why did you do it?' I ask.

'Do what?'

'Take that money. Steal Yamagawa-san's drugs.'

The hand fondling my lower back grows still. 'For us. I told you already. So we could leave Japan. It was fucking stupid, I know . . .'

'But the drugs went missing *before* you needed the money to leave Japan. Hiro told me they broke into your apartment because of the missing drugs. And it was after that you wanted to leave.'

A geyser of smoke plumes from his mouth. 'I had planned to leave long before I told you about it. That time after the break-in was the first time I mentioned it to you, that's all. I wanted to keep all that shit separate from you. It wasn't until we knew each other better that I asked you to come.'

Yuji's eyes break with mine and he gingerly touches his swollen eyelid. I am hurt. All those months and he never said anything. The candlelight weaves through the blades of the ceiling fan, casting baroque shadows up above. He turns away slightly, telling me the subject is closed, that I'd better stick to the language of flesh and touch. But I have to know more.

'What happened to the drugs, Yuji? Did you sell them?'

Yuji is quiet for a while, brooding. Finally he says: 'I really don't want to talk about this. You live in a different world, Mary. You wouldn't understand . . .'

This riles me. 'How do you know I wouldn't understand?'

'I want to be honest with you but I don't want you to hate me.'

'I could never hate you.'

Yuji resumes staring at the ceiling. I kiss him again, on the shoulder this time. *I could never hate you.* Not a lie exactly. More a statement of faith. A train screeches by, a pterodactyl on rails. Shadows oscillate, and the walls judder, flimsy as a low-budget soap-opera set.

'Why does Hiro hate you so much?'

Yuji sits up, wincing at the parts that hurt when moved. Reluctantly he meets my eyes. 'We used to be friends,' he says. 'Until we both started working for Yamagawa-san.'

'What made you fall out?'

'Yamagawa-san took a shine to Hiro. After a few months he was always taking him aside, talking to him in private. It pissed everyone off, me most of all. I got jealous, we stopped talking, drifted apart. It was immature, I suppose.'

'That's not the only reason, though.'

'No. About a year ago someone set Hiro up to make it look like he had screwed Yamagawa-san over. He was punished and sent away from Osaka. He thought I was the one who set him up.'

'Do you know who it was?'

Yuji shakes his head. 'No.' He stares into the empty space beside me. 'They put acid on his face,' he says. 'I saw them do it. I didn't hold him down or anything. But I had to watch, I had no choice. I still have nightmares about it – his screaming, the smell.'

I reach out and touch his hand. I am sickened that he stood by and watched it all, but at the same time I believe

him when he says he had no choice. This is what we have
to leave behind.

'Have you seen him since?'

Yuji pulls his hand away from mine. 'He came here today
with a gun.'

My heart thuds. I thought he said it was safe here. 'Are
you serious! To shoot you?'

'In the face.'

'Oh God.' I can't see my face but I am sure it is a
caricature of fear. 'But you're OK, though. Why didn't he?
What stopped him?'

'He had the barrel in my mouth, finger on the trigger,
when his phone rang. If I hadn't had a mouthful of gun right
then, I would have laughed. I thought he would ignore it, but
he answered, listened to whoever it was, then turned and
walked away. Just like that. Without a word. I lay on the
floor, sweat pouring off my face, waiting for him to come
back and finish me off. Then I heard his car drive away.'

I try to imagine what that must have been like, but my
mind is blank.

'Who was on the phone?'

Yuji shrugs. 'Yamagawa-san, or maybe he answers to
someone else now. That boy who works for my mother –
you know, the boy who is strange in the head. He was with
him, and stood over there . . .' Yuji points to the door and
I look over, almost expecting to see a figure in the shadows
'. . . just *staring* at me. When I get out of here he's not
gonna be making pizzas for my mother any more. I'll make
sure of that.'

'*Watanabe*?'

'Is that what he's called? Watanabe?'

Watanabe? Mixed up in all this? Is anything as it seems
any more?

'Did Hiro do all that to your face?'

Yuji taps the gash below his hairline. 'Maybe this one.
It's hard to remember who did what. In the last twenty-four
hours I've been everyone's favourite bitch.'

He grins and I try to smile back, dumbfounded his sense of humour has survived all this.

'What's to stop him from coming back?' I ask.

'Trust me, he's not coming back,' he replies, with easy assurance.

'How can you be so sure?'

'Trust me. He won't.'

Yuji strokes the back of my head and I lean towards him, my head in my hands, despairing. I yearn for the semi-ignorance of before, to slam the lid on Pandora's box and never go near it again.

My memory snags on another item on the long list of Yuji's crimes. 'Hiro said that you told his fiancée he was dead.'

Yuji stiffens. 'I had no choice. She took it well. No tears; she just asked me to leave. She went to work as usual the next day. Never mentioned it to anyone.'

'How did you say he died?'

'Gunshot wound.'

'She knows the truth now. She must hate you.'

'She knew the truth from the start. And she doesn't hate me; she knows I was just doing my job.'

I fall quiet, turning things over in my head.

Yuji mistakes this for the silent treatment. 'Look, Mary, what do you want me to say? Do you think that I don't already feel guilty, every single day? I stood by and watched them torture my best friend. I've known that Hiro has been back for weeks now. I've been expecting him. When he held that gun to my face today, do you know what I thought? *Good. Pull the trigger. Give me what I deserve.*'

'Don't talk like that. How does being shot in the face help anything?'

'I fucked everything up,' Yuji says. 'All I want to do is pay my dues and get out. I just want this to be over. I'd cut off my own hand just to get out of this.'

'Stop it. We are leaving, remember? We can leave and never come back.'

I put my arms round him, breathing in the antiseptic rising from his pores. The night has cooled, but his flesh is hot, like all the sins he has yet to atone for are burning him inside. I hold him quietly, feeling the pressure of something left unsaid. Some words of reassurance, to ease the weight on his conscience. Now is the right time, but nothing comes to mind.

All that remains of the candles are pools of wax, moulded against the grain of the floorboards, opaque splashes on table legs, where drips hardened mid-descent. We lie in each other's arms, our eyes soaking up the darkness like sponges. It is midnight and our stomachs are growling together. We smoke Marlboros and swig from an ancient bottle of sake to ease our hunger pangs (Yuji hasn't eaten for over twenty-four hours and swears he can feel his stomach is digesting itself). Between swigs from the dusty bottle Yuji talks about his past, the school he was sent to, how he used to resent his mother for being a hostess. I listen, interrupting only to ask the meaning of a word I don't know. Yuji never usually talks like this to me; he is aware of the departure too. He keeps pausing, apologizing for boring me. I ignore his apologies and tell him to go on, not wanting to miss a thing.

The phone rings while Yuji is talking. Set on vibrate, it writhes over the floorboards in cellular exorcism. Yuji pounces, breath held in suspense. I listen to the low grumble of static, the authoritative monotone. It lasts for half a minute. Yuji says nothing until the caller hangs up.

'Well?'

'That was my mother. A car is on its way. It will take us to Yamagawa-san. He wants to talk to me first, then we are free to leave Osaka.'

'What does he want to talk to you about? Shit! What if he wants to do to you what he did to Hiro?'

Yuji puts a hand on my shoulder, squeezes it. 'Listen. If my mother brought this about, then we are not in any danger. Yamagawa-san wants to see me so he can lay down the law. Then he will let me go. My mother has spoken to him and he has promised her.'

'And you trust him?'

'Well, no. I think he wants to break my fingers . . .'

'*Yuji!*'

He laughs. 'Sorry . . . Listen, he knows I've already had the crap kicked out of me. He just wants to give me a talking-to. No one skips town without the farewell speech. My crime wasn't serious and my mother is his close friend.' He picks up his bloodied T-shirt, shakes it out and pulls it over his head. 'You don't have to come with me,' he says.

'I go where you go,' I say.

Yuji threads his arms through his T-shirt sleeves. I reach for my crumpled skirt.

'Are you scared?' I ask.

'No.'

'I am.'

'Mary, they're not gonna do anything to you . . .'

'It's not me I'm scared for.'

'Just think, in a few hours' time we won't be in Japan any more. My mother is sorting out our passports and plane tickets as we speak.'

The BMW pulls into the yard, headlights glaring. The chauffeur who drove me here lurches out, as poker-faced as an undertaker. He stares through us as though we are transparent, ghosts of the condemned, unworthy of his acknowledgement. He pulls open the back door without so much as a glimmer in the direction of Yuji's battered face.

In the back seat I whisper: 'He's strange. Do you know him?'

Yuji shakes his head, thoughts engaged elsewhere. The ignition sparks and the BMW pulls out of the yard, over the stony track, back past the bamboo and corrugated-iron fences. We roll into a built-up area, and are stared at by two *bozoku*, straddling Harleys, in a 7–11 car park.

Graveyard-shift workmen in yellow boiler suits are drilling up the road. A man in a hard hat and reflector vest waves us through the detour with a flashing wand. Yuji is silent, but his nerves generate a near-audible hum. He was lying when he said he wasn't scared. I want time to speed up for us, so that the meeting is already over, or to slow down, so it never arrives. We avoid looking at each other. I squeeze his hand. And he squeezes mine back, transfixed by the world beyond his azure-tinted window.

Though Yamagawa-san's bar is just a few streets away from The Sayonara Bar, this is the first time I have been here. It is tucked into a cobbled side street filled with tiny bars with façades of pink neon and names like Pink Panther and Tuesday World. One or two places don't have names, just blacked-out windows and heavy-set doormen. Outside Diamonds Are Forever two Japanese drag queens flourish cigarette holders aloft, rouged as pantomime dames, lending the street a carnival atmosphere. A disembodied karaoke howl rips through the night as somewhere, not so far away, a falling-down-drunk salaryman insists he did it 'My Way'.

Yamagawa-san's bar is called The Seven Wonders. The clientele are exclusively salarymen, grouped round large tables. Above each table a large plasma screen is suspended, each boasting a virtual construct of one of the seven wonders of the world. The one closest to me shows the Pyramids. The perspective dips and glides, soaring overhead, exploring the Sphinx from the viewpoint of a circling bird. As well as the plasma screens each table has its own hostess in a beautiful dove-white kimono. Ebony hair secured into chignons, skin translucent from whitening lotions, the hostesses smile and pour drinks, possessed of an understated elegance that suggests hidden toil.

'What kind of bar is this?' I ask Yuji.

Yuji doesn't hear me. A handful of salarymen overshadowed by the Hanging Gardens of Babylon are having

a sly gawp at the wreckage of his face. The hostesses blank
us completely, in a forced manner that makes me think they
know exactly who we are and what we are doing here.

Yuji turns to me and says: 'Listen, Mary, I want you to
wait at the bar while I go and speak to Yamagawa-san.'

'No. I'm coming with you.'

'I won't be gone for long. Just wait here.'

I shake my head, determined not to back down. 'I'm
coming with you.'

He drops my arm. 'OK.'

The hostess concocting drinks makes no attempt to stop
us when Yuji leads me behind the bar. Yuji opens the door
leading to a stairwell and I glance back in time to catch her
violet irises flash in my direction. A click of recognition and
her eyes break away. She is the young mother I saw at
Mama-san's bar fourteen hours ago, wearing coloured
contact lenses. I thought she said that she hated hostessing.

Yuji pulls me by the hand. 'C'mon . . .' he says.

We go up a flight of stairs leading to a short corridor,
where the starkly plastered walls act as sounding boards for
the thud of blood in our hearts. The fluorescent strip light
is broken, stuttering like a defective stroboscope. Yuji
inhales, as though oxygen will lend him the courage he
needs, and knocks on the door. A gruff voice shouts at us
to wait; then, in the next breath, to enter. Yamagawa-san
rises from behind his desk as we walk into the dark room.
The walls are blacker than black, as though they have been
painted with some light-absorbing pigment. A plasma
screen, sister of the multimedia downstairs, emits the
only source of light. Virtual tropical fish flit about, their
rainbow fins gliding through waters too sparkling and
aquamarine to be real. It is 2 a.m. and Yamagawa-san is
immaculate: his shirt is whiter than white, his hair a carefully sculpted wave.

'Good evening, Yuji.'

'Good evening, Yamagawa-san.'

'Mary.'

'Good evening, Yamagawa-san.'

We bow, deep and prolonged. If it's humility he wants, we've got it in spades. Anything to get out of here with a minimum of fuss. Yamagawa-san is relaxed and informal, like we've just dropped in to say hi. He gestures to two leather chairs, then walks round and perches on the edge of his reconstituted granite desk. As the computer-synergized light falls upon Yamagawa-san's face, I begin to suspect that all is not well. At first it looks like an illusion caused by the ripples of the virtual water, but then I see there is definitely some kind of muscular disturbance going on beneath his skin. His jaw clicks. He is coked up to the hilt.

'You have blood on your shirt,' he remarks to Yuji.

He gets up and slides open an invisible compartment in the wall. He pulls out a brand-new shirt, folded and cellophane-packaged, and tosses it to Yuji. This is an encouraging sign: you don't go to the trouble of giving someone a clean shirt just before you smash his face in. I smooth my skirt and slide my toilet-slippered feet under my chair. Yamagawa-san re-perches, tapping out a rhythm on the table top, creaking his jaw. He smiles. Perhaps his being off his head could work to our advantage.

'You like the Tigers, Mary?'

What? I am flustered for a moment. 'Excuse me?'

'The Hanshin Tigers. Do you like them?'

Oh, baseball. 'Yes, I do.'

'Good girl.'

Yamagawa-san chuckles. I have passed the test. He turns to Yuji, his tone changing.

'Gave you a good beating, didn't they?'

'Yes,' Yuji says. 'I deserved it.'

Yamagawa-san tuts and shakes his head. 'No, Yuji. This is far less than you deserve. Be thankful your mother is who she is, because it is only the sheer accident of birth that saved you from getting what you deserved.'

Yuji nods, listening attentively.

'Anyway, Yuji, what's done is done. Let me run through the terms your mother and I have agreed upon.'

Yamagawa-san lifts his backside from the table again, wiping his palms on his trousers. Light from a virtual fish tints his face with riotous stripes of colour.

'First you must leave Osaka and never come back. And when I say you can never come back, this means *never*. You might be tempted to test the water after a decade or so, or even after a few months, if I know you, Mr Oyagi. Try it and you will be killed. Even after my death – not too soon, touch wood –' he raps the granite desk three times, 'you won't be forgotten. Whoever replaces me will take you on, just as I took on the enemies of Ogawa when he was killed.'

His voice is mellow, even verging on affectionate at times. I am so desperate to be out of here, the condition that we never come back is the most reasonable thing I've ever heard. I am sure Yuji sees it differently, though.

'What else . . . ?' Yamagawa-san asks, directing the question to his memory. 'If you start hankering after the glamour and violence again and toy with the idea of joining another syndicate, don't. I will find out and come and cut out your tongue. Understood?'

Another nod.

'Anyway, it's unhealthy to dwell on the past. Let's toast your new life, your new love.' He smiles at me in an ingratiating way. 'What do you say?'

Yuji nods and Yamagawa-san claps his hands, once.

'Aya-chan, drinks.'

The door opens and the girl from The Sayonara Bar walks in. A fan is tucked into the broad sash of her white kimono. She does not acknowledge me, her rosebud painted lips shut tight, giving nothing away. Beneath her lacquered geisha hairstyle she has eyes for only Yamagawa-san. She shuffles over to him and bows deeply.

'Three whiskies, no ice.'

Aya nods and moves to the wall opposite the plasma screen. She places her palm flat against the wall and it opens into a liquor cabinet. A phalanx of bottles sit upon a mirrored platform of blazing light. As she clinks about with glasses and screw caps I watch the ivory pillow folded from the back of her kimono sash, the downy unlacquered hair at the nape of her neck. Does Yuji know her from when she used to work for his mother? If he is confused by her being here he doesn't show it.

'So, exciting, isn't it, going off into the big, bad world? What are your plans?'

'I don't have any,' Yuji says.

I can hear the hesitancy in his voice. He talks to Yamagawa-san as though treading an active minefield.

'Rubbish! Your mother has booked you on a flight to Seoul that departs from Kansai International at 5 a.m. Still, you are wise to try and keep it from me.'

He smiles and winks at me, molars grinding. The sooner we drink up and leave the better. Aya turns to face us, bearing the tray like a porcelain serving doll. She comes to me first and proffers the whiskies, impervious to my attempts to penetrate the blankness of her face. I take a glass. The geisha robot disarms me with a crafty wink. Then Aya turns her tray to Yuji. As he selects a whisky she leans towards him, smiling. She removes a hand from the drinks tray and pinches the flesh of his cheek. Yuji keeps perfectly still, the whisky held limply in his lap. Aya moves her face closer to his, her teeth glistening behind parted lips, like she wants to take a bite out of him. Then she half sucks, half kisses his bloodied, unresponsive lips. Stunned, I glare at her, suppressing the strongest urge to jump up and yank her off him. At her lapse in professionalism Yamagawa-san only chuckles. Aya runs the tip of her tongue up the side of Yuji's face, over the battlefield of cuts and grazes. She whispers something in his ear, then releases him and turns to Yamagawa-san with the last whisky.

'Thank you, Aya. That will be all.'

Aya bows and glides out of the room. The door closes behind her and blends seamlessly into the black of the wall.

Yamagawa-san raises his glass. 'A toast, Yuji. To your future. May you be happy and grateful for your ill-deserved freedom.'

Yuji and I lean forward to clink glasses with Yamagawa-san before drinking our whiskies.

'Music,' Yamagawa-san announces.

I smile politely. Is he insane? Is he so hard up for company that he is willing to consort with a disgraced gang member and his girlfriend? Can't he see how desperate we are to get out of here? Perhaps he gets a kick out of our discomfort. Yamagawa-san opens a thin laptop on his desk and skims his fingers over the keyboard. Within moments the tinkle of piano keys rains down from speakers in the ceiling. The intro to a forgotten song followed by the genderless, spine-tingling vocals of Chet Baker.

'You like jazz, Mary?' Yamagawa-san asks.

'Yes.'

I'm not so keen really, but, fuck it, what does personal taste matter right now? We sit in silence as Yamagawa-san closes his eyes and sways his head to the music, lost in his jazz connoisseur's delight. In any other circumstances Yuji and I would be in hysterics, exchanging grins at the very least. As it goes we daren't even look at each other. Yamagawa-san's eyes spring open. The head swaying has perked him up and he embarks on some crackhead monologue about Miles Davis that is excruciatingly hard to follow. He then complains about the bad season that the Hanshin Tigers are having, and how he had to confiscate his daughter's credit cards after her recent splurge at the Hankyu ... and so on. I don't get why he is being so friendly. Isn't he angry at Yuji? Maybe he is just in a talkative mood. Tomorrow he'll wake up wondering what the hell he was going on about the night before.

I tune out, lulled by the hypnotic singing and the whisky spreading its warmth right down to my toes. I am surprisingly relaxed now; Yamagawa-san's mindless stream of consciousness must be having a soporific effect. On the plasma screen the virtual fish flit. I let my eyes swim out of focus, so the fish dissolve into a myopic blur, a kaleidoscope of shimmery fish scales. Thrown by this acid montage, I try to flip back into the correct gear, but my eyes continue to swim lazily. Somewhere beneath my drowsy stupor, panic begins to stir. What the fuck is going on? I turn in the direction of Yuji and try to reach across the space between our chairs. Gravity reclaims my arm before it even makes it to his armrest. No reaction is registered on Yuji's part.

Yamagawa-san cuts off mid-sentence. 'Well, Mr Oyagi, it's been a pleasure but I expect you are anxious to be off. You have exactly one hour to collect your belongings and leave Osaka.'

Yuji nods and rises from his chair with enviable ease. My limbs are dense, as though I am at the cusp of a fever.

'Yuji . . . ?' Why is my voice so weak? 'My legs . . .' *My legs feel strange* . . . I reach for his hand, but it seems to evade mine. Panic eddies and corkscrews in my gut. This cannot be happening. 'No . . .'

I try to reach again but my arm is not co-operating. The room will not stay still. Jazz crashes atonally in my ears, and the walls swell and oscillate. At the door two blurry figures are shaking hands. The door closes. I struggle to bear with it, flailing at the last dregs of consciousness, but find myself letting go. It's easier.

20

WATANABE

I lie on my back, fallen from heights beyond imagining. A pale day moon waxes and wanes, framed by the rungs of the fire escape. I lie on a bed of damp cardboard, enclosed by the walls of the Tiger Den and Karaoke La La Land. For the thousandth time I lift my hands to my face and stare into the fate furrows of my palms, valleys and deltas, sedimented with alley silt. I strain so hard my brain cramps. Nothing happens. Frustration and loss pounding in my chest, I flex and flex until I am nearly spent.

A cold drop of water splashes down from the sky onto my brow. Heaven must be weeping me a tear. Or subjecting me to Chinese water torture. Stare into these palms long enough and I will go mad. But I will not surrender. So I stare once more and flex, as somebody very close by begins to scream.

Earlier this afternoon the poseur-mobile swerved all over the road as we piston-crunched back to the city, serenaded by the blaring horns of oncoming cars. One pick-up truck veered into a rice-paddy ditch to escape our kamikaze path, a mishap that barely dented Red Cobra's conscience. We tyre-squealed on through the sleepy suburbs, Red Cobra manhandling the steering wheel as though it had done him harm.

By denying him the fulfilment of revenge, the phone call from Yamagawa-san had torn a great existential cavity in Red Cobra's world. As his white-knuckle passenger I was unsympathetic; I told him not to answer the damn phone. My primary sentiment was anger. At the Lotus Bar we had had fate in our clutches, only to let it flutter away, like a winning lottery ticket in the breeze. Now Mary and I were back where we started, uncertain as two quantum specks in a sea of relativity. God may not play dice, but our good Lord, He does like to rattle them about in his loosely clenched fist.

Red Cobra slammed on the brakes at a bend in the road. The Mercedes spun to a halt, momentum throwing me into my seat belt.

'You. Out,' he hissed.

The road was deserted. Either side of the car potential landslides of bamboo forest were held back by concrete embankments. Red Cobra clutched the steering wheel, ravenous for the solitude in which to indulge his manic despair. That was fine by me. The symbiotic potential of our union was long exhausted as far as I was concerned. I opened the car door and estimated a 17.2-minute hike to the nearest station.

'If you are still worried about Mary,' he murmured, eyes on the windscreen, 'she will show up later at the Seven Wonders.'

I nodded, as if this was something I didn't already know – his self-esteem needed the boost. No sooner had I closed the door than Red Cobra slammed his foot down and tore away, like a man with only an hour left to live. At the time I saw this reckless passion as weak. But I understand enough now to withhold judgement.

I moved along via various modes of public transport to the Street of True Love and hid in the alleyway opposite Yamagawa-san's headquarters. Though Mary would not

WATANABE

arrive for several hours, and my surveillance capacity is independent of spatial proximity, I saw no harm in being prepared. The alley was a rat bonanza, with a vermin density of 4.3 per square metre. As I crossed the stinking threshold, one skulked by with the paws of its offspring dangling from its mouth. This did not perturb me. Pavements, manhole covers and drains: all these barriers between human city dwellers and the rat population dis-integrate beneath my hypersenses. The subterranean activities of these cannibalistic, disease-spreading critters are no mystery to me. And credit where credit's due, they are a damn sight more astute than humans. As I sat on the cardboard, one surveyed me from the fire escape, its tiny eyes glinting in acknowledgement of the paradigm shift I represented for humanity. I gave him a sombre nod before reconvening my extra-sensory espionage.

I somersaulted four streets east to look in on the hostess bar. Alone in the lounge, Mama-san was on the phone to a catering company, trying to secure a replacement chef. Her cranial sacs were still inflamed after having to put to rights the pot plant I knocked over earlier that day. *That boy is long overdue for a sacking*, she seethed, Beethoven's Fifth failing to soothe her as she waited on hold. I moved up a flight to the tiny room where Mary paced the tatami, eat-ing her heart out over Yuji. Barefoot she strode in her cotton bathrobe, the peach down of her limbs gently chaf-ing. Like an infinity of Cubist paintings, her visceral being glistened from every possible aesthetic plane. Twice my hypergaze had to be averted lest it overdose in rapture.

As Mary chewed her lower lip, molecules shuffled in the thought factory of her mind, generating anxiety after anxiety. How easy it would be for us if the blueprint of the universe was Newtonian and mechanistic, I thought. If I could leap ahead in the chain of cause and effect, and fore-cast the next twenty-four hours, then the necessary steps for rescuing Mary would be clear to me.

Alas the universe does not conform to Newton's

clockwork schema. Ours is a cosmos governed by fuzzy logic and paradox. And in this chaotic and random void the future morphs by the nanosecond. What will hatch from these eggs called now? I cannot say. I figured my best bet was to employ my hypersenses to monitor the situation, and then, when the time was right, I would act. Returning to the hostess bar and warning Mary off will not work when she is so hung up on Yuji. And my poor verbal presentation skills would not do justice to my dark prognosis.

Mary knelt beside a low table. Gases exchanged in her lungs and the protein of her toenails regenerated. Life teemed in every cellular unit of her being. I pulsed with pride, for soon she would be my companion in hyperspace. We had only the immediate future to live through first.

Projected into the room above the hostess bar I saw the blind optimism that flooded Mary's mind. I saw the life epicycles of the mites in the woven mats and the silverfish in the book bindings. But the wondrous complexity of it all paled next to my monomania for Mary. My projection into that room above The Sayonara Bar was just another expedition into the mind of god, a trip I long took for granted. Though not for much longer.

My demise began as a hot flush. My micropores leaked sweat. The electrical conductance of my skin leapt up. Tiny fireworks exploded on my retina. Thinking it would pass, I stayed by Mary's side. The mental palpitations did not concern me so much as her welfare. At least not until the fall.

It was like plummeting from a skyscraper. A moment of sheer cardiac terror. The urban landscape sank into absolute flatness. One moment all was bright and fourth-dimensional. Then it flatlined, spewing me back into the alley in the Street of True Love. Numb with shock, I tried to comprehend what had happened. With the exception of my first ever excursion, my sixth sense has never acted independently of my will before. Choking back my panic, I sat up and tried to vault back. Nothing. Rodents whispered in the wheelie bins. Ousted from the guttering, a drip splashed at my feet. Mustering all my strength, I flexed once more. When I saw I was still stranded in the alley my mouth filled with the metallic taste of my worst fear. The spiked jaws of the mantrap had clamped shut on me, incarcerating me in the third dimension. I could feel the blood leeching from my cerebellum as consciousness gave way to the dark splendour of despair.

I came round about six or seven hours later. I cannot say precisely when because the fabric of space-time is no longer accessible to me. How long this spatial castration will last I do not know. I am positive, though, that it is not permanent. One is not bestowed with divine powers only to have them cruelly repossessed. This malfunction of my extra-sensory apparatus will resolve itself in time. I must be patient.

Adjustment has been tough, though. No longer can I read the intimate secrets of passers-by; they have become strangers to me. No longer can I perceive the city as a single entity; an organism of concrete and flesh; gorging on fast food, caffeine and electricity; excreting rubbish, sewage and heat. I am not even privy to the mundane carry-on behind the walls that enclose me. What is the chemical composition of the air I breathe? What thoughts occupy the mind of that rat watching me so intently? Your guess is as good as mine. Most devastating of all, I do not know Mary's whereabouts. For the first time in months my only organs of sight are my eyes. And what wretched, pathetic organs they are.

As soon as I regained consciousness I attempted to contract my hypersense. When I failed, I banshee-screamed the street down. Throughout the night my screaming has enticed many onlookers. Earlier two girls from the Tiger Den came and stood in the alley entrance. They wore tiger-striped catsuits, their detachable ears and whiskers silhouetted against the neon nightscape.

'D'you reckon we ought to call the police?'

'I think he's having a bad trip.'

'He keeps staring at his hands like there's something inside them.'

'*Hey . . . If you've taken too many mushrooms, you just have to ride it out. Chin up, little guy.*'

Later the manager of Karaoke La La Land came out the back way to ask what was the matter. At my non-reply he shrugged and told me to keep it down. At that point I realized it was imperative I got a grip. I had to be alert for the coming of Mary. Without my extra-sensory sense I had begun to fear that I had missed her.

My sense of loss is overwhelming. The evolutionary short circuit in my mind has erased not only my ability to transcend but my memories of transcendence too. Though my mind's eye can summon any colour, sound or smell of the ordinary realm, it cannot summon that which lies beyond. It is as though my travels into the fourth dimension never even happened. Only two things now persuade me to draw my next breath: Mary and the faith that my powers will return.

Since recovering from my breakdown I have been monitoring The Seven Wonders. So far, nothing of interest – just a trickling influx of salarymen and yakuza. The windows are darkened and I cannot see inside.

'Hello.'

'Hello.'

'Still here, then?'

The question is too ridiculous to answer. The girl in the lycra tiger costume lights a cigarette, standing one foot in the street, within sensible fleeing distance should I turn nasty. Her whisker attachments quiver as she sucks on the filter. Behind her the odd punter saunters by, casually checking out her artificial tail. Had I met her a few hours ago I would have sent binary pulsars into her mind to fathom exactly where her need for self-humiliation stems from. Deprived of my resources, I just have to surmise that she is stupid.

'Gone all quiet now, haven't you?'

I ignore her, hoping to bore her into retreat. I focus on the door of The Seven Wonders. No one has gone in or out for at least half an hour now.

'You wanna go in across the road, don't you,' Tiger Girl says.

I look up in surprise. My desire must be stamped on my face. I nod.

'It's a private members' club. Full of hoity-toity hostesses. Like, a million-yen membership,' she says.

'Yakuza,' I add meaningfully.

Tiger Girl laughs. 'Who isn't round here?'

Without my hypersense I am unable to supply her with an accurate answer.

Tiger Girl smokes in silence for a while. Her ponytail is so tight it pulls her face taut, making it sleek and cat-like. 'What was up with you earlier, when you were screaming and all that?' she asks.

I look at her and try to formulate an answer. Is Tiger Girl someone I want to confide in? Whereas before I would have read her psi quotient, now I have only her human interface to go by – that which is on show for the rest of humankind: a tiger impersonator, with sticky-out ribs and a ponytail facelift. 'Nothing,' I say.

'Nothing!' she hoots. 'I'd hate to see how you act when there is *something* the matter with you.'

I gaze stoically past her.

'You know, it's, like, two in morning. Don't you have a home to go to?'

Two o'clock? I straighten up in alarm. How did so many hours sneak by without my noticing?

Tiger Girl's cigarette has now smouldered right down to the butt. 'You can come and sit in the Tiger Den if you like. You can sit at the bar. They ain't gonna let you in across the road, not without membership.'

I look up at her. Is she joking? Her eyes narrow impatiently. Her hand rests on her hip in aggressive come-on. It must be a slow night.

'Well, yes or no? I haven't got all day.'.

Behind her a BMW pulls up.

My heart leaps to attention. At my failure to reply, Tiger Girl utters a few choice words of insult and returns to her bar with a bad-tempered shake of her prosthetic tail. Like a wing beat the back doors of the BMW open in unison. From this acrylic-painted chariot Mary appears. This is the first time I have perceived Mary out of hyperspace. The three-dimensional Mary is a flat, cardboard cut-out of her fourth-dimensional incarnation. Nevertheless, I am deeply stirred by her. Her hair still streams like rivers of gold, her *bijou* eyes still sparkle. Mary possesses a beauty that would make itself known if it had only had one dimension to work with. The nefarious Yuji lurches out too, resembling an extra from *Dawn of the Dead*. I watch Mary follow him inside, my chest tight as a sumo wrestler's embrace.

The door closes behind them and I stand up for the first time in eight hours, only to fall down again, disabled by leg cramp. The auspicious coming of Mary has been and gone. What comes next I do not know. I stand once more and stagger to the Seven Wonders, entering in time to see a shimmer of blond disappearing behind the Staff Only door. I stand at the bar, dead-ended. The corporate drones beneath the television screens are too drunk to notice my entrance, but one of the hostesses does. She glides over in her white kimono, pure as the driven snow. Her skin is pale as angel dust, her hair a black snake coiled round her head.

'I know you,' she says, with an infinitesimal squint of her piercingly violet eyes.

I have no recollection of our acquaintance. Were my hypersenses restored, I would know at once if she was mistaken or not. In the interim I just hope this means she'll let me stick around without coughing up the million-yen membership fee.

'You're the kitchen boy from the hostess bar a few streets over.' She smiles, her voice not exceeding a whisper. 'Get out, kitchen boy. You can't afford to be here. Get out before I get someone to break your arms.'

I slope round to the back door of The Seven Wonders, only to hear the bestial rumble of a yakuza poker game in the kitchen. So I go back to my alleyway and monitor the bar from there, gradually summoning the courage to sidle out from the shadows. Surely no one will break my arms in full view of the drag queens, and the doorman of Tuesday World . . . Who am I kidding? Black eyes and broken noses are all in a night's entertainment for this crowd. I just have to risk it.

Time drags excruciatingly. The neck of the hour glass has narrowed so only one grain of sand can escape at a time. Civilizations fall and rainforests are bulldozed in the time that lapses between each rarefied beat of my heart. Behind the upstairs windows of The Seven Wonders nothing stirs. Waiting is agony. What the hell are they doing in there? Stripped of omniscience, I fall prey to grisly imaginings. I am persecuted by visions of samurai swords, of Mary's blood spilt on the carpet. So vivid is my imagination that I fetch up some battery acid from my stomach and spit it on the street. Another ten minutes and I will go in. I will storm the place. Even if it means the sacrifice of both arms. I cannot stand by and let this happen.

Ten minutes and ten minutes more. The drag queens outside Diamonds Are Forever are falsetto-laughing their heads off at something. The one in the tattered ball gown keeps lifting his hands up and staring into his palms, ferociously bug-eyed. When I look over, they laugh harder and I see that he is doing an impersonation of me. I must be flexing compulsively without even realizing it. Their laughter does not offend me. They know nothing. I would like to see how old Ball Gown would cope if he lost his post-human ability the evening his astral true-love called on the local yakuza boss.

The door of the hostess bar opens to the drum roll of my heart. Out into the Street of True Love stumbles Yuji. Alone.

He is ashen and haunted, aged by a decade in forty minutes. His bruised eyes flicker instinctively in my direction. Gone is the alpha male with the superior gloat. Yuji is vanquished and broken, the weedy kid kicked to the back of the lunch queue. He turns away, his quick step betraying his urgency.

It occurs to me what I must do. There is a phone box round the corner. I run to it and hit the button for the operator. The operator end rings. And rings and rings. The receiver slips in my fear-lubricated hand.

'Good evening. This is your operator Makita. How may I help you?'

I am momentarily thrown by my inability to trace the disembodied voice back to its biological source. I remember what is at stake and recover myself. 'I have planted explosives in the Street of True Love, Shinsaibashi. They will blow up very soon, so you had better evacuate the whole street. *Now*.'

'_____'

'I hail from a dangerous doomsday cult.'

Makita the operator giggles nervously. 'Just a moment. I'm putting you through to the police.'

There is a click and then more ringing.

After the third ring: 'Hello. Police.'

'Hello. This is an anonymous tip-off. In ten minutes explosives will detonate in the Street of True Love, Shinsaibashi. The area needs to be evacuated.'

The mouthpiece is covered and I hear the sound of muffled urgency. The receiver is passed along to a different person. 'OK. We need you to be more specific. Where is the bomb? What kind of explosive is it?'

I gulp back some air. 'It is not a bomb. It's a nerve gas.'

Now it is the policeman's turn to inhale deeply. 'Where?'

'I cannot say. My cult master will punish me. Just evacuate the street.'

I hang up before they can trace the call and return to the alleyway to wait.

The nearest precinct is only a couple of streets away. I am not even halfway up the fire escape when the patrol cars arrive. Sirens wail in sonic blitzkrieg and flashing emergency lights douche the cobblestones with blue. The queens canter about in excitement as brakes screech and policemen spring out. The policemen come equipped with hard hats, white surgical masks and day-glo batons. They disperse among the bars, shouting through their masks for everyone to vacate the premises quickly and calmly. Blinking salarymen begin to spill out onto the street to be waved along by day-glo batons. One man emerges from a basement brothel, buttoning his shirt over a chest slick with massage oil, hopping about as he jams a foot back into a loafer.

A megaphone lisping with static commands the crowd: '*Vacate the premises immediately. Repeat: vacate the premises immediately. Please remain calm. There are ambulances waiting should anyone require medical assistance.*'

From the top of the fire escape I watch a policeman lift a paralytic salaryman over his shoulder and carry him towards an ambulance. The salaryman is deposited on a stretcher and pounced on by three waiting medical attendants, who clamp an oxygen mask on him and shine lights in his eye. The policeman returns to the fray, adjusting the cotton armour of his surgical mask.

'*Everybody out. Please remain calm. Please leave all belongings behind.*'

Two barmen in bow-ties and waistcoats try to evacuate the Pink Panther at the same time, only to get wedged in a shoulder jam at the door. Pummelling fists assist them from behind until they fall streetwards and are stampeded into the cobblestones.

'Hey you! Get down from there.'

A white-masked officer of the law waves his day-glo baton at me. I mime climbing down, which seems to do the trick. He turns and gives an almighty baton-shaking to a girl trying to sneak back inside the Tiger Den to retrieve whatever she has left behind. Dozens swarm the street in a surreal exodus that is part costume parade, part adjourned business meeting. I glimpse a blonde amid the mob and am queasy with hope. But it is only a girl in a Marilyn Monroe wig.

The customers vacating The Seven Wonders are the only ones to heed the megaphone instructions not to panic. Kimono-clad angels guide them, soothing with intimate whisperings. One of the last to leave is Yamagawa-san, a shadow of a bemused smile on his lips. His henchmen follow, snarling into their mobiles and hawking spit onto the floor. No sign of Mary. She must be trapped inside against her will, listening in terror to the call to evacuate. I need to get to her.

Before long every bar and club has been purged of its inhabitants. Everyone has been herded up at the end of the street where the patrol cars and stand-by ambulances are. Orange hazard tape is stretched out to seal the street off at both ends. Soon even the policemen, satisfied that the evacuation has been a success, duck beneath the tape to safety. The Street of True Love is now cordoned off from the rest of Osaka.

Perhaps it is the alcohol-enhanced dopamine levels, but everyone relaxes, as if the caution tape and traffic cones create an official safety zone. The evacuees switch to spectator mode, necks craned to peer down the empty street, somehow confident that the chemical agent will not dare to cross the threshold of the orange tape. They don't know how lucky they are that this whole thing is a hoax.

I hurl myself down the fire escape as phase two of Operation Chemical Attack gets under way. A truck pulls into the street and out climb four men in butyl-rubber boiler suits, their faces obscured by hulking gas masks. An awed hush descends upon the crowd. The quartet of men have armbands on their orange boiler suits that say: TOXIC PATROL SQUAD. They each have a chemical probe, which they swing about like metal detectors as they proceed towards the bars. The bizarre science-fiction aura they lend the proceedings has a curious psychosomatic effect on a girl in the crowd, who faints. No sooner have they loaded her onto the stretcher than another one keels over. I can tell this is going to swell to epidemic proportions.

The Toxic Patrol Squad progress slowly, moving their chemical divining rods about with scientific thoroughness. When each squad member is poised at the entrance to a bar or club I duck my head down and dive bomb from the alley over to the Seven Wonders. An excited tumult rises in the crowd. A number of police batons rise up, brandishing themselves at me in a *mise-en-scène* of day-glo outrage. I crash through the door into the abandoned bar.

The bar is a Marie Celeste of abandoned whisky glasses and pushed-back chairs, the video screens playing out to an empty audience. I make a bee-line for the Staff Only door and take the stairs behind it two at a time. At the top, three doors confront me. The first door opens into a conference room with a long table surrounded by chairs. The second door opens into a bathroom with a jacuzzi and sauna. The third door is locked, and becomes the focus of my attentions. I shoulder-slam it, launching my entire body weight, again and again. While I am hard at work dislocating my shoulder a chemical probe sweeps up the stairs towards me, green lights blinking. Attached to the end of the probe is one of the Toxic Patrol Squad, an apocalyptic vision in his boiler suit and aardvark gas mask. He watches me, respiring noisily through his charcoal chemical filter.

'There is a girl in there,' I pant, clutching my damaged shoulder.

I stand back and he opens the door with a powerful rubber-soled kick. The room is pitch black, and in its centre is Mary, slumped in a chair, like the recipient of some lethal injection. Polychromatic light falls from a video fish tank, tinting the pale face of my languid beauty. My chest heaves and I start towards her. A butyl-rubber hand clamps down on my shoulder and pulls me back. Signalling for me to stay where I am, the Toxic Patrol man goes to Mary in search of a pulse.

A shudder rips through me as I realize what must have happened. Mary must have finally transcended. Unable to comprehend the enormity of what lay beyond, her mind must have shut down. If only I had been there. I could have helped her through the trauma that I have endured myself. I could have been her one-man welcoming committee, gently initiating her into the pantheon of hyperspace. But I had failed.

Satisfied that life pulses through her arteries, the Toxic Patrol man lifts Mary into his arms. 'Wrap your T-shirt over your mouth and nose . . .' he husks through his breathing apparatus '. . . and follow me.'

The heroic Toxic Patrol man strides out with the rescued foreigner in his arms, her blond tresses streaming as he carries her to safety. The local media snap like crazy. I follow behind with my baseball cap yanked down and my T-shirt lifted to cover my lower face. In the crowd I spot a white kimono, who spots me back and shoots poison at me with her piercingly violet eyes. At least Yamagawa-san is nowhere in sight. Toxic Patrol man hands Mary over to the paramedics, who place her on a stretcher and suction an oxygen pump to her face. Toxic Patrol man salutes the adoring crowd before heading back into the danger zone to save a few more lives. The stretcher is lifted into the back of an ambulance.

'Wait,' I say. 'Where are you taking her?'

A doctor in a white coat materializes as they close up the ambulance. 'Osaka General Infirmary,' he says. 'Can you take a deep breath for me? Are you experiencing any difficulty breathing?'

I shake my head, then change my mind and nod, with an asthmatic wheeze thrown in for good measure. I could do with the free ambulance ride to hospital. I need to be there when Mary comes round. If she begins to transcend again she will need someone there to explain things to her, even if that person is a member of the dimensionally enslaved. Despair crushes my chest. All these weeks I have been waiting for Mary to join the new dawn of human enlightenment, only to lose my powers the very day she gains hers. Oh, the cosmic injustice!

Dr White Coat looks at me, concerned. 'This ambulance is full. But you look as though you could do with a respirator. Try to breathe deeply until the next one comes.'

The ambulance with Mary in it starts up, wailing its ode to life and death as it pulls away.

'Are your pupils contracted?' asks the doctor.

I nod, hoping this will bump me up the ambulance-ride priority list.

As the doctor jots this down on his clipboard a policeman in a black overcoat cuts in. 'Detective Honda,' he says with a flash of his badge. 'May I have a minute with your patient? I have a very important matter I want to discuss with him.'

The doctor nods and moves away. I give Detective Honda a mute, dazed stare, hoping he will assume post-traumatic shock.

'Listen,' Detective Honda says in a low voice. 'I'm going to be straight with you here. I know you made that hoax call. We could get you pulled in on a number of charges for what you did. Look at all the resources you've wasted here, all the panic you've caused.'

Detective Honda gives me a hard stare. Every last drop of blood drains from my face.

'But let's forget that for now. Help me out with my investigation and I'll get you off the hook for your little stunt, so don't look so frightened. I just need you to fill me in on a few things. Like how did you know that foreign girl was locked in that room? How much do you know about Yamagawa-san and his . . . activities?' Detective Honda looks about with a suspicious squint. 'We need to talk somewhere private. C'mon, we're going back to the precinct . . . ' He raises his head. 'Hey, Mori,' he shouts to one of the masked policemen, 'I'm taking this one here back to the station. Tell everybody it's safe to go back inside the bars now.'

Detective Honda steers me by the elbow through the crowd, which has swelled considerably, the flashing emergency lights drawing the late-night drinkers from neighbouring streets. The medical attendants have their work cut out noting down the phantom symptoms amassed by the evacuees. I hear complaints of cramps, palpitations, nausea, cold sweats, visual impairment and hyper-ventilation. All this from one prank phone call. More ambulances arrive and an NHK news crew tumble out of the back of a network van. As we weave out of the chaos, Detective Honda's grip tightens on my elbow.

We reach his car and Detective Honda takes his keys from his overcoat pocket and shoots an infra-red beam at the central locking system. We climb into the leather-scented interior, which is littered with empty aluminium coffee cans.

'Some very serious allegations have been made about Yamagawa-san,' says Detective Honda, clicking shut his seat belt. 'He has been connected to incidents of abduction, trafficking of drugs and prostitutes, illegal gambling, con-struction . . . I have been investigating him for two years now. Can't pin him down on anything. That's why we need a statement from you confirming that the girl was locked in the room.'

I stay quiet. Imprisoned in my own private hell, I have no

wish to partake in this battle of good versus evil. I have no
interest in bringing down the Yamagawa faction. All I want
is to get my powers back and find Mary. As the car moves
through the streets I have a nasty epiphany: that Mary's
freedom has come about at the expense of my own powers.
What if this is true? What then?

After a short distance the car stops outside the police
station. I climb out, despondent and leaden. 'How long will
this take?' I hear myself ask Detective Honda.

'This is a criminal investigation,' he says sharply. 'It will
take as long as necessary.'

I follow him into the empty lobby of an office block. We
progress through the beige landscape, down a corridor
reeking of filing cabinets and sick-building syndrome.

'In here,' Detective Honda says.

He pushes open a door to a room containing a conference table so long it looks like it is attached to the wrong
end of a telescope. At the head of the table sits Yamagawa-
san and a circle of men in dark suits. Two men, the Kaku
twins mark II, seize me by the arms. Not that restraint is
necessary: I am near-paralysed with terror. I look to
Detective Honda. He is lighting a cigarette from a Zippo
flame, a look of boredom in his eyes.

'Watanabe!' Yamagawa-san greets me warmly. 'At last
we meet. Firstly, let me tell you how much your antics of
the last few weeks have entertained us. We will be sorely
disappointed to see it all come to an end.'

A roomful of yakuza eyes bore into me.

Yamagawa-san rises from behind the table, an Armani-
suited Titan. 'But your vigilante efforts have crossed the
line tonight, I am afraid, Watanabe,' he says. 'Now, what
do you think we should do with you?'

21

MR SATO

I let myself into the Daiwa Trading offices five minutes ago. As you'd expect there is not a soul to be seen this Sunday morning. The building is still, the computers shut down and the waste-paper baskets empty. In the Public Accounts office is the lingering odour of spilt correction fluid and old coffee grounds. It serves to remind me what a good friend caffeine can be to the sleep-deficient, especially those with hard work ahead of them. My head is a jumble, so I shall set up the coffee-making machine and sit and take stock of all that has happened. Part of me, the cowardly part, would rather not tell you what I am about to tell you, for I am not proud of what I have done. But I will leave no detail untold. I cannot allow myself to keep secrets from you.

There was a dreadful commotion going on outside Osaka General's Accident and Emergency when I got back. Paramedics leapt from still-braking ambulances to race their human cargo into the hospital. A Kansai network TV crew scuttled about, spinning out a web of electrical cables across the car park. When I tried to get by, a reporter with thick, wavy hair and a charismatic smile aimed a microphone at me and asked if I had been in Shinsaibashi around

3 a.m. that night. Cameras and lights swung round, dazzling me in the quest for news. I shook my head and shuffled away, even though Shinsaibashi was precisely where I had been at 3 a.m. I had seen nothing that would interest them, and, as you know, I am very camera-shy.

I took the side entrance, bypassing Accident and Emergency, and went up a flight to the head-injuries ward. On my way to Mrs Tanaka's private room I passed the rows of sleeping patients, mummified in white starched sheets, a muted choral group of snorts and murmurs and nostril wheezes. Neck braces appear to be very much *de rigueur* on this particular ward. Dr Ono has granted Naoko and me twenty-four-hour access to Mrs Tanaka. He says she might respond to familiar voices and that we should talk to her. Though Naoko converses with ease, I am uncomfortable with the idea of talking to my comatose neighbour. To dominate the conversation for once would be to reverse the natural order of things. Mrs Tanaka would be very frustrated by her inability to interrupt with her two-yen worth.

Naoko had been chattering when I left for Shinsaibashi and when I returned she was still in full flow: 'I made Uncle a hot toddy before I put him to bed. Uncle has been through a lot today, and I thought a drop of brandy would help him to sleep ...' As you know, Mrs Tanaka is vehemently opposed to her husband's consumption of alcohol. I think Naoko was trying to infuriate her poor aunt into wakefulness. Naoko looked exhausted. Anguished hands had raked her chic career-girl hair into a bird's nest, and her skin was blotchy and tear-worn. Earlier she ran her uncle back to the flat she shares with her lady friend and then rushed back to the hospital to be by her aunt's bedside. I doubt that she has slept a wink all night.

'Mr Sato!' Naoko said when she saw me hovering in the doorway. 'You've only been gone a couple of hours. That's hardly a good night's sleep.'

'And how about yourself, Miss Tanaka? The night nurse

says you whisked your uncle home and came back in less than an hour.'

Naoko sighed, her fingers squeezing her aunt's limp hand. 'There hasn't been any improvement.'

Naoko was overtired and emotional so I persuaded her to go and take some fresh air on the roof. When she left I took her place in the hard plastic chair by the bed.

'I am sorry to have left you, Mrs Tanaka,' I said awkwardly. 'I had to dash off and take care of a work-related matter.'

Mrs Tanaka was in a bad way. She had a drip attached to her wrist and a tube taped to her face that snaked into her left nostril. The sunken yellow of her eyelids alarmed me, as did the white gown they had put her in, with openings gaping between the stud buttons along the sleeves. Her grey curls had been flattened by the white bandage they wrapped round her head. I think they had to shave some of her hair away for the emergency surgical procedure. This will make her very cross when she wakes up.

At five thirty the ward was showing signs of life. Two nurses chatted quietly as they scraped burnt toast over the hallway bin. A linen trolley squeaked by. Seeing that the sun had begun to establish itself in the sky, I opened the curtains so that it would shine some of its health-prompting vitamin D down on Mrs Tanaka.

'What fine weather we have this Sunday morning,' I remarked with spurious cheer.

Mrs Tanaka lay unresponsive in her starched white sheets. The only thing that moved was the liquid in her drip. My throat clenched and the room became cloudy with the cataract of tears. I sat back down in silence.

Naoko is under the impression that I went home to sleep last night, but this was a lie. While Naoko had been conducting her selfless bedside vigil, the comatose Mrs Tanaka couldn't have been further from my thoughts. I was beset by new worries, you see, worries I had to address immediately. The truth, it seems, is a nebulous thing, shifting like an image in the clouds.

The telephone conversation with Mariko destabilized my centre of gravity. After replacing the handset I slumped against the wall. 'That poor girl,' I whispered aloud, 'that poor, poor girl.' I took out my pocket book, thumbed for the number I wanted, and dialled it with shaking hands.

Ten minutes later a taxi drove me through the streets.

'This time of night most people are headed the other way. Back home,' the driver said in his thick Kansai accent.

In the rear-view mirror an inquisitive eye angled back at me.

'I have urgent business to attend to,' I retorted.

'You seem like a man in a hurry,' said the driver, and wisely left it at that.

The taxi could not get by on Suomachi street because there was some kind of disturbance with police cars and ambulances.

'Gangland shooting, has to be,' the driver tutted.

I told him to let me off in Amerika-mura. I decided to walk the rest of the way to the hotel to let off some steam.

I fastened my light summer jacket up to my chin and set off at a fast clip. The streets were a neon-smudged blur, littered with empty cigarette cartons. Police sirens shrieked in the distance as I ran through my intended confrontation. I wanted to chasten and shame and make absolutely clear that I would not stand for such wickedness. Common sense told me that I should wait until I had calmed down first, but I was too fired up to pay it any mind. Rather than letting off steam as I pounded the streets, I whipped myself up into a cyclone of anger.

Two night doormen stood sentry outside the Plaza Hotel. They bowed and each held open a glass door so I could enter the hotel lobby. It was a lobby that catered for the tastes of the obscenely rich; the floor a lake of marble, a grandiose staircase leading up to a mezzanine. But it was no match for me and my sour mood. I strode over to reception as though I had just stepped into a potting shed.

On the twenty-ninth floor the bellboy guided me to a large conservatory that led out onto the roof. As I stepped through the French windows onto the patio the wondrous view leapt at me like a boisterous dog. The whole city appeared to be strung with fairy lights, all that is concrete and grey considerately buried beneath a landslide of night. Cars crawled along the Hanshin expressway like wingless fireflies. The hazard lights on top of the Umeda Sky building blinked in warning to lazy pilots. The rooftop had been converted into a leafy garden (a policy Osaka city council has been encouraging to diminish carbon-dioxide emissions), but I did not stop to admire this horticultural feat. From beyond the jungle of palm leaves, flowering cacti and ornamental urns came the sound of disco music. I cut through the landscaped undergrowth to its source.

Beyond the vegetation glistened a swimming pool, and to the side of the pool was a sunken hot tub, encircled by a mosaic of tiles. In the middle of this bubbling decadence sat Murakami-san, bare-chested and drinking from a champagne flute. Alongside him was his disciple, Taro the graduate trainee, wearing a diving mask with an air-tube attachment. A laughing girl kneeling on the mosaic tiles poured champagne from the bottle directly into the air tube, making him choke and splutter into the jacuzzi. Two more girls were dancing like wind-up dolls by the poolside tables and chairs. The girls were dressed for a beach party rather than a mild spring evening. The orgiastic sight froze me in my tracks.

'Sato-san!' Murakami-san bellowed when he saw me. Water splashed down his body as he rose from the fiercely chlorinated bubbles, his belly overhanging his navy trunks, which clung to him with a gaze-deflecting snugness. He lifted his champagne flute towards me buoyantly. 'I was delighted to hear from you earlier. You have to join our celebrations.'

Murakami-san spoke with an undignified wobble. As I

had feared, he was already intoxicated. But I decided to persevere. What I had to say would soon sober him up.

'We've got a spare pair of trunks, Sato. Pop them on and join us. There's a good boy. You won't believe it when I tell you what we are celebrating tonight!'

I pushed my spectacles up the bridge of my nose and eyed him coolly. I was in no mood to hear of his silly celebrations.

'Have a guess, Sato, go on – you won't believe it.'

Jet streams roared at his knees as he staggered about, too drunk to wonder why I had gatecrashed his party in the early hours of a Sunday morning.

'Murakami-san, I would like to speak to you privately,' I said.

'Eh?' At my serious tone Murakami-san sank back down, reimmersing himself in the water. 'What can't be said in front of old Taro here?' He patted the pigeon-chested creature in the diving mask. 'Or Honey, Coco and Cynthia, our Hawaiian friends? Say hello to Mr Sato, girls!'

The girls smiled and waved at me and continued to dance. Murakami-san closed his eyes and smiled lazily. Strewn about the poolside were trousers, socks and ties. By the champagne bucket was a silver tray bearing a lobster torn limb from limb, though most of its flesh still clung to the shell, uneaten. The extravagance turned my stomach.

'Very well, Murakami-san, I shall speak to you here, then. I have come to tell you I have discovered your little scheme with Mariko.' I squeezed my fists tight as I said this, to stop my hands from shaking. How I despised that man in the jacuzzi.

Murakami-san raised his eyebrows in feigned surprise. 'What? Mariko? Mariko from the staff canteen?'

'No, Mariko the hostess.'

He took a leisurely sip of champagne. 'I'm afraid my memory needs refreshing.'

'Mariko from The Sayonara Bar.'

His charade of ignorance made me want to give him a

good shake. Taro sunk deeper into the jacuzzi foam. All the things he had teased me about over the past week were beginning to fall into place. He had been in on it as well. My nails dug deeper into my palms.

'Well, I want you to know your plan did not work. I know exactly what is going on and I intend to contact head office first thing on Monday to tell them what you and your accomplice Miss Yamamoto have been up to.'

Murakami-san blinked, as if he had just experienced a mild hallucination. 'I'm sorry, Sato-san. I missed the end of what you just said. Could you repeat it, please?'

'I said I know exactly what you and your accomplice Miss Yamamoto have been up to. And I am telling head office about it first thing on Monday. You will be sent to prison.'

Taro tore off his scuba mask; his mouth was open wide enough for a tonsil inspection. Of course, I had no idea whether Murakami-san would be sent to prison or not. I was simply furious about the way he had treated Mariko.

Murakami-san chuckled, his self-assurance unruffled. 'Come off it, Sato! Miss Yamamoto is a lovely girl but far too serious for my liking. Besides, I am a married man.'

'*That is not what I meant, and you know it!*'

My forceful delivery took us all aback. Murakami-san's chuckle lost its suave conviction. The three girls silenced their pop music and looked over at me. Had you been there you would have marched me straight home. You would have placed me under house arrest until I was fit for civil society again.

'Well, you had better enlighten me, Sato-san. What is it that you mean?' Murakami-san said.

'Under your instruction Miss Yamamoto has been stealing money from our clients' accounts. You planted her in the Finance Department for this specific purpose.'

Murakami-san ran his fingers through his silver hair, deprived of its usual volume by the humidity of the hot tub.

'What nonsense!' he scoffed. 'Miss Yamamoto is a fine young lady who graduated first in her class from Kobe University. I put her in your department because my secretary selected her from a list of people qualified for the position. And this is the first I have heard of any money being stolen.'

'Mariko told me everything.'

'Mariko the hostess?'

'The hostess you paid to seduce me, to distract me from the affairs of the office.'

Murakami-san and Taro exchanged a glance. Taro whirled his index finger at his temple, and mouthed the word 'Crazy'. Really! The insolent cheek of that boy! Had we been in the office I would have given him a good dressing-down.

Murakami-san placed his champagne on the side and rose once more, his hands held out in the open-palm, you-can-trust-me gesture they teach at management seminars. 'Mr Sato, why don't you come and sit with us. Have some champagne. Things have been very stressful lately in the Finance Department, haven't they? I assure you I haven't been paying any hostesses to seduce you. You're a handsome man: you don't need my help to find yourself a woman. Let us sit at a table together. It would be criminal to let this good champagne go to waste.'

Murakami-san turned to Taro and made a quick, inscrutable gesture. Taro nodded and belly-flopped over the side of the hot tub – a somewhat inelegant manoeuvre owing to the large rubber flippers on his feet. He uprighted himself and waddled into the landscaped jungle, his flippers slapping the tiled floor. The trio of dancing girls pattered along after him. I did not budge from the spot.

'Do not patronize me, Murakami-san. It is not work-related stress that has prompted me to make this accusation. Mariko has told me everything. You have been paying her a handsome sum to preoccupy me so that your illegal activities would go unnoticed.'

Seeing I was unswayed by his offer of champagne, Murakami-san snatched up a cotton robe from the side and threaded his damp arms through the sleeves. The robe was a tropical riot of parrots and palm leaves. Murakami-san frowned in a thoughtful way. 'Sato-san, I have been nowhere near the accounts. And I assure you I would not hire a hostess just to distract you from that.'

'You have been caught red-handed,' I said.

'Really? Caught red-handed? What evidence do you have of any of this?'

The enormity of what I had done suddenly hit me. I had just attacked my superior when the only evidence I had was what Mariko had gleaned from her private dealings with him.

'Evidence will be found,' I said confidently. 'And there will also be a proper inquiry into the disappearance of Takahara-san. His absence is a little too convenient for my liking.'

Murakami-san squinted at me as though I were an inscrutable magic-eye poster. It then occurred to me that by confronting Murakami-san I had effectively given him an advance warning; he could go to the office and erase whatever evidence there was before Monday. I panicked, then remembered that Kyoto bank have records of all our transactions.

'So you think that I am responsible for Takahara-san's disappearance, do you?' Murakami-san laughed. 'That I hired yakuza hitmen to kill him so my embezzlement would go undiscovered? You really have no idea what you are talking about, do you, Sato? You are very lucky tonight. Firstly because I am very drunk, and secondly because I am sympathetic to all that you have been through in the past few years. Otherwise I might take offence to all these things you accuse me of.'

'Take offence? What right have you, the guilty one, to take offence when accused of your own crime?' I said. 'You did a very wicked thing. You took an orphaned child, and exploited the fact she is all alone in the world and riddled with her late father's debts. You tried to corrupt an innocent.' Hypertension made me short of breath and quickened my blood.

Murakami-san waded through the jacuzzi to the metal steps. With the aid of the railings he hoisted himself out onto the tiles. 'I really don't know what you have got yourself involved in here, Sato,' he said, 'but hostessing is a deceitful profession. Many of these girls will stop at nothing to manipulate a client. Has this girl, this so-called orphan, asked you for any money?'

'No. *You* are the one who is giving her money.'

'What proof do you have other than her word?' Murakami-san hiccuped.

I had no tangible evidence, but my logic was conclusive. 'Someone has been feeding her private information about me. She knew I was a widower, she knew all the vicious lies that were spread about my wife after her . . . her passing. All those vicious untruths. Only one customer she has come into contact with at the hostess bar could have taught her these things. And now I know your motive.' Emotion deformed my voice and hot tears needled my eyes. This vexed me terribly. The humiliating reality of my confrontation no longer corresponded to what I had intended.

'Sato-san,' Murakami-san said softly, 'I promise you I have never once discussed you with that hostess. Someone else must have. She is playing you for a fool. I will speak to the Mama-san at the bar where she works: she needs to keep those bitches under better control.' He took a step towards me, his hand held out in a gesture of comfort.

'Then, how did she know all the lies you spread about my wife?'

'I have *never* spread any lies about your wife.'

I went mute with fury. How dare he deny all the lies he spread about the company? I even overheard him with my own ears once, gossiping with his cronies in the designated smoking area.

'*Liar*! I heard what you said! Thanks to you, even now, years later, everyone thinks that my wife took her own life. Do you have any idea how you dishonoured her? How you dragged her name through the mud?' I was shouting like a madman, but I did not care.

The champagne lustre was finally gone from Murakami-san's eyes. 'Sato-san, you are a good man, a first-rate employee, but I think you need to take a break for a while, seek some psychiatric help . . .'

His hypocrisy sent my heart askew. It pounded all over that hotel rooftop, everywhere at once.

'Who are you to tell me that I need psychiatric help? I am not the one who makes up sick lies for his own amusement.'

'It was broad daylight,' Murakami-san persisted. 'There were many eyewitnesses who saw what she did. It was reported in the newspapers.'

Do you see the wickedness I was up against? When exposed as a bare-faced liar, Murakami-san's tactic was to lie and lie *ad nauseam*.

'One more word about my wife,' I said, 'and you will regret it.'

But the Deputy Senior Managerial Supervisor could not stop himself. 'I understand your guilt, Sato, but it wasn't your fault. You have to stop blaming yourself. Everybody knew about her mental-health problems . . .'

Murakami-san paused to let out a despondent, drunken hiccup. It was one mark of disrespect too far. Before I knew it I had leapt across the four or five metres that separated us and taken a clumsy swipe at him. He swerved before it connected and toppled backwards into the jacuzzi with a great splash, sending a chlorinated tidal wave over my shoes and slacks. At first he vanished completely beneath the white, frothing bubbles as I looked on, amoral with rage. Then his head bobbed up, wide-eyed and gasping, his silver hair plastered otter-like against his scalp. Coughing and spluttering with panic and disbelief, he splashed away from me and made his way to the side of the jacuzzi. He heaved himself out and lay on the side, as if beached, his parrot robe clinging wetly to his bruised behind. Palms flat against the tiles he coughed and coughed, trying to clear his watery lungs. The hot-tub interior was moulded plastic, so if he was concussed I doubt it was all that serious.

I swelled with remorse at my bungled act of violence. No matter how terrible the provocation, there is no excuse to carry on like a barbarian. I hung my head, just as I hang my head now, because I know you disapprove.

'I did not mean to do that,' I said, as Murakami-san wheezed into the tiles. A pair of angry, bloodshot eyes met mine. 'I will go now. It was foolish of me to come here. This is a matter best left for Head Office to deal with on Monday.'

Leaving him to cough the agony from his lungs, I went inside, deeply ashamed by my behaviour. How can you be proud of a husband who carries on in such an aggressive manner? It wasn't only Murakami-san who had dishonoured you tonight.

Repentance did little to quell my anger, though. How dare he suggest I seek psychiatric help? He who has turned to illegal activity to fund his hedonistic addictions. He who has sacrificed all integrity for the sake of lobster, hired go-go dancers and panoramic views of the Osaka skyline? What disease lurks in the heart of a man ready to take advantage of a penniless young girl? *Come Monday morning he will no longer be in a position to abuse others. I will see to that*, I thought, retreating down the dim corridor.

I decided to return to the hospital to check on Mrs Tanaka's progress. Then I would go to the Finance Department to commence an investigation of every file and account Miss Yamamoto has so much as sniffed at in the past week. Whatever evidence I find will be backed up by Mariko, who will come with me to explain everything to Head Office on Monday. The thought of Mariko and her deception was accompanied by a stab of pain. But we both know that she is a good girl at heart – a girl who needs help to turn her life around, so that she may never have to compromise her dignity again.

At the lift I pressed the call button and saw that the lift was already in use. I watched the numbers on the display above the door climb to twenty-nine, and then the doors ping open. At first I did not recognize the man in the lift. He was with a stout, foreign woman, who had a mannish haircut and rounded, hamster cheeks. The man was a middle-aged hippy, bronzed by the sun, his long fringe hanging in his eyes. They both wore tie-dyed sarongs and flip-flops woven from straw.

The man smiled at me widely. 'Sato-san! *Aloha!* Taro said you'd come along to celebrate tonight!'

It was Takahara-san, back from Hawaii.

Takahara-san had brought his wife and her five children to Japan for a family honeymoon. The rooftop party had been at his expense and the go-go dancers were his wife's two Japanese-Hawaiian cousins and eldest daughter. Taro had woken the newly-weds to inform them, in his melodramatic style, that I had gone berserk. Takahara-san placed a bronzed hand on my shoulder and said it concerned him that I thought Murakami-san was stealing money. He told me that Murakami-san had offered him his old job back – hardly the behaviour of a man with something to hide . . . And how had my health been lately? Had I been getting enough sleep? After listening to Takahara-san, his wife smiling enthusiastically along (stone deaf to the meaning of her husband's words), I mentioned my accident with Murakami-san by the hot tub. As Takahara-san and his new bride sped off to check he was OK I stepped into the empty lift.

Takahara-san's last-minute intervention took the edge off my conviction. But for all I know Takahara-san could be in on it as well. The only way to know the truth is to seek it out myself.

*

Before leaving the hospital I sat at the bedside of the comatose Mrs Tanaka, breathing in the odour of bactericide and surgical dressing. Mrs Tanaka resembled a waxwork as she lay there, pale to the point of translucency, her inner arms threaded with blue and green. I was concerned that this discoloration was a sign that her drip was malfunctioning. When Naoko returned from the roof, flushed and smelling like she had been in attendance at a chain-smoking convention, I asked her opinion. Naoko removed her leather coat and hung it on the back of the door.

'I think her arms have always been like that. Yes, come to think of it, I remember asking her about it when I was a kid.' She bent over her aunt and stroked her brow. 'You always had bad circulation, didn't you, Auntie?'

I stood up again and told Naoko that I had an errand to attend to, but would be back in an hour or two.

Naoko looked at her watch, a slender band of silver round her wrist. 'What kind of errand do you have to attend to at six thirty on a Sunday morning?' she asked in bafflement. Then she shook her head at herself. 'Sorry, I am forgetting my manners. You really look as though you haven't slept, Mr Sato . . .'

'I will be only an hour or two. And I will bring you back something nice for breakfast,' I said. 'And a portable television set too, so Mrs Tanaka can listen to her favourite programmes.'

And off I went once more, determined to get the investigation under way, so as not to keep Mrs Tanaka waiting too long.

The early sunlight stung my eyes. Through the smeary lenses of my spectacles I inspected the hospital car park, peaceful now it was empty of television crews. More than anything I wanted to sit and close my eyes for a minute. Just a minute. But I knew this was a tempting trap laid out for me by sleep. Though the trains were running I decided to take a taxi to the Daiwa Trading offices. One can always rely on a taxi driver in want of his fare to wake passengers who nod off in the back. The taxi rank was across the road from the hospital. As I stood at the pedestrian crossing, waiting for the lights to change (there was no traffic, but one mustn't neglect the rules of road safety, under any circumstances), I heard a foreign voice call out: 'Hey, can I ask a favour?'

I turned my head, expecting to see a boy because the voice was husky and low. But instead I saw a girl with wavy blond hair falling to her shoulders. It was Mary from England. Do you remember how I met her at the hostess bar? How she had picked her nail varnish and got told off by the Mama-san? I was very surprised because I did not expect to see Mary from England again, let alone in the car park of Osaka General Infirmary. The night I met Mary in the hostess bar she had been wearing too much make-up. Now she wore none at all and was so washed-out she resembled her own ghost. Her eyes were dark and shadowy like a racoon's, and her clothes rumpled and dirty. On her thin wrist was a hospital band, so I assume she had just been discharged. On her feet were toilet slippers. Didn't she know they are only meant to be worn in the toilet? I wondered if it would be rude of me to tell her.

'I've lost my purse, see, and I need to borrow 1,000 yen to get to my friend's place. If you give me your address I promise to send the money back to you right away. If you don't have 1,000 yen, anything will do.'

She spoke in excellent, if somewhat slangy, Japanese. She did not seem embarrassed about accosting a stranger in such a matter-of-fact manner. Perhaps this behaviour is acceptable in England. Mary did not recognize me. But I expect she encounters a lot of faces in her line of work, and mine is not the most memorable.

'If you have lost your purse,' I said, 'you should go to a police box. Someone might have handed it in. I can direct you to the nearest one.'

Mary sighed impatiently. 'I lost it in Shinsaibashi. I doubt it would have been handed in round here.'

'But they could still help.'

'Right.'

The pedestrian crossing flashed green and played a melody, signalling it was safe to cross. Mary turned away from me, regretful of the time wasted. It was obvious that she would continue to waylay strangers until she got the money.

'Wait,' I said: '1,000 yen, was it?'

Mary turned back and nodded.

I rummaged through my wallet. 'I have nothing smaller than a 5,000-yen note,' I said. 'Here, take it.'

She had not struck me as a sentimental girl but as she took the money her eyes shone with gratitude. I remembered how terribly young she was. What would her mother and father think if they knew she was scavenging for money in a hospital car park in Japan?

'Thank you,' she said.

'That's quite all right. I know you from the hostess bar,' I said. 'It's Mary, isn't it?'

'No,' she said, shaking her head. 'It isn't.' Then she darted ahead of me, ignoring the traffic lights, which had gone back to red.

I've just sent the last of a second cup of coffee down the hatch. Good thing it's a Sunday and there is no one about, because I could really do with a good spit and polish. The beginnings of a beard rasp beneath my fingertips and my teeth are unclean. While on my first cup of coffee I went about collecting the files assigned to Miss Yamamoto and have piled them in front of me. I am not sure exactly what I am looking for. But there is no excuse to delay any longer. I want to put an end to Murakami's wrongdoings once and for all. I let you down tonight, and I want to earn back your respect. I want to do good in your eyes again.

File number one, here I come.

22

MARY

The taxi pulls through the quiet streets, past a silent row of vending machines, a wooden tenement building, its curtains drawn in postponement of dawn. I think of all the people behind the curtains, asleep in their beds, breathing the same air as the people they trust. The grass is not just greener, every blade is gold-plated.

I fidget on the back seat, jittery in my skin. It is a poor substitute for what I really want to do, which is scream, for as long and hard as my lungs can endure. Inside my head is a terrible place to be right now. I could have sworn right up until the drugs kicked in that he loved me. Fool.

The blast of our horn drowns out my thoughts. The taxi driver curses and thumps the steering wheel. Sliding out from a side street is a car, silent as a shark. It brakes ahead of us, creating a road-block, and we skid to a slantwise halt on the edge of a building site. 'Idiots!' the taxi driver cries. 'What are they playing at?'

The windscreen of the car is all reflected sunlight, but I make out the shadows of two men. My stomach bottoms out. That was too decisive a manoeuvre to be engine trouble. The driver and I watch as the car door opens. Out steps a man in a suit and sunglasses: Yamagawa's one-man search-and-retrieval unit, Hiro.

I lean towards the driver. 'You'd better reverse the taxi,' I tell him, urgency undermined by the calm in my voice. 'He has a gun. Reverse back down the road.'

The driver does not reverse, speak or even look round. In a breath-taking display of chivalry he opens his door and legs it into the building site, where he vanishes behind the scaffolding of a nearly completed house.

Hiro smiles at the sight of my driver loping off, or maybe it was just a trick of the light. Adrenalin doesn't allow me time to speculate – it has me out and flying down the road, harrowed by the thought of a well-aimed bullet shattering my spine. Hiro gains on me in a few seconds and seizes my arm. I wheel round and lash out, striking air. He catches my other arm and I scream, almost dislocating my wrists as I try to wrench them free. He says: 'Mary, stop. I am not going to hurt you . . .'

Bloodstains like crimson raindrops splatter his shirt. Things do not look good.

Behind him comes his friend, running to help him. 'Mary! It's OK. Stop, it's me.'

I stop my thrashing. *Katya*? My wrists are released and Katya slots herself between us, her hands squeezing my shoulders. A man-sized T-shirt and loose jeans swamp her small frame; her brown hair is tucked out of sight beneath a baseball cap.

'We were waiting outside the hospital for you, but you got in the taxi before we could get you.'

I look back down the empty road, at the two abandoned cars. There is no one but Hiro and her.

'Good thing we got you before you got to my apartment,' Katya says. 'They'll have someone waiting for you there.'

We drive to a lake and park in the clearing by the trees. Hiro skims stones from a small jetty. They skip the water, concentric circles spreading from the instances of impact.

The new, tomboyish Katya tugs off her trainers, the visor of the baseball cap shading her face. Breathing in the brand-newness of the upholstery, I watch as her boyfriend reaches down on the ground for another stone.

'So you remember nothing,' Katya says.

'The last thing I remember is the drugs starting to work; after that, waking up in hospital.'

'The police evacuated the street. There was some kind of gas leak – I don't know the details. Watanabe knew you were in Yamagawa-san's bar and told a policeman. It's thanks to him that you got out. Hiro told me that Watanabe had been watching out for you.'

I think of Watanabe in his stained chef's apron, and feel violent gratitude. I always liked that boy.

'And then they took me to hospital?'

'Hiro said they put you in an ambulance. Didn't you speak to a nurse or anyone?'

'No one. I left five minutes after I woke up.'

'You just left?'

'Yeah. What was the point in staying?'

The reasons for staying were many and obvious, but Katya nods as if I was right to leave. The first thing I saw when I woke was the green of my cubicle curtains. I had been crying in my sleep, tears spilling from my eyes and wetting my ears. I asked myself some questions. Why am I in hospital? What did they do to me in that office? Have I been raped? I sat up, swung my legs over the side of the bed and looked myself over, checking under my skirt. I was groggy but not in pain, not sore or bruised. So I found my shoes under the bed and left. I keep seeing Yamagawa-san leaning over me, breathing on me, doing things to my unconscious body.

From the lake comes a sequence of splashes, two faint, one loud, as a stone skips and breaks the surface.

'Do you know if I was raped?' I ask.

Katya does not flinch at this question; she gazes calmly at me. 'Highly unlikely. They got you out of there quickly.

And even if Yamagawa-san had a fortnight I doubt it would have made a difference. The man is impotent.'

'Impotent?' I smile my first smile of the day. Not-quite relief lightens my heart. 'So why . . . ?'

'It's one method of recruiting girls to work for him. The man is scum . . .'

Katya continues to vent her rage in Ukrainian. I recognize the swear words she taught me, expletive after expletive, a string of poison pearls. Her words of hate and condemnation soothe me, but they come too late.

'Why didn't you tell me what these people are like? You never said a bad word against them . . .'

Katya looks to Hiro and back again, almost in a silent appeal for help. 'I have not been a very good friend to you. I'm sorry. I knew they were after Yuji . . . He had it coming for a long time now. But I promise you, Mary, I thought you were safe. I don't know, maybe I should have said something . . .' A guilty pause. 'Yamagawa-san never messes with English or Americans. Everyone knows it. When you didn't show up for work last night Mama-san told me you'd gone to Korea with Yuji. And I knew you two were planning to leave Japan. I thought she was telling the truth . . .'

'Do you think that Mama-san knew what they were going to do to me?'

'Mary! She set you up. She sent you to him. And I bet Yuji was in on it too. I'm sorry . . . I know you trusted him.'

Katya leans over the handbrake to put her arms round my neck. The embrace is awkward, her arms too thin. She rubs my back, as if trying to diffuse comfort through my shoulder-blade. I can tell she means it, but I am strangely detached.

'I want to go to the police,' I say. The desire makes itself known as I speak it.

Keeping hold of my shoulders, Katya pulls back, her eyes fierce with opposition. 'You have not been hurt and the only evidence you have is your word. They have friends in the police. Think about it. You will only make things worse. You have been very lucky.'

Lucky? Is she serious? Branches sway above the car, sending fitful shadows across the windscreen.

'So I just let them get away with what they did?'

'I don't like it either, but there is nothing that can be done.'

Hiro abandons stone-skimming to watch the breeze unsettle the surface of the lake. I almost ask Katya how she felt when she first saw what they did to his face, but there is a fine line between curiosity and cruelty. I know she is happy anyway. Radiance diffuses from her every pore; it hit me as soon as I got in the car, sharpening my heartbreak.

'Hiro didn't mean to scare you yesterday. He hasn't made a very good impression on you, has he?'

'He scares me more each time I see him . . .' I say this in jest, then realize it is true. 'What next for you two?'

'America. Hiro has a cousin who can get us a job on a farm out in California. We've picked you up on the way to the airport.'

'America. Wow!' I am happy for her, I really am. Especially after all the shit she has been through. But I don't want her to go. Not just yet. 'I'm going to miss you,' I say.

Katya opens the glove compartment and takes out a brown envelope. 'Here.'

Inside the envelope is a British passport and a sheaf of ten-thousand-yen notes. I hand it back. 'Katya, I can't take this. It's too much – I can't pay it back.'

'Take it. No arguments. What else are you going to do? Go back to working at The Sayonara Bar? Count the money later. Hiro got the passport for you this morning.'

I take it out and flip it open. It belongs to Casey Rhodes, a blonde born in June 1979. Nondescript enough to pass for. Just.

'Mama-san has your real passport. This was the best we could do at short notice,' Katya tells me. 'Mary, I want you to come with us to the airport. You have to leave Japan: it is too dangerous here now. Hiro's cousin can get you a job if you want to come with us to America. Otherwise I advise you to return to England straight away.'

Idyllic as it sounds, I can't bring myself to gatecrash Katya's new life. I am not too keen on England either, but any destination that puts a fourteen-hour plane journey between me and Yamagawa-san can't be all bad.

'Looks like I'm going back to England, then. When do you fly out?'

'In two hours.'

'*Two hours?*'

I am fraught; how can she go so soon? Katya's smile is a strange hybrid of guilt and love-struck indifference.

'How come you never mentioned Hiro before?'

'I never said anything to you because it was safer to keep my mouth shut. It was just too risky with you seeing Yuji. I knew he was coming back, I just didn't know when.'

'A year is such a long time. How could you stand it?'

'I would do it again. I would wait ten years, my whole life if I had to.'

The man Katya would wait her whole life for stands with his hands in his pockets, introspecting on the glinting surface of the lake. I remember something he said in Yuji's apartment. That he couldn't contact his girlfriend because they'd threatened to send her back to the brothel he rescued her from. I look at Katya, beatific even when she is un-smiling. At the hostess bar I always saw her as hard and cynical, but I know better now. I knew ten per cent of her before this morning. Five per cent. And now that she is going away I will never rectify this.

'When did you know Hiro had come back?'

'Two hours before we met you. He had been back in Osaka for weeks, but Yamagawa-san told him he had to stay away from me. Hiro got sick of being told what to do and resigned from his position early this morning. Then he came to get me.'

'And Yamagawa-san just let him go?'

'They didn't part on good terms. Which is why we are leaving on the first flight out of here. After what happened at The Seven Wonders, I advise you to do the same.'

Katya also advises me to change my clothes. She takes a black vest, a linen suit and espadrilles out of her bag. I climb into the back, where I strip and change into the outfit, lifting my hips off the seat to pull on the trousers. Then I set to work on my hair with a comb. Katya sits with her bare feet up on the dashboard and smokes a cigarette, one eye on the clock. The skirt and blouse I wore last night are next to me on the seat, covered in Yuji's fingerprints, his sweat and blood, dust from the floor of the Lotus Bar. I hate the sight of them. I ball them up, shove them in a carrier bag and kick it under the driver's seat. Katya notices but says nothing. I would kill for two minutes with a borrowed toothbrush, but Katya is getting twitchy.

She twists round in her seat. 'Ready?'

'Yes, but it's a shame I can't go back and say goodbye to Watanabe. Or at least say thank you. I owe him that much.'

'Watanabe is dead, Mary. They killed him for informing the police.'

My heart splutters. *Dead*? 'How?'

'They tied him up and drowned him.'

'Jesus . . . Why?'

'Because they can,' Katya says. 'Now do you see what the rush is for?' She leans over to the steering wheel and presses down on the horn. It honks across the lake, scaring the birds from the treetops. Hiro begins to walk back to the car. 'We have to go,' says Katya. 'Or we'll end up dead like Watanabe.'

We tear down the Hanshin expressway, churning up the asphalt and spewing it out with the exhaust. The city is a distant concrete haze, throwing up a skyscraper here, the artificial green of a golf course there. This motorway gives me déjà vu, like I have dreamt this journey before, all the carbon monoxide and grey. I keep hearing my last words to Watanabe: 'Can you clean the ice machine?' Not even a please. Be honest, Mary, you treated him like everyone else did: like shit. He was just a kid, a teenager.

Hiro drives and smokes and doesn't say much. None of us say much. Hiro took a clean shirt out of the boot before he got in the car, and threw the one with blood on it into the lake. Katya sits with one knee up like a restless child. Her hand moves from the back of Hiro's neck to his arm, always touching some part of him. She kisses him as often as she can, right where the acid has eaten into his face. Cars hover alongside us before peeling away into the background. I close my eyes and pretend to sleep.

We abandon the car and follow an indoor route of glass walkways and escalators to the International Departure lounge. The air-conditioned hall chimes with multilingual announcements, foreign inflexions and echoes. Tourists stand around hillocks of luggage, frowning up at electronic indexes of gates and boarding times. Children dangle from luggage trolleys, begging to be pushed.

The sinister charisma of Hiro's scar draws stares from all around. Some timid, others vulgar double-takes. A boy in a Spiderman T-shirt points and shouts: 'Mummy, what's wrong with that man's face?' Blushing, Mummy hisses fiercely and drags her child away. I wait around the Delta airline counter as Katya and Hiro calmly show their fictitious passports to claim their boarding passes. The flight for California leaves in thirty minutes. There is no time for lingering goodbyes.

The designated farewell zone is the metal barrier ahead of the security check. A corporate chieftain is sent on his way by a gathering of company men. Two teenagers bid farewell in the tragicomic style of a holiday romance. This is happening too fast.

Hiro takes Katya's bag, and nods at me. 'Sorry about yesterday.'

'Don't worry about it. Thanks for the passport.'

We shake hands, no less uncomfortably than the first time we met in the karaoke booth.

Hiro steps back, hesitates and says: 'Watanabe, he was a good kid. Really cared about you.'

I nod, not knowing what to say.

Hiro turns away to give me and Katya privacy. We hug quickly.

'Look after yourself.'

'You too. I hope America works out for you.'

'Good luck back in the UK.'

'Thank you.'

'Listen,' Katya whispers tersely. 'I know how you feel right now. Yuji will make enemies wherever he goes. He will get what he deserves one day. They all will.'

I shake my head. I don't want these to be our last words to each other. 'Stay in touch,' I say. But how can we? Neither of us has a contact address or email.

Katya must be conscious of this too, but she says nothing. She nods. 'I should go before I make us late.'

One last hug and she turns away. Hiro takes her hand and they join the line for the security check. On my side of the barrier left-behind friends and family smile, waving until their loved ones are swallowed up by the metal detectors. I turn and walk myself out of sight.

What now? Breakfast? The date-rape whisky was the last thing to pass between my lips, but I don't have any hunger pangs or even thirst. I have to make the effort, though. I head for a coffee shop beyond the souvenir precinct. The automatic doors wake the waiter dozing on the counter. Bleary-eyed, he welcomes me. The windows overlook the aeroplane safari park below; commercial liners drinking petrol or tracing slow, distinguished circles on the runways. One lifts off and I watch it until its Thai Air logo vanishes into the cloudscape. Chances are before nightfall I too will be belted up inside one of these winged cylinders. Why does the thought depress me so much?

I sit with my back to the window and watch the counter TV, which is tuned into *The Powerpuff Girls*. The waiter brings over a hot flannel and water and takes an order pad from his apron pocket. I scan the menu for something easy to eat and order ice cream, then coffee as an afterthought. A boy of Yuji's height and build stops at the door of the coffee shop to read the menu. My pulse quickens with dread though I know it is not him. He is long gone, like a rat that gnawed off its tail to flee a trap. I hold the flannel against my face, letting the heat coax open my pores. I remember the envelope that Katya gave me, take it out and count the money. I count it once, hyperventilate, then count it once more. There is over five hundred thousand yen. Where the hell did she get it from? Katya is insane. I love her. Forget England. I can go wherever I want with this.

The waiter stands over me, politely clearing his throat. I shove the money back into the envelope, but not before his eyes widen in intrigue. He sets down my order and withdraws to the counter, where he shakes open a newspaper.

I pour my coffee over the ice cream.

'That taste nice?' he asks.

'Very. You should try it some time.'

I eat a spoonful of ice cream, wincing as the cold shoots down the nerve endings in my teeth.

'Your Japanese is very good,' he says.

I smile and shake my head in knee-jerk modesty. The old man seems nice enough, but when I am this lonely I prefer to be left alone. Those few crumbs of friendliness only make me feel ten times worse.

'What part of the world are you off to?' he asks.

Good question. The lenses of his spectacles magnify his eyes, lending him an air of owlish curiosity.

'I am trying to decide.'

The waiter lays down his newspaper. The tufts of grey above his ears are separated by a generous dome of bald. His fingers wander to the dome now, and give it a confused scratch. 'You're a strange one,' he says. 'Have you just been on holiday in Japan?'

From nowhere comes the heartburn of nostalgia.

'Yes. I need a change of scene.'

'Anywhere in mind?'

'Asia, I guess.'

'Been to Korea?'

'No.' I shudder. 'I don't want to go there.'

'I went to Guam on my honeymoon, years and years ago. Beautiful, that's the only word for it.'

'Guam . . .' I've heard good things about it. And it is easy to find work there if you can speak Japanese. 'Why not?'

'Guam it is, then.' The waiter laughs, delighted I have taken his recommendation to heart. 'You can buy a ticket on the second floor. Flights leave every two hours. Aren't you lucky to be young and free to do what you want?'

This is the second time I have been called lucky today. I stir my coffee ice cream slush.

The automatic doors part for a party of ten or so healthy-looking young people. The waiter welcomes them and jumps up to fetch flannels and water. They move to a table by the window. 'Shame that Maiko of the secretariat division couldn't make it.' 'Did they refund her ticket?' They must be co-workers going on a company holiday. I listen to them laughing politely, the ice yet to break, the romances yet to happen. Quite a few salarymen I know met their wives on trips like this. It's a big, contrived group date really, the first stop on the nuclear-family production line. Most of the time I am scornful of this sort of thing, but sitting here without a friend left in the whole of Japan I almost envy them.

The waiter stops by my table as he ferries a pyramid of hot towels to the newcomers. 'You'll like it in Guam. There's enough sunshine to chase all your troubles away . . .'

I push my melted ice cream aside, wishing I could inhabit his innocent world, where sunshine is a miracle cure-all.

The news distracts me from my loneliness. The TV is unable to sustain an image for more than a second: drab rows of suits in parliament; a pod of whales; a typhoon in Okinawa; a photofit of a Brazilian armed robber. The volume is too low for me to grasp much of what is going on and the result is disorientation. Out of the fray a giant crab, clacking its claws like some crustacean enforcer, pulls me back from the brink of disengagement. I know that crab; I know the Shinsaibashi restaurant it sits on top of. Beneath the mechanical crab a reporter talks into a microphone. The camera pans back to take in some more of the entertainment district, washed-out and dirty in the daylight. I swallow a mouthful of coffee and watch the reporter's lips move with media-honed solemnity.

A face I know but cannot place floods the TV screen. It could be an actor, but he is too pinched and misfit-like to appeal to any casting agent. He looks scared, spooked by something lurking beyond the camera. Only when the screen returns to the reporter do I realize who the face belongs to. I look round to see if anyone else is as stunned as I am. Then I dash to the counter, jumping up and pressing all the buttons, trying to crank up the volume. That was no actor. That was Watanabe.

I move closer to the TV, the picture now green and horizontally realigned after my button pushing. The camera cuts to a bridge over the Yodogawa. Sunday shoppers swing glossy bags, talk into mobiles or stare blankly. One or two notice the camera and glance self-consciously into the lens. A shaven-headed monk chants and collects alms. The reporter's voiceover says: 'Blah blah blah . . . Shinsaibashi.' I raise my hand to the TV screen, now showing the murky waters of the Yodogawa. As if sensing the touch of my fingers the picture flits to a roomful of people doing wheelchair aerobics.

'Are you all right?' The waiter is next to me, scratching the inside of his ear with his ballpoint pen. In his other hand he clutches an order pad full of scribbles. He must think I have never seen a television before.

'He was my friend,' I say.

'The joker who threw himself in the river?' he asks.

Is that what they are saying? That's outrageous! How can they get away with that?

'He didn't throw himself in,' I say.

'But they just said so, on the news. The police chased him and he jumped . . .'

I open my mouth in protest, then close it again. So I correct one misinformed opinion. How many thousands of others out there have just seen this news bulletin?

'Oh, he was sick in the head, that one,' the waiter says. 'Pretending to be from the Aum and making Sarin threats to the police. It's just sick.'

'Sarin threats?'

'The police had to clear out the whole area last night. Sent everyone into a real panic . . . Er . . . He wasn't a *close* friend of yours, was he?'

'No, not close. But you are wrong about him: he was a good person . . . a little strange maybe, but not sick. He didn't deserve to die.'

The waiter gapes at me, a thin strand of saliva between his lips. He makes a startled sound, severing the silvery thread. 'Didn't deserve to die? He's not dead! They fished him out of the river this morning. They said they were keeping him at Osaka General.'

I charge back the way I came. Around me the airport rewinds in slow motion: the crawling check-in queues, the kids playing dodgems on the trolleys, the overpriced souvenir stalls swindling last-minute shoppers. I know there is no need to hurry – the boy is not going anywhere, at least not out of police custody. But I hurry nonetheless. I speed down the escalator, the woven soles of my espadrilles slapping the metal of each step. A Chinese woman I collide with shouts at me in Cantonese. I shout back an apology in

English and tear down the walkway linking the airport to the train station. Will they let me see him? What will I say? Thank you, then what else? The rest will come to me. I remember Katya's warnings. I will avoid Shinsaibashi. I was too trusting before, not wary enough. This will change.

In the train station is a video billboard, advertising some exotic destination with palm trees, a perfect shoreline lapped by surf. I join the queue for the ticket vendor. I am not through with Japan just yet.

23

WATANABE

I was thrown into the boot of the car and light vanished with a slam of the lid. The world shrank to the dimensions of the boot, and all I knew for the duration of the journey was motion sickness and the rough jarring of darkness. When the boot reopened Ace and Omi seized and delivered me to the night air.

'Shit, he puked on himself.'

'So he has. Disgusting.'

They dropped me like a thing covered in anthrax spores, then gave me a vigorous kicking. Cursing, Ace transferred my gastric juices from the back of his hand onto the sleeve of his jacket and kicked me again. Omi sparked a flame-thrower lighter and held it to his cigarette. We were on an embankment north of Umeda, in a land of warehouses and slums. Lights from a Pachinko parlour across the river scintillated on the water. Street-lamp reflections writhed on the current like liquid snakes. Our twin planet the moon hung in the pre-dawn sky. The sight of this lonely satellite induced a stab of longing. How I yearned to be up there, unmolested by yakuza henchmen and the Earth's gravitational field.

One of them took something out of the car. A hammer and

a rope. He threw them beside me on the embankment. A metal hailstorm of nails followed, chinking the concrete in their dozens.

'Enough rope?' growled Ace, the more dominant of the two.

'Don't need much to tie this one up. Look how small he is.'

River water churned and my stomach withered.

Ace shot his friend a sly look. 'Watanabe,' he said, mock-friendly. 'We're meant to put you in the river, but I tell you what, if you can hammer a nail all the way into the ground, we'll let you go. What do you reckon?'

What did I reckon? I reckoned it a mean trick. But what choice did I have? The surf of blood crashing in my ears, I took up hammer and nail. On my knees, nail secured between finger and thumb, I poured all my strength into the first blow. As my tormentors shook themselves stupid with laughter the absurdity of my endeavour was clear to me. Without my hypersense I was unable to detect any weaknesses in the concrete. Relying on physical strength alone I was screwed.

At my non-progress, the taskmaster smacked his forehead in exasperation. 'I can't watch. He is too pathetic.'

'Do you think he'll stay underwater? Maybe we should tie him up in a sack with bricks.'

'Go to Lawson's and see about buying some bin liners,' Ace ordered. 'And pick me up something to eat too . . .' He turned to me. 'Oi! I wouldn't stop hammering if I were you . . . Not if you want to live!'

Omi set off to Lawson's. Ace began thumbing his mobile, and I hammered on.

As I hammered I thought happily of Mary and her future of liberation. But the happiness soon caved into bitterness as I remembered I would not share her new-found emancipation. I thought of my future corpse, bloated with the gases of decomposition, surfacing in the river. Did I fear death as I hunched over that nail, pitiful clanking sounds emanating from my hammer? Yes, I confess that I did. Even the knowledge that, in one short lifetime, I had outshone all of human civilization left me unconsoled. As my jailer thumbed his text, I agonized whether to sprint to freedom across the embankment, but then remembered that bullets are made to travel faster than men.

'My dog can hammer better than you,' Ace remarked.

The hammer slipped and flattened my thumb. Sucking at the smarting flesh, I noticed that dawn had begun to flood the sky.

'Cool stunt you pulled,' he said, 'pretending you were from the Aum and all. But you know we got the police switchboard tapped, don't you? Well . . . maybe it'll come in handy in the next life . . .' Ace then cleared his throat, a sound bearing likeness to the start-up cord on a chainsaw being pulled. 'Say you were a girl,' he said, 'and you had to choose between me and Omi – the guy who's just gone to Lawson's – which one of us would you choose?'

Ace kept his scary prison-inmate eyes turned to the river. Which one of them would I choose? It was like being asked to pick the better of two apes. On what criteria do I judge? Which is least in need of rhinoplasty?

The desire not to get my head trampled on strongly swayed my decision. 'You,' I said.

'Honest?' he asked.

I nodded and Ace breathed a sigh into the vanishing night. The exchange made me feel dirty and cheap. Fury pulsed as I swung the hammer onto the nail. It sank into the concrete, by two millimetres.

'Hey, where's the bin liners?' Ace shouted when Omi got back.

'They'd sold out. But I got food. And look: this month's issue of *Tentacled Invaders*.'

Omi emptied his haul of cigarettes and snacks onto the floor. As I hit the nail deeper into the ground, they sat and breakfasted on potato crisps and the chewing gum from their baseball cards. The sun rose and they idly smoked and studied a pornographic comic depicting women having sexual relations with tentacled robots. All the while the nail neared its destination. When it got there I was too exhausted to be anything but underwhelmed. I stopped hammering and waited for my accomplishment to be noticed. The dialogue that took place when it was went something like this.

'Hey, look.'

'No way! He's done it!'

'Well, not quite . . .'

'Yeah, I see what you mean. Hey, let me see that hammer a second, Watanabe . . .' *Bang*. '. . . That's more like it.'

'Perfect. But you've helped him. Helping him is cheating.'

'So it is. Better sink him, then.'

They secured my arms behind my back and tied my ankles together. Rope-burn ate at my wrists and ankles, and before long my hands and feet were sensationless as phantom limbs. They debated whether to unload a bullet into my cranium, but fortunately decided it unnecessary. They lifted me to the embankment's edge and began to swing me back and forth, building up launch momentum. Earth and sky changed places as the grey parallax of horizon rushed by. Most people would have screamed; one last howl for mercy, or to scorch the air with the last breath of existence. Not me. Six years of beatings at the hands of the Kaku twins had schooled me well in the art of silent suffering. I clenched my eyes tightly shut.

'On the count of three?'

'OK. So long, Watanabe. Thanks for earlier . . .'

'What are you thanking him for?'

'___'

'One, two, three . . .'

I hung in mid-air for a moment, before the river rushed up to meet me, a cold wall slamming into me, towing me under. My eyes sprang open in panic as I went down, a human dead weight. Stirred by terror, murky darkness gyred round me. Gone was the nurturing caress of the troposphere; my veins were now icy with the embalming fluid of river water. I bucked and flayed against the rope at my wrists and ankles, my exertions leeching precious oxygen. My knees and crown hit the mud of the riverbed, then I rose back up, thrashing like a fish on the end of a hook. Oxygen deprivation began to take its toll, my lungs in paroxysms, screaming fit to rupture. The river swam red before my eyes, as though its belly had been slit open, spilling guts and blood. I couldn't hold out any more. I was ready to dash my skull against a rock to end the agony. Little over a minute had passed underwater before I did what I knew would kill me. I inhaled.

A backdraft of fire rushed into my sinuses and lungs. I thrashed wildly, inhaling again, and then again. And amid all the pain numbness began to seep into my skull, like the cold trickle of anaesthetic in those last moments of consciousness in the operating theatre. Dark apathy washed over me until everything became calm and still. My last thought was: *So this is it*. But I was wrong.

I had not been drowned long when it happened. The big bang of human consciousness, blasting me beyond the limits of perception. A sky lit by a thousand suns ousted the dark void, raining molten droplets into the water. A zodiacal light came and illuminated the monads of creation. Psyche speeding with joy, I cast my gaze inwards, into my bloodstream, and read my carbon-dioxide levels. As my unconscious body was borne along by the river, my vital organs languished in a state of respiratory acidosis. The Death Clock was ticking. One hundred and three seconds remained before I would be forced to pronounce myself clinically dead. Life after death was no consolation. Who wants to be an omniscient ghost, his corpse rotting in a watery grave? My powers had been restored for a higher purpose.

My hypergaze penetrated the knots that bound my wrists and ankles, deconstructing them into post-Euclidean geometric forms. Just as a two-dimensional prison cannot make a prisoner of a three-dimensional being, knots are meaningless in a realm that violates the laws of everyday geometry. By shifting into a spatial position exempt from the laws of three space, I could escape.

My pulse was deathly faint, but there was just enough adenosine triphosphate left in my blood to execute the manoeuvre. Summoning all my psychokinetic strength, I stimulated the requisite motor neurones. Electrical signals firing, muscle filaments began to slide and contract. My fingers twitched like those of an incubating foetus as my hypermind guided their transposition, right down to a bio-molecular level. The sleeping Houdini slipped his shackles. So subtle were the kinematics that to an everyday observer I would have appeared motionless, my escape nothing short of miraculous. Only I know the truth behind this mystic parlour trick.

Unfettered, my limbs spread-eagled, dispersing my weight so the upthrust of the water molecules could lift me to the surface. The current deposited me face down on a sandy bank. My pulse murmured faintly. My diaphragm contracted and I choked up some river water.

My hyper-being sky-rocketed over my barely sentient body and let out a whoop that echoed over the city. Down below, the nation yawned, shuffled feet into slippers, or rolled over and went back to sleep. I sought out Mary and swooped down on the hospital bed where she sat, still stunned by her first encounter with the higher reality. I corkscrewed round her in a ghostly vortex of an embrace, wishing her courage and joy, searing away her loneliness, telling her to hold tight for me. I flew back to where my body lay, and forgave the river its attempted manslaughter. The polluted river rampaged on, rushing over the sunken necropolis of broken bikes, shopping trolleys and other non-biodegradable relics of our civilization.

Further down the embankment three pensioners in canvas hats stood skewering maggots onto fishing hooks.

One of them, Kumamoto, a retired traffic warden, gave a cry as he caught sight of the limp, washed-up body on the sand. Hollering like schoolboys, the three fishermen threw down their rods and bait and ran towards me, endorphins surging in macabre excitement. They halted at the embankment edge and peered down at me, at the soaked T-shirt clinging to my back, debating my mortal status in stage whispers. Sighting me first gave Kumamoto a sense of responsibility towards my drowned carcass. Carefully, he lowered his ageing body onto the sand and bent over me. Then he lifted my wrist, placing his fingers two centimetres shy of my pulse point. 'Dead,' he intoned solemnly to the two above him. Kumamoto shook his head sadly and lowered my arm. Fortunately, climbing back up the embankment proved more troublesome for Kumamoto than climbing down. He lost his leverage, slipped and reeled back a step, stamping the rubber sole of his galosh onto my splayed fingers. Face down, I coughed river water up my windpipe. The three fishermen let out cries of surprise.

On the ambulance roof the siren sang in shrill soprano, a transonic air raid on the morning streets, mutating in Doppler shift. Inside, I lay shrouded in a silver-foil wrap, cold-blooded as a reptile, my eyelids bloodless membranes. One-handed, the paramedic compressed my oxygenation mask, resenting me for having the bloody-mindedness to drown fifteen minutes before the end of his shift. To the grouchy paramedic my life hung in the balance, though it was plain to me that his primitive resuscitatory technique would revive me. I heard the lusty battle cry of my immune system fighting back, of neutrophils engulfing river bacteria. Hypothermia had made my body vulnerable to pneumonia, but it would be nothing some bronchodilators couldn't manage. By sending some extra-sensory pulsars into his brain, I advised the paramedic that a squirt of anti-bacterial spray would bring down my lung inflammation a notch.

Bored by the biological minutiae of my recovery, I swept above the ambulance, leaving the shrill agitation of the siren to circumnavigate the city. Metaphysical compulsion drew me to Shinsaibashi like electric charge to a lightning rod. I descended on the Street of True Love; quiet now, its neon signs were bled dry of voltage and its vile habitués had been sent scuttling back beneath their rocks by the risen sun. I stole through the walls and ceilings of The Seven Wonders, to the stairway that Hiro climbed. His neurological state was clear to me straight away. It was identical to the condition of his psyche when he had flushed Yuji out of hiding. He twitched under the artillery of synapses firing out of control, his skin damp with nervous perspiration. At the office door Hiro steeled himself for what was to come. His knuckles struck the door before he could back out.

'Come in! . . . Ah! Hiro, good morning. Come to join us for breakfast?'

In the darkness of Yamagawa-san's headquarters, five men sat round a low table drinking Ebisu beer and eating rice with grilled beef and spring onion. Though Hiro had broken the rules by turning up without authorization, Yamagawa smiled (the guileful smile of a crocodile surfacing in the glade, but a smile nonetheless). Without disrupting the hungry to and fro of chopsticks from rice to mouth, the thugs looked up at Hiro. He in turn regarded them, registering every detail with the ultra-lucidity of fear. On the screen hanging behind them a Noh play shifted pixels, a virtual demon and priest dancing to the slow, hypnotic beat of drums.

'Why so mute?' Yamagawa-san asked. 'Been gargling with hydrochloric mouthwash again? Trying to fix your tonsils to match your face?'

Yamagawa belched. The thugs snorted into their bowls. Hiro decided to scrap the farewell speech he had rehearsed and move directly onto phase two. Stony-faced, he reached into his suit, into the holster hooked over his shirt, and pulled out an HK MP 5K standard 15-rounds magazine.

The breakfast party barely had time to register what was happening before Hiro slid the bolt back and squeezed the trigger. Cartridge after cartridge fired down the barrel, spent shells cascading to the floor. The air thickened with deafening gunfire and blood-curdling screams. Screams it took no more than 9.2 seconds to silence for all eternity. Crockery shattered in geysers of white rice. Bullets punctured organs so they exploded like water balloons, exit wounds splattering the walls with haemoglobin. The sub-machine-gun tore countless new orifices into each man, spraying the virtual Noh play with bloody precipitation. Hiro swung the nozzle left and right, grimly shuddering from the recoil. Life had departed from the bodies of his oppressors long before he could bring himself to stop. Only when he lowered the gun did he realize the extent of the carnage. Heads were thrown back and chests torn open. Hands held up in ineffectual protest had been blown clean away. Not one of them was identifiable as the individual he had once been. Ear-drums ringing with HK MP 5K reverberations, Hiro slid back the safety bolt and tucked his gun inside his jacket. He walked over to the desk, pulled open the top drawer and extracted a bundle of notes worth 1.4 million yen. Pocketing the money, he took one last look at the blood bucket of evisceration that had been Yamagawa-san, then turned towards the door. Leaving the remains of his former boss and colleagues slumped beneath the eerie glow of the Noh dance, Hiro stepped out of the room.

In the aftermath he was devoid of victory or triumph. Hiro had been the agent of a will far greater than his own, called upon to redress a cosmic imbalance far beyond his understanding. I was in no mood for rejoicing either. I telescopically contracted my hypersense and returned to the ambulance. Grim witness to justice served, I collapsed into an exhausted sleep.

Antibiotics trickle into my arm and a cardiac monitor reassures passing nurses that I am not yet in need of a trolley ride to the morgue. It pains me to see myself this way, pale and insensible on a hospital bed. I look barely alive, but an auto-biopsy of my deoxygenated tissues tells me I am bound to pull through. My hyper-destiny dictates that I live, and the elixirs of life continue to irrigate my veins.

They could not destroy me. They will never destroy me. For I am the hidden ideological agenda of the universe; the most extraordinary thing to happen to man since he crawled out of the primordial slime. How can they destroy he who is scripted into the cosmic blueprint? Our human destiny is written in my atoms, encrypted in my DNA. It has weathered the carnage of natural selection, millennium after blood-spattered millennium, to bring us to this new dawn of evolution. Hear my laughter ring. For the universe is a conscious force. And it is not indifferent to my fate.

I lie feverish, a ghost of a boy. I lie inert until a shimmering bioluminescence enters the room, and I spiral into being, a phoenix reborn. A girl made from stardust comes to my bedside and her cool hand descends upon my brow. Her touch expels life force as my forehead is caressed . . . How long I have waited for this.

Now we will transcend together into the future Garden of Eden, where we will live in peace, free of misery and sin. The sticks and stones of the ordinary world will no longer harm us, and all our scars will fade.

I do not have the strength to open my eyes, but Mary knows I am watching her. She takes my hand and smiles. She smiles and, hand in hand, we rise, shedding the former reality like dead skin as we transcend. To a realm of perfect happiness, and perfect love.

24

MR SATO

I

I woke this morning on the floor of the Finance Department. Daylight cast bright aureoles round the lowered blinds, and vibrations from the offices below travelled through my back. I lay dazed and still for a moment until a lively cry of 'Good morning' bouncing down the corridor nudged my dim sentience into panic. I quickly sat up and looked about myself. Never have I seen the office in such a state of emergency; every filing cabinet drawer hanging open, the floor unseen for ransacked files. The hands of the clock pointed to quarter past eight. Only a miracle would enable me to tidy everything away before the arrival of my colleagues. In my twenty-hour investigative frenzy over two thousand files, dating back to June 1992, had been exhumed. I had a dim recollection of deciding at two o'clock in the morning to abort my mission and tidy up, but, certain the truth was only a mere spreadsheet away, I pressed on. Until exhaustion terminated the investigation on my behalf.

I listened helplessly as sunny laughter and footsteps neared the door. The door opened. It was Miss Yamamoto and Miss Hatta, their smiling entrance quickly eclipsed by shock.

'Mr Sato!'

Miss Hatta sprang towards me, knocking a stack of ledgers to the floor. 'Mr Sato! Are you OK?' She crouched down in her peach twinset and blouse, eyes aglow with drama and excitement.

Miss Yamamoto ran over to hoist up the window blinds. Daylight lent no clarity to the chaos.

'Mr Sato!' Miss Hatta cried, giving my shoulders a little shake. 'Say something. You're scaring me!'

'It looks like we have been burgled,' Miss Yamamoto said. 'Maybe I should call the police.'

Miss Yamamoto's assumption that we had been burgled gave me a shameful idea: that I could pretend the office was in this condition before I arrived. How dark the workings of my mind! I decided to nip temptation in the bud immediately. 'We have not been burgled,' I said. 'I came here yesterday to do some overtime.'

Miss Hatta's jaw lost all means of support. She turned to Miss Yamamoto, who had pressed a hand to her mouth.

Was she distressed by my discovery of her illicit dealings? Or by the damage inflicted upon the filing system in the name of overtime? I could not tell. But I was not going to take any chances. 'I must go and speak to Head Office at once,' I said, the authority of my tone somewhat undermined by the mess surrounding me. 'It is very urgent. Money has been embezzled from the accounts.'

'No!' Miss Hatta gasped. 'Which accounts?'

Unable to name any specific account I said: 'Evidence will be found.'

'Perhaps I should call the company nurse,' Miss Yamamoto whispered. 'Mr Sato looks unwell.'

'Really!' I protested. 'I am not in need of a nurse. Please both just go about your business as usual.'

The girls watched as I gripped the corner of Matsuyama-san's desk and tried to pull myself upright. The third attempt was met with success, but accompanied by an animal moan as agony flared in my lower back. Standing afforded me a clearer view of the pandemonium. With a sinking heart I realized that the clean-up operation would take up the best part of a day. The floor shifted in a dizzy montage of files and I remembered that my only sustenance since Mariko's birthday dinner had been several litres of strong black coffee. All at once the floor gave way and Miss Hatta swooped in, catching me by the shoulders.

'Quick, call the company nurse. He is unwell.'

'No, really, I am quite all right . . .'

But Miss Yamamoto had already gone.

Miss Hatta sat me down in a chair and fetched me a glass of water from the tap. Her eyes roamed over the chaos of files in bewilderment. I rose from the chair, insisting that I would commence putting the office to rights, but Miss Hatta begged me to sit down again. Embarrassed, I stroked the thistledown growth of beard on my chin. My jacket and slacks were rumpled, and my mouth tasted like one of the many sodden coffee filters I had thrown in the waste-paper basket.

'I must go to Head Office,' I told Miss Hatta. 'I must speak to them urgently.'

'Oh, Mr Sato, perhaps you should wait here until the company nurse comes. You look so ill,' she tentatively advised me.

In the end, Head Office saved me the trouble of making the trip up to their plushly carpeted headquarters by coming to me. A breathless Miss Yamamoto rushed back in, having summoned not only Nurse Hisako, but, horror of horrors, Deputy Senior Managerial Supervisor Murakami and Chief Supervisor Sanjo. In my two decades of loyal service at Daiwa Trading, Chief Sanjo has only appeared before me on a handful of occasions. That he had journeyed all the way down from the eighteenth floor, in violation of his near-mythological status, meant this was a very serious matter indeed. Murakami-san entered the room with a civil nod, then let out a low whistle as he took stock of the inversion of normalcy. I made no secret of my displeasure to see him and did not return his nod. Chief

Sanjo remained in the doorway, impassive as a cliff face. I was certain that Murakami-san had already poisoned his mind against me.

Only Nurse Hisako in her crisp white uniform spoke: 'Hello, Mr Sato. I hear you're not feeling very well today.' She came and placed a cool hand on my forehead before taking my pulse.

Taro the graduate trainee materialized, peeping impishly over the Chief Supervisor's shoulder. Heaven knows why today of all days the wretched boy had to be punctual. When he asked what was going on Miss Yamamoto gave him a quickly whispered account.

'Whoah!' he cried. 'Nervous breakdown!'

Nurse Hisako lowered my wrist with a maternal smile. 'Mr Sato, your heart rate is very quick and irregular,' she said. 'You are overtired and need some rest.'

Murakami-san smiled at me in an impartial, management-seminar-taught way. 'Section Chief Sato,' he said, 'how about taking the rest of the day off?'

I opened my mouth in outraged protest. I had much to do. I had to tell Chief Sanjo all that Mariko had told me. I still had the 1989–1991 accounts to investigate.

'If you don't mind, Chief Supervisor Sanjo,' I said, rising to my feet, 'I would like to speak to you privately . . .'

Chief Supervisor Sanjo silenced me with a stern and powerful glance. 'Assistant Murakami,' he said, 'please see to it that Section Chief Sato is escorted from the premises. He must see a doctor and have a full medical examination. Then he will come and see me in my office at nine on Friday morning, with the doctor's report.'

He turned to Miss Yamamoto. 'Call him a taxi, please,' he said. 'Tell the taxi firm to bill Daiwa Trading.'

And then the Chief walked away, leaving us in a silence that heaved with discomfort.

As the car-park barrier rose to let the taxi depart I looked back at the building. All of my colleagues were assembled at the office window, staring sombrely down into the car park. Anyone would have thought that I was being taken away in a hearse, not in the back of a Kwik Kab. The fever of humiliation upon me, I wondered how I would ever regain their trust and respect. Why in all those hours of searching had I uncovered nothing? Not even a rogue decimal point? Despite the deficit of evidence, I was determined that Head Office should hear Mariko's testimony. As the taxi dawdled through the rush-hour traffic, I devised a plan. I would go home, shower and shave, and change into my smartest suit. Then Mariko would accompany me to Head Office, where she would tell them how Murakami-san had paid her to distract me from his misconduct. Though officially suspended until Friday, I was certain Chief Sanjo would perform a volte-face on the matter when he learnt the truth. Then, once this ghastly state of affairs had been resolved, I intended to go back to Osaka General Infirmary to see Mrs Tanaka. I hated to put the company above my comatose neighbour, but desire for vindication consumed my heart. I decided that the second I got home I would call the hospital to enquire after her progress.

As the taxi negotiated the narrow streets of Osaka Bay, my palms and chest prickled, as if I were the plaything of an invisible acupuncturist. In the midst of all the greater calamities I was still nervous of my reunion with Mariko, whom I had not seen since the failed seduction attempt of Saturday night. I reminded myself that the manipulative seductress who cornered me in the spare room had not been the real Mariko, but a role she had been financially coerced into. I thought it an act of deplorable exploitation, and anger derailed my fear.

The taxi pulled up outside our house. As I climbed out and slammed the door, I noticed that all our curtains were drawn, which I thought odd, as Mariko is not one to laze about in bed. I hurried to the front door, worried she had fallen ill again. The hallway was very dim, and smelt of musk and crushed petals, as though a bottle of fragrance had been smashed not far away.

'Mariko?' I called.

The house was silent in reply. As I went to the stairs the hallway mirror caught my eye. It had been vandalized with lipstick, a bold and flagrant shade I have never known you or Mariko to wear. Written in the lipstick was a message: *You did not listen to your wife.*

I shuddered in offence. Then I began to wipe furiously at the lipstick with the sleeve of my summer jacket, not caring about the long-term damage to the fabric. I wiped until the characters had been smeared into illegibility. Beneath the message an arrow pointed to the stairs. One of my work-shirts hung in the stairway, hooked on the upper banister rail by a coat hanger. I pulled it down at once. On the back of the shirt she had written: *I will tell them what you did to me.*

I threw down the ruined shirt. What had I done to her? Nothing more than provide her with refuge during her bereavement. A second arrow urged me up the stairs. Docile servant of the lipstick commands, I followed. Marking the door of the spare room, belligerent as a banner at a political demonstration, were the words: *This is your punishment for ignoring your wife.*

Choked with fury, I ran over and hurled open the door. The cello was in the middle of the room. It lay slaughtered on its back, a large hammer lodged in its side. It had been clawed, dented and brutalized. The tuning pegs were broken, the bridge collapsed, and loose strings mangled and curled. The neck had been totally severed from the body, leading me to suspect that Mariko had lifted the instrument over her head and slammed it to the tatami. Never again would the cello produce another note. What hatred lay behind this vandalism? Mariko had even gone to the trouble of snapping the bow in two. I sank to my knees, mourning the demise of this thing of wood and carpentry. A make-up counter's worth of lipstick obliterated the walls.

The boldest message stretched from one end of the room to the other: *I will tell them you raped me.*

I physically reeled. Why threaten me so? To discourage me from reporting her crime to the police? Vicious lies and vulgarisms were scrawled elsewhere. I could not bear to read them, for each one found a new way to pierce my heart. Down on my knees, I pulled the dead cello into my arms, trying to reattach the neck to the body. Broken wood caught on the polyester of my slacks. I turned the cello over. A large cavity had been beaten into its back. Armed with only lipstick and a hammer, Mariko had laid waste to the spare room. On the skirting board she had scribbled: *Seen the family shrine yet?*

I put the cello on the floor and ran down the stairs.

Mariko had smashed a bottle of ink and splashed it over the shrine. She had broken the glass in every photo frame and had used a chopstick to scratch out our parents' eyes. Our mothers had inky beards and our fathers had been transformed into monsters, horned and fanged. Only your photograph had been left untouched, save for a message written along the bottom: *Your neglect made me kill myself.*

I choked back my sobs. It was silly of me to get so upset, I know. But I couldn't help it. *Why?* What had we ever done to her? Above the desecrated shrine, finger-painted in blue ink, was one final message: *Still have your job, Mr Sato?*

Oh, what a fool I have been. For I honestly do not know.

I swept up the shards of glass into the dustpan and threw away the photographs Mariko had spoilt. I did not have the energy or courage to tackle the rest of the damage. Instead I ate a piece of toast, showered, and changed into a clean pullover and casual slacks. Then I took the portable TV out from the cupboard under the stairs and caught the bus to the hospital. Mrs Tanaka's condition has not improved, but she is stable and Dr Ono is very optimistic. Naoko has taken time off work to camp by her aunt's bedside, and was nattering away when I got there, as if her stream of conversation had been unbroken since I left on Sunday morning. In her involuntary sleep Mrs Tanaka was sallow and serene. Both aunt and niece had identical bruises under their eyes, as though they had taken it in turn to punch each other while the nurses weren't looking. Preoccupied by her aunt, Naoko did not think to ask why I was not at work, or why I had not kept my promise to return on Sunday. Instead she smiled and clapped her hands at the sight of the portable TV and insisted that we set it up so Mrs Tanaka would be able to listen to her favourite lunch-time serial, *The Lives and Loves of the Lift Girls.*

I stayed at the hospital until nightfall. I considered staying overnight, but thought it wrong to use the comatose Mrs Tanaka as an excuse to avoid the house. I mustn't allow Mariko to scare me away. Tomorrow will be a day of spring cleaning. I will go round with a scrubbing brush and remove all evil defamation from our walls. I will also put your butchered cello out for collection and call the locksmith to change the locks on our front door.

I went back to the spare room earlier. The atmosphere seemed charged with the memory of violence. To see the cello lying there, broken and vulnerable, made me very unhappy. I went to the linen cupboard and took out an old red silk kimono. Then I laid the kimono over the dismembered cello, to bequeath it a small amount of dignity.

So many upsets plague my heart tonight. Flashbacks from the office this morning detonate cluster bombs of shame. I will just have to accept with good grace whatever disciplinary action is levelled at me, and work like a demon to earn back the respect of my co-workers. Climbing Fuji in ballet slippers seems an easier feat at present.

Still have your job, Mr Sato? How cleverly Mariko devised my downfall. How cunningly she duped me. Each layer of deception peels away to reveal another beneath. How far do they go? Had her father really passed away? Did she really dream of our beach in Okinawa? What baffles me most is, when I checked your jewellery box, nothing had been taken. And no money either, not even the loose change on the sideboard. Why would she do what she did if there was no financial reward? I had nothing else to offer her. Nothing at all.

II

Wonderful news! Mrs Tanaka has woken from her coma. As I arrived at her ward this morning carrying a bag of fresh fruit, Naoko beckoned to me from the doorway of Mrs Tanaka's private room. I feared the worst until an ecstatic smile broke across her face. She flung her arms round me in happy abandon, jumping up and down and nearly knocking the spectacles off my nose.

'Oh, Mr Sato! Auntie woke up last night! Come and see! She is sitting up in bed and she can move her head and everything.'

All the bananas and pears I was carrying fell to the floor when I saw her. Mrs Tanaka was indeed sitting up and watching *Good Morning, Japan*, a throne of pillows supporting her back. She gave me a friendly nod, as though we had just bumped into each other collecting the mail.

'Mrs Tanaka! You woke up!' I cried, superfluously.

It was truly astounding. Just the day before, Mrs Tanaka had been completely unconscious, and now, less than twenty-four hours later, she was sitting up and watching a light news item about a kindergarten sumo wrestling tournament.

'How are you feeling?' I asked. 'Is your head sore?'

'Auntie cannot communicate yet,' Naoko said. 'The doctor says she is still in shock and it will take a while for her voice to return.'

Smiling, I chased about after my fallen fruit, then pulled up a chair beside the bed. Naoko and I spent the morning fussing over Mrs Tanaka and laughing in happy disbelief.

Mrs Tanaka did not partake in our astonishment. When Naoko praised her ability to feed herself semolina pudding at lunch-time, she put her spoon back down with a withering look.

After Mrs Tanaka had finished her lunch of nutritious semi-solids, Naoko's housemate Tomoko came to visit with Mr Tanaka in his wheelchair. Mr Tanaka had been spruced up especially, his white hair combed and neatly parted. A large bouquet of roses sat on his lap and made him sneeze as he was wheeled into the room. He nodded at his wife and presented her with the flowers, depositing them on her lunch tray. Then he settled back in his chair to watch a documentary programme on the dangers of financial pyramid schemes. Tomoko laughed and told us that he had been asking after his wife all morning, assuring us he was quite lost without her. Naoko and I laughed too, agreeing that this was most certainly the case. It was the first time I had met Naoko's travel-agent housemate. Tomoko was a big girl, though one would hesitate to call her fat. The extra weight rather became her and was complimented by her fetching mop of corkscrew curls. She wore aggressive leather boots and one of those black trouser suits in vogue with young career women. She was very talkative, as overweight people often are, and told me that Naoko had spoken highly of me. This surprised me, as I did not think I had made much of an impression on her.

As the weather was fine Naoko suggested that we find a wheelchair for Mrs Tanaka and take her out for some fresh air in the hospital gardens. With the nurse's permission we bundled Mrs Tanaka up in a couple of blankets and wheeled her into the hospital quadrangle. We made for a very orderly expedition. Naoko acted as pacemaker, pushing Mrs Tanaka's wheelchair, and I walked alongside them, holding the metal drip stand, careful to maintain the slack between the drip and Mrs Tanaka's wrist. Tomoko and Mr Tanaka trundled at the rear. The hospital quadrangle was small and well maintained. Two stone paths dissected the lawn, which was bordered by shrubs and flowerbeds. An ornamental bird-bath marked the centre, and round the edges patients sat on benches. Supervised by a nurse in gardening boots, youngsters from the children's ward sat on the grass with sketch pads and a tin of coloured pencils, drawing the daisies.

'Isn't this nice, Auntie!' Naoko exclaimed. 'Such lovely weather.'

Actually, at that point the sky was rather overcast, but nothing would dampen Naoko's good mood. Because the grass was bumpy and might capsize the drip stand, our little procession moved slowly up and down the stone paths.

Quite a few people were out enjoying the fresh air, among their number a doctor, smoking a cigarette and flicking ash into the flowerbeds. *Really!* Those in the medical profession should know better than to smoke in front of sick children. They should know better than to smoke at all. You will be pleased to hear I gave that doctor a very stern look of disapprobation. It was while I was conveying these sentiments that I noticed the foreign girl sitting on a bench quite close to him. Not just any foreign girl. It was Mary from England. So unexpected was the encounter that it stopped me in my tracks, and I almost dislodged the drip from poor Mrs Tanaka's arm. Mary wore a black T-shirt and linen trousers and was sitting beside a frail boy in a white hospital gown. She had an open book on her lap and was reading to the boy as he stared into mid-air. The boy was malnourished-looking, the cadaverous physique beneath his gown suggestive of some terminal, wasting disease. As our procession drew nearer to Mary I saw that she was reading from an illustrated book of Japanese folk tales. This surprised me, as not many foreigners can read Japanese. A butterfly with lavender wings fluttered up to Mary, distracting her from the folk tale she was narrating. She smiled and pointed the butterfly out to her companion, who stared at it blankly until it flew away. As I rattled by her bench with the drip stand, Mary met my eyes, but did not recognize me. She must have thought I was a hospital porter or suchlike. I did not mind this, nor did I care to ask her to return the money I had loaned her. It pleased me to see her sitting so contentedly with her sickly companion.

I bade farewell to the Tanaka clan at 3.30, as I had arranged for the locksmith to come at 4 p.m. While the locksmith set upon the front door with his selection of tools, I went about with a bucket of soapy water cleaning Mariko's savagery off the walls. The spare room was so badly soiled that no matter how furiously I scrubbed the residual pink lipstick stain would not come off. The only solution is to give the walls a fresh coat of paint. Extravagant, I know, but we want the walls back as they were, don't we? I shall make a trip to the DIY store to-morrow. You will be pleased to hear that the shrine has been restored. I had a good rifle through the family albums and replaced all the damaged pictures. In your frame I put that photo I took of you on the Kyushu ferry crossing. How very beautiful you are, laughing beneath your own halo of sunshine. It really brightens up the shrine.

After the locksmith had demonstrated the workings of the locks and handed over the shiny new keys, I went upstairs to see the cello. It lay on the floor, still draped in your red silk kimono. Carefully, I lifted it in my arms and carried it down the stairs and into the backyard.

Sundown darkened the sky and I could barely make out the bushes at the end of the garden. Fortunately the light from the kitchen was just enough to work by. I laid down the cello and began to dig up the lawn with the potting trowel. The trowel could only scoop a little earth at a time, making the task more laborious than I had expected. Perspiration stuck my shirt to my back and a painful blister wept from my hand. When the hole was ready I lifted the silk-sheathed cello and lowered it into its new resting place.

I stood for a moment in silent remembrance, before returning to my hands and knees to refill the hole. When I had finished I used my shoe to tamp down the mound of earth so that it was smooth. The lawn is a mess but I shall remedy that tomorrow with some grass seeds. I put the potting trowel back on the window ledge and went inside for a well-deserved bath.

Our house is almost purged of Mariko's cruelty. With cream cleanser and elbow grease I have reclaimed it and made it ours again. If only it was as easy to purge my heart. Even after all that Mariko has done I find myself regretting her absence. While cleaning my teeth in the bathroom earlier, I found one of her hair-grips in the toothbrush holder. It had a cotton rosebud sewn onto the end and was slender enough to pick a lock. I turned it over in my hands. It made me quite nostalgic for those short-lived days when Mariko had been a kind and considerate house guest. It annoyed me that the wisdom of hindsight did not stop me from missing her. In the end I flushed that hair-grip down the toilet, not even caring if it got stuck in the pipes.

III

How peaceful it is at night, the entire neighbourhood tucked beneath a blanket of sleep. Only the breeze stirs, chasing its tail about the garden, restlessly shaking the leaves. Once again I am sitting at the kitchen table. The kitchen is very dark – the light bulb died earlier and I have not replaced it. This may strike you as melancholy behaviour, but I assure you I am far from discontent. I feel very alive, my chest astir with possibility and hope.

Though the clock struck midnight a while ago I will not be retiring. Sleep tonight is nothing more than wishful thinking. It is better to remain at the table than to fidget to the brink of insanity in my futon. Let me stay here and talk to you instead.

Mrs Tanaka's recovery advances in leaps and bounds. When I went to see her at the hospital this morning she was sitting up in bed, knitting, and looking much more like her old self in her claret quilted housecoat and turquoise turban (her skull bandages just visible beneath the gold trim). For once she was all alone, her niece and husband nowhere in sight.

'Good morning, Mrs Tanaka,' I said. 'You seem very lively today.'

She smiled and nodded, looping wool round her knitting needle. As her ability to speak had yet to return, I dispensed with small talk and sat on the chair beside her bed. The television was turned off and, in the absence of bouncy television presenters and jolly ad jingles, the gentle *clack clack clack* of Mrs Tanaka's knitting needles possessed the room. Without breaking the rhythm of her knitting, Mrs Tanaka eyed me expectantly, waiting for me to say something of interest.

I felt quite awkward and wished I had some of Naoko's chatterbox talents. 'You look quite well today,' I said. 'Our outing to the hospital garden yesterday must have done you some good.'

Mrs Tanaka did look a great deal more sprightly. She bowed her head and counted her stitches.

'I am sure it won't be much longer until you can go home. Is there anything that I can do in preparation for your return? Any shopping I can buy? Or housework I can do?'

Needless to say, Mrs Tanaka could not answer these questions. She scowled into her knitting and I wondered if my inattentiveness to her handicap had offended her. Then I saw that she had dropped a stitch a few rows down and a hole had crept into her knitting. Crossly, she began to unravel her work. She did not stop at the hole, though. She unravelled and unravelled until nothing was left. Then she pointed at my hands, making frail sign language and waving her wool at me. It took me a while to realize that she wanted to use my hands as a wool-winding frame. I held them out as instructed, leaning over in my chair so Mrs Tanaka could reach. When Dr Ono came in to take Mrs Tanaka's temperature he laughed to see me tangled up in this bondage of wool, and joked that I was Mrs Tanaka's 'little helper'. Mercifully, when the nurse came with a mid-morning snack of fruit salad and milk, Mrs Tanaka let me rest. The nurse chided Mrs Tanaka, saying she had heard from the night nurse that she had sat up all night doing her knitting. 'Now is not the time to indulge your knit-o-holic tendencies,' she said. 'You ought to be recuperating.' When the nurse left, Mrs Tanaka fed herself fruit salad and I read to her from the *Daily Yomiuri*. Midway through an article about a proposal by the Ministry of Fisheries to bring in a new regulation of net sizes, I looked up to see that Mrs Tanaka had nodded off in the upright position.

'Mrs Tanaka,' I whispered. 'Mrs Tanaka, are you sleeping?'

She made no reply, so I surmised she must have worn herself out night-knitting. I folded up the newspaper and lifted her tray onto the nightstand. Then I went over to the window and pulled the yellow curtains to, darkening the room.

As I crept to the door a tiny croak issued from the bed: 'Has she gone?'

I gave an excited little start and spun round. Mrs Tanaka was wide awake against her pillow throne. Her eyes sparkled in the gloom.

'Your voice has come back!' I cried.

Mrs Tanaka was not in the least bit surprised by her resurgence of speech. 'Well,' she persisted, 'has she?'

'You mean the nurse?' I asked.

'Not the nurse,' Mrs Tanaka said. 'That girl.'

'Mariko? Oh, yes, she has gone.'

A tremor betrayed my unease. I had forgotten about Mrs Tanaka's vehement dislike of Mariko. Not wanting to upset her, I decided not to mention the unhappy circumstances of her leaving.

'Good,' said Mrs Tanaka. 'Let's hope we never see that poor girl again.'

Poor girl? Mrs Tanaka had changed her tune! The way she spoke made me feel she was better acquainted with Mariko than I had thought.

'What do you mean?' I asked. 'Did she say anything to you?'

Mrs Tanaka softened at my alarm, her claret quilted arms folded over the bed sheets. 'I knew she would not break you,' she said, strength returning to her voice. 'And I was right, wasn't I? I was not so easily broken either.'

These strange words only heightened my alarm. 'Mrs Tanaka,' I said, 'did Mariko ever try to hurt you?'

A memory of Saturday night resurfaced. Mariko shivering on the front lawn, one sock rolled down round her ankle, the flowers on her dress faded by dusk. 'I heard a noise,' she had said. The memory sprang claws that penetrated my heart.

'Mrs Tanaka, that night you fell and hit your head . . . Mariko didn't . . . ?'

'My fall had nothing to do with Mariko. That young girl was responsible for nothing,' she said. 'We will talk about this no more. I just wanted to make certain she was gone. That was all. Now let an old woman get some sleep.'

For all her frailty there was a hardness in her eyes that warned me off pursuit of the subject. I was on fire with curiosity, but decided there and then that Mrs Tanaka will tell me what she knows when she tells me. I refuse to press an invalid pensioner.

'Very well, I will let you get some sleep,' I said. 'I will see you again tomorrow. I have to go home and paint the spare room anyway.'

As I said this, Mrs Tanaka's face became sad and

defeated. She seemed to age before my eyes. 'Mr Sato,' she whispered, 'I want you to know that I feel it too sometimes, very strongly. You really shouldn't live in that house any more. She is angry at you, don't you see? She will never let you live in peace . . .'

Mrs Tanaka ran out of breath at this point, which is just as well really – her head was obviously still quite muddled by concussion.

'Mariko is gone now,' I reminded her. 'And I have changed the locks on the front door, so don't worry, she can't get back in.'

Then I told her to make sure she got plenty of rest, waved goodbye and left. I simply couldn't wait to telephone Naoko with the good news that her aunt was talking again.

I was up the stepladder, using a roller to anoint the walls of the spare room eggshell off-white, when the telephone rang this afternoon. It had been weeks since I last heard its noisy jangle, and it sent me flying right out of my skin. Nerves a-twitter, I climbed down the ladder and rested my painting equipment on the frame. Then I hurried down the stairs and snatched up the receiver, exhaling an anxious 'Hello' into the mouthpiece.

'Ah! Sato! Enjoying your holiday?' Deputy Senior Managerial Supervisor Murakami boomed.

I winced and at once regretted not having one of those devices that informs you of the identity of the caller. Murakami-san was number one on the list of people I did not wish to speak to . . . Well, number two. The privilege of first place belongs to a certain hostess.

'I am very well rested, thank you,' came my curt reply. 'I hope everything in the office is back in order?'

'Don't you worry yourself about the office, Sato,' Murakami-san said. 'Miss Yamamoto took the opportunity to co-ordinate a complete overhaul of the filing system. Ambitious little minx, isn't she?' Murakami-san gave a throaty chuckle.

I thought it quite improper of him to refer to Miss Yamamoto as a 'little minx', but held my tongue. I wondered when he would apologize for all those lies he told about you. 'I hope it did not take them too long,' I said.

'Oh, they worked until seven or eight on Monday night. When they finished I took them out for a slap-up meal at the Octopus Hut. A little reward for all the work they put in.'

The thought of all my grossly inconvenienced colleagues gathered at the Octopus Hut sent a rush of heat to my face. I dread to think what was said about me as the sake flowed.

'Are they managing well enough without me?'

'Oh, they've been managing just fine. Ogata-san, the Assistant Warehouse Manager, stepped in to fill your shoes. Did you know he has a certificate in accountancy? I have never seen a man with such an appetite for number-crunching, Sato!'

The news of my replacement brought relief. Ogata-san is an upstanding, well-liked employee, who will ensure that the Finance Department runs smoothly in my absence. However, his appointment did little to compensate for all the disruption I had caused.

'I cannot begin to convey,' I began, 'my apologies for what I did to the office. I would also like to apologize for my behaviour on Saturday night . . .' The next word caught in my throat. After all, I was not sorry for everything. I was not sorry for what I said when he lied about you, for instance.

'Er . . . Sato, can you hold a moment? I've got a call on the other line . . .'

Without waiting for my reply, Murakami-san put me on hold. A recording of 'Greensleeves' (arranged for panpipes) forced me to move the phone away from my ear. It was a pleasant afternoon. Sunlight slanted through the glass of the front door, casting the hallway in a mellow buttercup light. In the street children played, rubber balls and roller-skate wheels clashing pavement. I heard a mother call for her son to come home and take his bath, followed by the boy shouting back that he was too old for baths. The next thing I heard was the boy's cries as his mother gave him a smack. Two more minutes of panpipe music was endured before Murakami-san returned to my ear.

'Sorry, Sato! Urgent call, couldn't wait. Now, where were we? Oh yes! How are you enjoying your holiday? Getting plenty of rest?'

Murakami-san had clean forgotten our exchange of words prior to the interruption. I was obviously of little consequence to his short-term memory.

'Yes, I am very well rested, thank you.'

'And your hostess, Mariko, is she still . . . ?'

'She is gone,' I said.

How stiffly delivered, these three words. And yet how tangible my sorrow. Amazingly, Murakami-san stemmed the flow of stupidity from his tongue. In his silence I heard myself explaining matters further, behaviour I can only put down to the ventriloquism of my subconsciousness.

'You were correct in your suspicions about Mariko,' I said. 'She was deceiving me all along.'

Murakami-san cleared his throat and said: 'I went to The Sayonara Bar last night. When I was there I called the Mama-san over and told her about you. I told her that she will lose customers if she lets her girls go about playing dirty tricks on salarymen. I tell you what, Sato, I have never seen that Mama-san in such a pig of a mood! She was stark raving drunk and bitchy as you please. She called Mariko over and told me to deal with it myself. Then she stormed into her office. Well, when I confronted Mariko she denied everything, saying she had met you only twice before, each time at the hostess bar. At first I thought she was lying, but when I pressed her she began to cry. She said that she had been seriously ill in bed for the past two weeks and could not remember anything. Strange as it sounds, Sato, I believed her. At least, last night I did. She ran away and hid in the kitchen, crying her eyes out as she went. Taro and I drank up and got out of there quickly. We went to the Copa Cabana instead. I am thinking of closing our company account at The Sayonara Bar. That place has gone downhill!'

Mariko's denial stung my heart, but it did not surprise me. The tears, however, did.

'Don't feel too bad about being duped,' Murakami-san said, in confidential undertones. 'I want you to know that I sympathize. We've all gotten mixed up with bad hostesses before. I once had a mistress who blackmailed me for months, forcing me to buy her the whole autumn range of Issey Miyake shoes and handbags . . .'

Well, I interrupted him right there! 'Mariko was never my mistress.'

One could almost hear the smile of disbelief on Murakami's face. 'Call it what you will, we've all been there. You learn from your mistakes. Exercise more precaution next time.'

There will be no next time. But trying to persuade Murakami-san of this is as futile as trying to persuade him Mariko was never my lover. I reproached him with my silence, an ineffectual means of reproach indeed.

'Anyway, Sato, we must press on. I want you to know that Chief Supervisor Sanjo and I have discussed your position within the company and arrived at the joint conclusion that you might benefit from a change of scene. The Shipping Department has a vacancy for an assistant file clerk. I know it is a bit of a leap into the unknown, Sato, but how does it suit? Your new post starts on Monday, provided you see a doctor and supply us with a clean bill of mental health.'

Ah! The sound of the guillotine blade in descent. They were shunting me as far down rank as one can get before one has to don a pair of rubber gloves and scrub dishes in the canteen. And to be honest, I would much rather work in the canteen than the Shipping Department, with its battery-farming cubicles and pervasive odour of damp and mustard gas. *Eighteen years until retirement*, I thought. *A life sentence!* Strangely enough, the news did not devastate me as much as it once would have done. The nasty incident with Mariko had left a substantial buffer zone against pain.

'Sato? Sato? Are you still there? Don't go upsetting yourself now. You do understand why we are doing this, don't you? I assure you this is only temporary. I will do my best to get you promoted back up to the Finance Department . . . Sato? Can you hold for a moment? I've got another call coming through . . .'

The line clicked and the panpipes made an unwanted return. How carelessly Murakami-san ordained my fate.

I put the phone down in its cradle, then took it off the hook. Only when I heard the dial tone purling did I understand what I had done. *My God, there will be repercussions*, I thought. *But only if I remain an employee of Daiwa Trading*. And that was that. I decided to tender my resignation the very next day.

I went to the kitchen to make a cup of tea. As tap water drummed the aluminium base of the kettle, I experienced the onset of a mild panic attack. What had I done? What company will want to employ a middle-aged salaryman changing jobs mid-career? I lit the hob and put the kettle on to boil. I thought of the savings that I had in the bank and assured myself that I would survive for a year or two, provided I stuck to a frugal existence. But everyone needs a job. Everyone needs purpose in one's life and a means of contributing to society. I recalled the position in the fishmonger's I had found Mariko. What law decrees that I must push a pen for a living? A community needs fish just as much as it needs accountants. Why not have a job that lights up a different province of the brain entirely? It was a radical idea and I had to stand by the window to allow it time to sink in. A whistle, low at first, then rising to a persistent shriek, interrupted my thoughts. The time it took for the kettle to boil was all the time it took for me to become accustomed to my new plan. I brewed a cup of green tea and took it upstairs with me, to drink while I finished painting the spare room.

How much has changed in these past weeks. The more I think about it, the more I can see the good that has come out of my dalliance with Mariko. Though cleaning up in her aftermath has been time-consuming, the experience has made me think. One ought to be careful about whom one invites into one's home. Mariko was a short, sharp lesson in the perils of being too quick to befriend. I shall be much more mistrustful in future.

My heart is mending fast, though. Can you believe that I have almost forgotten her face? Her delicate features, once so sharp and real, are now fickle and ill-remembered, drifting into nebulous imprecision. A train journey into Shinsaibashi is all that I need to rectify this. But why would I want to do that? This amnesia ought to be encouraged. And as I told you earlier, I never want to go near The Sayonara Bar ever again. In a roundabout way all that happened with Mariko was what I deserved, for being inconsiderate enough to visit a hostess bar in the first place.

How silent it is at night, as if I am deaf to the world. Perhaps I have mentioned this before, but I feel closest to you at night. This is strange because night-time is when you used to be at your most distant, always leaving our warm bed to pace about downstairs by yourself. But let us not dwell on the past. I made you unhappy once. I know that now. And I promise I will never make you unhappy again. I want nothing more than for us to continue to live in peace. Let this night and the silence last for ever.

But the silence is broken. Did you hear that? Out in the garden? A sound that demands investigation. See how clumsily I push back my chair. How my bare feet stick to the linoleum, every tacky step reminding me the floor needs mopping. It is almost as though I move in a dream as I open the back door to step beneath a sky dense with stars, damp blades of grass stroking me underfoot. Even the goose-bumps beneath my pyjamas do not seem real. The only thing that is real I advance towards now. As I kneel down upon our newly made plot of earth and lower my ear to the soil, I hear it clearly and, enchanted as ever, I close my eyes. For the cello is singing: a midnight sonata in D minor. A melody you have played for me before.